Samantha Grosser

# *Another Time and Place*

MACMILLAN NEW WRITING

First published 2006 by Macmillan New Writing,
an imprint of Macmillan Publishers Ltd
Brunel Road, Basingstoke RG21 6XS
Associated companies throughout the world
www.macmillannewwriting.com

ISBN-13: 978–0230–00235–7 hardback
ISBN-10: 0230–00235–8 hardback
ISBN-13: 978–0230–00733–8 paperback
ISBN-10: 0230 00733–3 paperback

10   9   8   7   6   5   4   3   2   1
14   13   12   11   10   09   08   07   06

A CIP catalogue record for this book is available from
the British Library.

Typeset by Heronwood Press
Printed and bound in China

*For Steve*

He wasn't coming back.

She waited for him at the hotel near the airbase, roused from dreams by the sortie of bombers flying east overhead, lying shattered and sweating, awake but still in the nightmare.

Dragging herself from the warmth of the bed, she shivered as the winter air touched bare skin, and dressed hurriedly in the semi-darkness of the morning. Downstairs, the hotel was just beginning to stir, and outside, shadows made their way here and there across the village.

She walked all morning to fill the space before the bombers returned, unable to find peace, her steps always drawn towards the airbase, waiting, waiting. She bought a *Daily Express* from the shop in the village and saw the words Monte Cassino in the headline, but the name held no meaning for her and she tossed the paper aside on the hotel bed, unopened.

It was lunch-time when the planes returned, a distant drone that rose to the familiar roar, and she raced down three flights of stairs to stand on the street, watching the damaged aircraft flying low across the village, searching among them for the *American Maiden*, but unable to make out the names. She almost ran to the base as the planes came into land one after another, and the silence of the afternoon was deafening when the last engine finally died. Pacing back and forth, never far from the gate, she waited till the chill of the evening began to settle around her and the light was leaving the sky before she returned to the hotel, arms wrapped around herself against the cold; useless because the cold was inside her.

She waited all night for him, refusing to believe that he hadn't returned, wrapped in her arms, cold and in pain, hating each footstep on the stairs that wasn't his. Staring into the fire, she hoped against hope that there was some other explanation, that some miracle might bring him to her even now. But the morning light brought no relief, just the thunder of another mission flying overhead and the growing realisation of the truth. He wasn't coming back.

But she waited still, unable to leave, walking again in the lanes near the base as though by being close to where he should be he would come. Once, she approached the gate, wanting to ask the sentry, desperate for information, but at the last moment she backed away, knowing he would tell her nothing, that she had no proof of who she was.

Late in the afternoon, as the winter light ceded easily to the darkness, she retraced her steps to the hotel and another night of fitful sleeping, dreams of fire and falling planes. Then finally, as the sun rose once more behind its shroud of grey, she understood that he would not come, so she packed her few belongings, paid the bill with the money he had given her, and went outside to wait for the bus that would take her home.

# One

It was early afternoon when Anna Pilgrim turned into Byron Street and walked with reluctance towards the only home she had ever known, hands dug deep in her pockets, head bent against the wind that bit between the rows of houses. A sudden gust almost took her hat and she reached up a hand to save it, surprised by the existence of an outside world. The children from the house at number four were playing hopscotch on the pavement and George's thin legs had turned bluish purple in the cold. She watched them absently as she approached.

'Morning, Miss Pilgrim,' George said.

'Morning.' The word left her lips as a whisper.

Susan buried her face in her scarf and peered up at Anna with sad brown eyes.

'Mum said you were missing,' George said. 'Captured by Germans most likely and never to be seen again.'

'Really?' The shock of such a ridiculous assumption forced words from her throat. 'Did your mum say that?'

George nodded.

'Well, I'm back now,' she replied. 'Safe and sound.'

'Was you really captured by the Germans?'

'No George. No, I wasn't.'

'Not even a little bit?' His young thin face was long with disappointment.

'I'm sorry, not even a little bit,' she said, and she smiled at him before picking her way through their chalk lines on her way up the street.

At number eight she paused, rested one hand on the broken gate and looked around her, reluctant to go in. It was an ugly house, red brick and pebble dash on the end of a short terrace, protected from the road by a small garden and a flight of four stone steps. Above it the sky bulged with low, dark clouds. Too heavy to fly she decided, and was glad. They promised rain.

Swallowing hard, she resisted the urge to turn away and run back to the hotel, to be close to the base and other airmen, part of his world amongst their uniforms and the music of their accents. Then, breathing deeply, collecting her resolve, she pushed open the gate on its one remaining hinge, climbed the steps to the door and slipped inside. She was home.

In the dingy hallway, lit by the greenish light that filtered through the stained glass window, she breathed in the familiar musty smell. Swallowing again, tasting the vomit that threatened to rise, she shrugged herself out of her coat and hung it on the rack by the door. Everything seemed strange, somehow, changed since she had been here last, and she was acutely aware that she no longer felt at home.

Her mother would be in the kitchen at the back of the house, and she wondered if the old woman had heard her yet, whether she was waiting, her anger prepared and ready, or if she might get to the kitchen unannounced and take her mother by surprise. Hesitating, Anna caught the flicker of her reflection in the mirror on the wall. She stepped up to it, observing eyes that were red from weariness and crying, hair tangled and unkempt. Then, turning away, depressed by what she saw, she pushed open the dining room door and trod across the tiles that led to the kitchen.

Her mother was waiting, facing the door, hips spread wide against the sink as she rested her bulk against it. Red pudgy hands gripped the counter either side of her body, knuckles white with the force of her grasp. She was not a big woman, but her presence filled the small kitchen, and her fury swept through the room in a flood of foul air.

'Hello Mother,' Anna said. 'I'm back.' She stood inside the door and leant against the wall, facing her mother, ready for the fight she knew was coming.

'Aren't you even sorry? I've been worried sick about you. You disappear for a week in the middle of the war and you've got nothing to say? And you aren't even sorry? Don't you care that I've been out of my mind with worry?'

'I'm sorry,' Anna said mechanically.

Her mother nodded, mollified a little by the apology, and there was a pause. Then, 'So where were you?'

Anna kept her eyes lowered resolutely to the tiles and said nothing.

'All the neighbours noticed you were gone. I didn't know what to tell them.' Mrs Pilgrim stopped and looked enquiringly at her daughter, the small eyes narrowed in the fleshy face. 'So I told them you were staying with a friend.'

Anna nodded in response.

'Were you? Were you staying with a friend?'

'Yes,' Anna whispered finally. 'I was staying with a friend.' Tears burned at the back of her eyes, and her mother's voice, insistent and shrill, cut through her mind like a chain saw.

'Who?' her mother demanded. 'Who did you stay with?'

'No one you know,' Anna answered. 'A woman from the factory.'

'Well why didn't you tell me? You could have let me know. I was sick with worry wondering where you were. There was a bombing over at Ditchfield and I couldn't sleep I was so worried you'd been caught in it.'

'I'm sorry,' Anna said again, but her own detachment surprised her. She felt no guilt, no sense of remorse for her mother's unhappiness, and the old woman's anger had lost its power to frighten her.

Because of Tom, she thought. Because I have Tom.

'I'm sorry you were so worried,' she said.

Her mother was still breathing heavily, still staring at her daughter with a mixture of disgust and incredulity.

'I even thought of calling the police. You've got no idea what it's like to be so worried, and no one to share it with.'

There was a silence.

'I need to sleep,' Anna said finally. 'I'm going to bed.'

She pushed herself away from the wall and walked slowly away from the kitchen. Upstairs in her room she slept immediately and deeply, untroubled by dreams, exhausted.

Anna woke with the dawn the next morning, and in the half-light between sleep and waking, still in the warmth of forgetfulness, she reached out a hand for Tom's body next to hers. But there was only the emptiness of the bed, and with a start she came to full consciousness, the memory returning, taking her breath away.

She lay unmoving in the darkness, resting her hand where his chest should have been, her head against his shoulder. Tears fell unwiped across her face, her eyes still closed so that behind them she could see him there, just waiting for her to wake. Soon they would get up, go for breakfast somewhere, and he would make her laugh with his quiet humour and teasing eyes.

Her mother's footsteps on the narrow landing outside her door roused her from the make-believe and she sat up, wiping the wetness from her cheeks, brushing the sodden strands of hair from her face. The cold air stung her skin as she reached out in the darkness to the lamp and turned it on. In its light she touched one finger to the small photograph of Tom that was there, tracing the lines of his face, the creases beside his eyes, the high cheekbones and slightly crooked nose, the wide lips that always seemed hesitant to smile even when his eyes were full of humour.

'Please sweet Jesus,' she whispered. 'Please keep him safe.'

When her mother's footsteps had receded down the stairs and along the hall into the kitchen, Anna climbed out of bed and padded barefoot into the bathroom to wash herself at the sink, standing naked in the cold room, watching the goose bumps rise as she splashed tepid water on her skin. Afterwards, she dried herself quickly, warming her body with the rough towel, rubbing the skin until it reddened, and when she was dry and warm she put on the green wool dress that Tom had picked out for her their last day in town. The memory of it was still woven in the fabric; his fingers against her skin as he helped her with the buttons in the shop, the scandalised expression of the assistant who couldn't look away from them. She shivered, wondering what his hands touched now, if there was still life in them, then she set to combing her hair, patiently working from the ends, using her fingers to untangle the worst of the knots.

Downstairs in the kitchen, Anna could hear the clatter of her mother washing up, and though she was hungry after so long without eating, the tears were too close to face her mother. So she stayed in her room, tidying things, killing time until the morning began to lighten behind the heavy curtains. Then she turned off the feeble lamp and looked out across the street to another row of houses like her own. Behind them the sky had turned to gun metal grey, and the empty road was still damp from yesterday's rain. For a moment she was puzzled by the quietness of the street, but then she remembered that it was Sunday and that people were at home with their families. Depressed by the greyness, she turned from the window, left the sanctuary of her room and went downstairs.

'Morning, Mother,' she said as she entered the kitchen.

Mrs Pilgrim looked up in surprise. 'Morning.'

Anna stepped round her mother's chair to light the stove for the kettle.

'There's tea already made,' her mother told her.

'I think I'll make some fresh, thanks.' The tea in the pot would be cold and stewed.

'Tea's rationed, you know,' Mrs Pilgrim said. 'You shouldn't waste it.'

'I know,' Anna replied. 'But I want a hot cup of tea.' It was hard to talk and she wished her mother would leave her alone. There was silence except for the hissing of the kettle as it warmed.

'Are you coming to church?' her mother asked.

Anna nodded and made her tea.

They walked to church without speaking and Anna missed the bells that had been silent since the war began. The air was fresh and crisp after yesterday's rain, and the sky had cleared to a beautiful blue with a few leftover strands of cloud that whispered above the tops of the houses. The freshness of the day lifted her spirit a little and she held her head up to the sun's pale warmth as they walked through the quiet streets.

A half-recognised buzz in the corner of her mind became more insistent and swelled into the drone of approaching bombers. They're late today, she thought, and looked up, shielding her eyes with a hand against the sun. Fortresses. The planes that Tom flew.

Her mother stopped and grabbed at her arm. 'Ours?'

'Ours.'

The roar was a part of her now, almost comforting in its familiarity, a connection to Tom. They stood and watched the planes pass over, all thought suspended in the vibration, metal glinting in the sun until the sound began to die away. Then they moved on slowly into the Sunday morning silence, Mrs Pilgrim's steps quick against Anna's long stride.

The vicar arrived late at the church as usual, his frizzy grey hair springing uncontrollably from its proper position as he hurried through the chapel. He smiled a greeting at each one of the small congregation before he turned and took his place at the lectern. Anna returned the smile. She liked him. She liked his warm eccentricity and his kindness. She glanced sideways at her mother who sat stony-faced and impassive, waiting for the service to begin, then she knelt, resting her forehead against her hands as she prayed.

Blessed Jesus, help me. Bring me news of Tom. Bring me good

news of him, news that he's safe and well. Bring him home unharmed. Give me patience, Lord, and strength to wait.

The early morning service was short; a brief sermon on overcoming fear amid uncertainty, and then Communion. Afterwards, they walked home in silence, not waiting to chat with the others as they usually did, her mother still too full of her anger to socialise, and their heels on the pavement cut into the peace.

There were no signs of the war in this middle-class suburb except for the stubs of railings atop the walls. No damaged buildings, no soldiers, no screams and cries, and the tranquillity was beguiling. A tortoiseshell cat basking in the sun raised sleepy eyes to them as they approached, then jumped up and slunk off over the low stone wall into a garden. Anna watched and wished she could disappear into hiding as easily. The prayer and Communion had helped; there was a fragile peace inside her now, and she held on to it tenaciously until Mrs Pilgrim stopped abruptly and swung round to her daughter. She slowed and waited, and as they stood on the pavement near the shops that were closed, an elderly couple passed them, labouring up the slope towards the church. As they went by they smiled and said good morning. Only Anna replied.

'So have you still got a job?' her mother asked.

She sighed and lowered her eyes, brushing aside the twinge of guilt.

'Didn't you go to work last week either?' Mrs Pilgrim demanded.

Anna glanced up. Her mother was glaring, trying to force a response.

'No,' she answered. She felt foolish, scolded in the street like a child, and the peace inside began to dissipate under her mother's attack.

'And just what are you going to tell Morris?'

'I'll tell him I was ill or something,' she shrugged. It didn't matter. It would soon be forgotten.

'I'm very disappointed with you,' her mother said. 'I thought I'd brought you up to be more reliable. And more considerate.'

'Yes,' Anna agreed. 'You did.'

Mrs Pilgrim nodded to herself and bustled on, and Anna followed behind, squinting into the blue clarity of the sky, scanning for aircraft.


'What will your mom say when she finds out about me?' Tom had asked.

Then, curled and warm, his gentle hardness against her body, her mother seemed trivial, insignificant. 'She'll be cross,' she replied.

'What'll you tell her?' He stroked the soft hair from her forehead, winding its silkiness around his fingers.

'I don't know. Nothing probably. I'll tell her nothing.'

'You'll have to tell her something, won't you?'

'No. It's better that I don't tell her anything or she'll pursue it forever.'

He was silent, eyes scanning the rough worn cotton of the sheet between them before he looked up at her, searching and intense. 'Why can't you tell her about me?' he asked.

'She wouldn't understand.'

'Are you ashamed of me?' He was uncertain suddenly, and vulnerable.

'No,' she said. 'Of course I'm not ashamed of you.'

'Then why?'

She lifted her fingers to his face and stroked the unshaven cheek, liking the roughness of his skin against her hand.

'I'm sorry,' she whispered. 'I'm sorry I can't tell her about you. But she wouldn't approve and she'd say awful things and …'

'I've asked you to marry me.'

'It doesn't matter. I've spent the night with you. She won't like it. She's … old-fashioned.'

'You should have told me,' he said. 'I'd have taken you home.'

'Then I'm glad I didn't tell you,' she retorted, and he smiled in spite of himself. 'I'm sorry, Tom. I can't tell her. I just can't.' 'It's okay,' he said, but she knew that it wasn't, that it hurt him.

'We'll be married soon,' she told him. 'And then after the war we'll go to Montana and forget all about my mother.'

'Sure.'

'Tom, it doesn't matter,' she persisted. 'Please believe me.' She took his hand in hers, touching the calluses there with her fingertips, caressing his fingers gently. Rough hands, a carpenter's hands. 'I don't care about my mother any more,' she said. 'I don't care what she thinks. All I care about is you and being with you.'

There was a silence and then he asked again. 'Will it be all right with your mom? Really?'

'It'll be fine,' she had promised, knowing that it wouldn't, and hating herself for lying.

Now, in her room, gazing out of the window, she sat in depression. It had seemed impossible then that she would ever come back here like this, that her life could return to what it had been. She had sat here so many times like this in the past, held by pity and guilt for her mother's unhappiness.

But now it was different. Now she had Tom to sustain her and though the pity remained, the bonds of guilt had diminished. Her life was her own.

*Floating – they are floating through air that is black with smoke, looking down, seeing nothing but smoke below them.*

*Where is it all coming from? she thinks. Why is there all this smoke in the sky?*

*A sliver of red reminds her of fire, trying to light fire with damp wood. So much smoke and then there are flashes of red all around her, tingeing grey prettily with pink and suddenly she is afraid. Afraid of the evil smoke which leers at her in messages of red.*

*Look out! someone shouts, a disembodied voice reaching her through the fug, the sound surprising her in the thickness of the silence. Flak ahead!*

*She tries to twist sideways, away from the shell burst, aware now somehow of its danger, but her body is leaden and she cannot bend it as she wants. The shell approaches slowly, heading for her belly. She is screaming in silence, calling his name, watching her death approach but when it hits her it passes right through, leaving a big gaping hole, the edges blackened and charred as if she were made of steel like an aeroplane. She laughs at the game.*

*Look Tom, she says. I'm all right, there's just a hole. I'm an aeroplane. The* American Maiden. *You can see right through me to the other side. She laughs again, reaches for his fingers outstretched to her but he is too far away so she can't reach him and as they float downwards they watch through the smoke for more shells.*

*There's one for you, she says to him. He smiles and waves, slow motion, the smile fixed and strange, then he looks down to watch the shell and when it hits him, he explodes into fragments and covers her with his blood.*

Anna woke sweating, frantic, curled and shivering under the covers, too afraid to sleep any more. She lifted her hand, searching at her breast for the little cross he had given her, clutching it, praying he had survived. In the utter darkness of the early morning, she waited for the alarm clock to ring and force her out of the terrifying safety of her bed.

A shout from the street, a man passing the time of day with an air raid warden, drew her gently from her nightmare, offering some normality within her mental chaos. Stretching out onto her back, the bottom of the bed icy against her feet, she heard her mother rise and shuffle stiffly to the bathroom. When, finally, the alarm began to clamour, she slammed down a hand to silence it, then waited for the old woman to go downstairs before she dragged herself out of bed. She dressed hurriedly, fumbling with the buttons of her dress, combing her hair blindly in the dark and gripping it back with practised deftness, shivering with cold.

Behind the curtains the sky began to lighten over the roofs of the city and each band of grey that filtered through the blackness was paler and more insistent than the last. Anna paused at the window, waiting for the planes that today didn't come. She glanced at her watch, the figures blurred and mobile in the gloom, and struggled to focus. Time to go down. She sighed, procrastinated a little longer and took the photograph from her bag. Tom smiled out at her with his shy half-smile, but it was hard to shake from her mind the memory of her dream. Be safe, my darling, be safe, she whispered. Then she hurried downstairs to the kitchen.

'So,' her mother said, 'you've decided to go to work today, have you?'

Anna nodded and poured some tea from the pot. It was cold and stewed.

'Well?'

'Yes, Mother. I'm going back to work.'

'What are you going to tell them?'

'I'll tell them I was ill,' she said with a half-shrug of one shoulder. 'That's all.'

Mrs Pilgrim said nothing, watching her daughter with narrowed eyes, wondering, and Anna drank more of the tea, needing the energy from its sweetness. When she had drunk the last of it she stepped across the kitchen and put the cup in the sink.

'Goodbye,' she said. 'I'll see you this evening.'

The bus, when it came, was packed, and Anna spent the long ride out to the factory sweating in the heat generated by the crush of close-packed bodies. The smell was overpowering and she breathed deeply to combat the rising sickness in her stomach as she swayed from the strap, her eyes closed. She tried to think of Tom, to remember something joyful, but she could find only the images from her nightmares. The journey took for ever as she swung between the sadness of her grief and the nausea of the bus ride.

She stepped down at the factory into the cool dampness of the air with relief, and stood for a minute, head bowed, waiting for the sickness to subside. Then, when she was sure that she wouldn't vomit, she started towards the factory gate, returning the guard's cheerful good morning with a small smile as she passed him.

At the steps to the office she paused to compose herself, touching fingers to her hair, straightening her coat before she marched firmly up to the door. The three young typists that she supervised looked up from their desks as she entered, and, squinting in the sudden artificial light, she nodded a good morning. They replied politely but she saw the surprise in their faces and the only half-suppressed smiles.

Mr Morris was at his desk when she opened the heavy door to his office. He looked up at her with interest. 'Good morning, Anna,' he said, the Scottish burr distinct over the hum of machinery from the building next door, low and insistent. 'It's very good to see you again.'

She hesitated, holding on to the door for a moment before she let it go. It swung shut with a clang that startled her as she stepped across the bare floorboards towards her boss, her eyes lowered. She whispered, 'I'm sorry, Mr Morris … I was ill.' The words were difficult to form, difficult to voice.

'Is that so?' he asked in such a way to let her know he was not convinced. She wondered what gossip had reached him, and glancing up, she saw the thin lips pursed in disapproval, the brow drawn into a frown beneath hair growing thin at the temples. Then she stared at him in defiance, hazel almonds meeting Celtic blue for an instant of self-assurance before he turned away, unnerved.

'Yes. It is,' she stated. Her own nonchalance surprised her, no trace of the guilt she had expected to feel.

The conversation ended abruptly as she re-entered the typing pool and giggles were stifled.

Let them think what they like, she thought. It doesn't matter.

Nothing matters. Except Tom.

She took her place at her desk, paying no attention to the girls, and began sorting through her in–tray. It was clear the others had done very little without her there to supervise them. She waded gradually through the pile of work, concentrating with eyes that were sore and tired, pausing now and then to answer questions with her usual patience.

Just before lunch one of the girls asked, 'Were you ill? We were all worried about you. Especially Mr Morris. He said it wasn't like you not to telephone in.'

Anna nodded, ignoring the glance the other two typists exchanged. 'Yes. I was ill.'

'And you're all right now?' the girl enquired.

'Yes, thank you Rita,' she lied. 'I'm more or less fine now.'

'That's good then,' Rita replied, and returned to her desk.

At lunch–time there was a concert party in the canteen, an attempt to keep up the morale of the workers, but they were loud and talentless and Anna sat as far away from them as she could. Other workers sang along with enthusiasm, so she left her meal untouched, not hungry, and slid out the back to the comparative quiet of the office, grateful for the solitude. She knew the other girls were talking about her, that she and Tom had been seen that day in the tea room when they first met, a nine-day lifetime ago. She saw the lewd grins and the nudges as she walked past their table to escape and their crudeness angered her.

*17 January 1944*

*Dear Colonel,*

The clatter of the typewriter was loud in the deserted office.

*I am writing to enquire if you have any news of the whereabouts of First Lieutenant Thomas Blake, whom I*

*believe may have been shot down on January 14th. As his*
*fiancée, I am sure you can understand my concern and*
*I would be very grateful if you could give me any news.*

*I look forward to hearing from you,*

*Yours sincerely*
*Anna Pilgrim*

She knew it was a long shot, that it was unlikely he could tell her anything. But she folded it carefully into the envelope, sealed it with her hopes, and dropped it into the outgoing post tray. Then she turned back to the pile of unfinished papers on her desk.

The day dragged in spite of the work load, her eyes drawn irresistibly to the post tray again and again. She worked in a daze, eyes unfocused on the words in front of her, forcing herself to concentrate, reading and rereading simple sentences before she could make sense of them. The girls noticed her strangeness and kept their distance, uneasy, no longer laughing at her. Once she went to the bathroom and let the tears come for a while, watching herself cry in the mirror, observing how the water welled and spilled. Then she splashed her face with cold water to wash away the redness. The clock ticked slowly round and it felt like another lifetime before the hands settled into a straight line at six o'clock and she could finally leave.

On the bus, in the seat she was offered by a young soldier, she sat huddled against the cold of the window pane as they chugged through the evening. Once, she peered out through the small hole she had rubbed with her hand in the mist, but outside was only the impenetrable darkness of the blackout, so she rested her aching head against the glass, and slept.

Mrs Pilgrim watched her daughter, the vexation and unsated curiosity simmering behind the expressionless face, brimming and ready to boil. Still in shock, still weary from worrying and lack of sleep, each morning she sat for four hours in Ruth Llewellyn's narrow sitting room, fiddling to assemble the small aeroplane parts that sat on the trestle table in front of her, her mind churning.

Stayed with a friend indeed, she thought. A likely story.

But it was unlike Anna to lie. She'd always been such a considerate girl, so amenable. It had never been her nature to be so defiant, so indifferent to the worry she had caused.

It had to be a man, Mrs Pilgrim thought with disgust. Only a man could turn a girl's head like that and change her almost beyond recognition. She shuddered, and hoped for both their sakes she was wrong.

The other outworkers passed no comment but the old woman's sullenness infected them all and the usually cheery banter dwindled to a tense hush, audible above the *Music While You Work* that crackled from the radio set.

Over morning tea on Thursday Ruth Llewellyn ventured to ask if everything was all right. 'Only you've been ever so quiet the last few days.'

A silence fell over the room and all eyes turned expectantly towards Mrs Pilgrim.

'Yes, thank you. Everything's fine,' she replied. 'I've just got a lot on my mind at the moment.' She would never dream of sharing her problems with this bunch of gossips. 'But thank you for asking.'

'That's all right. Well, if there's anything we can do. We've all got to help each other in these times. Things are hard for all of us.'

The others nodded in sage agreement.

But it's harder for some than for others, Anna's mother whispered in her head, and forced a smile. 'Of course,' she said. 'I'll ask if I need anything.'

Ruth Llewellyn cleared away the tea things and the women went back to work.

\* \* \*

The days passed slowly for Anna as she dragged herself from sleepless night to stupefied day, losing herself in the roar of the bombers that passed over each morning. Tom never left her thoughts. At times he was a presence so real that she was certain he was still alive, thinking of her, working his way back to her, but at others she was convinced of his death, and then she would struggle through the day in a haze of grief that could not yet be expressed. The uncertainty nearly tore her apart.

She was almost oblivious of her mother. The old woman's resentment failed to penetrate completely the depths of her anguish and the two women barely spoke. Anna knew that it would not last, that the anger would break in the end, but for nearly a week she lived in a circle of solitude, profoundly grateful for her mother's silence.

It broke on Saturday.

Mrs Pilgrim found her daughter in the kitchen, washing out her clothes in the sink, her hair twisted up in a scarf, sleeves up over her elbows. She was smiling.

'And just where did you get the money to spend on all this?' her mother demanded. She waved a reddened finger at the little heap of pretty underwear that sat on the draining board, unseen by her daughter who stood with her back to the door. But Anna knew what she meant.

'I saved up,' she answered hurriedly, startled by the intrusion into thoughts that were far away. She reddened, as though her mother could read her mind, and let the wet washing slip back into the water, let go of the memory she was holding. The day Tom had picked out the underwear for her at the little shop they had found in the back streets in town, choosing the most expensive items, the prettiest. Taking her back to the hotel for her to put it on and show him. His hands cold against her skin as he had done up the hooks of the brassiere, his lips warm against her neck as his fingers had lingered beneath the lace.

She turned to face her mother and waited, tense again, remnants of the smile still at the corners of her mouth. She had been waiting for this, but still when it came it left her breathless.

'I don't know what you've got to smile about, my girl,' the old woman went on. 'I've just about had enough of your attitude.'

Anna stared at the floor, at the bunions on her mother's slippered feet and hoped her own feet would never get like that.

'You don't even answer me when I speak to you any more. You used to be such a nice polite girl. I don't understand what's got into you. You disappear for a week without so much as a word of explanation. Sent me half out of my mind with worry. And you've shown no sign of remorse. It's certainly not how I brought you up to behave.'

'What do you want me to say?' Anna asked quietly, raising her eyes to her mother, who glared, arms crossed defensively across the low-hung breasts.

'I want to know the truth,' her mother said. 'I want to know where you were last week.'

Anna looked down again and shook her head slightly. She would never tell. She would rather die than let her mother utter his name.

'Why won't you tell me?' Mrs Pilgrim's voice was shrill with frustration. 'I'm your mother. I've a right to know.'

'No,' Anna answered firmly. 'No.'

She could hear her mother's breathing, hard and fast, and she looked up slowly, surprised by her own bravery, at how easy it was. She should have stood up to the old woman years ago. 'I told you,' she said. 'I stayed with a friend.'

'What friend?'

'Just a friend. No one you know.'

Her mother leant her bulk against the door frame. 'How dare you be so defiant?' she breathed, her voice beginning to crack. 'The least you owe me is an explanation after what you put me through. I expected more from you, Anna, after all these years of struggling on my own. I had no one to share the worry with. No one to help me. You wait until you have children of your own. Then you'll know.'

'I'm sorry,' Anna said, guilt beginning to stir at last with her mother's tears. 'I didn't mean to worry you.' She leant back against the sink, heart beat rapid now with the confrontation, her body light with adrenalin. In a wave of dizziness, her mother blurred, became an indistinct shape of grey and pink, then solidified once more into squat bulkiness.

'I'll find out in the end,' Mrs Pilgrim snorted. 'And then it'll be so much the worse for you.' She turned and stomped away through the dining room.

When she had gone Anna turned slowly again to the underwear, rinsing it through mechanically, without interest. She tried to recapture the joy of the memory, but it had gone, and in its place there was a big hole inside her, a dark void of numbness.

# Two

Tom swung like a pendulum and the parachute harness dug painfully into his legs. He must have blacked out soon after he jumped; he couldn't remember seeing trees from the air. He looked down. Below him, the forest floor was fifteen feet away, dark earth that he knew would be hard with cold beneath a layer of fallen pine needles. His right leg dangled, useless and broken, full of shrapnel.

Gritting his teeth against the pain he looked up, wondering if he could tease the parachute free and let himself down gently, but the silk and string were hopelessly tangled in the canopy of pine above him. He swore silently. There was no easy way down.

Gradually the swaying stopped, and he hung there, immobile for a moment before his fingers reached to fumble in the heavy gloves for the release button on the harness. Then he hesitated, bracing himself for the drop; it was a long way down. Finally releasing himself, finding the courage in the end because to stay there would be a stupid way to die, he instinctively twisted his body, trying to protect the injured leg. He landed awkwardly and the pain was blinding, left him gasping for air as he lay motionless, breathing hard, sweating in the cold morning.

Gradually, as his breathing quieted, Tom hauled himself up into a sitting position, moving his body slowly and with care. Then, when he was settled, he picked away the fabric of his pants to expose the wound beneath. The bone was visibly broken, the flesh around it a pulpy mass of blood and shrapnel. It was worse than he'd imagined, the pain more intense now that he could see the damage, and he wondered if he would make it through after all, or if he was going to bleed to death here in this forest, his frozen body to be found by local children days or weeks from now.

Shaking his head against the thought of it, he searched his mind for an image of Anna to keep the fear at bay, and found one of her with an uncertain smile, the way she had smiled after the last raid, when Matthew was killed and he had wanted to cry. She had looped her arm through his and led him back to their room in the village. For a moment he was there, warm and safe in bed, wrapped in her, and with the memory a ferocious determination was roused in him, a refusal to die.

He would get back to her somehow, he promised himself. He would see that smile again whatever it took.

Breathing deeply to calm himself, the chill of the air hard in his lungs, he began to feel behind him with his hands, searching beneath the carpet of pine needles until he found what he was looking for and prised it from its bed in the earth. He made the tourniquet deftly, the way his father had shown him before hunting trips in the forests back home, and when he was finished he ripped off more of his shirt and wound it tightly over the wound so that the worst of it at least was covered. Then he shifted his weight back slightly to lean against the tree trunk and rest. His father would have been proud of him.

He wanted to stay there, exhausted by the pain and the effort, but the memory of Anna's smile goaded him on. He had to move and get help, get away before the Germans came looking. The *American Maiden* was not the only bomber shot down; the area must be crawling with airmen.

Gently, he took his weight onto his hands, trying to lift his right hip clear of the earth, and began to drag himself very slowly along the earth, westwards, towards home, towards Anna. It took all his strength, pain pulsing through him with each small movement, and after only a few yards he needed to rest again. Discouraged, he reached to the breast pocket of his tunic, tempted by the single vial of morphine. But he resisted the desire to use it. Yet. He needed his mind to be alert, and later he might need it more.

He moved on with agonising slowness, trailing the damaged leg, wincing each time it bumped against tree roots or stones or just the unevenness of the earth. He rested often, loosening the tourniquet each time to let the blood flow to the limb as his father had taught him, biting his lip in the effort not to cry out. The rests became longer and more frequent as his body weakened and his mind emptied of all but the effort of his journey.

Morning wore into afternoon and scattered dapples of light began to penetrate the canopy of branches as the trees thinned around him. Through the fog of his fatigue he realised he was nearing the edge of the forest at last, and the knowledge revived him, marking some measure of progress. He hauled himself forward with renewed energy until the trees stopped abruptly in a line and he was staring out across fields lying fallow that led down to a village some half a mile away.

He rested, ate the chocolate he had found in his pocket and wondered if he should wait until nightfall to move on. Cooling quickly in the bitter cold, he could feel the clamminess of the sweat-soaked clothes, and overhead a lone Focke Wulf droned across the sky, flying low, its engine rough and erratic. Instinctively Tom shrank back into the shelter of the trees.

Anna, he thought, and wondered if she had missed him yet. Anna.

He would wait until nightfall.

By the time he reached the village Tom's energy was spent. Chilled by the wait at the edge of the trees, his body had stiffened and shock had begun to set in. Later, he would look back on that endless journey across the fields and wonder where the strength had come from to keep moving so long after the point of exhaustion.

Now he lay sprawled across the back doorstep of a cottage,

banging against the door with a fist he barely had the power to raise. In the silence that followed, he prayed for help, fighting the urge to hide, no resources left anyway to go elsewhere, and all the stories he had heard of butchered airmen crowded in on his mind. He tensed as footsteps approached, the sweat profuse between his shoulder blades, trickling in streams down his spine. His breath came hard and quick in the long moments of anticipation before the door opened, blood pulsing in his ears like in the moments before take off when there was no going back and he was scared. Then an elderly face with snow white hair emerged through the crack.

'Help me,' Tom croaked. His throat was parched, his voice no more than a whisper. 'Please.'

The face looked down at him sharply, apparently shocked, then disappeared back inside, closing the door. Tom waited, wondering if the next moments might be his last. Then the door opened wide to reveal the warmth of a cottage kitchen and the familiar figure of his navigator. \

'Harry,' he whispered, and relief surged through him. He was not alone after all, and the adrenalin of his fear began to ebb.

'Hi Tom,' Harry answered, as if it were the most natural thing in the world that they should meet like this. Then he stooped, lifted the pilot's arm over his shoulder, and with a hurried glance into the night, dragged him quickly inside.

The kitchen was warm, a bright fire burning in the stove, and Harry lowered him into an armchair that stood to one side of it. The elderly lady who had opened the door fetched a footstool and Tom loosened the tourniquet. Blood dripped onto the flagstones.

'You okay?' The navigator squatted down close to Tom's chair.

'Just peachy.'

'You look like shit.'

'Thanks.'

Harry grinned and laid a reassuring hand on the pilot's arm before he stood to take the mugs of milk the old lady held out for them. Tom drank greedily, the milk cool and soothing on his tongue and the dryness of his throat. Then he turned again to his friend. Harry's face blurred once or twice before settling into focus, the room behind him indistinct and hazy. He had to concentrate hard to keep the image before him.

'What's happening?' His voice sounded strange, distant and weak, like someone else's.

'They're going to help us,' Harry told him. 'There's a daughter who speaks English, Marie. She's gone to get the mayor.'

Tom nodded.

'There are Germans everywhere. Must be a base or something around here.'

The old lady hovered near them, thin hands twisting nervously in front of her. She waited to catch Tom's eye, then gestured to his leg.

'*Médecin*,' she said.

'Yes,' Harry answered. 'He needs medicine.'

The old lady nodded and spoke in a low voice to her husband who sat quietly near the door, cleaning some small piece of machinery with an oily rag, unnoticed by Tom. The old man said nothing but took down a heavy overcoat from a rack near the door and headed out into the night. The old lady smiled at the Americans and repeated, '*médecin*'.

They sat in silence, waiting, Tom too exhausted to speak, sinking gratefully into the warmth. He was safe now, his fate out of his hands. A pot of soup bubbled on the wood burning stove and the aroma reminded him of home, of his mother's cooking. He wondered how long it would be before his family had news of him, before they learned he was still alive.

When the others returned they brought a doctor who spoke in a low anxious voice.

'He says we must lift you on to the table,' Marie translated into slow but fluent English. 'So he can properly examine your leg.'

'Give me morphine,' Tom whispered, and Harry pulled the precious vial from his pocket. The doctor took it and jabbed it into the muscle of his patient's thigh. The drug wormed its way through Tom's body, fuzzy and warming as the doctor worked to cut away the sodden makeshift bandage, cleaning the wound, lifting shrapnel from the mangled flesh. Occasionally the doctor spoke and Marie translated for Tom, who lay rigid, his jaw clenched against the pain in spite of the morphine, his eyes closed. It seemed as though it would never end.

'The bone is broken,' she told him. 'He's going to put it in a …' she stopped, not knowing the word, and Harry supplied it for her. 'A splint.'

'Yes,' she said. 'A splint.'

When it was over, Tom was almost unconscious, the world about him drifting in and out of focus, objects swimming in a blurred and hazy reality.

'You must rest,' Marie said, 'and get strong.'

Then she turned to Harry and Tom half heard the conversation at the scrubbed table where the family was now eating. He remembered that he had been hungry before and the smell of the soup, but now he felt sick and wanted only to sleep. He closed his eyes and fell into the space between sleep and waking, a world where his thoughts were jumbled and made no sense.

'You're very kind,' Harry said to Marie. 'You're taking a great risk having us here.'

She shrugged. 'We have to fight against them any way we can.'

Later, she helped the navigator to carry Tom upstairs to a bedroom. Together they undressed him and he shivered in the cold before they lifted the covers over him and he felt the warmth of the sheets where the old lady had put heated bricks.

In the night he woke many times, startled and disorientated until he remembered. Then he lay staring up in the darkness, listening to the creaks and groans of the unfamiliar house, thinking of

Anna to take his mind from the pain in his leg.

She would have left the hotel now, he thought, and gone home, uncertain and afraid, to the mother she could not tell about him.

'She wouldn't approve of you,' she had told him. 'She would say awful things.'

'Why?' he had asked her.

'Because you're a man,' she had tried to explain. 'Because you're a Yank. Because I love you. Any number of reasons.'

Still hurting, he ran through the conversation again and again, wondering what he had missed, why he couldn't understand. It had made no sense even lying next to the reassurance of her body in those last few minutes at the hotel, almost the last words they had spoken to each other.

'We're going to be married,' he had argued. 'You'll have to tell her.'

'Yes,' Anna replied. 'But not yet. Not yet.'

Then when? he had wanted to ask. When would he be good enough to be more than her secret? But he had said nothing because it was almost time for him to go and he couldn't bear for them to argue as they said goodbye. So instead he had swallowed down the shame and the hurt and pretended that it didn't matter.

Now in the darkness of a strange house so far from her, immobile and in pain, it was easy to believe she might be the same as the other women he had known before her after all, that the difference in her was no more than smoke and mirrors. Perhaps it was too good to be true, as he had feared from the beginning.

He shoved the thought aside, irritated by its insistence, and forced himself to remember every other moment of the time they had spent together, every other moment of certainty. But as he drifted in and out of sleep through the night, it was the memory of that last conversation that stayed, leaving its footprints of doubt in his mind.

\* \* \*

The night reached its end with the first seeping of grey through the curtains. Out of habit Tom reached for his watch but the numbers swam before him, not yet light enough to pin them down, so he dropped the watch back on to the windowsill, too weary to care. Downstairs, in the kitchen below his room, he could hear people talking, the voices carrying through the old walls and floors of the cottage. He strained to listen, to hear the words, but he could hear only the music, the fall and rise in intonation. He identified Harry's voice among them before he drifted back into a sleep that was punctuated by dreams of flying.

When he woke again, Harry was there, waking him, offering him coffee.

'You okay?'

'Yeah,' he whispered. 'I think so.'

'Your leg?'

'Painful.'

'Here. Drink this. It's good.'

Tom reached an unsteady hand for the cup and lifted it to his lips, sucking in the hot sweet coffee. Harry was right; it was good and strong and cleared his head enough for him to ask his friend what was happening.

'I'm being taken to a safe house tonight,' Harry told him. 'Something to do with the Resistance. Apparently they've helped Allied airmen before.'

Tom nodded, concentrating on the navigator's words. 'And me?'

'You're not going anywhere for a while. You need to rest. You have to stay here until you're strong enough to move.'

'I want to go with you.'

'Marie's going to look after you. It's going to be okay.'

Tom shook his head, frustrated by his incapacity, his dependence on others. Anna would be waiting. 'I'm not staying here. I'm going with you.'

Harry smiled at the pilot's determination, the unquenchable belief that all things were possible.

'It's already been decided, Tom,' he said. 'It's too dangerous to move you. Not just for you, for everybody. You have to stay here till you're stronger.'

Tom said nothing, sipping coffee to quell his irritation, and beneath the window they could hear a German soldier haranguing someone in the street who could not or would not understand him. His proximity unsettled them both.

'It's dangerous here.'

'You can't move. You have to stay.'

'And them?' Tom gestured with his head to indicate the family downstairs. 'Are they okay with this? It's a huge risk for them.'

Harry shrugged. 'They don't have much choice.'

They were silent, listening again for the soldier's voice outside but he had moved on, and the street was quiet again.

'I know it's hard,' Harry answered. 'But look at you. You can't even focus properly. You need to get better.'

Tom half smiled at the navigator's bluntness.

'Sorry. But it's true. You hungry?'

'No.'

'Maybe you should sleep some more. I'll come back later.'

'Tell Anna I'll be back for her soon as I can. Tell her I love her.'

'Sure.'

'8 Byron Street.'

'8 Byron Street. I got it.'

'Thanks.' Tom drained the last of the coffee and dropped back down into the softness of the pillows. He was asleep again before Harry had even stood up.

The navigator smiled. 'Sweet dreams,' he said. 'And get better soon.'

They had only a few minutes warning when the German army patrol began their house-to-house search for the missing airmen the following day. Shouts in the street, the revving of engines and cries of complaint from other villagers alerted them, and Marie came racing to Tom's room as soon as she realised what was happening.

He had manoeuvred himself from the bed by the time she arrived, and he stood waiting by the door, needing her help to continue, exhausted by the effort. Her usually calm face was contorted with panic and as he placed his arm over her shoulder he could feel the tension in her muscles. He wanted to reassure her, tell her that it would all be okay but he knew their chances were small and his own fear kept him silent. Boots thudded on the road outside and she half dragged him down the narrow stairs.

'My things,' he reminded her. 'Tell your parents to get my things.'

She nodded and shouted to her mother who stood wringing her hands at the base of the stairs, eyes flicking anxiously from the American to the door. From outside, they could hear the shouts of the soldiers, guttural and foreign, moving closer. The elderly woman came towards them, squeezing past them on the stairs up to Tom's room to retrieve the bag. They moved quicker in the hallway, the flat ground enabling Tom to swing himself forward, supporting his weight on Marie's shoulder, his hip against hers. Her father stood ready with the trap door under the stairs.

Between them, bent almost double beneath the low ceiling, father and daughter lifted him down the wooden ladder into a dank coal cellar. Marie wrapped a blanket around him, dropped his bag to the floor beside him and then he was alone, cold and shivering in the dark as the trap door thudded into place. He heard them move some piece of furniture over it and then their footsteps over his head, slow and deliberate, trying to be calm.

Tom could see nothing, not even his hand before his face, and he held his breath against the surging pain in his leg. He was shivering, cold in spite of the sweat on his body, and he drew the blanket closer round him, huddling inside it in a dismal attempt to be warm. Something moved not far from his outstretched leg and he jumped, his nerves on edge, before he realised it was just a mouse or a rat.

The patrol reached the cottage and he heard Marie's protestations as the soldiers forced their way in, the men's terse rebuttals. Boots scuffed and tramped above him and it seemed impossible that they would not find him as they paused in the hallway, shouting at one another and at the family, who couldn't understand them. Even through the filter of his pain he hated them, a visceral hatred of their arrogance and the harshness of their language, a disgust at the fear that they stirred in him.

Then, at last they left and there was silence, more waiting until it was safe enough to release him. He was patient now, the danger past, but he was lightheaded from the pain and the exertion and when the trap door finally opened, light pouring into the blackness of the cellar, it took all the strength of his will to haul himself out of his hiding place.

Later, Marie told him that two airmen were found in the searches. The women of the family that were hiding them were deported, probably to Buchenwald, the men shot in front of them before they left. The fliers themselves were taken away for interrogation amid rumours of the Gestapo. She told him without emotion, and he wished he could recover faster and spare them the danger that his presence brought with it.

'You must stay here until you are well,' Marie insisted with a smile. 'You must stay until you're fit enough to travel.'

'Okay, okay,' Tom agreed, and he was moved by her courage.

# Three

Anna learned gradually to live with the pain, the not-knowing that left her half-grieving, half-alive, swinging between her faith in Tom's life and the certainty of his death, working in a haze of exhaustion and depression.

He was with her always, in her thoughts and before her eyes, in her dreams and nightmares, and this helped to ease the loneliness. She talked to him often. Switched off from wherever she happened to be, she could hear the low gentle voice within her head, guiding her, encouraging her, making her smile.

It was only four days before she began to feel life stirring inside her, to sense the part of Tom that she carried within her. She knew even before her period was due that she was pregnant, and she waited patiently, sure of herself, counting the days until there could be no doubt, stroking her still flat belly with delight.

We're having a baby, she told him, and saw him smile his shy boyish grin, the lines around his eyes crinkling the handsome face. Then she cried, afraid that he would never see his child.

Mrs Pilgrim watched, noticing a new lightness in her daughter that she did not recognise, and she retreated for a time, still determined to find out but resigned to surly patience. Oblivious, absorbed in her new role, Anna retained her distance, and the fragile veneer of civility remained unbroken.

The letter from the base took three weeks to arrive and Anna panicked when she saw the slim envelope on the mat in the hallway as she came down for breakfast, almost tripping down the stairs in her anxiety to reach it. She took it to her room, safe from her mother's prying eyes, fingers trembling as she fumbled to open it, eager and afraid.

*4th February 1944*

*Dear Miss Pilgrim,*

*Thank you for your letter.*

*I appreciate your obvious concern for the whereabouts of First Lieutenant Thomas Blake, but unfortunately I am not able to divulge the status of United States Army Air Force Personnel to a member of the public. I can only suggest that you contact his parents who will be notified immediately there is news of him.*

*I very much hope that you are successful and that the news is good.*

*Yours sincerely*
*Colonel Sherman White*

Anna stared at the words, black lines on white, a meaningless jumble. She had known, deep down, that it was a slim hope, but it was the only hope she had, and now she was crushed. She gripped the letter, fingers curled tight with frustration, holding it close to the feeble light of her bedside lamp, staring at it, waiting for the words to make sense again. But they hovered and shimmered over the page and she let it fall, let the tension seep out of her, sitting on the edge of her bed, head in her hands.

Too tired to cry, she thought, and reached down to grasp the letter once again. She read it over, slowly, pinning the words to the page, searching for meaning, for answers.

... 'contact his parents', she read, 'who will be notified immediately there is news of him.'

No news. There is no news of him yet. No one saw him die for sure. That means there's hope. Thank you Colonel, thank you for your clever letter.

She folded it neatly and placed it back inside what was left of the envelope. Her mother's door opened and she heard the uneven shuffle along the landing into the bathroom. Anna shivered and waited. Let her mother go downstairs to the kitchen, then slip away silently to work, unnoticed.

Work dragged on through the week. The girls in the office no longer bothered her. The giggling and snide remarks had died down within a few days as other juicier gossip came to light, and they left her to herself. She was relieved, and she sympathised with the married woman whose love affair had taken their interest. Her absence was not mentioned again and she assumed that it was forgotten. Now, back in the routine of the long working days, the week with Tom seemed such a distant memory that she thought sometimes she had dreamed of it, until she remembered the growing child inside her and knew that it was true.

Morris softened quickly, his gruffness giving way after a day or two to his usual appreciation of her help. Then, slowly, he became kinder to her, and she wondered if perhaps he had understood her distress. She spoke little to anyone beyond what was necessary, conversing mentally with Tom, her mind always with him. Her relationship with the other girls, always cool, became more distant as she wrapped her solitude tighter around her. And she worked hard, burying herself in the paperwork, quiet and efficient, doing more than her share because that way she had less time to think.

One lunch-time she wrote to Tom's parents, the envelope only half-addressed with all the information that she knew, praying it would find its way across the world to them, hoping they were good people as Tom had said.

On Saturday she arrived at work with a sense of relief, anticipating the early finish at noon. The girls barely worked all morning, making plans instead for their evening, discussing clothes and make-up, sharing thoughts on their chances with the men they had chosen for targets that weekend. She let them be, picking up the slack, their conversation a background hum to her industry. She saw them watch the clock tick round and at twelve on the dot they left, hurrying to the canteen to join the larger group of friends from the factory floor. Watching them go, she felt the tiredness seeping through her limbs, and worked for another hour.

'Goodbye, Mr Morris,' she said at one o'clock, leaning in through his office door. 'I'm off now.'

'Goodness me! Is that the time already? Have you had lunch, Anna? Will you have a bite with me in the canteen?'

'No, thank you, Mr Morris. I'm meeting a friend, so I'd best be off.'

'You'll waste away if you don't eat, you know,' he said, and she smiled.

'I'm fine, thanks. Have a nice weekend.'

'You too. See you Monday.'

Anna walked to the gate the long way round to avoid the smell of the canteen. She had already vomited once that morning and just the thought of food made her stomach heave. Sitting on the bus with the window wide open, cold wet air blasting into her face numbing all other sensation, she ignored the grumbles of other passengers, and thought of Lottie, her best friend since childhood, the friend she had been supposed to meet the day she met Tom. As she stepped down from the back of the bus into the rain, she wondered how Lottie would react to her news, and a slight tingle of apprehension warmed her cheeks.

A sudden squall lashed the rain around her face and neck and she turned up her collar against it, eyes downcast to the glistening pavement at her feet. She ambled from the bus stop, taking deep breaths of damp air, allowing the sense of sickness to subside, sheltered from the rain by the awnings of half-empty shops until she turned off the main road into Howard Street. Quickening her pace in the wet, she arrived at the little terraced house at number seventy-one, the yellow door faded and peeling, and banged hard with her fist so she would be heard in the parlour at the back of the house over the rain. The door opened finally, and the familiar smell drifted out to where she stood on the step.

'Hello Lottie,' Anna smiled, spirits lifting, nervousness forgotten. 'Can I come in?'

'Anna!' Lottie replied. 'It's lovely to see you. Come in, come in. I'm so sorry I couldn't meet you that time. I couldn't get away from work. You know how it is ...' She reached out to hug her friend, and Anna held the tiny frame in her arms, surprised as always by how slight Lottie was.

'That's all right,' she answered, and as Lottie turned back to the living room she said quietly, 'Can we talk?'

Lottie stopped and raised an interested eyebrow in the semi-darkness of the hallway. 'Shall we go upstairs?'

Anna nodded and followed Lottie up the narrow staircase to the bedsitting room she shared with her husband at the back of the house.

'It's a mess,' she apologised, throwing a pile of clothes from the bed into a cupboard.

'I don't mind,' Anna smiled, and they sat close together in front of the fire on the floor beneath the sloping roof as they done since they were children. The room had changed little in all those years. There was the double bed now of course, and new curtains, but Lottie's simple creativity was still evident in a carefully placed shawl on a lampshade, and unusual pictures that dotted the walls. Lottie gave Anna a towel and she wiped away the film of moisture that had settled on her hair, rubbing the ends lightly and then leaving it, uncombed and tousled. She stared into the fire, thinking, distant, and Lottie watched her with curiosity, her head tilted a little to one side.

'What is it?' she asked finally. 'What's happened?'

'I don't really know where to start,' Anna began. 'How to put it all into words …' She glanced up at the elfin face which smiled in encouragement.

'Just start,' Lottie told her. 'Anywhere.'

Anna looked away again, eyes distant and unfocused. It was hard to bring the words to her lips; all conversation that mattered had been mental for so long. Tom smiled at her, smoothed the damp hair from her forehead, gave her strength. She breathed deeply, four or five breaths, touched her finger to the cross at her neck and then turned to her friend.

'Lottie,' she said. 'I'm pregnant.'

Lottie was speechless, her mouth open, eyes wide with surprise.

'Oh my God … are you sure?'

'I'm sure.'

'What … who … who's the father?'

Anna swallowed, the memory still raw to touch, to utter for the first time.

'His name is Tom,' she said. 'He was … he is an airman. American. I met him the day you didn't come to the tea room. He's a pilot. A lieutenant.' She pronounced it the American way, as Tom did. 'First Lieutenant Thomas Blake.' Her voice was soft and low and Lottie leaned forward to catch each word above the hiss of the heater. 'We stayed in town at first and then just before the end of his leave we went to a hotel in the village near the base so I could be close to him. I stayed with him for almost a week and he flew twice. The second time, he didn't come back.'

She turned away from her friend and stared again into the fire, remembering.

They had caught the last bus to Little Sutton, buying cups of sweet weak tea from the stall at the bus station to warm them as they stood on the concrete in the wind. Other airmen waited too and exchanged brief words with Tom, smiling enviously at the woman on his arm.

'They think you're beautiful,' he whispered to her. She looked away and blushed, aware now of their attention. 'And so do I.' She turned back to him and smiled, her face close to his, and it was hard to resist the temptation to kiss.

The bus came at last and the other airmen stood back to let them board first. They sat on the top deck, away from the draught of the open doorway at the back, and Anna nestled into the arm that held her as the old vehicle chugged slowly through the night. The sound of men's laughter reached them often from downstairs and made them smile, but mostly they were silent, content just to hold each other for the long ride out of town.

It was late when they finally reached Little Sutton, and the airmen wished the couple a good night, the darkness hiding their grins before they headed off into the night towards the base. Voices, still chatting, floated back disembodied, fading gradually as Tom and Anna walked quickly in the cold to their hotel.

'It's a nice room,' she said.

They stood for a moment in the doorway blinking in the light before they went in and Tom lit the fire.

It was small and old fashioned, but clean and well-kept with a small lead-lighted window that looked out over the main street of the village. They stood by the fire, warming themselves, cold hands stretched to the heat. Tom watched her staring into the flames, her eyes distant and sad, and wished he could say something to make it all better.

He said, 'I love you, Anna.'

She turned and smiled at him, her cheeks flushed from the fire.

'I wish you were my wife already.'

'So do I,' she whispered.

They held each other, and he rested his cheek against her head, his skin rough against her hair.

He woke several times in the night and held her again, and the strength of his need woke her also so she turned to him, finding his lips with hers in the darkness, making love again with silent desperation. In the morning when it grew light, they drank tea in their room and afterwards she followed him down to the street and walked with him to the base, her long stride keeping pace easily with his.

They were a little way from the gate when the first engine shattered the stillness of the morning and they stopped dead in the middle of the lane, paralysed for an instant before they ran to a gate and climbed on the rickety bars to watch the airfield come to life, drowning in the ocean of noise that surrounded them. They sat watching the bombers taxi slowly into line and take off one by one in close succession, less than a minute between them. She had never seen the bombers so close, had never understood their size, and she barely breathed, overawed. They stayed until the last one had lifted her bulk from the runway and climbed slowly into the overcast, and the quiet began to settle once more. Then they jumped down and stood together in the lane, awkward, not knowing how to say goodbye.

Finally Tom said, 'I'd better go.'

Anna bit her lip and nodded and looked away.

'Look at me,' he asked.

She lifted her face, fighting back the tears she didn't want him to see.

'I'll be okay,' he told her, but there was doubt in his eyes, and the lines of the young face were etched in worry. She reached out and touched his brow, smoothing the cool skin with her fingers.

'I know,' she replied, and gave him a small, brave smile.

'I may be able to make it out this evening to see you. Maybe. I can't promise. It depends on a lot of things. But I'll try.'

'I understand.'

He reached out with his hand, lifted her chin with his fingers and bent slightly to kiss her. Both of them wondered if it would be the last time.

'I love you,' she said, as he let her go and began to back slowly away.

'I love you too, Mrs B.'

She smiled, and then he turned and walked quickly away. He didn't look back. He couldn't.

Anna had waited since the roar of the bombers taking off had woken her early. She had lain in the warmth of the bed, shaken by the din, paralysed with terror in the silence that followed in their wake. She tried to picture him, to see him in the Fortress, serious and brave, a different side of him from what she knew. But the picture was hazy, she hadn't enough detail to make it complete, and she realised how little she knew about flying. She wanted to know with an urgency that overwhelmed her; a need to understand this side of his life, to understand what it was that he went through each time that he flew.

She lay on her back in the dark, wondering where he was, what he was doing. Then she forced herself up out of the covers and dressed hurriedly in the cold, shivering, fumbling with the buttons on her skirt.

Outside, the morning was grey and damp and people hurried about their business. Two children were playing leapfrog in the road. City kids perhaps, evacuated here at the start of the war, country kids now, whose lives would never be the same. She watched them for a while, envying them their energy and innocence until they saw that she was looking and ran away, screaming and giggling out of sight behind the houses. Anna turned slowly from the door of the hotel, not sure where she was going but needing to walk. To stay still filled her mind with the horrors of flying; movement calmed her, gave her something other to do than simply wait.

The village was small; a church, a post office, the pub where she stayed, and some cottages, all built in stone two or three centuries before. There was a tranquillity about it in spite of the closeness of the war, as though the past generations of life unchanged had stamped themselves irremovably into the stones and the road and the air itself. At the end of the village, where the buildings stopped and the flatness of the fields began, there was a small memorial with the names of fifteen or so men who had not returned from the last war.

*Greater love hath no man*, she read above the names, *than that he give his life for the life of his country. Lest we forget.*

She read down through the list of the men who had died, *John Parr, Stanley MacIntyre, Frederick Day*. Then she turned and walked away, scared and depressed. Such ordinary sounding names. Thomas Blake wouldn't look out of place among them.

The minutes ticked slowly by on the small face of her wrist-watch as she wandered aimlessly along the lanes between the fields, bordered by dense and barren hedgerows that barred her view of the landscape. Inevitably, she wound her way towards the base, as though her closeness to it made him nearer or safer or something. She climbed up on a gate and looked out over the vast network of concrete that crisscrossed the fields, the tower, the huts and the planes that stood at their hardstands, small figures clambering over them, groups of men playing ball on the grass. She sat on the gate for a while and tried to identify the buildings, working out in her mind which was the mess hall, or the briefing room, the small hut where Tom lived with Harry and two others, until the cold of the morning began to penetrate her coat. Then she jumped down and walked on, back to the village with a sudden need to get away from the base to something more familiar, a normality where the war seemed more distant and unreal. A jeep passed her as she walked and three young officers lifted their hats to her as they slowed to go past.

'Howdy ma'am,' one of them said. He looked so young, almost a boy, and she looked up and smiled at him, grateful for the contact. Men like Tom who were surviving.

At the hotel she ordered tea and a sandwich and took it to her room, away from the curious stares of other people. She flicked through the newspaper, four pages of war news, skimming the headlines, unable to concentrate on anything more. Then, too restless to remain alone in the room, she left again and walked once more to the base, taking her time, passing the entrance and exploring the country beyond.

A horse, a chestnut cob, shaggy in his winter coat, stood sleepy at a gate. She went to him, stroked him and talked to him, told him about Tom. Her voice sounded loud to her in the silence of the early afternoon until, at last she heard the low drone of engines. She turned quickly as the buzz became louder, more compelling, identifying itself as the bombers returning. The chestnut butted her shoulder with his head, wanting more attention, but she ignored him and stepped down from the gate to retrace her steps towards the base, walking swiftly now, with purpose, the agony of the waiting almost over.

The drone swelled and filled her mind as more planes came slowly into view and she watched them as she walked, saw them coming into land, saw the holes and the engines that had failed, the Fortress that had to belly land, sliding and scraping on the concrete of the runway before it hit the grass, the wail of the ambulance and the fire truck screaming as they chased it across the airfield. She wished she had binoculars or some other way of knowing which plane was Tom's.

She passed the entry to the base once again, wandered slowly a little way towards the village and then lifted herself on to a gate so she could see the length of the lane in the weak afternoon sunshine. She settled down to wait in the tranquillity that had returned now that the bombers were home, knowing it would take time for him to come.

Finally, when she thought perhaps that she should go, that he would not come after all, a lone bicycle turned from the base and wove unsteadily along the lane towards her. She dropped down from the gate to stand in the centre of the lane, shielding her eyes with her hand, praying that it was him, unable to see his face against the sun until he was almost level. When she was sure that it was Tom, she ran to him, wanting to hold him. But she stopped when she saw his face, the exhaustion and the pain.

He swung his leg over the seat and stood next to the bike, resting his hands on the handlebars, facing her.

'Hi,' he said.

'Hi.' She smiled, unsure of herself, uncertain how he wanted her to be.

He stepped forward, pushing the bike, and she turned and walked with him, looping her hand through his arm.

'Welcome back,' she said.

He glanced sideways at her and tried to smile.

'How was it?' she asked, and thought immediately how trite the question sounded.

Tom stopped walking and turned to her. 'We lost our tail gunner. Matthew.' His voice was low and hoarse, as if he barely had energy to speak. He looked away, out into the distance, not at her. 'He was nineteen. Just a kid. It was his first time out and he was killed by the flak.'

Anna dropped her eyes to the crumbling concrete of the road. She had no idea what she could say, what she could do to make him feel better.

'I'm sorry,' she whispered. 'I'm so sorry.'

She reached up a hand to touch his face and his eyes flicked to her in surprise, as though her presence so close was a shock. His jaw was clenched with tension and he looked away again, unable to hold her gaze.

'It's all right to cry,' she told him. 'It's all right.'

He shook his head and lifted a hand to his face, pinching the bridge of his nose between his fingers and thumb, his face screwed tight with pain.

'No.' He lifted his eyes to hers with determination. They glowed with some emotion she could not name. 'No. It's not all right. You don't understand. I can't give in to it. Not yet. Not till it's over.'

He breathed deeply and shook his head, and later he told her that to have given into it would have crippled him, made it impossible to fly again.

'I'm sorry,' he whispered finally. 'I'm sorry you have to see me like this.'

'It's okay,' she said and smiled, touching his hand as it gripped the handlebar, the knuckles white with the force. 'Let's go back to the hotel. You can sleep for a while.'

He nodded, smiled a little at her with his eyes, then they moved off along the silent lane towards the village.

He had woken just after dark in the lamp-lit room, and nuzzled into the warm arm that held him. This was where he wanted to be, and he stayed in the half-lit world between sleep and wakefulness, breathing her warmth. He reached out with his arms, pulled her closer to him, and her body was soft and forgiving, a place to hide. It seemed impossible that the war existed any more, that soon he would have to leave this place of safety and go back to it. Anna lay still in his embrace, running her fingers through his hair, until finally he looked up and she was smiling.

'What were you thinking about?' she said. 'You were miles away.'

He moved away from her, rolled onto his back to stretch. Then he cradled his head in his hands and stared up at the ceiling, considering, searching for the best way to explain. After a moment he said, 'I was wondering if it would be better or worse in the army.'

'Worse, I should think,' she said.

Tom turned his head to look at her.

'Why d'you think that?'

'You'd have to kill people close up and live in a foxhole and you'd be away for months at a time, years even.'

He half smiled. 'Maybe you're right,' he agreed, but he didn't tell her that he saw the faces of the people he killed in his dreams anyway, the faces of women and children. That maybe it was easier to kill a man trying to kill you than drop bombs on unknown lives below.

'Why did you choose the air force?'

'I guess I thought it would be exciting. I wanted to fly Mustangs or Thunderbolts and be a fighter ace like in the Great War.'

Anna smiled.

'I read a lot of war stories as a kid. I wanted to be a hero.'

'You are a hero.'

'Not really.'

'You're my hero.'

She smoothed strands of loose hair back behind her ear with her fingers then touched the bare muscle of his arm.

'You do what you have to, Tom,' she whispered, so that he wondered if she had read his thoughts.

There was a silence then, her fingers resting on the skin of his underarm, her touch light and ticklish.

'Are you okay?' she said.

'I'm okay,' he replied. 'I'm fine.'

'You were exhausted. It's good that you slept.'

Tom yawned, glad again to be alive. 'Kiss me,' he said.

She leaned over, kissed him and he closed his eyes as their lips met. The raid was forgotten. All he wanted was this woman who was next to him.

'Again,' he said, and she laughed, leaning over once more, but this time he wrapped his arms round her back, held her against him and kissed her hard. She struggled, still laughing until he let her go and as she lay back he moved with her so that he was over her and she was no longer laughing as they kissed again, hard and with passion, her legs parting, wrapping round his thighs.

After, they lay breathless, still holding each other, afraid to let go, each moment together blissful and precious. Then she turned her face up to his and smiled.

'Are you hungry?' he asked.

'Yes. Starving. I barely ate while I was waiting for you. I was so scared you wouldn't come back.'

Tom stroked her hair, let the long silkiness trail between his fingers. 'What did you do?'

'I just walked mostly. I tried to read the paper but all I could think of was you. So I just walked and walked all around the lanes near the base and that helped.'

'It must be hard for you,' he said. 'I couldn't bear all that waiting if you were in danger. I'd go crazy.'

She nodded and lifted herself away from him, rolled from the bed and dressed quickly in the cold. He watched her as she turned away, the firm muscles of her back and her shoulders, the soft roundness of her buttocks, the long strong legs. He began to harden again, but wanting her in a way that he knew not even making love to her could satisfy.

Dressed, she turned to him, and he grinned.

'Are you coming down for dinner like that?' she teased, throwing back the covers, laughing when she saw him, naked and hard. He looked away, smiling and embarrassed, shivering in the sudden cold, wondering what she would do.

'Get dressed,' she said, still laughing. 'I'm hungry.'

'Okay,' he replied, and took the clothes that she handed him from the floor where he had dropped them earlier in the haze of his fatigue.

In the hotel dining room they were subdued, talking in whispers in the prim and proper hush, aware of the disapproving stares of some of the older guests, and they ran away back to their room as soon as they had finished. Anna straightened the bed as Tom lit the fire and they sat once again on the floor until the room began to heat, then they moved to the comfort of the big soft bed where they lay, leaning on their elbows, facing each other.

'I can't stay here tonight,' Tom told her. 'I've got to sleep at the base.'

'All right.'

There was a silence.

'Will you have to fly again tomorrow?' Anna asked, hesitant and afraid.

He shook his head. 'I doubt it. The plane needs repairs. The tail section was damaged. It'll be a couple of days before she can fly again.'

'I'm glad,' she replied.

'But I have to be there. There's always training, ground classes, things to do. They think that if they keep us busy it'll stop us being so scared. I should be able to get out in the evening though.'

'Good.'

'What about you? What will you do tomorrow?'

She looked down at the fraying bedspread between them, traced the lines with her thumbnail.

'I don't know.'

'What about work?'

'I don't want to go,' she said, and lifted troubled eyes to his. 'It's so far away from you. It would be so late by the time I got here. And then, when you fly again, I'll be there, not here, close to the base. And I won't know whether you're safe or not. Not until late in the evening. I'd go crazy not knowing, Tom. I couldn't bear it.'

He nodded, understanding.

'Is it all right if I stay here? I want to be near you.' She looked up at him, pleading, and he knew she was asking about the money, if he could pay for the hotel room for longer. She had little money of her own.

'Of course you can stay.'

'Are you sure? Are you sure it's all right?'

'I'm sure. I like having you near me.' He hesitated. 'I just worry about you waiting. Being alone for so long with nothing to do.'

'I'll be fine. I want to be here.' She smiled up at him with her great almond eyes. 'Maybe once we're married we can find a room in a house somewhere near. And then I'll work, except for the days that you fly.'

'Okay,' he smiled, but it was hard for him to think that far ahead; life existed only from mission to mission. Beyond that there was nothing. 'Okay.'

They talked almost into the morning until he tore himself away from her and went back to the room he shared with the other officers of his crew. She had walked down the stairs with him, out into the village, and they had stood in the darkness holding each other, not wanting to part and sleep alone.

'I never saw him again,' Anna whispered now to Lottie. 'He didn't come back from the next one. I waited and waited but he didn't come. That was a month ago and now I don't know if he's alive or dead, and I feel like I'm somewhere in between.' She looked away from the fire for the first time, looked at her friend, focusing with difficulty through the film of tears. She fumbled in her bag for a handkerchief.

'I'm so sorry, Anna. Not knowing must be so hard.'

'We were going to be married. We went to the Registry Office and everything but they make you wait a day, and he had to be back. He was going to get time the next week. We were going to be married.'

She held the handkerchief to her face, dabbing just below her eyes, catching the tears that spilled over. Then she reached up to the slender gold chain round her neck and lifted it over her head. It caught in the tangles of damp hair and Lottie had to reach forward to help. The small gold cross swung as her fingers worked to undo the knot, tapping at Anna's lips. When Lottie had worked it free, the small pile of gold sat in her palm. She looked at it silently, waiting for her friend to go on.

'He gave it to me when he asked me to marry him,' Anna said

finally. 'Because he had no ring, he said. It was his mother's. It's got her initials on the back if you look closely enough. She gave it to him when he joined up. For luck.'

'It's beautiful,' Lottie said. She lifted it and wound the chain round her fingers, let the cross fall free so that it swung on the long chain.

Anna held up her hand for it and Lottie dropped it into her palm. The fingers closed tightly around it, holding on to it like a memory she never wanted to fade.

'He promised me I'd know if he was still alive,' she said, 'and I thought I would. I thought I'd just know. That I'd be able to sense him somehow. But I can't. And I don't know. Some days I'm so sure he'll come back and then others … And nightmares. Terrible nightmares. Always watching him die.'

Anna fumbled with the chain, fingers clumsy with emotion, placing it carefully over her head. It fell against her skin between the folds of her shirt and the cross sat low down on her breast bone, in the shadow of the dip that led to her breasts. She took it once again in her fingers and lifted it so she could look.

There was a silence.

'And the baby,' Lottie remembered. 'When did you find out?'

Anna's lips twisted into a smile, painfully, swallowing down the tears. She folded her hands lightly over her belly.

'It's strange but I knew within days,' she said. 'I just knew. I could feel the life there. And now my period is more than three weeks late, I know for sure.' She looked down at her stomach and smiled again.

'I have a piece of him, still alive, inside me, and that makes it bearable. Just.'

Her friend smiled, grateful for the small humour, concerned.

'How are you physically? I mean, is everything all right?'

'I think so. I've been quite sick, and tired. So tired I could sleep for weeks but I think that's normal. I just wish …' she trailed off, staring into the fire again, distant.

'Anna?' Lottie whispered. 'Are you all right, Anna?'

Anna turned her head slowly. 'I just wish he were here to share it. That's all. He'd be so happy.'

Lottie reached out and took her hand and squeezed it. Anna returned the pressure, biting her lip, tears always just behind her eyes.

'I'm sorry to come here and cry. It's the first time I've spoken about him. To anyone.'

'That's all right. After all, it's not the first time you've come here and cried ...'

They laughed and the tension was broken.

'Have you told your mother yet?'

Anna grimaced and shook her head.

'Oh Anna,' Lottie sighed. 'You poor thing.'

The rain had stopped when Anna stepped out of the door into the garden, and in the half-light of the late afternoon a fine mist of drizzle hung in the air. She glanced up at the heavy laden clouds and wondered if she would make it home before they emptied again. But she walked slowly, reluctant to reach the house at Byron Street.

On the main road a bus lurched past, overfull and heavy, spraying the pavement. She stood back until it had gone and then strolled on, hands in pockets, eyes down. The drizzle began to thicken and small drops of water splashed onto her hair, and onto the ground in front of her. She watched the wetness flicker and dance as the rain began to hit the pavement and huddled deeper into her coat.

It was almost dark when number eight Byron Street loomed into view, the outlines of the roof still just visible against the murky sky. She paused at the gate, bracing herself before she lifted it on its one hinge and strode up the steps. The key turned silently in the lock and she slipped inside, left her sodden shoes on the bottom stair and crept up to her room.

'Anna?!' her mother's voice cut through the gloom. 'Is that you, Anna?!'

'Yes, Mother. I'm just getting changed. I got wet coming home,' she called, hoping the old woman would return to the living room and leave her in peace. 'I'll be down in a minute.' But the irregular thud was already on the stairs, approaching, and she towelled herself hurriedly in the cold room, wanting to be dressed.

'Where have you been this time?' Her mother stood inside the door, arms folded, observing her half-naked daughter.

Anna slipped into the green wool dress and drew comfort from its warmth and the memory.

'I went to Lottie's after work.'

'Oh, did you?' Mrs Pilgrim sneered. 'And what did she have to say for herself?'

'Nothing much. We just chatted.'

'You must have talked about something.'

Anna finished buttoning the dress and sat on the edge of the bed to dry her feet. She worked slowly and carefully, drying each toe in turn, her attention averted from the resentment of her mother's glare. She shrugged slightly.

'Like I said, nothing much. Nothing worth repeating.' She was used to this grilling each time she came back from her friend's, this obsessive need to know each thought that she had.

'I suppose you told *her* where you went? And did you tell Mrs Lawrence as well? Sharing things with them you won't even tell your own mother.'

Anna looked up from her drying. Her mother was staring, eyes narrowed, waiting for an answer. She shook her head slightly and returned to her toes.

'Well, obviously you did then, since you won't deny it. How do you think that makes me feel? Knowing you tell that … that … family things you hide from me? And you've always done it. I know you have. God only knows what you've told them. I don't

know what you see in them. I really don't … that Mrs Lawrence
is a dreadful woman … and as for Charlotte …' She shook her
head, trailing off with a sigh before she began again. 'It's all very
well for them to be nice about it. They didn't have the worry.
They didn't have to go to bed each night alone, wondering what
had happened to you. With no one to share it with.'

Anna finished drying her feet. She reached across from the
bed to the chest of drawers, pulled open a drawer, awkwardly,
from one end, and withdrew a pair of socks. They needed darn-
ing. She put them on anyway, enjoying the rough texture against
the softness of newly dried skin. She pushed the drawer shut and
it slammed on its roller. Her mother winced.

'You don't even answer me when I speak to you. I don't know
where you went but you've become very insolent since. You were
never this rude before. You used to be such a polite girl.' She
sighed again. 'Well, you could have told me you were going to see
Charlotte. I didn't know where you were. I didn't know what time
you'd be home. Three people were killed by a bomb yesterday,
you know. I know it's not like it used to be, but it still happens and
I worry.'

'I'm sorry,' Anna said, placatingly. 'I only decided to go at
lunch-time.'

'Well, next time, I'd like to know. If it's not too much trouble.'

She turned and stomped out and Anna sat on the bed, listening to her thump down the stairs and into the kitchen. She
touched her belly softly with her fingers, still in awe of the life
that lay there. It seemed more real now that she had told someone. Now that the knowledge wasn't only in her head.


'Has Anna gone already?' Mrs Lawrence asked when Lottie
stepped down into the parlour and lifted herself onto the wide
arm of the sofa. 'Not like her not to say hello.'

She turned from the newspaper that was spread on the narrow
dinner table by the window and faced her daughter.

'She's got problems, Mum. Lots of problems.'

Lottie slid off the arm into the deep seat and sat cross-legged like a child. The heavy curtains were pulled against the early evening darkness and a single lamp on the table cast a yellowish glow through the small comfortable room.

'Her mother?' Mrs Lawrence enquired.

'Not this time. Well, not exactly.'

Her mother folded the flimsy newspaper in half and smoothed it flat. She glanced round the cluttered room with satisfaction. A homely room, she thought, a room to feel safe in.

'Am I allowed to know?' she asked, eyes returning to Lottie over the top of her spectacles.

The daughter nodded slowly and said, 'She's pregnant.'

'Anna?' Mrs Lawrence exclaimed. 'Pregnant? That is a surprise.'

'The father's an American airman missing in action.'

'Poor girl,' Mrs Lawrence said. 'Does her mother know yet?'

Lottie shook her head.

'Oh dear,' her mother sighed. 'That's going to be very nasty. I can't imagine Mrs Pilgrim taking that too well at all, can you?'

'No.'

'Poor girl,' Mrs Lawrence repeated. 'And you said the father is missing in action.'

The two women sat in silence for a moment, each contemplating the possibilities.

'Well,' said Lottie's mother finally. 'Tell her we're always here if she needs anything. She only has to ask.'

'I already have.'

Mrs Lawrence nodded in satisfaction and turned back to the paper. 'Who'd have thought it,' she murmured to herself, eyes scanning again the headlines of the paper. 'Anna Pilgrim pregnant.'

# Four

St Valentine's day, Anna's birthday, and Tom wondered if she would celebrate it without him, if another man might take her out instead of him. Even as he thought it, he knew it was stupid, but the memory of that last conversation cast its shadow across all his thoughts of her, and it was hard to keep bright his faith. Stuck in the cold confines of that little room, watching the soldiers come and go in the street outside, there was little else to fill his thoughts. So he wrote to her, trying to explain all he felt about her, sharing with her his dreams for their future, long happy years ahead in the house back home he would build for her. A home with children and love and laughter. It was a long letter that he knew was impossible to post, but pouring out his heart seemed to bring her closer, and helped dispel the doubts.

'You seem sad today,' Marie said when she came to change the dressing on the slowly healing wound. 'What's wrong?'

Tom shook his head and crumpled the letter into a ball, crushing it in his fist, frustrated by its futility.

'Aah,' Marie said, turning from her care of his leg to look at him, one eyebrow lifted. 'Your sweetheart?'

He laughed then and rubbed his eyes with the fingers of one hand, embarrassed to have been so transparent. 'It's her birthday today,' he told her. 'She's twenty-five.'

'She's a lucky girl. To have you, I mean.'

'Except I'm stuck here, and she probably thinks I'm dead.'

'If she loves you, then she'll wait for you,' Marie said. 'Does she love you?'

He laughed again. 'I think so.'

'You only think so? You are not sure of it?'

Tom thought for a moment, and touched the calluses of one hand with the thumb of the other, noticing that they were beginning to soften, remembering how he had been ashamed of their roughness against her skin. He said, 'She loves me.'

'Then stop worrying.'

Tom smiled, knowing she was right.

'It's getting better,' she said, patting the new dressing into place. 'Much better.'

'It's not as painful any more.'

'That's good. Perhaps soon you'll be able to do some exercise, and leave this room.'

'I'd like that.'

'I know it's hard but you must be patient. We must all be patient.'

'You sound like my mom,' he said, and in his mind he saw his mother in the doorway of the house back home, waving him off to the war, chin lifted in that way she had when she was trying not to cry. The house would be all but snowbound now, his father clearing the paths without him, no snowball fights this year, and he wondered if his leg would ever heal enough to ski again, or to skate on the creek that ran behind the mill.

'Your mother sounds like a very sensible woman.'

'She is, most of the time. D'you have kids?'

'I have a daughter. Her name is Monique,' Marie replied. 'She lives in Paris now. She visits sometimes and we hear news from others. But it's hard for her to get away. This was her room.'

He looked around him at the simple wooden furnishings, the patchwork counterpane, little trace now of the girl who had once lived there, except a solitary picture on the wall above the bed, a fading painting of a lake and mountains somewhere.

'She always loved that picture,' Marie said. 'She said that one day she'd like to live somewhere so beautiful.'

'I like it too. It reminds me of home.'

Marie smiled. There seemed to be nothing more to say, so they sat in the comfortable peace, no longer unsettled by the sound of German voices outside, accustomed to the constant danger. Eventually Marie rose from the bed and stood looking down at him.

'You'll be strong again sooner than you think. You'll see. Then you will have less time to doubt that your girlfriend loves you.'

He laughed again, cheered by her humour, but after she had left and gone downstairs it wasn't long before the frustration of his confinement began to gnaw at him again.

The days passed slowly and in the nights Tom woke often to the noise of troops and vehicles outside, falling only gradually back into sleep again, uncomfortable, distracting himself from the pain of his wounds with thoughts of Anna. She should have been his wife by now. One, maybe two, more missions and they would have been married. He tried to imagine her in her daily life without him, at the factory or at home with her mother, but he could see her only as he'd known her, her life apart from him hidden and mysterious. At times she seemed unreal to him, and then he hardly dared to believe in her, afraid that she might elude him and prove to be only a shadow from his dreams after all. More than anything, he thought of her waiting, the not-knowing tearing her apart, and he hoped that Harry had made it back quickly so she would know at least he had survived. It seemed it would be a long time before he was fit enough to travel.

Now and then Marie brought him news of the war, illicit information garnered and spread by the Resistance, a lifeline to the world beyond the harsh realities of occupation. The bombers flew more often now, they heard, further afield as far as Berlin and Nuremburg, and Tom wished he could fly with them, do his part in the war against a people he was learning to despise. Back in England, or at 30,000 feet, it had been different, a less emotional battle. But now the war had touched him personally. It had taken him from Anna and threatened the lives of the family who took care of him. Now he understood what he had risked his life to fight for. He still had nightmares, dreams of dying, but he no longer dreamed of those beneath the bombs.

In the empty hours of the day when he was alone in his room he read. Marie brought English books for him from the school where she worked, and he read them carefully and slowly, rationing himself to half an hour at a time so that they would last longer. He discovered classics that he had not known before, becoming immersed in Homer's *Odyssey* and the plays of Shakespeare, and as he struggled through the unfamiliar language, he wished he had paid more attention at high school instead of gazing out of windows to the freedom beyond, muscles twitching to be outside and active. But he was delighted when one afternoon she brought him a copy of *Huckleberry Finn* that she had found, and he could lose himself in a world that was familiar since childhood.

Occasionally the doctor came, a different face that broke the monotony, checking the wound and mumbling in French as though the American didn't exist.

'He says the wound is very clean,' Marie translated. 'And that the scars are very neat.' Then, conspiratorially, 'I think he's quite pleased with his work.'

Finally, Tom was allowed to move around a little. Three times a day, he would hobble downstairs for his meals, and the warmth of the kitchen and the company of the family eased his loneliness and helped the time to pass. The freedom of movement too, even so small a distance, gave him the comfort that he was improving, that at least his body was no longer getting weaker. He moved about far more than he should have, anxious to get strong again, walking around his room in the mornings when he thought the family was too busy to hear him, and doing sit-ups and push-ups that were hard because he could not yet use his injured leg that way.

'Don't do too much,' Marie warned him once when she caught him.

'I won't,' he lied, because already he could feel the strength seeping back into his limbs and the waning of the frustration that his idleness had wrought.

She smiled and turned away with a shake of her head, but he didn't mind. He knew what he was doing. And gradually, with persistence, his mobility increased, so he was able finally to imagine a time when he might be strong enough to leave on the dangerous journey back to England. Back to Anna.

They had met on the Saturday of his last leave. He had been alone amongst the couples in a crowded tea room that was filled with the fug of steam and cigarettes. Around him, servicemen sat with their girls in hurried intimacy, their time together snatched eagerly from the war, precious and too short. He had ordered more of the tasteless coffee and observed them casually. Watching them, their laughter and their closeness, he felt a rising sense of envy, a need to love and be loved. Then he thought about flying, and how much harder it would be if he had a good reason not to die.

The door opened with a tinkle of the bell and a blast of bitter cold air from the street, and she entered the tea room wrapped warm in a woollen coat and a hat pulled down almost over her eyes. He shivered, mesmerised, as she peeled the hat from her head and shook her long hair free, roughly pushing it into place with her fingers. She peered through the pall of mist that hung over the diners, searching for someone but not finding the person she was looking for. Hesitating, searching for a free table, her eyes lit on one near the window not far from his own. Tom watched as she wound her way through the jumble of chairs and tables, disturbing the couples she passed as she made her way between them to sit down.

The window was misted. The warmth of bodies and steam and breath had condensed against glass almost frozen by the wind outside and she rubbed a small patch clear with her hand so she could gaze out at the people walking swiftly by, hands dug deep in their pockets, shoulders hunched against the cold. Once or twice she turned her head in to the room, waiting for the waitress to come to her and then she looked out again and scanned the street.

Tom watched her, fascinated, all thought of the war wiped from his mind in her presence. The young waitress noticed her finally and hurried over, harassed and overworked and apologetic, but Anna just smiled and gave her order.

'Tea please.'

The waitress returned the smile and slid back through the tables to the counter, disturbing no one.

Tom watched her, waiting for her to turn again from the window. He could see her in profile, the almond eyes and full lips, the long slim elegance of her back and her arms, but he wanted her to turn so he could see all of her.

The waitress brought the tea and Anna smiled and said thank you, and the smile lit a warmth in him he didn't recognise, a warmth that went deeper than his fear of dying. When the waitress turned again towards the counter, the empty tray held loosely at her side, he gestured to her with a movement of his head and she came over to him and smiled.

'More coffee?' she asked.

'No thanks. But I'd like to pay for the lady's tea.'

The waitress grinned and glanced in Anna's direction. 'She's pretty, isn't she?' she whispered.

'She sure is,' Tom answered and they both stared for a moment, then turned to each other and laughed.

'I'll just get the bill for you,' she said, and wove her way back to the counter.

Tom turned again to Anna, still smiling. He knew he was

staring, but she was beautiful and he couldn't help himself. He wondered how long it would be before she noticed, before the heat of his gaze burned holes in her cheek, but she was absorbed in the scene outside, watching the greyness of the road for whoever it was she had planned to meet. She checked her watch, rubbing at the face with her thumb, and he checked his own automatically. It was a quarter after one. Whoever she was meeting was late, he decided, or perhaps they had stood her up. He smiled to himself and hoped so.

She waited for almost an hour, oblivious of his attention, her mind elsewhere. The lunch rush subsided and the tea room emptied and became quiet as the couples spilled out into the bleak cobbled street to make what they could of their short time together. Tom became aware of their absence and the passage of time only vaguely when Anna called to the waitress for the bill.

'It's already been paid,' the waitress said.

He could hear their conversation in the quietness of the almost empty tea room.

'By the American airman just there.' The waitress nodded to him and smiled but he barely noticed. He was waiting only for Anna's response. She turned to him quickly in surprise and held his eyes for an instant before she looked away and blushed.

Tom hesitated, unsure whether or not to approach her. She fingered her hair nervously, tucking it back behind her ears with rapid graceful movements, her fingers trailing over the heat of her neck. The blush had risen over her throat and her cheeks, infusing the natural pallor of her skin with a hot pinkness that he wanted to touch, but he stayed seated, giving her time to recover herself. It seemed an age before she raised her face again to his and he saw that the flush had faded, leaving her glowing in her shyness and the warmth of his attention. She smiled slightly, then rose from her seat, picked up her coat and hat and bag and walked the few paces to his table, her heels loud on the tiled floor.

'Thank you,' she said. 'You're very kind.'

He smiled. 'My pleasure.'

She stood nervously before him, fingering the brim of her hat, and he hesitated again, surprising himself by his awkwardness. He had never felt shy with a woman before. He swallowed hard before he stood and extended his hand.

'Thomas Blake,' he said. It felt strange to talk to her and his voice sounded unlike his own. He hoped she wouldn't notice, that she wouldn't think him strange. 'Nice to meet you.'

'You too,' she said, and let him take her elegant fingers in the hand that he offered. Her skin was smooth and cool to touch and inwardly he shivered. 'Anna Pilgrim.'

They stood for a moment, their hands touching above the small table that stood between them and then, reluctantly, he let her fingers go.

'Would you like to join me?' he asked, and though he was terrified she would say no, she nodded and slid into the chair across from him.

'Thank you.'

Tom ordered tea for them both.

'Your friend didn't show up?' he began cautiously. He didn't want to sound too eager.

'No,' Anna replied. 'She probably had to work overtime. You know how it is.'

He nodded slightly. 'You were meeting a girlfriend?' He lifted his eyes in enquiry, hopeful, and she laughed.

'Yes,' she told him. 'I was meeting a girlfriend.'

'That's good.'

'Is it?'

'Yeah. It's real good.'

She laughed then and he dropped his eyes, shy again under her smile, exposed and transparent.

'It's all right,' she said. 'I'm flattered.'

There was a pause and their tea came and she poured for them both. A group of girls bundled in from the cold, shrieking and laughing, and the waitress steered them to the other side of the tea room where she dragged together two tables. The metal legs scraped loudly on the tiles. The girls were raucous and good-natured and Tom and Anna smiled.

'D'you work?' he asked between sips of the tea. It was better than the coffee. He watched her lift her cup with two hands, cradling it in the long fingers he wanted to touch again.

She nodded. 'I'm a secretary at a munitions factory.' She shrugged. 'It's all right, I suppose. It's better than the factory floor and at least it isn't dangerous.'

He smiled slightly and drank more tea.

'And you?' she said. Her eyes wandered over his uniform and the heavy leather jacket slung over the back of his chair. 'You're a flier?'

'Yeah, I'm a flier.' He didn't want to talk about it. Didn't want to bring in the war to this place of peace he had stumbled into.

'Bombers?' she persisted.

'Fortresses. B17s,' he answered. 'I'm a pilot.'

She nodded and looked down at the table, eyes thoughtful and distant and he waited for her to reply. Finally she lifted her gaze to his and held it.

'It must be very frightening,' she said. 'I hear the planes every morning. Sometimes they fly right over our house and the windows shake in the vibration.'

'Yes,' he said. He wanted to stop the conversation, to change the subject before he told her how terrified he was each time and lessened himself in her eyes, but he couldn't, and he found himself telling her anyway. 'It's real scary. Everyone feels the same but there's a kind of unwritten rule that you don't talk about it; like a superstition or something that if you don't talk about it, it won't happen. I have a lot of nightmares.' He looked up to see if he had said too much. 'I hope you don't think now that I'm a coward.'

'Not at all.' Her answer was quick and definite. 'I think you're very brave.'

'Even though I'm scared?'

'Especially because you're scared. Isn't that what bravery is? Being afraid and doing it anyway?'

He smiled. 'I guess so. I just never thought of it quite like that. I never really thought of myself as brave.' Then, 'I'm sorry. You don't want to hear all this. I'm real sorry.'

He was embarrassed now, sharing thoughts he'd never admitted to anyone before with a girl he'd just met, a girl he wanted to impress more than anyone he'd ever known.

'No, don't apologise. It's fine. I'm touched that you wanted to tell me.' She smiled at him and the hazel almond eyes caressed his face in a way that made him fall a little deeper.

'Are you sure?' he asked. 'You're not just saying that to make me feel better?'

'I'm sure.'

'You're very sweet,' he told her. 'I'm glad we met.'

'So am I.'


They ordered more tea and she left him for a moment to go to the bathroom. He watched her walk leisurely between the tables, elegant in the plain black skirt and sweater that hugged her tall body as she moved away from him. The raucous girls shouted something as she passed them and she turned and laughed, then she disappeared for a while and he wondered what he was doing falling in love. He should stop it now before it was too late. He should just go while she was in the bathroom and disappear from her life so she wouldn't have to know his fear, and to die would not be to lose her. But she was a part of his life already as if he had known her always so he stayed.

When she came back she smiled as she sat down, and he leant forward onto his forearms, decreasing the distance between them, his shyness gone.

'Where are you from?' she asked.

'Montana.'

'Montana?'

'North West of America. Lakes and forests and mountains. It's beautiful.'

'You must miss it.'

'I do,' he said. He wanted to take her there, away from the war and the uncertainty, and show her the place he would build them a house.

'And your family?'

'They're there. My mom and dad and little sister.'

'I'm sure they miss you.'

'Especially Mom. She worries.'

'Of course she worries. It must be just awful to have a son or a husband in the war. Or a lover.' The almond eyes flicked up to his. For a moment she held his gaze and then, realising what she had said, she dropped her eyes and the colour flooded her face. 'Oh God.' She stared down, her breathing hard and quick in her embarrassment. 'Oh God.'

Tom watched, not sure what he could say to help, pleased by her words, sure of her. The warmth flooded him again, more distinct, and this time he knew what it was.

'It's okay,' he murmured, reaching out across the table with his hand for hers. 'It's okay.'

She jumped at his touch, lifted her eyes. They were startled and excited and afraid, but he sensed the fear most of all and slowly withdrew his hand.

'I'm sorry,' she whispered, still breathless. 'I don't know what I was saying ... I don't know where that came from ... I've never ... I mean, I hardly know you ...'

'It's okay,' he said again.

Their hands lay close together on the table, fingers almost touching, and the desire to feel her skin against his almost overwhelmed him. There was a silence and slowly the tension ebbed. The bell on the door tinkled as a group of Tommies came in and milled in the doorway until the waitress led them to tables not far from the raucous girls. Anna shivered in the gust of cold air they had brought in with them.

'Are you okay?' Tom asked. She seemed to have withdrawn from him, hiding in her embarrassment, and he was terrified that he had lost her. But she raised her eyes briefly from the table to his face and whispered, 'Yes, I'm okay.'

'Are you sure?'

She smiled and the tips of their fingers brushed against each other on the surface of the table as she shifted slightly in her chair. He almost held his breath, half expecting her to snatch her hand away from his, but she let it rest and they sat for a while in silence, just touching. On the other side of the room the group of soldiers moved nearer to the girls and the laughter softened to the coyness of giggles.

'More tea?' Tom asked to break the silence.

She shook her head slightly. 'No. No thanks.'

'Cake?'

She laughed and shook her head, then leant forward towards him, let her hand slide into his. He held her fingers very gently, caressing them, and she gave him a small shy smile.

'Where are you based?' she asked.

'Little Sutton.'

She smiled and seemed relieved. 'I know it. I went there once as a child although I can't remember why. I think perhaps my father knew someone there.'

'It's about an hour from here on the bus.'

She hesitated. 'How long is your leave?'

'Seventy-two hours. I have to be back Tuesday morning.'

She nodded, as though she were considering the possibilities. 'Have you got any plans?'

'None.'

She waited for him to go on but he was silent, words unable to express what he wanted to tell her, and an awkwardness fell between them. She lifted her hand from his to flick hair back over her shoulder and when she replaced it, she gripped his fingers tightly so that he looked up at her in surprise.

'I will have more tea,' she said.

He smiled and called to the waitress and it was as though the dam had broken. They talked all afternoon, hands still touching, unravelling each other's thoughts and emotions and fears in a river of conversation that seemed to have no end.

When the tea room closed at six, they were unaware of it and they stared at each other in disbelief when the waitress, hovering tactfully nearby for some time, finally stepped forward and told them she was sorry, but they would have to leave now. They laughed and apologised to her and Tom left a generous tip when they walked out through the empty shop to the bitter darkness outside.

The waitress watched them go, envious of the woman, charmed by the American. Then she locked up behind them and turned tiredly back inside to start cleaning up for the night.

Outside, they stood close together on the step, made breathless by the freezing wind. Anna shivered and he wanted to put his arm around her, pull her to him and warm her with the heat of his body. They stood for a moment in the silence of his hesitation and she moved nearer to him. He could hear her teeth chattering through the darkness.

'Hey,' he said. 'Put your hat on.'

Her body brushed his as she lifted her arms and he shivered with her touch. She jammed the hat on her head like a child and he laughed even though he could barely see her. He liked the way she didn't fuss about her appearance, the softness of her face with no make-up. She would look the same in the morning when he woke to her beside him.

'Where shall we go?' he asked. He wanted to get out of the darkness, get to somewhere he could see her.

'Dinner somewhere?' she suggested.

'Sounds good. Where?'

She shook her head in the dark. 'I don't really know anywhere. I don't go out much. I'm sorry.' There was shame in her voice and he was sorry he had asked.

'I know somewhere,' he said. 'Not far from here.'

'Good. Then let's go.'

He offered her his arm and she took it, holding herself close to him as they picked their way through the blackness, their path lit by the small beam of a torch. At first he walked slowly, but she kept stride with him easily, her body graceful and lean against his, so he quickened their pace through the cold night.

They went to a small self-service restaurant that was brightly lit and crowded. It was busy and there was a queue, so they stood with the other couples in line by the till, whispering self-consciously, holding hands.

'Have you been here before?' she asked him.

'Once,' he replied.

'Who with?'

He grinned and squeezed her hand and made her wait for an answer.

'Who?' she insisted.

'Just guys from the base,' he said.

She laughed, relief in her face as he watched her, and he wished he had taken her somewhere nicer.

They ate quickly in the hectic atmosphere, barely speaking over the hubbub, the food good and warming, better than Anna had eaten for a long time. Even eating fast in the cheap and tatty restaurant, she ate elegantly, taking small mouthfuls. Tom ate without appetite, barely tasting the food, hurrying so they could leave and go somewhere quiet where they could talk again.

A man at the next table leaned over to Anna and slurred something offensive, his voice thick with alcohol. Tom rose instantly, fists clenched, and the man cowered back in his seat and cringed.

'Let's go,' Anna said, taking Tom's arm. 'Just leave him. He's not worth it.'

'What did he say to you?'

'Nothing. It doesn't matter. Let's go.'

Tom stood over the man, breathing hard, his anger roused.

'Tom, please.'

The man stared down at the table, not daring to look up.

'You're lucky,' Tom told him, then he took Anna's arm and they hurried out down the stairs and stood close together on the pavement, two silhouettes in the blackout. Another couple, the man in army uniform, brushed past them, laughing, and the pavement was flooded briefly with light as the soldier opened the restaurant door. A wave of noise washed over them and ebbed again as the heavy door swung slowly shut behind the couple. They smiled at each other as the silence closed round them again. Heels clicked on the street a short distance away, but they could see no one in the darkness, and high overhead a lone aeroplane droned, heading home for the night.

'Are you okay?'

'I'm fine,' Anna said. 'Just fine.'

'What did he say to you?'

'Nothing. I don't know. Does it matter?'

Tom paused. 'No. I guess not.'

His anger had surprised him. He had never wanted to protect a woman like that before, had never been so offended by someone else's insult.

'I just wanted to protect you,' he whispered, hoping she would understand. 'He had no right to talk to you like that.'

'I know. And thank you. But it's not important. He was just a drunk.'

They stood in silence on the freezing street and he let the anger drain away from him, felt his heartbeat gradually slow. Then he turned to her and took her hands in his.

'Anna,' he said. He wanted to see her, hating the blackout that hid her face from him. He knew she was watching him. He could feel her gaze in the darkness, but he hesitated, nervous now.

'Anna,' he said again. She waited patiently, her hands small and cold in his, her fingers pressing against his palms. He wondered what she was thinking, what she was feeling. He wanted to see her face.

'What do you want to do now?' he asked at last. All he could hear was his breathing.

'What do you want me to do?'

He paused, not knowing how best to say what he wanted to say, afraid of offending her.

'Tom?'

'I want you to come back to my hotel. I want to spend all night with you.'

Her fingers tensed against his palms.

'It's okay,' he said. 'I don't care if we just talk, or just sleep, or just hold each other. If you don't want to make love, that's fine. I understand, it's very soon. But I don't want to be apart from you. Not tonight. Not ever.' He stopped, hoping she had understood how much he needed her, praying she would agree. He could feel her tension, the slight fear she still had of him.

'Of course I'll stay with you,' she answered. 'Of course.'

In the darkness he stretched his hand to her face, touched the cold smoothness of her cheeks with his fingers and felt the warmth rise up in him again, the bitter night receding around him.

'Thank you,' he said softly. 'Shall we go?'

'Yes.'

He put his arm around her shoulders, gently lifted her arm round his waist, and held her tightly against him, her body lean and yielding against his hardness as they walked in silence through the night to his hotel.

The room in the cheap hotel was cold and spartan, a fading threadbare rug the only colour. She glanced around from the doorway and shivered. Tom hurried to light the gas fire and invited her over to the warmth as the flames glowed blue then orange and the room became homely. They stood in their coats, hands stretched to the flames and he watched her face in the bright light of the uncovered light bulb. She was thoughtful and the almond eyes stared deep into the heater.

'Are you okay?' he asked. He was concerned that she was afraid, that perhaps she didn't trust him.

'I'm fine,' she said, and turned to him and smiled. 'Really. I thought I might feel … cheap or something being in a hotel room with a man I just met. But I don't. It feels like the most natural thing in the world to be here with you.'

Tom smiled. 'I'm glad. I'd hate for you to feel cheap.'

'I don't. I feel fine.'

He took off his jacket and helped her with her coat, found a hanger in the wardrobe and hung it neatly next to his shirts. Then he returned to the fire and they stood next to each other in the glow of its heat. There was only one chair, on the right of the heater, and he offered it to her but she refused and sat instead on the floor, her back against the end of the big bed, still close to the warmth. She smiled up at him, her long legs curled under her and he sat on the floor too, a little distance away by the chair, careful not to be too close to her.

'I'm sorry it's not a nicer room,' he said. 'It was all I could find.'

'It's fine,' she replied. 'It's cosy.'

He looked around it briefly. She was being kind.

She saw his expression and laughed. 'It doesn't matter anyway. It could be a hovel and I'd still be happy.'

'I'm glad,' he said. 'I don't often bring girls back here, you know. Only sometimes. Only if they're very special.'

She frowned for an instant before she realised. 'You're teasing me,' she said, and laughed.

'Yes. I'm teasing you. But you are special.'

There was a silence and they listened to the hiss of the fire.

Her face was flushed now with the warmth and excitement and he was aware of his breathing and the heat inside him. It took effort not to move towards her and she was shy under his gaze, smoothing the wool of her skirt against her thighs, her eyes dropped to the floor.

'I'm getting quite hot now,' she said, and gracefully lifted herself up onto the big bed in one languid movement. 'Come and sit over here with me.' She moved back across the candlewick bedspread towards the pillows and he watched as she settled herself and made herself comfortable. She lay on her side, her head propped up on one hand, and his eyes followed the inviting contours of her body, the small roundness of her breasts, the dip of her waist that led to the curve of her hip. Then he pushed himself to his feet and sat close to her on the bed.

'I've never done this before,' she said. 'There's never been anyone.'

'I know,' he answered gently. Then, to ease the tension, he said, 'Tell me more about your family,' and in a low voice she told him that she lived with her mother, that her father had left them for another woman when she was six years old.

'I told everyone he was a famous explorer,' she said, 'and that he'd gone to find treasure in Africa. By the time my friends stopped believing me I was old enough that I'd got used to not having him around.' She stopped and looked up from the bedspread and smiled. 'Sometimes I wonder where he is now and what he's doing, if I've got brothers or sisters I don't even know about.'

'How did your mom take it?'

'Very badly. She became very protective after he left, and distrustful of everyone, especially men. Especially attractive men. My father was very good looking, you see.'

Tom said nothing, wondering how much of her mother's dislike of men had rubbed off on her, if her nervousness of him ran deeper than she knew.

'It was hard for us both for a while,' Anna went on. 'Sometimes she would hold me and cry and I hated that. Then she'd go back to being stern and puritanical. But she became spiteful too, and I didn't understand why at the time. I realise now that I was all she had, but I was also a constant reminder of the man who'd left her, so she was torn between the two emotions.'

'And now?'

Anna half shrugged, and paused, searching for the right words.

'It's all right,' she offered finally. 'I mean, we have our ups and downs. She's a bit old-fashioned in her views, and she can still be spiteful, but most of the time it's all right. I suppose I've got used to her ways.'

'You've never thought of leaving?' He hated to think of her being bullied by her mother, unhappy, knowing instinctively it was worse than she said.

'Yes, I have. Of course I have, but it's difficult for a woman on her own. And I'd feel guilty leaving her. She's lonely. And sad. I'm all she has.' She gave him an apologetic smile.

'She's lucky to have you,' he said, and reached with his fingers to her face, the tips just brushing the smooth skin of her cheek. She dropped her eyes and turned her face away, the intimacy too much now that they were alone in his room. He let his hand drop, disappointed, understanding that she needed time, but his eyes stayed on her face and when she slowly looked up again, she could barely hold the intensity of his gaze.

'I'm sorry,' she whispered.

'What for?'

She looked down again and bit her lip, embarrassed.

'You don't have to be sorry,' he said, but he knew she could see the desire in his eyes, and he had no way to hide it from her.

'I didn't ask you here just to make love to you, Anna. I wanted to be with you.'

'But you want to make love to me.' Her eyes were still lowered as though she were ashamed of herself.

'Of course I want to,' Tom said. 'You're beautiful.'

She smiled.

'But I can wait until ...' He stopped abruptly, uncertain if he should say what was on his mind, frightened by the violence of his love for her. He swallowed and there was a silence.

'Until what?'

He shrugged. 'Until you're ready. Until we ...'

'Tom?'

He took a deep breath. 'Until we're married,' he said quickly, and looked up at her lying opposite him on the big bed, his heart knocking hard, his breathing tight with nerves, waiting.

She blushed, then smiled and lifted her eyes to his face. 'Are you proposing?' she whispered.

He nodded with a half-shrug of shyness, hardly believing it himself, afraid she would think he'd lost his mind.

'I don't know what to say,' she murmured, still smiling, and he was glad that he had asked.

'You don't have to say anything,' he told her. He was sweating, shaken by his own impetuosity, yet sure of the rightness of it. He wiped a sleeve across his forehead. 'Think about it for a while. I know it's very soon.'

She nodded and in the silence that followed he had known what her answer would be.

# Five

Anna lay in the darkness of the early morning, nauseous, head pounding. She touched her hand to the small swelling in her belly, lifting her nightdress so she could feel the tautness of the skin across the bulge. She rubbed it gently with her palm, massaging, reassuring herself. If she looked sideways she could see the luminous figures on her alarm clock but she ignored them, instinctively knowing the time, holding each precious moment of rest for as long as she could.

She rose finally, slowly, the pain in her head intensifying with each movement, and squeezed herself into the skirt she had altered last night, working secretly in her bedroom to let out the waist. Someone must notice soon, she thought, buttoning the cardigan that hid the growing life.

The house was still silent, her mother still asleep, and Anna crept along the landing and down the stairs, barefoot, the threadbare carpet rough against her soles. She almost ran the last few steps when she saw the pale rectangle of an envelope on the mat and as she squatted to pick it up, she could make out unfamiliar handwriting in the gloom of the hall. She snatched it up, glanced up to check she was alone, and trod quietly into the kitchen. Standing close to the window in the first greyness that filtered through the glass there was just enough light for her to read the bold black handwriting.

Montana, she read in the return address. Flathead Valley, Montana, USA.

She ripped open the envelope and held the letter close to the glass, squinting in the half-light.

*12th March 1944*

*Dear Anna,*

*Thank you for your letter, which came to us eventually, in a roundabout way! You must have been so worried, waiting for our reply. We have had news of a sort, which is that Tom is missing in action. I've written out the telegram word for word for you below.*

*'Regret to inform you report received states your son First Lieutenant Thomas B. Blake missing in action in European area since fourteen January. If further details or other information of his status are received you will be promptly notified.'*

*It's not much information really but at least we have hope that he is still alive. Of course, we will write to you again as soon as we hear anything.*

*I know you will pray for him as we do.*

*With our love and best wishes,*
*Emma and Alex Blake*

She had almost given up hope of hearing from his parents. As the weeks had slid by, she had begun to despair of ever knowing the truth. But now she would know. Whatever happened, at least she would know. She read the letter over and over, burning the details into her mind until she heard her mother stomp into the bathroom overhead. She checked her watch, drank some milk from the bottle on the counter and left hurriedly, letting the front door slam behind her.

The bombers came as she walked to the bus stop, the silence shattering, and she stopped, looking up, watching them approach.

They flew way over to the north today, but the roar still vibrated inside her and the euphoria she felt from the letter dissipated in their wake. She placed her hand on her belly protectively, sad again.

'I hope you never have to go to war, my little one,' she whispered.

'Do you want to have children?' she had asked Tom once. They had been walking in the city, weaving through the crowds of people late in the afternoon, their arms interlocked, dodging the trams.

'What, now?' he had replied, teasing.

'Yes, why not?' she joked back, and then he became serious, shaking his head.

They slowed to a stop and stood facing each other. People walked around them in the busy street.

'No, not now. Not until this war ends. If it ever ends. This is no world to bring a child into.'

His words made her sad and he must have seen it in her face because then he smiled and said, 'Yeah, of course I want kids.'

'Boys or girls?'

He thought for a moment and they meandered on, arm in arm again. 'Oh girls, I think, so I can have a house full of women to love me.'

'Tom!' she exclaimed and pulled away from him, dragging her arm out of his. She turned quickly and punched him in the arm, right in the muscle where it hurt and he looked up at her in delighted surprise.

'Where did you learn to punch like that?' he asked, nursing his deadened arm, playing the game.

'Billy taught me years ago. My best friend's little brother. Bless him,' she replied, laughing, backing away, almost bumping into a soldier, who sidestepped smartly to avoid her.

'I'm going to get you for that,' Tom had laughed, coming after her. She had turned and run through the crowd, but not far before he had caught her and kissed her in the busy road.

She smiled at the memory, the last of hum of the bombers receding into the morning. Then she realised that other workers bustling to the bus stop were staring at her, standing in the street smiling to herself, so she hurried on to the bus stop to join the queue.

At the Lawrences on Saturday afternoon, the two women lounged on Lottie's bed, their conversation easy and never ending.

'Have you been to the doctor yet?' Lottie was asking.

Anna looked down under her friend's questioning gaze, and traced the lines of the bedspread with a thumbnail. 'No. Not yet.'

There was a silence and they could hear the soft murmur of voices from the living room below.

'You should go,' Lottie said. 'How far gone are you now?'

'Fifteen weeks.'

'Already?'

'From the date of my last period. Not from the one I missed.'

'Oh.' Lottie nodded and absorbed this piece of information. 'I see.'

'I've been doing some reading.' Anna was half-apologetic. 'There's all sorts of stuff I didn't know about before.'

'Don't tell me. I don't want to know.'

'I'm sorry.'

'It'll happen when it's meant to,' Lottie shrugged. 'Then and only then. But I don't want to talk about that. I want to talk about you. You've got to go to the doctor soon.'

'I know. It's just … All those snide glances. And once it's official it'll probably get back to my mother. You know what people are like.'

'Yes,' Lottie conceded. 'But the health of your child, of Tom's child …'

There were ripples of laughter downstairs.

'You'll be a great mother,' Anna said drily.

Lottie laughed. 'I'm sorry. I'm just concerned about you.'

'All right. I'll go next week. I'll take a day off sick.'

'Good. Now, how's the morning sickness?'

'Better. I've stopped vomiting. I just feel like I'm going to now.'

'Ahh, the joys of motherhood.'

'And headaches. Really bad headaches. But I think that might be tiredness.'

'It's probably both. You're still working long hours. That's exhausting in itself.'

'I'm trying to save money for the baby.'

'When are you going to tell your mother?'

'I don't know. I don't think I'll be able to keep it secret much longer. I've let out all the clothes I can but I'm struggling to get into them already.' She pulled at the waistband that was stretched tight across her stomach.

'You can't really tell though.'

'Are you sure?'

Lottie nodded. 'I'll ask Mum if she's got anything you can have. She might have something.'

'Thanks.' She paused. 'What did she say when you told her?'

'She was shocked. We all were, Anna. You've always been the sensible one. No one ever expected you to get into trouble.'

Anna bit her lip, hurt, wondering how to reply. 'I'm not in trouble,' she said softly. 'I'm carrying Tom's child.'

'I'm sorry,' Lottie replied. 'I didn't mean anything by it.'

'I know.'

There was a silence between them, and more laughter downstairs.

'Shall we go down and be sociable?' Anna suggested. 'I haven't seen your brothers for ages.'

Downstairs, the living room was alive with conversation and

laughter. Billy was entertaining his parents, and the younger brother, Richard, was trying unsuccessfully to do homework at the table. Billy paused when his sister and her friend came in, and Mrs Lawrence wiped a tear of laughter from the corner of her eye.

'Hello Anna,' he smiled. 'How's the tummy?'

'Billy!' his mother scolded.

'Fine,' laughed Anna. 'Getting bigger. Look.' She turned sideways and smoothed her skirt across her belly so that he could see the small swelling. Billy reached a tentative hand towards her and touched her stomach lightly. They grinned at each other and Mrs Lawrence turned away in exasperation.

'Anna's almost family, Mum. She doesn't mind. Do you Anna?'

'No. I don't mind.'

Mrs Lawrence shook her head, sighed and stood up. 'Tea?'

'Yes please.' Anna sank into one of the dips in the sofa as Mrs Lawrence went out to the kitchen. 'So how are you Billy? How's school?'

Billy flicked his sister a look of surprise. 'Lottie hasn't told you?'

'Told me what?'

'I thought you'd want to tell her,' Lottie said, sliding from the arm of the sofa into the other dip.

Billy looked embarrassed and sat on one of the dining chairs next to the window so that he was close to Anna.

'I joined up,' he told her softly. 'Infantry. I start my basic training next week. On Wednesday.'

'But you haven't finished school!' Anna was shocked, horrified, that this boy she had known all her life was becoming a soldier.

'I can finish school afterwards. I want to do my bit.' He sat up straight on the hard-backed chair, the narrow shoulders pushed back, chest thrust forward.

'You volunteered?' Anna was incredulous.

Billy nodded.

'Your mum must have loved that.'

'Touchy subject,' Lottie murmured.

There was a silence.

Finally Anna said, 'I don't know what to say.'

Billy looked down, disappointed by the reaction. 'I bet whatever his name was volunteered. I bet he didn't wait to be called up.' He lifted his eyes, sullen and hurt, and dropped them as soon as he saw the pain in Anna's face. 'I'm sorry,' he said quickly. 'I didn't mean that.'

'It's okay. You're right. He did volunteer.' She smiled slightly, remembering what Tom had told her; how he had driven all night with a friend in his father's car to the recruiting office, fired by his own love of freedom and the belief that he'd be a great pilot. He wanted to shape his own future, he'd said, not wait for someone else to decide it for him, and he told his parents afterwards, when it was done, the same as Billy. The look on their faces when they heard would stay with him always, he'd said, the same shock and fear and pride in him that she felt now for Billy.

'I understand,' she said. 'And his name is Tom.'

Billy smiled, gratefully. There was a pause and Mr Lawrence lifted himself out of the armchair that was on the other side of the small room. He stood and stretched the tall lean body for a moment, then went out to his wife in kitchen. He was shaking his head, and murmuring.

'He thinks I'm a bloody fool,' Billy said.

'I don't,' Anna answered. 'You have to do what you believe is right. He knows that. He's just afraid of losing you. We all are.'

'Tea's up.' Mrs Lawrence bustled in with the tea tray, disturbing the tension with an atmosphere of determined good will. Nothing was going to spoil these last days with her son.

Later, at home, Anna sat with her mother in the living room.

'*The hour of our greatest effort and action is approaching,*' Mr Churchill intoned over the radio set. '*The flashing eyes of all our*

soldiers, sailors and airmen must be fixed upon the enemy on their
front. The only homeward road for all of us lies through the arch of
victory. '

'What do you think he means?' demanded Mrs Pilgrim from
her place on the sofa. 'Does he mean the second front is finally
coming?'

'Perhaps,' Anna replied, reluctant to speculate. 'I hope so.'

'So do I. Then it will be over and we can go back to a normal
life. I'm sick of it. Really I am.'

Anna nodded, placating.

'It isn't right that a woman of my age should have to work. It's
just not right.'

'It's only part time, Mother. Everyone has to do their bit.'

'Well, I'll be glad when it's finished.'

'We all will.'

Vera Lynn began to croon softly on the radio set, and Anna
got up to turn it off, depressed by the sentimentality. The two
women sat in silence in the overfurnished room, the gloom made
heavier by the blackout curtains at the window. Unconsciously
Anna rubbed at her belly, watching her mother. She could think
of nothing neutral to say and the silence was uncomfortable.

She won't mention it again, Anna thought. Even after all this
time it's still driving her mad that she doesn't know where I went.
But she won't ask because she knows I'm not saying and she can't
bear to lose the argument again. She won't bring it up any more.
Until she finds out I'm pregnant. Then all hell's going to break
loose.

'Billy Lawrence has joined up,' she said, to dispel the mood.
'He's doing his basic training up north somewhere, he thinks.
He's off next week.'

'Well, it's no more than he should do. I don't suppose he volunteered.'

'He did actually.'

Ignoring the reply, her mother said, 'And I suppose he's doing just wonderfully. You seem to think the Lawrences do everything just perfectly.'

Anna swallowed and said nothing.

'Well?'

'I'm sure he's doing just fine.'

'And is Charlotte pregnant yet? They've been married almost two years.'

'No. Not yet.'

'My guess is that there's something wrong with her. She was always such a skinny little thing.'

'Perhaps,' Anna said, but her body was tensed with anger. 'But I think they might be waiting until things improve. Evan is away such a lot.'

'Well, she should be thankful he isn't fighting.'

'She is.'

'I can remember when your father was away fighting in the last war. You've no idea what I went through, worrying and waiting. Of course, he never wrote.'

Anna was silent then, her hand resting lightly on the little life inside her.

# Six

The days inched by and the worst bitterness of the winter cold gradually yielded to the longer warmer days of spring. Tom saw the season change from his chair in the warmth of the kitchen, and watched the garden beginning to show hesitant signs of life beneath the melting snow. Or he sat in his bedroom and looked out from the small window over the street, the German soldiers young and loud and abrasive, stamping their authority into the stones, the villagers hurrying past, eyes dropped to avoid confrontation.

He ached to go out, to be active and on his way, the boredom of confinement chafing him inside. He had to fight to hide his feelings, full of guilt at his impatience and frustration when the family was risking so much to keep him.

In an effort to distract himself he studied French, much to the amusement of Marie's father who would sit with him in the evenings for hours, patiently correcting and encouraging but unable to suppress his laughter until slowly the American's pronunciation began to improve and he learned to communicate in shy faltering sentences. The study helped to pass the time, and chased Anna from his thoughts for a while. But later, alone in bed, in the solitary darkness of his room, his mind led him inevitably back to her, wondering always how she was, anxious that she might not yet know that he was still alive and that he loved her. Then he could feel the tension in his muscles and would get up from the bed and stretch to ease the stiffness, moving carefully and silently in the sleeping house.

\* \* \*

He sat quietly in the kitchen, struggling with the French grammar exercises that he studied now each day as Marie worked, preparing the food she had collected on her bicycle on her way home from work. He wondered how she made it stretch to feed him too, and wished again he could move on, spare them the extra hardship.

Bored with the future tense, he looked up from his book and watched her. She was deep in thought, her hands moving deftly above the kitchen table among the vegetables and the luxury of the small chicken she had bartered for with vegetables from their small garden.

Like a second mother, he thought, and remembered again his mom in Montana; the big kitchen that was the centre of the family, the air aromatic with the scent of strong coffee, and in the background the buzz of the saws from the timber mill. They were alike, Marie and his mother, women with a gentle manner that belied the core of toughness beneath.

She glanced up from her cooking and caught him watching her. He smiled. 'You remind me of my mother,' he said.

'Thank you,' she replied, pleased, and returned to her work for a moment, before she looked up at him again. He waited for her to speak, aware of her hesitation. 'Would you like to go out for a walk this evening?' she asked finally. 'One of us will take you. We can go before supper, just before it gets dark. You need to exercise, to gain strength before you can go from here.'

'I'd like that very much,' Tom replied with a smile. He had been waiting, hoping she would ask him soon, forcing himself to be patient and defer to her judgment of the right time. Then, anxious for her safety, he said, 'Maybe I should go alone.'

Marie shook her head emphatically 'No,' she insisted. 'You're still weak and you do not know the area. You need to have one of us with you. I won't hear of you going out alone.'

He smiled. She was very like his mother.

* * *

Later, he stood on the back doorstep where he had crawled more than six weeks before, and felt the cool of the evening air against his face, and the smell of the early spring. He lifted his eyes and scanned the sky, the heavy cloud that pressed down against the undulating earth, the tips of the trees in the distance hidden by the mist. He inhaled deeply, his senses excited by the freshness, then he turned to the old man who stood with him, waiting patiently. With a nod from him, they set off slowly across the garden towards the fields that stretched to the forest where he had fallen, but even walking with a stick he stumbled often, his muscles unaccustomed to more than a few short paces at a time. Marie's father walked at his side, turning to him often, smiling praise and encouragement. Tom nodded in reply but it took all his concentration just to walk, and the little French that he had learned was soon forgotten in the effort.

He was quickly exhausted and they went only a short distance before he was struggling, his wounded leg painful, his other muscles sore and aching. They turned back, and he shuffled with determination through the fading light of the evening, too absorbed in the effort of the task to even think about the danger of being caught. At the cottage he collapsed in his chair in the kitchen, and the old man teased him good-naturedly until, with rest and food, he began to recover. He slept well that night, undisturbed by the racket from the street, and with a tiredness that had come at last from activity.

The walk became a nightly ritual, and always one of the family walked with him, taking him a different way each time in case their habits should be observed. He became bolder as his strength increased and they walked further and longer each day. Once, not long after he had begun to go out, he and Marie stumbled across a group of German soldiers who were lolling idle in a street near the cottage, smoking silently in the half-light of the evening. Their appearance was sudden and unexpected and instinctively Marie grasped at Tom's arm. He covered her hand with his own, an automatic gesture of reassurance, and they slowed their pace a little, but they were too close to turn back without arousing suspicion, so they walked on, conversing quietly in French.

A couple of the soldiers watched them approach, and Tom felt the sweat break out on his back as they moved towards them, heads bowed. He was less afraid for himself than for Marie; punishment for helping the enemy was swift and severe, their escape entirely dependent on good luck. He kept his eyes averted from the men, kept them lowered to the road, and murmured soft replies to Marie's conversation though he understood almost nothing of what she was saying.

It seemed to be a long way before they could turn off the road out of the soldiers' sight, and as soon as they did so, they began to walk quickly, silently, anxious to be home in the safety of the cottage. They said nothing of the incident to her parents, and after that, it was always Marie who accompanied him on his nightly walks.

With each day of exercise his strength returned and he watched the muscles beginning to harden with pleasure, pushing himself more each day, testing his will against the fitness of his body. He had been strong when he fell, the rigours of flying a heavy bomber clear in the power of his shoulders and arms, and he knew he would need such strength again for the journey home. But the energy he gained from the exercise made it harder for him to be still, or patient, and Marie's father scolded him often as his attention wandered from his study, his mind preparing itself for trials ahead. He tried to be patient, not wanting to seem ungrateful, and Marie helped him by giving him odd jobs to do around the place, weeding, or firewood to chop. Then he worked with energy and relish, thankful for the activity, anything that took his mind from the waiting and the wondering.

Discreetly Marie made enquiries, but she learned only the Resistance would make contact when it was safe for Tom to move.

Early in April, André appeared at last with the news that they would leave the following day. It was as they had expected it would happen, sudden, taking advantage of an opportunity to go, but still, the abruptness of his going took them all by surprise, and Tom found it much harder to leave than he had imagined. They had done so much for him, taken such risks to keep him safe, and he had no way to express his thanks.

That final night Marie cooked a special dinner and they drank a bottle of Bordeaux treasured from before the war and hoarded for a special occasion.

'To a safe journey,' Marie toasted.

'And the end of the war,' he returned.

It was almost like leaving his own family all over again.

André led him swiftly across the fields in the darkness and Tom followed at first with ease, the terrain familiar, his eyes used to picking his way through the night. They moved in silence, resting occasionally, travelling away from the roads. But he tired quickly, unused to the sustained activity, angry with himself for his weakness. André slowed the pace and the rests became more frequent as the night progressed towards dawn.

They reached the farmhouse in the early hours. It was quiet, nobody awake, and André guided him upstairs to a hard bed where he could sleep. He fell into it and slept immediately, deeply, exhausted by the long walk, waking only in the bright morning sun when a pretty teenaged girl with freckles brought him coffee and bread, telling him to come down to the kitchen when he was ready. He woke groggily, still tired, but he dressed hurriedly and ate, anxious to go down, to find out what was happening.

The kitchen was busy. There were two other evaders, and André sat at the heavy wooden table in the centre of the room that was spread with papers and maps, in deep conversation with three other men. The girl with freckles was tending the stove and another older woman in a headscarf washed dishes near the back door. There was a silence when he entered. All eyes turned to him and he hesitated at the door, self-conscious under their scrutiny.

'Come in,' André said. 'Have more coffee.'

The Frenchman spoke to the girl, who lifted a pot from the stove and filled a cup for him. Tom took it from her with a smile of thanks and made his way across the large room to where the other airmen sat on a low couch.

'Hi,' he said.

They nodded their greetings as he pulled up a chair and they sat awkwardly for a moment before Tom introduced himself.

'Tom Blake.'

'Mike Lewis.'

'Ralph Soloman. RAF.'

He sensed hostility towards him in the attitude of the British flier and wondered what he had done to offend him. There was an uncomfortable silence.

Eventually Ralph spoke again. 'When were you shot down?' The hostility was still there, as if Tom had no right to be with them.

'January fourteenth.'

Both men stared at him in surprise. 'You've been here since then?'

'I was wounded. I've been staying with a family.'

'You okay now?' Mike asked, and Tom smiled at the American accent he hadn't heard for so long. It was strange and comforting to be once again with people whose language was his own.

'Yeah. Pretty much. How about you guys?'

Tom turned to the Englishman and noticed for the first time how young he was. Just a kid. He seemed in awe of all that was around him. 'How about you, Ralph?'

'I came down about a week ago. We were on our way back from Berlin when some night-fighters tagged us. We crash landed in a field and I was the only one still alive when we stopped.' The young voice quavered with emotion, his eyes downcast, and the two Americans exchanged brief glances.

'I ran like hell all night, just heading west, then I spent a day in a barn and moved on again after dark. I did that for a couple of days, text book stuff, I suppose, what they tell you you're supposed to do. But then I got hungry so I asked a farmer for help and he contacted these chaps for me. And here I am.'

Tom sat back and sipped his coffee, nodding, trying to determine how close the kid was to breaking point. He had heard that brittleness in men's voices before.

'You're in good hands now,' he said. Then he turned to the American.

'I was shot down a couple of days ago,' Mike said. 'And these guys picked me up almost straight away. I guess I was lucky. But it was a pretty bad mission.'

'Fighters?'

'Everything.' He looked away, remembering, telling them how it all went wrong from the beginning. A long slow haul that the whole crew knew from the outset was the final one, a bad feeling, just a case of when and where, the plane disintegrating piece by piece as if she had given up before they even started. 'It felt like the longest time.' He gave a wry smile. 'But I guess you know how it feels, right?'

Tom nodded. But the last one hadn't been the worst. It had been over too quickly for that. It was the mission before, the first since knowing Anna that he relived again and again in his dreams, and that still troubled his waking thoughts.

He had examined his reflection in the mirror in the washroom at the base that morning, looking for traces of the fear he knew were hiding behind the eyes. He had aged, he thought, since he started this, the brightness of his youth dimming a little with each mission that he flew. Ten more to go. Only ten, but it still seemed a hell of a long journey home. The face stared back at him impassively, pale brown eyes clear and intense, dark circles of tiredness beneath them, and there was no trace of the emotion that chewed at his innards.

He missed Anna already. He had woken in the night and reached out for her, but his hand had found only air and the rough air force blankets before his half-consciousness had remembered and he had fallen back into dreams about flying, not making it home.

Swallowing down the rising bitter taste from his gut, he shaved in the dim light, running his fingers over his skin, checking the smoothness until he was satisfied it was good enough that the mask wouldn't itch and drive him crazy. He checked his watch. A quarter after two. The duty corporal had woken him fifteen minutes earlier with a flashlight in his face, shouting times for breakfast and briefing and stations. Wherever it was they were going, it was going to be a long trip.

Tom made his way across the base through the darkness of the morning, guiding the bicycle carefully over the frozen mud, one hand holding the flashlight. The bike skittered and slid on the rough furrowed ground, and twice he nearly came off. At the mess hall he left it with the others in an untidy heap not far from the door. Inside was quiet, the tense hush broken only by the scraping of utensils on china and the scuff of boots on concrete. He sat alone, eating eggs and toast and jam without appetite, forcing the food down for the energy he would need later, but the coffee was good and hot so he drank two cups, letting the warmth trickle down and soothe his stomach.

No one talked much. Each man was alone with his private thoughts, eyes lowered to the food on his plate. At ten to three Tom drained the last of his coffee, rose from the table and walked reluctantly out and across the rutted mud to the briefing room, which was filling fast. He showed his pass to the guard at the door and then paused for a moment, scanning the sea of heads until he caught sight of Harry, way down at the front. He threaded his way through the rows of men to the vacant seat next to the navigator. They nodded and half smiled, knowing each other too well for a need for words, and they sat side by side in silence on the hard wooden chairs waiting for the briefing to start. Harry's presence calmed him, as always, and the fear abated a little.

Some raucous laughter a few rows behind them broke the tension, then other voices began to crack jokes and insults. The laughter was high, and strained, but as three o'clock approached, the noise died down gradually. A headquarters officer called the men to attention. Chairs scraped on concrete as the crews rose unenthusiastically to their feet, the tension returning, all eyes on the covered map centre stage. The colonel strode in, business-like and purposeful, admired by his men. He stood next to the curtain that still hid the map, tapping the pointer in the palm of one hand, scanning his combat crews with satisfaction.

'At ease, gentlemen,' he said at last, and waited while they settled back into their chairs. There was a silence, a moment of apprehension before he threw the black cloth from the map.

'Today's target,' he said, 'is just south of Cologne. Marshalling yards.'

The crews stared at the long piece of red yarn that stretched from the base to Cologne, and a low moan, which began near the back of the hall, escalated into a collective groan. Tom glanced at his navigator, who grimaced, and slowly the men fell silent again. All attention returned to the colonel and the details of the briefing, the course they would fly, the weather, the flak and the fighter attacks, the fighter support they could expect, fears buried beneath their concentration. When the briefing was finished, they filed out of the barn-like hut, the scuff of unlifted boots loud on the concrete floor.

Later, in his flying suit, his kit collected and signed for, Tom stepped up into the truck amid the roaring of engines and the clatter of tailboards in air that was thick with exhaust fumes. The trucks pulled away from the huts one by one, hurtling dangerously through the mud and the ruts in the darkness until they hit the concrete of the runways. There the lurching lessened as they sped towards the hardstands where the planes were waiting. Tom held on to the tailgate, barely aware of the racket and the motion, his thoughts with Anna, curled up and sleeping, warm in their bed at the hotel. He closed his eyes to see her better and felt the softness of her skin against his, the warmth of her breath against his shoulder as she slept, strands of her hair across his face, tickling. He opened his eyes, her presence too painful.

The other men were silent, immersed in their own thoughts, and they jumped down quietly when the truck reached the *American Maiden*. The girl on the nose smiled down at them, encouraging and sensual, the curves of her body smooth and inviting. Tom grinned back at her for luck as always and the truck roared off with a crunching of gears.

'Lieutenant!' The crew chief approached him, the engineering report in his hand, anxious to get down to business. 'She's lookin' good,' he told the pilot. 'Everythin' fixed and ready to go.'

'Okay,' Tom answered. 'Let's look around.'

Together they checked her over.

'Number two engine's workin' fine now. Should have no problems with it.'

'And the landing gear? Scared the hell out of me last time; we had to hand crank it down part of the way.'

'Yeah, it's fine. The electrics were shot out; some bad connections. Easy enough to fix.'

They were silent walking round, Tom's eyes running over the externals. He would know more once he was up on the flight deck, touching the controls that would bring the *American Maiden* to life.

'Thanks Pete,' Tom said when the inspection was finished. 'You've done a good job.'

Pete nodded his acceptance of the praise. 'Just try and bring her back the same way, no fuckin' holes or nothing, will you? Don't try nothin' fancy with her. Just do what you have to do and come home. You got it?'

Tom grinned. The crew chief's bitching cheered him somehow, made him feel that things were normal. It was just the same as every other trip he hadn't wanted to go on, nothing different about it.

'Don't worry, Pete. I'll do my best.'

'Yeah, like hell.' He waved a hand vaguely above his head in goodbye and turned away. The pilot stood at the wing and watched him go, still mumbling, still complaining, to whatever else he had to do that day. He smiled. The guy was a miserable bastard, but he was one hell of crew chief.

The crew hung about in a scattered group, smoking, or thinking, their preparations complete, waiting for a word from their pilot. He talked with them briefly, wished them luck, and as they made their way to their stations he spoke quietly to the new tail gunner, drawing him aside, a hand on his shoulder. The new man was young, probably not yet out of his teens, and this was his first live run. He had not yet learned to hide his fear beneath the youthful features and he was shaking, furious with himself.

'Take it easy Matt,' Tom told him. 'You'll be okay.'

He hoped he was right, and remembered how scared he had been on his first raid, the mistakes he had made, how lucky they had been to get home in one piece. He knew how he must seem to the young man, impossibly calm, so unafraid. He had looked at older fliers once and thought the same.

'Just do it like they taught you back in school, same as in training,' he said. 'You'll be fine.'

The gunner nodded and tried to smile, embarrassed by his fear in front of the other men. Tom watched him walk away before he bent to the kit at his feet and stepped into his chute harness. The straps felt tight and secure against his legs, reassuring, how they were supposed to be. Then he hauled himself up by his arms through the nose hatch, and sat for a moment on the edge, legs dangling, to accustom himself once again to the sickening smell of the plane, gasoline and stale sweat and hydraulic fluid, the smell of fear. He swallowed down the rising sense of nausea that he knew wouldn't leave till the engines started to run. Then concentration would prevent him feeling much of anything, except the ball of fear in his gut.

He stood slowly, still nauseous, made his way to the flight deck and took his seat next to Randall, the giant Texan, his co-pilot. They smiled at each other and began the routine checks, the control surfaces shifting slightly under his hands as the wind buffeted the wings and the *American Maiden* stirred slightly in resistance. He checked his watch.

'You ready?' the co-pilot drawled finally.

Tom nodded. 'Energise number one.'

One by one, the four engines whined and spat and burst into life, the pilots checking each one before moving on to the next, the vibration shaking the plane, the roar deafening, drowning out all thought. As across the airfield the Fortresses roared into life, Tom thought of Anna waking and the hours she would spend while he was gone, waiting for his return. Anger scorched through him, a sudden intense resentment that he might lose his future with her, that perhaps they might not get old and wrinkly together how she had said. For the first time flying was more than a dirty job that he had to do. For the first time he truly hated the Germans.

'Let's get those bastards,' he murmured. 'Let's go.'

The *American Maiden* strained against her brakes, raring to go, as one by one the others taxied out on to the runway and took off in quick succession. Then it was her turn and they sped over the concrete, using every last inch of the run before she lurched airborne, holding her few feet of height with desperation until the airspeed increased and Tom could inch her upwards to begin the long climb into the greyness of the cloud.

They swept over the village in the first half-light of the dawn, still climbing, and Tom allowed himself one last thought of Anna as he picked out the hotel amongst the cluster of rooftops. Then no more, and he directed his mind back to the plane, to the task of keeping them all alive.

The ship bounced hard in the overcast and Tom grimaced, trying to judge where the prop wash was coming from, to alter their position a little and lessen the risk of flipping over. He was almost blind in the thick cloud and he could feel the tension of the crew, all of them praying he could guide them through it, that they wouldn't die in a mid-air collision with one of their own.

'We're approaching 10,000 feet.' Randall spoke over the intercom. 'Oxygen masks on.'

One by one the crew checked in. There was no thought of Anna in Tom's mind now, every nerve and muscle straining to hold their position until finally they broke through into clear sky. Above the clouds they met the sunrise, blood red and orange smeared across the heavens, and he was awed, as always, by its splendour. In the moment before he turned the plane away to head southwards he remembered that there was a God.

They found their group quickly, took their position, and levelled out at 21,000 feet. The shadows of the bombers flicked easily across the candy floss carpet beneath them, and the intercom was silent as they moved out over the sea, the channel kept clear for urgent communication. Tom gave the okay to test fire the guns, and he heard their stutter, the whir and clunk of the top turret above and behind him as the gunner swung slowly round. the *American Maiden* filled with the smell of cordite.

'Approaching enemy territory,' the navigator told them and they put on the heavy cumbersome flak suits that all of them hated. Tom tucked his down well between his legs, covering his genitals. Randall did the same and they grinned at each other as they always did, amused at this little ritual they shared. Somewhere below them and to the right a few bursts of flak exploded harmlessly, black plumes of smoke appearing above the clouds, a reminder of what waited for them at Cologne.

Then, later, the shout on the intercom.

'Bandits! Bandits! Four o'clock low!'

It was Matthew in the tail. His voice was excited but strong and controlled. He was going to be okay. The top turret whirred behind Tom's head. The formation tightened almost imperceptibly, and Tom braced himself for the impact of the attack.

'I see them!'

'Jesus! How many are there?'

'Hold fire until they're in range.'

'There's fuckin' hundreds of them!'

The guns rattled as the Messerschmidts swept past, tracer bullets flying past the window of the flight deck. Tom saw them break left, swoop down in an almost vertical dive to regroup and come back for more.

'*The Sly Fox* is hit!'

Tom turned instinctively to check his left wing man. She looked bad, fire and smoke trailing from number three engine, a chunk taken out of her nose. He looked back ahead, tearing his eyes away with difficulty, willing her to recover.

'She's diving!' someone yelled, 'Trying to put out the fire.'

'Bandits! Bandits!'

'Where, for Christ's sake?!'

'Ten o'clock, ten o'clock high!'

'I see them!'

Behind him Tom heard the turret turn and the gun's staccato fire.

'We've been hit! We've been hit!' It was Danny in the waist.

'Pilot to left waist. What's happened?' Tom's voice was calm in the tension, but the sweat oozed between his shoulder blades and under his helmet, hot and uncomfortable.

'Right waist gun is out. No one's hurt.'

'Okay.'

He watched the Messerschmidts surge forward through the formation, guns blazing.

'*The Sly Fox* is down!'

Tom turned again, saw her diving and spinning below him, the right wing snapped in two.

'Any chutes?'

'I saw two. That's all.'

*The Sly Fox* began to plummet. No one else would get out now. Up ahead, the lead squadron was getting the worst of the attack. The formation floundered as the B17s struggled to maintain position, engines burning, or feathered, the propellers turned edgeways into the wind to stop the drag. Two were down, an explosion of fire and smoke then an empty space in the sky, and the others pulled up, changed position to regain formation, trying to cover one another. The fighters came in again and the crew of the *American Maiden* watched as they took out the lead plane, watched her break up and counted the chutes as they fell from the wreckage; one, two, three, four. Only four. Six men still inside, falling with the bomber. Tom wondered how long the moment of consciousness before death lasted. How intense was the terror?

Then the fighters were gone, and he turned to check who flew now at his wing. It was *Lady Luck*, tucked in neatly beside them. He signalled to her co-pilot, his forefinger and thumb forming a ring, other fingers extended, and then touched his hand to his throat mike.

'Four minutes to bomb run.'

The lead squadron had already hit the flak, surrounded by little black bursts of smoke that looked utterly harmless. Then they were in it, and the *American Maiden* lurched and bounced in the turbulence. Small fragments tapped against the bomber's skin, and he moved her slightly away from *Lady Luck*, in case they should hit in the rough air.

'Pilot to bombardier. I'm putting her on auto-pilot. You're flying the plane now, Mac.'

'Okay,' Mac answered. 'I hear you.'

Tom hated this part of the ride, the time when he had no control of their movement, when all they could do was fly straight and level until the bombs fell away. He could feel the tension of the crew as they waited and he became aware again of the sweat between his shoulder blades. The flak burst around them and they could do nothing to evade it.

'How's the target looking?' He spoke to the bombardier.

'Pretty cloudy.'

'One minute to target.'

He heard the bomb bay doors starting to open, and the *American Maiden* lurched forward with a sickening jolt.

'We've been hit! In the tail section somewhere.' Again it was Danny in the waist.

'Anyone hurt?'

'We're okay.'

'Matthew? Pilot to tail. Pilot to tail. Are you okay?'

There was no response from the tail gunner.

'Pilot to left waist. Get back to the tail. Check if Matthew's okay.'

'Okay.'

In his mind he watched the gunner go, carrying the heavy oxygen bottle, weighted down by his flak suit, staggering aft as the bomber bucked and pitched.

'Pilot to bombardier. Can you see the target yet?'

'I can't see jack shit.'

Tom prayed they would be able to make the drop the first time over. He didn't want to have to go round again. Up ahead, the lead squadron had dropped their bombs and were rallying away in a large curve. Heading home.

'Bombardier to pilot. What do you want me to do?'

There was a silence and then the bombardier was on the intercom again.

'There it is! I can see it! Bombs away!'

The *American Maiden* leapt upwards as the load dropped away beneath her and Tom took control of his plane again, dropping the left wing, banking away from the target, keeping formation, heading home.

'Tail to pilot. Tail to pilot. Matthew's been hit. Repeat, Matthew's been hit.'

'How bad?'

'Don't know. He's out cold. But he's trapped. I can't get him out of there. The metal's all buckled round him. He's stuck fast.'

'Fuck.' Tom and Randall exchanged glances.

'Could you do it with help?'

'I could do it with a welding torch.' The sarcasm was heavy.

'Okay, just do what you can to make him comfortable. That's all you can do. Stay with him for a while in case he comes round.'

He could hear Danny cursing, still trying to free the trapped gunner.

'Poor bastard,' Randall said, to no one in particular. 'His first live run, and that happens. Poor bastard.'

Tom called the rest of the crew to check in, to know that they were still all okay, to assess any damage, and after, the intercom went quiet, the tension of the crew tangible. Then Irving's voice in the top turret.

'Little friends. Little Friends. P51's. Ten o'clock high. Lots of 'em.'

'Where are they when you fuckin' need them?'

'Be thankful they're here now. The odds on getting home just went up.'

Tom smiled slightly with relief.

'Co-pilot to crew. We're under 10,000 feet guys. You can come off oxygen now.'

Tom pulled the mask from his face and rubbed the skin where it had been.

'Can you take over for a while, Randall? I need some coffee.'

'Sure.'

He reached down for the thermos, poured himself some of the bitter black liquid. The heat in his throat and his belly was good and relaxing. Over the rest of the plane the men smoked or ate sandwiches, some act of normality after the stress of the bomb run.

'Co-pilot to tail. How is Matthew? Danny, you still there?'
'Yeah. I'm still here. He's still breathing. That's all I can say.'
'Stay with him.'

It seemed a long journey home, each extra minute lessening the tail gunner's chances of survival, and when they landed finally at the base, the crew waited while the medics cut him free. As they lifted him down the blood that had been held back by the twisted metal started to flow. Within a minute he was dead. The crew walked away from the bomber in silence. A jeep approached, offered them a ride back to debriefing but as one man they refused, the clean air and the firm earth beneath their feet too precious to give up.

Debriefing was short.

'Did you hit the target?'
'I think so.'
'How was the flak?'
'Lethal.'
'Light, moderate, heavy?'
'Lethal.'

The questioning officer looked up from his sheet of paper, the pen hovering over the options he had to circle. He raised an eyebrow at the pilot, a silent plea for cooperation. Tom raised his hands, palms facing outwards in a gesture of tired apology.

'This won't take long sir.'

Tom nodded. 'It was heavy.'

'Fighters?'

'Me-109s. Five minutes or so off the target.'

'How many?'

'I didn't count.'

The interrogator paused and his eyes flicked down the page at the rest of the questions he was supposed to ask. Tom watched him, sullen and exhausted and feeling belligerent. The interrogator looked tired. He had been on the receiving end of returning crews for some time. 'I think we'll call it a day,' he said finally and lifted his eyes to the pilot.

'Thanks.' Tom managed a smile and a raised hand and then he left the hut. He wanted Anna. He wanted to curl up beside her away from this place, forget about targets and flak and fighters. And dying.

Outside, he searched for his bike amongst the pile, throwing those in the way aside, his own energy surprising him. Then he lifted his clear of the heap, stooped to replace the chain, wiped the oil from his hands on his pants, and rode slowly away, bumping and skidding slightly in the wetness of the mud.

# Seven

Mrs Pilgrim stood in the queue outside the butcher's, sweating in her thick cardigan in the warm April sun, fanning herself with the ration book that she clutched in one hand. It was a long queue and she was in reluctant conversation with the two women either side of her.

'Well, it looks like spring is here at last,' commented the woman in the garish dress.

The other two women nodded in agreement.

'Perhaps the second front will happen now.'

'I don't think it was ever dependent on the weather,' the younger replied, bright lips parting in a smile. 'Do you?'

'No, but you never know.'

'What do you think Mrs Pilgrim?' the garish dress woman asked. 'Do you think it'll be soon?'

Mrs Pilgrim nodded. 'I heard Mr Churchill on the radio just the other week, talking about effort and action and victory, so it must be coming soon.'

'Well, let's hope so.'

They shuffled forward in the queue and Mrs Pilgrim glanced at her watch. She seemed to spend most of her time in queues these days.

'Terrible isn't it?' the younger woman said. 'Spend all bloody day either working or queuing.'

The others nodded.

'And how's your daughter, Mrs Pilgrim?' the garish dress woman asked. 'I haven't seen her for a while.'

'Oh working hard,' Mrs Pilgrim replied. 'She's up at the Royal Ordinance Factory, in the office.'

'Really? She's still there, is she?'

'Yes, really,' Mrs Pilgrim said, irritated by the woman's tone of voice.

'Oh, well, she must just have been having some time off when I saw her then. A couple of months ago, it was. Maybe more.'

The younger woman's red mouth parted into a grin and Mrs Pilgrim hesitated, aware they were having a go, unsure how to reply. The garish dress woman continued, enjoying herself. 'She was on the arm of an American. Airman, I think he was. Yes, he was definitely an airman because he was wearing one of those nice leather jackets, you know the kind I mean.'

The younger woman nodded her encouragement and Mrs Pilgrim was silent, desperate to know more, filled with humiliation.

'I don't think she saw me. She seemed to be otherwise occupied. Good looking lad he was too, but then I always liked a man in uniform. Obviously your Anna's the same, eh, Mrs Pilgrim?'

Mrs Pilgrim swallowed and forced herself to nod, her eyes glazed with shame and anger.

I'll kill her, she thought. I'll kill her when I get hold of her. So that's where she was. Fooling around with a Yank. Wretched girl. And to be *seen*. I was right. It was a man. But it never crossed my mind it might an American. Little fool. How could she be so stupid?

She clenched her fists, dropping the ration book unnoticed onto the pavement. The younger woman stooped to pick it up and Mrs Pilgrim snatched it from her, too engrossed in her fury to realise.

'Excuse me,' the woman said with sarcasm, exchanging glances with her friend. 'I'm sure.'

Mrs Pilgrim stared at her in surprise, then saw the book in her hand. She was confused for a moment, looking from one to the other before she stammered a belated thank you.

'My pleasure,' replied the woman.

'Anyway,' the garish dress woman continued. 'I'm sure she told you all about him.'

'Yes,' Mrs Pilgrim lied. 'Of course she did.'

The red lipstick grinned again and Anna's mother stood rigid, staring ahead, rooted in her embarrassment. She wanted to walk away, to put distance between herself and these awful women, but she couldn't. Let them wait before they rip into her back. Let them wait. I'll kill her, she thought again, for putting me through this. I'll kill her.

'Friday, thank God,' said the woman on the bus sitting next to Anna. 'You in tomorrow?'

'Just till twelve,' Anna replied.

'Me too,' and then she turned to peer out through the dirt on the window as the bus rocked and swayed and jolted its way into the city.

Anna folded her hands over her baby and dozed, waking automatically at her stop and strolling in the last light of the evening back to the house in Byron Street. In the almost darkness of the hall she felt immediately the tension, as if the air itself was angry. Shuddering, foreboding prickling her skin and quickening her pulse, she trod reluctantly towards the kitchen. The door was open, unusually, and her mother sat facing her as Anna stood just inside the doorway. She waited for the old woman to speak, uneasy, and when, finally, Mrs Pilgrim began, it was through teeth clenched shut with anger.

'How could you?!' she hissed. 'Staying with a friend, you said. Well no wonder you wouldn't tell me the truth. I'd like to wring your bloody neck.'

Anna placed a protective hand over her child and slid onto the stool by the door, looking down, breathing quickly, waiting.

'Who else knows?' her mother demanded. 'Am I the last to know? Am I always to be made a fool of? How could you be so stupid as to think you wouldn't be seen? That I wouldn't find out? How dare you lie to me like you have. If your grandfather were alive he'd belt you black and blue.'

Anna swallowed hard, trying to breathe deeply, trying to calm herself.

'Have you nothing to say for yourself?' Mrs Pilgrim paused, waiting for an answer, but none came. 'I don't know how you've got the gall to sit there,' she went on, 'saying nothing, after what you've done. No apology. No sign of remorse. Have you no sense at all? After all I've told you about men? And with a *Yank*, of all people,' she shrieked, as if it were his nationality that had made her act a crime. 'Haven't I taught you better than that? Haven't I taught you to have some self-respect?'

She hauled herself up from her chair and stood over her daughter, attempting to force a response. Anna felt her mother's breath against her hair and shivered with revulsion.

'I can't believe you could have done this. Made you lots of promises, did he? Told you that he loved you? And now where is he? Eh? Eh? How could you be such a fool after all I've told you?'

Anna took a deep breath, fighting to control the anger that swelled up from her gut, the instinct to defend the man she loved almost overwhelming. Her mother moved closer, bending, and the smell of the hot stale breath so close sickened and disgusted her.

'And with a *Yank*,' her mother spat again, spraying tiny drops of spittle at her daughter's cheek. Anna wiped them away. She was trembling with anger, afraid of herself.

'The worst kind,' Mrs Pilgrim continued, shaking her head in disbelief. 'An airman. An American airman. You're nothing better than a common slut. Aren't you going to say anything?'

Anna turned her head away from the hateful voice before she stood suddenly in one graceful movement. Taken by surprise, her mother shuffled clumsily backwards.

'You want me to say something, do you?' Anna asked, her voice low, trembling with emotion. Tears prickled the backs of her eyes and she blinked them back, refusing to let them come. Don't cry, she warned herself. Not now. Don't let her know how much you hurt. She touched a hand to her belly, drawing strength from the life there, her connection to Tom, before she levelled her gaze at her mother and spoke again.

'Well, all right. I'll say something. But you'll wish I hadn't because you're not going to like what I'm going to say.'

Her mother stared, horrified by this Anna she barely knew, this girl who would no longer be cowed.

'Sit down,' Anna said. 'I think you should sit down.'

Mrs Pilgrim backed unsteadily, reaching for the chair with one hand, lowering her bulk onto the seat. Her mouth worked, opening and closing, but no sound came out.

'Yes. You're right,' Anna said. 'I fooled around, as you put it, with an American airman for a week. I'm sure you don't care, but we loved each other very deeply. Now he's missing in action, shot down somewhere over Europe, fighting for this country. I don't know if he's alive or dead but I do know something.' She paused, knowing that this was not the time, knowing that she would regret it, but unable to stop herself. 'I know that I'm going to have that airman's baby.'

Her mother blanched and reeled, held on to the kitchen counter to steady herself.

'Yes. I'm pregnant. There. Are you happy now? Happy that I've said something?'

But her mother was no longer listening. She stared into space just past Anna's left arm, her world collapsing. Her lips moved soundlessly, trying to form words that wouldn't come. She shook her head slightly, as if to deny what her daughter had said. Anna watched until her mother whispered, 'Go. Leave me alone.'

Then Anna turned and walked unsteadily back through the dining room, along the hall, up the stairs to her room. She sat on her bed shaking, feeling cold suddenly, and light-headed. The euphoria of her anger began to wane, and a sickness to seep into her stomach, the realisation of what she had done. She rested her head in her hands, her elbows on her knees, her mind blank as the dizziness began to subside. I shouldn't have done that, she thought. I should have waited, told her calmly, picked a good time. I've made things much worse now.

Gradually her breathing slowed and she sat up and looked around her. Her mother had been tidying her room again, moving things round, prying, and the old woman's presence was palpable in the obsessive neatness of her things. Anna felt a childish urge to mess everything up but she had no energy and turned instead to the window, leaning on the windowsill, looking out into the blackness. She sat a long time in the dark, head resting on her arms on the windowsill, weary and depressed, listening for her mother, wondering, waiting. The house was silent.

'Where are you, Tom?' she whispered to the dark sky beyond the window, hoping her thoughts would reach him, wherever he was. 'Please come home soon. I need you.' She touched the small bulge beneath her skirt. 'We need you.'

Mrs Pilgrim sat slumped in her chair, dazed and reeling.

It isn't possible, she thought. It just isn't possible that my daughter could have done such a thing. It's bad enough that she slept with him. Bad enough that she was seen. But it could have been forgotten, hidden in time, nothing more to be said. But she's gone and got herself *pregnant*, and now there's no way of hiding it. Everyone will know and they'll say it's my fault. That having no father, I couldn't control her.

She thought of her own father and her fear of him, the power he had held over his family, her mother shrinking and spineless. She remembered the weight of his belt across her body, and thought perhaps she should have done the same to Anna. But it took a man's hand, and there had been no father for Anna.

For the first time in years she pictured her husband's face, breaking through the shutters in her memory. The same almond eyes as Anna, bewitching. The beautiful lopsided smile that had lost her the first time she saw it, the only man she had ever cared for. For a moment she saw him as he was that day at the fair when she met him, his smile as he watched her each time she passed him on the carousel. She had stayed all day at the fair just to be near him, and when it was late, he had left the carousel in the care of a friend and walked her home. It was a year before the fair came to town again but he remembered her, and when the fair moved on at the end of the summer he had stayed behind.

She shook her head to be rid of the memory, refusing to believe he had ever loved her, knowing he had only ever deceived. Then she saw him again the way she remembered him best, the day she discovered his infidelity, the day he left and told her that she had never loved him, that she didn't know how to love. The smile had turned cruel and sneering then and lost its beauty.

'But I've been a good wife,' she had pleaded with him, 'a good mother to our daughter. What else could I have done?'

'You could have loved me,' he answered.

'I did love you. I still do.'

He laughed as he stood at the door with one hand resting on the head of the bewildered child who was watching. 'I don't think so.'

'Who is she?' she wanted to know. 'Who is she?'

'What does it matter?' he shrugged. 'She's a woman. A woman who knows how to please a man. You never did that for me. You never even tried.'

'Just tell me what you want me to do,' she had said, but he'd already gone, footsteps light on the steps and through the gate.

Afterwards, when the first sense of shock retreated, she came to understand that it had been her own fault in a way, for trusting him, for believing that he had loved her. So she decided she would never let herself be deceived that way again, and she would make sure that Anna understood it too. She would never let any man do the same to her daughter.

Now, slumped and cold in the kitchen, still flushed with

humiliation from the memory, she thought about her daughter, running her mind over the choices that lay before her. A quiet maternal instinct struggled against the strident stronger voices of her hatred of men, and was defeated.

It was an age before Anna heard her mother climb the narrow staircase, the unrhythmic stomp of stiff limbs. She turned on the bed, away from the window, and fiddled with the cross at her breast, calling silently for help. Mrs Pilgrim entered without knocking and stood inside the door, her back to the wall, arms folded, jaw set with determination. She stared at her daughter implacably, her decision made.

'I'm sorry Mother,' Anna whispered. 'I didn't mean to be so rude.'

'And you think that's enough do you? You think with one word of apology that all is forgiven?'

Anna looked down, hating her dependence, her need for her mother's support.

'I am sorry,' she repeated, glancing up, but her mother's eyes were impassive, and she looked away, back at the floor.

'You're sorry that you were rude, are you?'

Anna nodded.

'But that's all you're sorry for, isn't it? You're not sorry about anything else, are you? You're not sorry about ...,' she paused, the words difficult to utter, 'about ... having it off with a soldier, or lying to me about it, or letting yourself get pregnant.'

The daughter's eyes remained lowered. She could not bring herself to apologise for loving Tom, nor for carrying his child.

'See? I was right. You aren't sorry at all. The only thing you're sorry about is that you've fouled your nest. Well, you've only got yourself to blame. You can't say you weren't warned. You can't say I didn't tell you. They're all the same, you know. All of them. And if you think this airman of yours is any different, you're in for a nasty shock.'

Anna bit her lip, fighting down the words that gathered dangerously in her throat.

'Well,' Mrs Pilgrim went on. 'It makes no difference whether you're sorry or not anyway, because I've made up my mind.' She waited for her daughter to look up, and Anna lifted her eyes slowly in the silence.

'You'll have to go,' her mother said. 'You can't expect me to keep you here after what you've done. You've got to go.'

Anna swallowed past the painful lump in her throat, searching for something, some words she could say to change her mother's mind. But there was nothing, and she stared at the floor in silence.

'You can stay tonight,' her mother continued. 'I'm not such a monster that I expect you to leave at this time of night. I'm giving you time to pack. But tomorrow you go. Do you understand?'

'But Mother …,' Anna began, finding her voice at last.

'I don't care what you think,' Mrs Pilgrim cut her off. 'If your grandfather were alive he'd have beaten you within an inch of your life and thrown you out with nothing. Or worse. So thank your lucky stars there's only me.'

'But where will I go?' Anna asked. 'I've no money, there's no housing …'

'You should have thought of that earlier, shouldn't you …'

'He was going to marry me …' Anna pleaded.

'But he hasn't, has he?'

'He was shot down …'

Mrs Pilgrim snorted in disbelief.

'It's your grandchild,' Anna said. 'If not for me, for your grandchild.'

For a moment her mother wavered.

'Please,' Anna begged, hating herself for it. 'Please, Mother.'

But the old woman would not be swayed, unable to think beyond her father's sense of justice and a need to punish. She said, 'Leave the keys on the hook when you go.'

Anna flinched as the door slammed shut and the sound reverberated through her tightened nerves. She bit her lip, vainly trying to stop herself from crying. Then, reaching into her bag, she took out the little photo of Tom, tracing his features with her fingers, but his face was blurred by her tears and for the first time she felt very far away from him. For the first time she couldn't summon his presence to her side.

# Eight

The evaders did nothing for the rest of the day, keeping out of the way as the Frenchmen came and went, talking amongst themselves, and the women prepared food for them all. Sitting quietly, Tom struck up conversation with Mike, anxious for news from England, the recent spate of bombing raids on English cities, and the larger Allied ones on Nuremberg and Berlin. He heard too about the German retreats on the Eastern Front, and the news that the tide seemed at last to be turning inspired him and lifted his hopes. They talked easily, two young Americans in a strange land, and though they tried to include the Englishman he refused to join them, preferring to sit brooding alone by the fireplace. Tom observed him, concerned, worried that if he broke he could compromise them all. Mike seemed not to notice, chatting with wry humour about the peculiarities of the Eighth Air Force, making the pilot laugh with his mimicry of senior officers they had both met along the way. Tom felt better now that the journey had begun, his instinct for activity appeased and the limbo broken, but he was grateful for the rest, and the day passed quickly.

They left the next morning, cycling to the station in silence at a distance behind the teenaged girl, their identity cards and their train tickets in their pockets, their new names memorised. She cycled slowly, aware that Tom was not at full strength, but even so, he found it hard to keep up, his injured leg aching and weak. Infuriated by the weakness he pushed himself against the pain, concentrating only on each turn of the pedal, not thinking of the distance ahead, and when he stepped off the old bicycle outside the station, his legs were quivering and unsteady.

The Paris train was late and they mingled with the other people who were waiting. There were few civilians and many soldiers who were mostly sullen and resigned. Tom stood quietly, disturbed by their proximity, breathing deeply to calm himself, but his unease remained and he hoped his face showed no sign of it. He wandered across the platform and read the notices on the boards so that he could turn his back to the soldiers, and the others stood near the edge of the platform, staring morosely down at the track.

Time passed with no train and the crowd became bored and restless. The soldiers muttered amongst themselves in complaint and Tom shifted his weight from one leg to the other, resting the injured one as much as possible. It was sore and swollen from the exercise and he hoped they would get seats for the journey to Paris.

High overhead a formation of Allied bombers flew east and Tom suppressed a smile as the familiar sound of Fortress engines filled the air. He glanced across at Mike, who lifted his eyebrows in a slight smile of recognition. A few of the Germans looked upward with irritation, just briefly, and then the whole crowd surged forward as the train arrived and squealed to a stop at the platform.

Tom pushed on with the others, jostling in the corridor until he could follow Mike and Ralph into a second-class compartment. A large family of peasants made grudging room for them, and then returned to talking loudly across the small compartment as the train dragged itself out of the station to continue its slow haul southwards. In the open country the heat of Tom's anxiety cooled, his confidence lifted by the absence of Germans, and the presence of the Allies overhead. For the first time since he had arrived at the station, it seemed possible that they might make it to Paris.

The journey was slow, with many delays, but it was uneventful. The ticket inspector came round alone and clipped their tickets without a second glance. Small stations slid by, and more passengers squeezed in to stand in the overcrowded corridor. Once or twice someone opened the compartment door hoping to find a seat but they were shooed away by the family, and Tom barely turned to look, eyes downcast, thinking of Anna, pleased to be on his way to her at last, always wondering how long it would take.

When the train pulled in finally at the Gare du Nord, he shuffled his way down the platform with the other passengers, knowing he was less likely to be stopped if he passed through with the crowd. He felt self-conscious, taller than most of the men around him, conspicuous. An armed guard stood at the barrier and Tom kept his gaze averted as he handed his ticket to the collector but the guard questioned no one. The airmen passed through and stopped on the other side, waiting for their next guide to make contact. For a moment the heat of anxiety returned as he scanned the crowd with nervous eyes.

It was Ralph who spotted her eventually, waiting near the ticket office. She was petite and pretty and dressed exactly as they had been told she would be. She smiled to acknowledge them, then she turned and walked quickly out into the street. They followed at a distance as they had been told.

Outside, the weather was cool and damp and Tom turned up the collar of the French workman's jacket against the drizzle. They walked as a group, not speaking, stepping off the pavement now and then to let others pass them in the busy streets. It was tempting to look around and observe the streets of wartime Paris, no longer a city for lovers, but he kept his eyes directed forward, never leaving the narrow back of the girl who walked ahead.

They had walked some way from the station before she dropped her handbag and stooped to pick it up, the signal for them to approach and introduce themselves. Tom spoke first in quiet halting French, reluctant to use English in a street where any passer-by might be an informer. She smiled and told them that her name was Monique, then she led them through a maze of back streets to a café in a quiet cul-de-sac, where they sat and ate lunch amongst workers who paid them no attention. The food was simple, soup and bread, but it was good and Tom ate hungrily, less anxious now, accepting he could pass as a Frenchman in spite of his height. He watched how the workmen ate, copying the way they broke their bread, and remembered how Anna had copied him that morning in the café when he was sad because she had asked him what it was like to fly. Watching her awkward with the fork in her right hand had made him smile, but it was still hard to talk about flying. He had wanted to forget all about it for a while and lose himself in her. But she wanted to know, had insisted, and so he told her what he could, putting into words things that were better left unspoken. Afterwards, she was sorry, and much later, after he had tried to imagine her in her life without him, he understood her need to know and forgave her.

Monique ate with them, looking up once or twice to smile, reassuring, and then they left, following her into a tall apartment building two doors down from the café. They climbed the stairs behind her to a small apartment scattered with dark heavy furniture on floorboards that were stained with age. Two large windows looked down into the street outside. Tom struggled to focus in the gloom after the bright light of the afternoon.

'Please stay here, and keep away from the windows,' Monique told them. Her English was excellent, barely a trace of an accent. 'You can talk, but keep your voices down and take off your shoes, so that your footsteps can't be heard in the apartment below. I'll bring food for you later and perhaps some papers or books, but now I must go.'

They thanked her and the others turned away, but Tom stood watching her fumble with the catch, something familiar in the sideways glance she gave him as she felt his eyes on her face.

'Have you a question?' she asked him.

'No,' he answered quickly. 'No. I just wanted to say thank you.'

'You already have.'

Tom nodded and returned her smile as she slipped out of the door, then he fastened the chain behind her. He knew what it was that he had recognised, and wished that he didn't. He wanted to know nothing he might give away under torture. Perturbed by the knowledge, wondering if Marie knew of her daughter's work, he wandered through the apartment, running his fingers over the furniture, feeling the quality of the wood beneath his fingers, noticing the cheap workmanship, the shoddy finishing. In the drawer of a desk he found a chess set.

'Game of chess?' he asked no one in particular and Mike nodded so they sat at the table and played. The young Englishman refused to be interested, pacing nervously across the floorboards in his socks until Mike began to grow irritated.

'Will you keep still!?' he hissed in a stage whisper. 'How the hell can we concentrate with you pacing up and down like that?'

Ralph stopped in his tracks, outraged, and Tom lifted his eyes from the board.

'How can you two sit there playing chess as if everything is normal?' Ralph demanded. His voice seemed loud after so long in silence. 'How can you think about anything except about the danger we're in?'

'Hey,' Tom warned. 'Let's not fight.'

'I'm not fighting,' Ralph said, petulant. 'I'm just appalled by your nonchalance.'

There was a pause, and Mike looked to Tom, the officer among them. Tom sighed, wondering how best to defuse Ralph's temper, aware of his mental fragility.

'Look,' he said. 'None of us knows what's going to happen. We're all on edge. We're all scared. But we deal with it in different ways. You think I'm nonchalant? You should see the game of chess I'm playing.'

Mike smiled, but Ralph sighed in exasperation and threw himself into an armchair. It juddered and shifted under the sudden weight and the legs scraped, squealing against the polished floor. There was an uncomfortable silence, and Tom swallowed down his rising irritation. The strain of so long spent powerless and dependent was beginning to tell. Mike tapped his arm gently.

'Your move.'

Tom nodded and forced his mind back to the chess game he was losing. It was hard to concentrate.

He woke abruptly in the early hours to the sound of engines and raised voices outside the apartment. Rolling out of his bed on the living room floor in the darkness he half crawled, half ran to the window and lifted the edge of the curtain, peering down into the street below. There were three Mercedes cars, headlights blazing, and several men in dark uniforms. The café was being raided by the Gestapo. He swore, dropped the curtain, and in one movement threw open the door of the bedroom where the others were sleeping.

'Hey guys,' he hissed sharply. 'Wake up, come on guys, wake up quick. We've gotta go. Now.'

The two men obeyed automatically, bleary eyed, unquestioning, rolling out of the single narrow beds. Briefly Tom wondered if they should stay, if perhaps the Germans didn't know about the safe house, if he would put them all in more danger by going, but he rejected the thought immediately. It was not a risk he was prepared to take.

An image of Monique projected itself across his mind, the same lively eyes as her mother, and he prayed that the Gestapo hadn't found her. Dressing hurriedly in the dark, he was glad that Anna was safe in England where scum like the Gestapo didn't exist.

Dressed and ready, the others followed him through the small kitchen at the back of the apartment. He opened the door quietly, peering down the fire escape into the silent gloom of the lane below. It was empty. He ushered the others in front of him, hurrying them, their boots slung loosely over their shoulders so that their feet on the steps would not rouse any neighbours. Then he followed them down the steep metal stairs, using his arms to steady his weight. He was lighter now than he had been, and leaner, but the muscles of his arms and shoulders were still strong and he was soon in the lane, crouching, lacing up the heavy boots that André had given him.

Mike and Ralph stood silently, waiting for him to make the decisions. There was no noise in the shelter of the alley, the buildings behind them cutting out the clamour of the raid, and Tom led them away along the lane, moving parallel to the street, running softly until they reached another road. At the corner he squinted out into the gloom, his body still hidden behind the corner of the building, his heartbeat loud and fast from running. He could hear nothing except his heart as they slid out from the lane to start walking close to the buildings in the pre-dawn light, still furtive, still alert, unsure if the curfew had yet been lifted. But they moved quickly, trying to put as much distance as they could between themselves and the café.

Slowly the morning lightened, the sunrise invisible behind clouds turning almost imperceptibly from black to grey, and other people began to appear on the streets. The evaders slowed their pace, relieved by the end of the curfew, but anxious now not to appear conspicuous to passers-by. They walked in silence, in a group, eyes dropped to the paving before their feet. Tom hunched his shoulders self-consciously and they came to a stop finally on a narrow bridge where few people passed them. They leaned over the rail, their backs to the street, staring down at the still, murky water beneath.

'Where are we going?' Ralph hissed. 'Just where the hell are you taking us?'

'I don't know,' Tom said, turning his head to look at the Englishman, jaw tense with the knowledge of their danger and his anger with the young flier. He wanted to punch him. He knew it was wrong, that the kid was just young and scared, but he was scared too, and sick of Ralph's bitching.

'What do you mean, you don't know?'

Tom bit down the rising anger, turned away and stared at the river below, looking for inspiration.

'We need to find help,' he said, more to himself than to the others. 'And fast.'

Ralph stared at him, the young face frowning and belligerent, arms crossed across the narrow chest.

'And how do you propose to do that?'

'We'll try another café,' the pilot replied. He glanced at Mike, who half shrugged in acquiescence.

'What?' Ralph's voice was raised and Tom glared at him. The young man dropped his voice. 'What do you mean, we'll try another café?' he whispered. 'You mean you're just going to walk into some café you know nothing about and announce that we're evading airmen?'

There was something in Ralph's tone this time that lit the fuse of Tom's temper. He turned on him, livid, their faces almost close enough to be touching.

'Yes,' he hissed. 'That's about exactly what I'm going to do. And I don't give a fuck what you think. If you don't like it, you can just fuck off and make your own way. You got that?'

The young man stepped back, shocked by the sudden change, realising perhaps that he had misjudged, that the American's soft speech and affability were not signs of a slow mind, or an inability to lead. He flicked nervous eyes towards Mike who looked away, loyal to his officer.

'Do you have any other questions?' Tom demanded.

'How can you do that?' Ralph asked in a small voice. There was fear and incomprehension in his face and Tom felt like a bully, anger draining. But it had served its purpose; he guessed Ralph would follow him now.

'Ssshh!' Mike hissed and they fell silent as a group of labourers approached and hurried past them. Swinging arms brushed against their backs on the narrow footpath, and they waited until the men had disappeared off the end of the bridge amongst the buildings.

'Listen,' Tom said. 'We have to find another Resistance group. We have no choice.' He had run through it all in his mind already; he'd been thinking of nothing else since they left the safe house. They had no money, their fake ID's would stand little scrutiny, none of them spoke French or German. They'd be lucky to last a day on their own. The others stood silent, waiting for his direction, Ralph's brow creased with lines of uncertainty and doubt.

'We have to take the risk,' Tom said, laying a hand on the Englishman's shoulder. The young man tensed beneath his touch. Then, quietly, so that Mike would not hear, he said, 'Keep it together. We'll be okay.'

Ralph nodded. 'Yes sir.'

'Okay, let's go,' Tom said.

They turned then and walked on, silent again, watchful for soldiers and the French *milice*, looking out for a café they could try.

# Nine

Anna lay awake on her back staring up into the dark, exhausted. One hand was under her nightdress, resting on the warmth of the small life that was there, drawing comfort from its presence. Her mind was whirling, a merry-go-round of possibilities and impossibilities, drifting between the oblivion of the sleep she craved and the nightmare of her waking situation.

The carousel stopped at Lottie's, and in her logical moments she knew that she would go there. That for a few days at least she could sleep in the big double bed with her friend, or in Billy's bed when Evan came home, but she couldn't expect to share a room with Richard for long. And though she longed to go there, as she always had, she knew there was no room for her there for more than a short while.

Montana, she whispered. She should go to Montana, but how would she go? A voice in her head said, don't you know there's a war on? and she wanted to scream in frustration. There was no one else. No other close friends, no one she could turn to.

She reached out and gathered up the little cross in her fingers, the metal cold against her palm.

Help me, Tom, she whispered, over and over, until finally she fell into a restless doze.

She woke with a jolt, a lone plane droning overhead. The bed was clammy with her sweat and her face was wet with tears. She must have been dreaming but she had no memory of it. She wiped the tears away with the heel of her palm and sat up, hugging her knees with her arms, wide awake now, too fretful to sleep again. Nausea rose up from her stomach, the compounded sickness of pregnancy and nerves, and in the thin light from the lamp she noticed that she was trembling.

'What shall we do, little one?' she asked the child inside her. 'What shall we do next?'

Climbing carefully out of bed, unsteady on shaking limbs, she took the small suitcase from the top of the wardrobe, placed it on the bed and opened it, then gazed uncertainly round the room looking for things to put in it. She went to the wardrobe and touched the green wool dress that no longer fitted her, feeling the soft fabric between her fingers, remembering the day Tom had chosen it, the day they had gone to the registry office, hoping to be married. She hovered with indecision, wanting to take it, knowing it was foolish to do so. Her fingers passed along the line of clothes and she pulled random items roughly from their hangers, letting the wire bounce back against the wood of the wardrobe, not caring if the sound woke her mother. She stuffed them into the suitcase, opened a drawer and took out a handful of underwear, throwing it too into the bag. A brush, a comb, some of her precious hair grips saved from a time before they became impossible to buy, and her post office book. She sat down next to the case and rummaged until it sat flat enough to close the lid. Everything would need ironing again, but it didn't matter. The case was heavy as she dragged it off the bed, carried it across the room and struggled down the stairs. I shouldn't be lifting things, she thought, and made no effort to stop it scraping against the wall.

Outside it was still dark and she shifted her handbag to the same hand as the case, carrying them together awkwardly, the case banging against her legs as she lit her way with the little torch in her other hand. It was too early to go to work, so she wandered slowly up towards the church where she sat in silence, too numbed to pray, waiting until it was late enough for the first factory bus.

\* \* \*

She was early to work, the first to arrive in the office, and she huddled down over her typewriter, typing slowly, utterly unable to concentrate on the words in front of her. She went to the bathroom and rested her forehead against the coolness of the tiles, but it made no difference at all to her dizziness.

The girls noticed that she seemed unwell but said nothing, accustomed now to her strangeness, her self-containedness, knowing she would not welcome their concern. Morris too was aware that something was wrong from the repeated mistakes that she made, the sloppy typing that she handed him and the mumbled apologies when he handed it back to her.

'Are you all right, Anna?' he asked at last, when she stumbled on her way to the door, clutching a chair for support. 'You seem a little under the weather.'

'I'm fine, thank you Mr Morris,' Anna replied. 'Just tired, I think.'

'Why don't you sit down for just a moment. Get your breath.'

She slid gratefully onto the chair and leant forward, holding her pounding head in her hands. She began to cry, silently at first, the tears contained by the palms that covered her face, and then harder, her shoulders rocking and heaving with the sobs.

Morris sat on his desk and watched her. After a while, when the sobs seemed finally to subside, he said, 'Whatever is the matter, Anna? You seem to be most upset about something.'

Anna looked up, dragged a handkerchief from her pocket and wiped her face savagely, appalled at herself. 'I'm so sorry, Mr Morris. I don't know what came over me. I'm really sorry. I'm fine. Really I am.'

'You don't look at all fine,' he replied. 'You look very upset. What's happened? You can tell me. You know what they say, that a problem shared is a problem halved.'

Anna smiled slightly at his kindness and shook her head.

'I insist that you tell me,' he said gently.

Why not? she thought then. What difference would it make? 'I've been thrown out of home.'

Morris sucked in breath between his teeth, making a gentle hiss. 'Oh dear. That's no good at all. And what have you done to annoy your mother so much?'

She smiled at the dour humour. 'I suppose you may as well know,' she murmured, 'that I'm expecting a baby.'

Morris drew in air again. 'And where are you going to go?'

'I thought I'd go to a friend's house tonight. I can stay there for a short time while I sort myself out, but long term, I don't know. I'll have to see. I suppose I'm hoping my mother may soften with time.' It was a reluctant hope, the child of desperation, but she was alone and afraid, and she could think of few alternatives.

Morris put his fingers against his mouth, tapping softly, and stared out of the window, deep in thought.

'Tell you what, Anna,' he said finally. 'How about you stay with my mother and myself tonight. We can make you up a bed in the back parlour, and I'll go round and have a quiet word with your mother this afternoon, see if I can't talk her round. How does that sound?'

'I ... I ... I don't know,' she stammered, thrown by the suggestion.

It was hard to imagine her mother relenting so soon, and part of her was reluctant to return, almost grateful for this brief escape. But this might be her only chance to go back, her only hope of a home for her baby. Tom's baby. She said, 'I'd be very grateful.'

'Well, we can't have you on the streets in your condition, now can we? You should be with your mother where she can look after you.'

'Thank you, Mr Morris,' Anna said, collecting herself, straightening her hair and her clothes with nervous fingers. 'I really am very grateful.'

'Think nothing of it.' He smiled, self-effacing. 'Now why don't you go and sit outside in the fresh air for a while and I'll finish up here. I'll send the girls home a few minutes early.'

The factory closed at mid-day and after a quick lunch in the canteen, they travelled together on the bus to the neat modern neighbourhood where Morris lived with his mother. Anna tried to remember Mrs Morris, trying to picture the face she used to see each day over the garden fence as a child in Byron Street, but the image was blurred and the only memory she had was of a double chin and a kind smile.

The house stood in the middle of a low terraced row, with front doors painted bright colours against the red brickwork.

'Hello Mum,' Morris said, when his mother opened the door for them. 'You remember Anna Pilgrim, don't you?'

He stood aside to let Anna in, and Mrs Morris stared for a moment before she found her voice. 'What a lovely surprise! Please come in. I never would have recognised you,' she gushed. 'You've grown up so pretty. You were such a gangly girl, all arms and legs.'

Anna dropped her head, embarrassed, and there was an awkward silence.

'Anna and her mother are having a few problems,' Morris explained. 'I said she could stay here tonight while I go and try to talk Mrs Pilgrim round.'

'Nothing too serious, I hope,' his mother said.

'She's thrown me out because I'm pregnant,' Anna replied. There was no point in keeping it secret. It would be common knowledge soon enough. There was a thirty-second silence and she stood waiting in the hall in her coat and hat.

'Come on in to the kitchen,' Morris said. 'Let me take your coat.'

Mrs Morris recovered herself. 'Yes, please come in. I'll put the kettle on. It's lovely to see you after all these years.'

They sat drinking tea at the table in the kitchen, the early afternoon sun a large bright rectangle on the linoleum. The house was uncluttered and tasteful and Anna began to relax at the round pine table next to the open window, the pale net curtain flapping against her in the breeze.

'It's a lovely house,' Anna commented. 'It's so nice that you get the sun in here.'

Mrs Morris looked around with a smile, pleased by the compliment. 'Yes, I like it. It's small of course, and the neighbourhood isn't as classy as we were used to, but it's light and airy. I used to find that house in Byron Street quite depressing.'

'Yes, they don't get much light,' Anna agreed.

'So,' Mrs Morris said, 'when do you think the big push will be?'

Anna shook her head. 'I don't know. Honestly, I've got no idea.' She had barely thought of the progress of the war the last few days; the second front had been the last thing on her mind. 'But I hope it's soon.' Because then she might get news of Tom. Because then he might come home. 'It'd be good to get it started.'

'Yes, I think so too,' Mrs Morris replied. 'There doesn't seem to be any point in waiting. We should just get in there and get on with it. Still, there are so many rumours flying around you don't know what to believe.' She paused. 'I've heard it's impossible to get a train these days. Apparently the military have all but commandeered the railways.'

Anna had heard the same rumour.

'And I heard on the news last night that virtually the whole south coast is out of bounds. No more day-trippers. So something big must be afoot. It's my guess it'll happen in the next couple of months.'

Anna nodded in vague agreement, wondering how long it would be until she knew what had happened to Tom. Wondering if he was in prison or hospital somewhere, thinking of her. Wondering if he was alive.

* * *

Morris approached the house at number eight with reluctance. He was dreading the interview with Anna's mother, remembering her dogmatic abruptness from years earlier, when they had lived as neighbours, the men good friends, the women tolerating each other for the sake of their husbands. He had gone with the men sometimes, riding in the back of the bus with them, sitting amongst all the tackle. But he had hated fishing, and when he discovered that if he was naughty enough they would refuse to take him, he would play up each time until finally they had given up on him altogether.

The house had barely changed, he thought, though perhaps it had grown a little shabbier, the paint peeling a little more. He took a deep breath, strode slowly up the steps and rapped on the door. No sound reached him from inside and for a while he thought she might be out. He rapped again and immediately the door swung open. She stood there in her tatty apron, glaring.

'Morris,' she said at last.

'Can I come in?' he asked.

She backed away from the doorway reluctantly to let him through, and ushered him into the living room where he took a seat in Anna's chair, close to the unlit fire. Mrs Pilgrim took her place across from him on the sofa, staring ahead of her, waiting for him to begin.

'How are you, Mrs Pilgrim?' he asked.

'I don't think you're here to discuss my health now, are you?' she replied, risking a glance at him. He leant forward and rested his forearms on his knees, trying to reduce the vast distance between them. 'Just spit it out, Morris.'

He withdrew a little, disarmed by the curtness, and observed her, looking for weaknesses. Nervous, he cleared his throat and leant forward again. 'I understand you've asked Anna to leave home.'

'Yes.'

'She's staying with my mother and myself tonight,' he told

her. 'She almost collapsed at work with the strain and I thought it best.'

Anna's mother glanced at him in irritation. 'And now she's sent you here on her behalf. Am I right?'

'I offered. The poor girl was distraught.'

'Well, she's only got herself to blame.'

'Mrs Pilgrim!' The Scottish accent was strong when he was angry, and she flinched slightly at the sudden harshness. 'The girl is expecting a baby. You can't throw her onto the streets.'

'I can and I have. I'm sure she'll find somewhere to go.'

'Where? Just where do you think that she's going to go? There's a war on you know.'

'Don't patronise me, Morris.' Anna's mother turned to face him now, angry and resentful. 'That's her problem now. She should have thought of that before she got herself ... pregnant.'

Morris lowered his voice, keeping it even against the exasperation inside. 'You've got a duty to look after her. With things as they are, it's downright unpatriotic to expect the state to take her on. Every penny that goes to house and clothe and feed her is money taken away from the war effort. How do you think people will perceive that?'

She was silent, sullen, furious with the logic of his argument. 'Mrs Pilgrim?'

'People will talk, whatever. They'll say I didn't bring her up right. They talked all right when Jim left, too, but at least they couldn't blame me for it. It wasn't my fault he took off with some tart. But now this. They'll say I couldn't keep a husband, and I let my daughter go to the bad. It's humiliating, Morris. It's downright humiliating. If she stays, it's tantamount to me condoning it. I've got my self-respect you know. Life's worth nothing without that.'

There was a pause, while Morris thought how best to push on. 'Attitudes are changing,' he said finally. 'I think people will be a lot less shocked than you think. And I think most people would expect you to stand by her. She is your daughter after all. I don't think people will hold it against you. I really don't.'

'I thought we were fighting this war to protect our values,' she replied, changing tack, silencing the quivers of doubt. She couldn't back down now. After all, she had her pride.

Morris sighed and looked down at his hands clasped loosely in front of him, then ran one hand over the thinning hair. 'For God's sake, have some compassion. Anna needs you. You're her mother. She's going to have your grandchild.'

'You know she disappeared for a week while she was out fooling around with that American? Not a word. I was out of my mind with worry. Then she walks back in as soon as he disappears and she isn't even sorry. Did she care how I felt? Not a bit. So don't tell me I'm responsible for her. She's quite old enough to make her own decisions and if that's what she wants well then she's welcome to it. But she can't come running back to me with her tail between her legs when it all goes wrong and expect me to pick up the pieces.'

'Then don't do it for her. Do it for the war effort. Do it because people will think better of you if you do. People will think you've been terribly hard on her otherwise.'

'Hard on her?!' Mrs Pilgrim exclaimed. She shifted forward on the sofa, warming to her subject. 'D'you know what my father would have done? He would have beaten her black and blue, and then he would have thrown her out on the streets with *nothing*. So don't tell me I'm being hard on her.'

'Your father was a tyrant. And well you know it.'

Mrs Pilgrim breathed hard and stared ahead of her, refusing to acknowledge what he had said. The muscle in her cheek twitched with tension.

'And,' Morris continued, with sudden inspiration, 'you'll probably have to let out her room. Perhaps to a homeless family. You can't live in this big old house just on your own when there are so many bombed-out families needing digs. We still need places for people up at the factory.'

She wheeled slowly towards him. 'Are you blackmailing me?'

'I'm doing nothing of the kind. I'm just telling you how the local council might see your situation.'

'And who's going to tell the council?'

Morris raised his hands in innocence. 'I'm just warning you of what might happen.'

'I'd thought better of you Morris. I didn't think you'd stoop to that.'

'I'm just stating the facts of the matter, as I see them.'

Mrs Pilgrim struggled forward on the sofa and heaved herself to her feet.

'I'll think about it.'

Morris sat waiting, refusing to rise as she expected, and she stood immobile in indecision before she moved heavily out of the room to the kitchen. He could hear her, rattling and clattering as she made tea.

Bloody hell, she thought, slamming the kettle onto the stove. The match broke with the force she used, and she swore again, stooping to pick up the broken pieces. She struck the box with the shortened end, holding it awkwardly in her stubby fingers, lighting the stove hurriedly before she burnt herself.

He's got me. He knows he's got me. I'm not having strangers in my house, not for anyone. I could end up with a whole family upstairs, or even just a couple of war workers would be bad enough. And he's just sly enough to drop a word in the right place. She stood and waited for the kettle to boil, regretting the hastiness that had forced her to this. She should have thought more about it in the first place, not let her temper get the better of her.

'All right,' she told him in the living room, dumping the tea tray on the sideboard behind him. 'She can come back.'

'I thought you'd come round in the end,' Morris said, smiling slightly.

'But she'll have to be a bit more cooperative.'

'I'll make sure she understands.'

* * *

'You can go back,' Morris told Anna when he returned home late in the afternoon and found the women still in the kitchen, exactly as he had left them. 'But you've got to be more cooperative.'

'Thank you,' Anna said. 'Thank you so much. I don't know what I would have done otherwise.'

Morris waved a deprecatory hand. 'Think nothing of it.'

'What on earth did you say to change her mind?' Anna asked, surprised and impressed.

Morris sighed and looked away.

'Come on, Mo,' his mother prompted. 'We're all ears.'

He pulled out a chair and sat down at the table. He looked exhausted. 'I, uh, mentioned …,' he began.

Mrs Morris nodded encouragement.

'I, uh, mentioned, uh, that she may, um, have to rent out Anna's room to a war worker, or a homeless family.'

Anna laughed and wished she had been there to see her mother's face.

'Well, it's all over now,' Mrs Morris said, patting Anna's arm. 'So you can relax. Will you stay tonight? I mean it's late to be travelling through the city on the bus, especially in your condition, and you're more than welcome to stay. You can go home in the morning. I think that would be the best.'

Anna nodded grateful acceptance, and offered to help with dinner. Mrs Morris refused. 'You need to rest, after all you've been through. You just sit there and keep me company.'

She stood at the sink scrubbing vegetables, chatting away, happy to have someone to talk to.

'He works too hard,' she said, glancing towards the open kitchen door and the living room beyond, where Morris lay on the sofa with the paper. 'He's good son and he'd make someone a lovely husband, but I'm beginning to think he'll never find a nice girl and settle down.'

Anna said nothing, uncomfortable with the conversation.

'I suppose it's none of my business,' Mrs Morris continued, 'but I don't think he makes much effort in that direction. He never has.'

'As you said, he works very hard. He probably doesn't have much time.'

Mrs Morris turned from the sink, carrot in one hand, peeler in the other, looked at Anna, sighed and turned back.

'He's never had a girlfriend, you know. Well, not that he's introduced to me. Thirty-eight years old he is. I wonder sometimes if he'll ever find a wife. Anyway, like I say, it's none of my business. He'll do what he wants to do.

'Mmm,' Anna agreed, but she had stopped listening. She was playing with the little cross at her breast and thinking of Tom.

# Ten

This was the third café they had watched, but the others had not felt right to him and they had moved on, walking in silence through the cool damp of the early morning.

Tom stood leaning his weight against the side of the building across from the café, a leaflet picked up from the street in his hand as though he were reading. The others idled nearby, Mike squatting at the edge of the sidewalk, smoking and looking at ease, and Ralph staring down at his shoes, hands dug deep in his pockets, shifting restlessly from foot to foot. Occasionally he glanced up at the pilot with a look of frustrated impatience, but circumstances kept him silent and Tom ignored him. He was watching the people that came and went, and the patron who appeared now and then in the open doorway to greet customers, to pause and look out for a while. Tom couldn't have said what it was he was looking for, but there was something here that was different from the other cafés they had observed, an atmosphere that attracted him.

The patron appeared once again in the doorway and glanced up and down the street. He rubbed his hands together softly in front of the apron he wore as if he were nervous, and stared briefly across at the three men who were watching the place. Then he turned abruptly and went inside.

Taking a deep breath, trusting his instincts, Tom gestured with his head to the others and they followed him rapidly across the street. The patron appeared at the door again immediately. He smiled as they approached and when they were close to him, just in front of the entrance, he spoke. '*Guten Morgen.*'

Tom froze for less than an instant, skin prickling as adrenalin flooded his body, his mind looking desperately for a way out. The Frenchman observed his reaction carefully.

'*Bonjour,*' Tom replied carefully, holding the man's eyes with his own, searching them to understand what was passing between them. He was bewildered.

'*Bonjour,*' the patron said finally. '*Entrez.*'

He turned and led them inside, guiding them to a table against the far wall. They sat waiting while he prepared coffee and rolls for them, then they ate hurriedly, sharing furtive glances of incomprehension.

Gradually, as one by one the other customers finished breakfast and went out into the street, the café emptied. No one else came in, and when finally, only they were left, the patron moved to the door and bolted it shut. Tom swallowed, bracing himself. The patron approached their table, taking his time to observe them.

'*Qui êtes vous?*' he asked softly.

Tom felt the eyes of the others on his face as he held the man's gaze, aware that it was his decision that had brought them here. He hoped that his instincts hadn't let them down, that Ralph had not been right to doubt him.

'*Aviateurs Americains,*' he said, gesturing slightly to indicate himself and Mike. Then nodding towards Ralph, '*Il est Anglais.*'

The Frenchman compressed his lips and sighed, shaking his head. A small smile began at the corners of his lips beneath the sleek moustache.

'I thought so,' he said, in heavily accented English, and pulled up a chair to their table. 'More coffee?'

Tom nodded, and the patron called to the woman working behind the counter. She made no sign that she heard, but a minute later she brought a tray with steaming cups of coffee for them all. She smiled and placed the tray on the table.

'I am sorry for my little trick,' the patron said. 'You were watching my café. You could have been spies. You could have been Germans.' He laughed. 'But I saw from your reaction that you were not. Definitely not.'

Tom smiled, remembering his horror, imagining how it must have registered in his eyes. The tension began to ebb from his body, his heartbeat to slow, and the coffee was strong and tasted good. Ralph smiled at him for the first time and nodded slightly, acknowledging Tom's leadership.

'Why are you 'ere?' The Frenchman asked. 'Who sent you?'

'No one sent us.'

'Then …?' The patron shrugged and lifted his hands in question.

'We were in a safe house,' Tom told him. 'But there was a Gestapo raid and we escaped.' He chose his words carefully, not to give too much away until he knew more about this man.

'Which safe house?'

Tom shook his head. 'I don't know,' he said.

The patron nodded. 'I understand. Of course, you are right.' He drained his coffee and sighed with satisfaction. 'You can call me Pierre,' he said, and smiled. 'I don't need to know your names.' He stood and looked down at them. 'Please, come with me. I will take you upstairs where it is safer.'

The airmen rose, following him across the café and up the narrow flight of stairs. At the top a corridor ran the length of the building with doors leading off to washrooms and toilets. Pierre showed them into a large room with bare floorboards that may once have been used for functions, but it was dirty now and unused, empty except for some chairs stacked against one wall. The Frenchman lifted some down.

'Please,' he said. 'Wait 'ere, and wait quietly. Keep away from the windows. I will come back later. Don't worry. We will help you.'

'Thank you,' Tom said, wary still, hoping the man was as he seemed.

The others sat on the chairs, looking lost in the middle of the oversized room, and Tom ambled round, eyes grazing the cheap reproductions of old masters that hung on the walls. Too restless to sit with the others, he squatted against the wall until his knee began to hurt, then he got up and began to wander once more.

It was nearly lunch-time before Pierre returned with a companion, and the airmen had sunk into the apathy of tiredness and boredom, so that it was hard to rouse themselves to alertness when the Frenchmen finally arrived. Tom rose to his feet, blinking, forcing himself fully awake. The men nodded greetings to each other, but there were no introductions. It was better not to know names.

'We know who you are,' the newcomer said in flawless English. 'You were lucky to escape this morning.'

Tom nodded. 'The others?' he asked. 'Our courier?'

'They took three members of our group. Your courier was not one of them. But we're all in danger now and we must get you away from here, to a house that those taken do not know. We can't be sure they won't talk under torture.' He examined the aviators with eyes that were shrewd and intelligent, and Tom warmed to him immediately. 'Have you got papers?'

The airmen nodded.

'Show me.' He examined them and handed them back. 'They'll do. Follow me.'

They went with him out through the café that was busy now with lunch-time customers, and into the street. Tom blinked in the day that had turned to bright sunshine, blinded for a moment by its dazzle, then, still blinking, still trying to clear his vision, he followed the man through back streets and on to the Métro.

On the third floor of the apartment building the Frenchman stopped and knocked on a door. The small group waited tensely, their guide impatient, glancing repeatedly along the hallway, anxious that they shouldn't be seen. When a middle-aged woman finally answered the door, he hurried them in and took the woman quickly aside, her elbow in his hand, talking to her with the same low urgency he had used with Pierre. The woman's eyes flicked towards the fugitives and there was an atmosphere of apprehension, of fear. For a moment Tom thought she would turn them away, and he would have understood if she had. Their guide turned from the woman and moved to the door.

'Natalie will look after you. She doesn't speak English but she's looked after evaders before. You'll be safe here while I make arrangements to move you on.'

The airmen thanked him and he was gone.

Tom lay on his back that night on the floor between the others, staring up into the darkness of the living room ceiling. Mike sprawled on one side of him, snoring softly, deep in sleep, long limbs stretched out, casual and relaxed. On the other, Ralph lay curled up, foetus-like, his young features puckered in tense concentration, even in sleep. Tom wondered what it was that he dreamed about, what thoughts he had that required such determined consideration.

He was too young for war, the pilot thought. Too sensitive. He should still have been in school, instead of watching his friends get killed around him.

But he was glad they were asleep, welcoming the solitude of their absence, a time to be alone with thoughts of Anna, reliving their time together over and over in his mind, and discovering new details in incidents he thought he had perfectly remembered.

They had spent their last day in town wandering, arms entwined, and Anna had shown him the old parts of the city that had survived the bombings of previous years, buildings that dated from a time before the white man had ever seen Montana. He was impressed, the cobbled streets strange beneath his feet, like something from a movie, and for the first time he saw their beauty because they belonged to her world and she thought them beautiful. They stopped often for tea, and the crispness of the air surprised their lungs each time they came out of the warmth of the tea shops.

'Have you ever loved anyone else?' Anna asked him.

He stopped walking and turned to her and smiled. 'No.'

She looked down, her hands in the pockets of her coat, considering. 'Really?' she said, looking up, almond eyes narrowed in disbelief. 'Honestly?'

'Really. Honestly.'

'I don't believe you.'

He laughed, and wondered if he should tell her about the girls he had liked, girls he had wanted. But there were none that he had loved. Not really. No one like her. 'How can I prove it?'

'Really? You've really never loved anyone before me?'

'Never.'

They meandered along the crowded pavement, arms touching.

'But I wasn't the first ... in bed, was I?' she said.

'No. You weren't the first in bed.'

'I didn't think so.'

'Are you jealous?'

'No,' she said, lifting her chin in defiance.

He turned his head away for an instant so she wouldn't see his smile. 'Really? Honestly?'

'No,' she said firmly. 'I'm not jealous.'

'Look at me and say that.'

They stopped walking and turned again to face each other. Anna looked down at the cracked pavement and her shoes for a while, and he waited until she lifted her face, met his eyes with a mischievous grin. 'I told you I'm a very bad liar, didn't I?'

'Yes,' he said. 'You did. And you are.'

'I'd be a very bad spy. I'd lie at first and then they'd say, you're lying and I'd say, well yes, actually it happened like this ...'

Tom laughed.

'Of course I'm jealous. Wouldn't you be, if I'd been with another man?'

'No,' Tom lied. 'Not at all.'

Anna stared at him, horrified, but his face betrayed him and cracked into laughter. 'Just teasing, sweetheart, just teasing. Of course I'd be jealous. I'd be wild with jealousy.'

'You're mean,' she said, laughing. 'You shouldn't tease me like that. It isn't fair.'

'I'm sorry. Can you forgive me?'

'Yes. But I'll get you back later.'

'I'll look forward to it.'

They strolled on again, laughing and talking, arms entwined until Tom remembered about the photographs and then they walked more swiftly, with purpose, excited at the prospect of the pictures. The old man recognised them and hurried out with the prints as soon as they entered his shop. One of each of them as they had asked, and two copies of them together. They were beautiful.

Outside the shop there was a bench in the sun and they sat down, admiring the pictures, basking in the warmth.

'So tell me about her,' she said.

'Who?'

'The first woman that you ..., you know ..., that you ... slept with.'

He swallowed and hesitated, taken off guard, not knowing how much he should tell her, and scared she would think less of him. He dropped his gaze to the photograph in his hand.

'I was seventeen,' he said, 'and she was a lot older.'

'How much older?'

He shrugged. 'Late thirties maybe. Forty something.'

'Tell me what happened.'

He hesitated again, recalling the details for the first time in years, navigating the memory until it was vivid once more in his mind.

'I worked most summers in the mill with Dad,' he told her, 'but the year I turned seventeen there wasn't enough work for both of us, so I got a job at the hotel on the lake, doing odd jobs, looking after the boats, that kind of thing.' He stopped and glanced at Anna's face, aware of the force of her attention.

'Go on,' she said.

'I'd seen this woman around the place. She was a rich divorcee, up from the city. I didn't ever know her name, but I remember she was better looking than most of the women there, good looking in a way that men notice.'

'What way is that?'

'She was sexy, and she knew it,' Tom replied. 'Men find that attractive.'

He waited for her to say something but she was silent, and he wondered what she was thinking, if she understood that she was different.

'So anyway, I didn't really take much notice of her. I was just a kid, you know. I never thought she'd be interested in me.'

'But she was ...'

'Yeah.' He smiled, still pleased by it, remembering the fumbling of his nervousness when she came to find him on the jetty, the warmth of the sun on his back as he rowed her down the shore a little way as she asked him. He remembered too, the quickness of the sex and the woman's disappointment.

'Tom?'

He turned to Anna, guilty that the memory had taken him from her for a moment, taken him to pleasure with another woman.

'So you slept with her?'

'Once.'

'What was it like?'

'You're very persistent.'

'I want to know all about you,' she said. 'Even the bad things. I want to know everything you've ever done. No secrets.'

He smiled, but said nothing.

'So you liked her?'

'I was flattered,' he answered with a shrug. 'I was just a kid, busting to be a man.'

'Did it make you a man?'

'No.'

'What did?'

'Flying,' he said without hesitation. 'Seeing men die.'

Anna was silent then and he wondered if he should have told her after all, if perhaps there were things that were better left unsaid, unknown.

'Are you okay?' he asked.

She smiled and nodded and touched his face with fingers that were cold. He shivered and rubbed his cheek against them.

'I'm glad you slept with her,' she said. 'You'd be a different Tom now if you hadn't.'

'I guess.'

'Did you ever see her again?'

'No. She left the next day …'

'And the others?'

'What others?'

'Other women you've slept with …'

'Another time,' he laughed. 'We'll save it for another time.'

She laughed too, and they got up from the bench and walked on.

Darkness had fallen early and surprised them with its cold. The sun had been warm and in the bitterness of the night they clung tightly together, arms wrapped round each other against the chill wind. They went for dinner at an expensive restaurant and as the waitress led them to their table Tom saw someone he knew, another airman who was there with a girl. He spoke to the waitress who stood back to let them make their own way towards their friend.

'Hey Tom!' the airman called when he saw them. 'Hey Tom! Come and sit with us.' His voice was loud in the hushed atmosphere.

Tom glanced at Anna to check her reaction but she smiled politely so he couldn't guess what she was thinking. He hoped she wasn't offended by the brashness of his friend.

'Hey waitress!' the airman called. 'Bring two more glasses and another bottle for my friends.'

Other officers looked up from their meals at the raised voice and the waitress worked hurriedly to fetch the drinks, anxious to keep him quiet. The airman rose to his feet and held out his hand. Anna took it and smiled as Tom introduced them.

'Anna, this is my friend, Harry Woods. Harry, this is Anna.'

Harry murmured a greeting, and the dark good-looking face broke into its most charming smile.

'Nice to meet you,' Anna replied, and sat next to him, so that she would be opposite Tom when he took his seat.

'Tom,' Harry said, and gestured to the girl he was with. 'This is ... uh ... Kate.'

Kate smiled, barely hiding her irritation. She was a petite girl with short blonde curls that neatly framed her little face, and she drew hard on her cigarette with a bright confidence in her attractiveness. She was sexy, Tom thought, and three days ago he might have envied his friend.

'Kate, this is Tom.'

'Nice to meet you Kate.'

She flashed Tom a brilliant smile. 'You too,' she said.

'Kate, Anna.'

The blonde gave Anna the superficial smile she saved for other women, and Harry was thoughtful as the men took their seats. He leant forward, resting his elbows on the table, and lit himself a cigarette. There was a silence and the two friends held each others' eyes for just a moment. Then Harry sat back and observed his friend's girl with open curiosity. Tom smiled as he caught

Harry's eye, and nodded once, almost imperceptibly, in answer to the unspoken question.

'What do you do?' Kate asked Tom. She turned her head to blow the smoke away from him and then leant forward on her forearms so that her face was close to his. Tom felt for Anna's foot with his toe and pressed it softly.

'He's a pilot,' Harry answered. 'The best in the whole damn bomb group.'

Kate examined Tom with interest. 'You're a pilot. How exciting.'

'Not really.' He dropped his eyes to the empty wine glass he was holding between his hands, embarrassed by her flirting.

'Oh but it is,' Kate said. 'I'd love to be a pilot; to have a plane at my command and fly through the air like a bird.'

Harry laughed, and she turned on him, eyes savage.

'Sorry,' he mouthed without feeling.

'But don't you think so, Anna,' she continued. 'Don't you think it would just be simply marvellous to fly an aeroplane?'

'No,' Anna said. 'Not at all.'

Kate was disappointed. 'But it would be wonderful,' she insisted. 'I've always wanted to fly. Why wouldn't you like to fly?"

Anna glanced at Tom and said, 'I'd be afraid.'

'Of crashing?'

'Of dying.'

Harry's eyes sobered for an instant and he looked across at the pilot, who looked away, gaze flicking to Anna in surprise; she had seemed so confident in their future. She half smiled at him briefly, the corners of her mouth just moving, and he realised that she was just as scared as he was.

'Oh that,' said Kate. She sighed, deflated briefly, and ground the half-smoked cigarette into the ash tray. There was a pause. Then she looked again at Tom, who averted his gaze and searched for Anna's hand across the table. Anna leant forward onto her forearms and took his fingers in hers. He could feel Kate's gaze boring into the side of his face.

'Hey,' Harry said, leaning forwards.

Kate ignored him, concentrating on the pilot.

'Hey,' Harry said again, touching her arm.

She turned to him, irritated. 'What?'

'You're with me, remember? Stop flirting with my friend.'

She slumped back in her seat with a sigh and drew another cigarette from the packet. She waved it theatrically until Harry noticed, and flicked his lighter for her.

'Thank you so much, Harry.' She flashed him a plastic smile.

The waitress arrived with the wine and there was another silence as Harry poured for them all.

'To long life and love,' he toasted, drily.

They raised their glasses and Anna drank some of her wine. Tom winked at her, and she smiled and took another sip. He wondered what she made of it all, if the girl's attention had made her jealous.

Kate swigged down half her glass. 'You should be a pilot,' she said to Harry. 'I'd like you better if you were a pilot.'

'A pilot needs a navigator,' Tom said. 'Or he'd get lost.'

'True,' she conceded, 'but it's the pilot who swoops about and has all the fun.'

The men looked at each other and burst out laughing. 'No one swoops about in a Fortress, sweetheart. No one.'

'You're not a fighter pilot? I thought you were a fighter pilot. You know, Spitfires and Mustangs and all that.'

'Sorry sweetheart, we fly bombers. Boring, heavy, unromantic bombers.'

'Oh well,' Kate sighed. 'I suppose it doesn't much matter then whether you're a pilot or a navigator.' She turned her brilliant smile back to the man she had come with.

Anna took another mouthful of wine and watched. To Tom's relief, there was a smile at the corners of her eyes. Harry shot his friend a look of envy, irritated now by the shallowness of the other girl. He shrugged her away from him and leant back, fingering the pack of cigarettes on the table in front of him before he drew one out and tapped it lightly on the table several times. He placed it carefully between his lips, lighting it with pleasure, inhaling deeply. He had told Tom once that the heat of the smoke in his lungs made him feel alive and capable of anything.

'So what've you been doing?' he asked.

Tom smiled, knowing that later, at the base, the questions would be more direct.

'Nothing much,' he said. 'Walking, drinking a lot of tea.'

'How long is it?'

'Since Saturday.'

'Then it must be love.' He gave Anna a meaningful look. 'Never known him to spend so long with a girl. He usually backs off after one night. He's scared of commitment, you know. Finds it hard to trust.'

Anna looked from Harry to Tom and back.

'How much have you drunk today, Harry?' Tom asked.

'A bit.' The navigator thought for a moment. 'Actually, quite a lot.' He laughed and then turned to Anna. 'Don't mind me, I'm just teasing. I get stupid when I'm drunk. Tom'd probably tell you I'm stupid when I'm sober. But he's a great guy, and if I was a girl, I'd love him too.'

Anna smiled.

'I'll tell you something else. It's a secret though.' He motioned to Anna and she leant towards him to hear. 'I get very sentimental when I'm drunk.'

She made to move back but he stopped her, beckoning her forward again. 'Wait. Seriously. Tom's my best friend and I'm very happy he's finally found someone so lovely to love him.'

'Thank you.'

'Oh for God's sake, lighten up,' Kate said, draining her glass. She leant across for the new bottle and poured herself some more.

'Hey,' said Harry. 'I'm just wishing my best friend the best.'

'We already know he's your best friend, now can we talk about something else?'

'Okay. Shoot.'

She turned to Anna. 'You don't say much. What's your story?'

'She's a nice girl,' Harry said, 'Not a loudmouth like you. Leave her alone.'

'I'm just making conversation.' She lit another cigarette. 'What do you do, Anna?'

'I work in a factory. In the office. You?'

'I got out of the draft. I was in the land army for a bit, but it didn't really agree with me, so I sort of hurt my back and I've been at home ever since. Daddy's a doctor.'

'I thought you said the war was exciting. I thought you'd want to do your bit for England.' Harry winked at Anna who smiled.

'Yes, but the work is so boring. If I could fly a plane, or be a sailor or something then I would. You boys get all the exciting things to do. We girls just have to slave in factories or on farms or something.'

'Pilots need planes to fly.'

'But you only do it because you have to, don't you? I mean, you wouldn't work if you had a choice.'

'We're at war,' Anna shrugged.

Kate rolled her eyes. 'You're no fun. You're all too bloody serious. I'm leaving to find some fun.'

'Sit down,' Harry said. 'We'll go have some fun after I have another drink with my friends.' He touched the backs of his fingers to her arm. 'I promise.'

Enticed, she lowered herself back into her chair. 'Promise? Cross your heart and hope to die?'

'Scouts honour.'

She smiled at him, appeased, and flicked her cigarette butt into the ashtray, waiting. Harry poured more wine and drank. Kate watched him. When he had finished she stood up and the two men got to their feet.

'Nice meeting you, Anna,' Harry said.

'You too.'

'Take good care of him. He's not as tough as he makes out.'

'I will.'

'See you Tom.'

'See you Harry.'

Anna watched their backs retreating through the restaurant. They were still arguing. The waitress came and cleared the table and Tom ordered food for them both. When she had gone he held Anna's hand again across the table.

'Sorry about Harry. He was a little drunk.'

'I liked him,' Anna replied. 'Is he really your best friend?'

Tom nodded. 'We've been together since training school. The rest of the crew reckon we're a lucky team.'

'Are you?'

'I sure hope so,' he said, because in the air luck was what mattered most of all. More than skill, more than guts, you needed luck.

'So do I.'

Tom picked up the half-empty bottle of wine that still stood on the table and made to top up Anna's glass but she stopped him with a motion of her hand. He filled his own and placed the bottle to one side. Anna twisted the stem of her glass between her forefinger and thumb, thoughtful.

'He's very different from you, isn't he.'

Tom laughed. 'Smart city lawyer and dumb country boy, huh?'

Her glance flicked up to him, and she smiled. 'You know I don't think that,' she told him, but she was still thoughtful, searching for the words to explain. After a moment she said, 'He seems sort of world weary, and a bit sad somehow.'

'Yeah.' Tom drained his glass and poured more. 'But he's good friend, and a hell of a navigator.'

Anna smiled and took the bottle from Tom to pour herself another half-glass.

'What did you think of Kate?' she said.

'Not my kind of girl,' he replied.

'Is she Harry's?'

His lips twitched into the beginning of a smile. 'No. Not really. You shouldn't be too hard on them. They're just two lonely people looking for some fun.'

'Have you ever done that?' she asked, looking up. 'I mean, picked up a girl for the night because you were lonely?'

Tom half laughed, caught and unable to lie to her, though he could hardly remember the loneliness of his last leave. It seemed a million years ago, his life before Anna ancient history.

He watched her, his gaze resting on her face as she twirled the stem of her glass between her fingers so that the wine swished lazily to and fro in the bowl. She was watching it glimmer in the candlelight with eyes that held the softness and the warmth of the wine, and he wondered if she knew how beautiful she was, and how much he loved her.

'A couple of times,' he said, fingering the butter knife on his plate, rubbing his thumb along the smoothness of the blade, head tilted in shy apology.

'Tell me,' she said.

He laughed again, reddening with embarrassment, the heat of the alcohol flushing his face and his neck. He should have stuck to beer, he thought. He wasn't used to handling wine.

'There's not much to tell,' he told her with a shrug. 'Just a group of guys getting drunk on leave.'

He tried to remember the girls' names, their faces, but only vague images peered through the obscurity of the drunkenness he had needed for it, knowing even then that it wouldn't be enough, that in the morning he would still be lonely and wishing for a girl he could love.

'They didn't mean anything,' he said, observing her closely. 'I was real drunk ...'

'I know.' She tried to smile, but he could see that she was hurt. 'I believe you with my head, but my heart is still jealous.'

'I love you, Anna.'

She smiled more then, and when the food came she ate hungrily, her appetite sharpened by the wine. She was beautiful in the candlelight and he watched her eat with pleasure, noticing how she ate slowly, choosing each mouthful with care.

'Is it good?'

'Mmm, it's delicious. I haven't tasted food this good since … last night.' She giggled. 'I think I might be a bit tight.'

'I think so too,' he said. 'But it's okay. I'll look after you.'

'Thank you. You're very sweet.'

When they had finished they drank coffee and sat leaning forward, holding hands again across the table, their faces close together.

'We should get going soon,' Tom said. He was reluctant. The restaurant was warm and quiet and intimate, and the base seemed far away. She nodded and rose from her chair. He watched her, his eyes following the languid elegance of her movement until she looked down at him and smiled.

'Are you coming?' she asked.

He smiled and got to his feet and they had walked out into the cold winter night.

# Eleven

The bus wove its way through the quiet suburbs into the city, the gearbox graunching with each change. Anna sat alone near the door, needing the fresh air. She had not slept well, overwrought by emotion and anxiety, and now the smell of petrol and the constant lurching of the bus as it avoided and then hit the potholes sickened her stomach. She stared out through the grime on the window with unseeing eyes, fingering the little cross absently, her connection to Tom, her source of strength.

She was dreading going home, dreading her mother's wrath, the unfinished argument still between them. There would be questions, now that the shock was over, and recriminations, the old woman's pride shattered by Morris's intrusion and her need to back down. She would see herself as blackmailed, put upon, the unfortunate mother of a wayward child. It was going to be hell living with her again.

Anna changed buses at the bus station and the respite from the motion eased her nausea. She bought tea, hot and sweet and weak, like the night in January when she had waited with Tom on the cold concrete for the bus to Little Sutton, their breath condensing under the high steel roof. For a moment she was with him, her arm through his, remembering the glances of envy from other airmen that stood nearby as he smiled at her, laugh lines creasing the corners of his eyes.

Her bus arrived, roaring, belching black smoke out behind, and Tom was gone. She wondered where he was now, if he was out there somewhere in pain or in danger, thinking of her. He's coming back, she told herself as the old vehicle lumbered through sleepy Sunday streets towards home. Then, folding her hands across her stomach, she held the life they had made together. He's coming back for both of us.

Someone rang the bell and the faint tink roused her from her daze. She rose and made her way down to the back of the bus to stand in the open doorway, clutching the pole, swaying with the movement. The road flickered past in a stream of varying shades of grey until the bus slowed to a stop and she stepped off the back onto the pavement.

She ambled home, the little suitcase dragging at her arm and bumping her leg. Outside the newsagent she stopped to rest and read the headlines on the boards. The Soviets had captured a place called Tarnopol and she wondered vaguely where it was, what it meant for the progress of the war, but her curiosity was quickly dulled, and she sank back into the lethargy of her weariness. She walked on, gazing into windows, procrastinating.

Finally, she stood on her mother's doorstep, hesitating in the awareness that this house was no longer her home. She waited before she knocked, gathering courage, remembering that her home was with Tom now, in the place inside her that kept her hope alive. Three slow even knocks, the paintless lion's head smooth and cold in her hand. She waited, the beat of her heart loud in her ears until she heard the irregular stomp, and the door swung open. They faced each other, held each other's gaze, and Anna saw only an expressionless coldness in her mother's eyes before the old woman turned and retraced her steps to the kitchen. Anna watched the squat back retreat and wondered if there was something she should say, but the door slammed shut and her mother had gone, secure again in the citadel of her kitchen. She picked up the case and oppression settled once again on her shoulders.

Later, when she had unpacked and rested, she found her mother in the living room, knitting, the fat fingers whirling deftly in the grey wool, slowing slightly as the door opened, then resuming their rapid dance as Anna sat in her chair by the unlit fire. Only the click of the needles punctured the silence and Anna wondered what she could say to break it.

Finally she said, 'Did you go to church this morning, Mother?'

Her mother shook her head, lips pursed, apparently in concentration.

'Shall we go together to the family service?' Anna said.

Mrs Pilgrim shook her head again, persistent in her refusal to talk.

'Why not?' Anna asked. She was determined to break the silence, to regain some normality.

'I don't feel like it.'

'But we always go.'

The fingers stopped and the needles fell onto the apron that Mrs Pilgrim always wore. She turned then and Anna could hear the rasp of her breath.

'We always used to,' the old woman whispered. 'But things are different now, aren't they?'

'Because I'm expecting a baby?'

Mrs Pilgrim reddened at her daughter's bluntness, trembling with fury.

'Yes,' she hissed, 'Because you're expecting a baby. Because you've let yourself be had by a *Yank* and soon all and sundry's going to know about it. How do you think that will be seen up at the church? D'you think they're going to like sharing their church with you, after what you've done? Well, they won't, you know. They won't like it at all.'

'They're supposed to be Christians,' Anna said.

'Have you no sense of shame?'

Tears began to prickle behind Anna's eyes and she sniffed and swallowed hard, determined her mother would not see her cry.

'I'm not ashamed of being pregnant, if that's what you mean.'

'You damn well should be.'

Anna rose from her chair. 'I'm going to church.'

Mrs Pilgrim said nothing but picked up her knitting and wound the wool round her fingers, troubled by the defiance in her daughter's eyes. At the door Anna paused for a moment, watching the whir and click of the needles.

'Thank you for letting me come back,' she said. 'I'm very grateful.'

By the time her mother turned to her in surprise she had gone.

Anna watched her belly swell with awe, and gradually, the consciousness of the growing life inside her became a reality. She lay in the darkness of the mornings, caressing the tautened skin, trailing her fingers over this new curve of her body. At nineteen weeks she was beginning to show but she made no effort to conceal it, proud to be carrying Tom's child.

She made an appointment with the doctor. Sleeping in late on the day, waking drowsily as the bombers roared overhead, she turned over and slept some more until her mother slammed out of the house, infuriated by her daughter's idleness. When she opened her eyes again, it was light outside, and she rose slowly, enjoying the luxury of taking her time, of being alone in the house for once. She ate breakfast in her room, and afterwards, she left reluctantly for the doctor's, feet moving slowly over the cracked and broken pavements, fingers reaching out to touch fences and overgrown hedges of privet.

The waiting room was full. Two young children were fighting around the coffee table, hurling the tattered magazines at each other, and their heavily pregnant mother shouted at them, too tired to get up and pull them apart. Anna skirted the battle carefully and the two boys looked up at the tall figure with interest. She winked at one of them who stared until his younger brother punched him in the back and the fight was resumed. Other patients, mostly elderly, seemed oblivious to the racket in their midst. Anna approached the receptionist, who hid her wrinkles under thick foundation. She flashed Anna a superficial smile.

'Can I help you?'

Anna said her name, and the receptionist checked the book, running a red fingernail over the list of names. The nail stopped at Anna's name and she looked up brightly.

'Oh yes, Miss Pilgrim. If you'd like to take a seat. He's running a bit late, I'm afraid …'

'That's all right.'

Anna sat on the only remaining chair beside two women who were discussing their ailments in graphic detail, shouting at each other over the children's screams. She picked up an old magazine, a *Time* from the previous year, but it was impossible to concentrate and she flicked through it absently.

'Mrs Knott!' The receptionist called, and the woman with the children hauled herself to her feet and dragged the two boys along the corridor towards the surgery. Anna could hear the younger one crying from the cuff his mother gave him when she caught him, but it softened to a whimper when she threatened him with a second. The room was hushed in their absence and the ladies next to Anna dropped their voices.

She sat for an hour, changing magazines, staring at the snippets of information taped to the walls, her hand reassuringly over her abdomen, rubbing it gently in her nervousness. The old ladies each took their turn with the doctor and left, and other people took their places in the shabby chairs.

'Miss Pilgrim!'

Anna stood up and made her way to Dr Weaver's room.

'Yes,' he said, without looking up from his desk. 'What can I do for you?'

She sat in the chair he had indicated and waited for him to stop writing. He glanced up at the silence, mid-sentence, then self-consciously laid his pen on the desk. He smiled. 'I'm sorry. It's been a difficult morning.'

'That's all right,' Anna said. 'You must be very busy.'

He nodded. 'So, Miss ... er ...' He stopped and consulted his notes. 'Miss Pilgrim. What seems to be the problem?'

'I'm pregnant,' Anna told him. 'About nineteen weeks.'

'You seem very sure.'

'I am,' she replied.

He sighed. 'Well, I suppose I'd better have a look at you then, er, *Miss* Pilgrim.' He lingered on the word, his face expressionless, eyes blank behind the thick glasses. 'I don't suppose you've any plans for a wedding?'

'The baby's father is missing in action,' she said, meeting his eyes as she stood up. Taken aback by the hostility in her gaze, he looked away.

The examination was brief and impersonal, the dislike mutual, a job to be done. He asked what he needed to know and she responded with the necessary details.

'Everything seems normal,' he told her when she had dressed and sat once more in front of him. 'As you said, you're about nineteen weeks pregnant and the delivery date should be about the tenth of October. Are you still working?'

'Yes.'

'What do you do?'

'I'm a secretary. It's very sedentary work.'

'Well, there's no need for you to give up quite yet then. After all, we need all hands for the war effort. Come back in a month unless there are any problems. That's all.'

From the doorway Anna said, 'Thank you, Dr Weaver,' and he looked up in surprise that she was still there.


Mrs Pilgrim woke just before dawn and lay in the darkness. She had slept badly again, tossing and turning in fitful dozing, her mind churning with anxiety. Exhausted, she rolled over onto her side, resting on one elbow, and listened to know if her daughter was up yet. There was only the steady ticking of the alarm clock and she assumed that the girl was still asleep. The luminous figures of the clock showed half past six and she should have been up by now, but she procrastinated longer, drowsy and reluctant to leave the warmth of the bed.

She sighed, and the problem of Anna's pregnancy barged its way once more to the front of her thoughts, filling her mind as it had through the night, wearying her. It was a constant burden, and she could think of no way out, no way to undo her daughter's predicament.

If only the girl had listened, she thought. If only she'd taken notice. But she hadn't, and now this, and her daughter's life was thrown away. She'd have no chance to marry, not with another man's child in tow. No future there, just more hardship and stigma. And the father would never be back. He had long gone, shot down or otherwise. She knew all about his sort.

Stiff-limbed and aching she sat up with difficulty, sitting on the edge of the bed for a moment to accustom herself to being upright. Then she searched for the familiar felt of her slippers with a probing toe and shuffled across to where her dressing gown hung on the wardrobe. She shrugged herself into it, tying the belt tightly at the waist. The early mornings were still cool in spite of the warmer weather. Quietly opening the bedroom door she paused on the landing, checking again for movement from Anna's room next to hers. She heard nothing and went along the landing to the bathroom at the end. Splashing her face with cold water revived her a little, but she wouldn't be happy until she was on her second cup of tea.

Then it came to her, an inspiration from the reddened face that stared from the mirror above the sink. They would have the child adopted. She scooped more cold water and rubbed her face again, wondering why she hadn't thought of it before. It was the perfect solution. Anna could go to the country somewhere, a place where no one knew the name of Pilgrim, and the child need never set foot in the house. No one would suspect. People moved all over the place these days and it would be easy enough to arrange. But she would have to go soon before people started to notice, before the bulge became too apparent. Satisfied, she plodded downstairs, not caring about her sleeping daughter, and let the latch off the front door. They had never used to bother locking doors before the war but now it was a habit.

Shuffling down the hall, she stopped when she heard a soft rattle behind her, turning in time to watch the letter fall through the letter box and float its way to the mat. They didn't get much post these days, except bills, and there was nothing due. She stooped painfully for it and carried it into the kitchen where the first light was beginning to creep through the window, a faint greyness just permeating the dark corners of the room. Squinting to see in the half-light, needing her spectacles, she could just make out that it came from abroad. She reached for her reading glasses to examine it more closely and moved the letter forward and back near her face until the jumble of letters swam into some kind of clarity.

*Miss Anna Pilgrim*, it said, in small neat handwriting. Her breathing quickened and instinctively she glanced up at the door to check she was still alone. She turned over the flimsy envelope in her hand and read the return address.

'*Lt. H. Woods, c/o Stalag Luft III, Germany.*'

She stared at the name in black ink, bewildered. Then she realised. Woods. The bastard who had seduced her daughter. The father of Anna's baby. So that was his name. Woods. The jigsaw fitted slowly together, one piece at a time. She smiled grimly at the information in her hand and stuffed the thin blue paper into her dressing gown pocket. She would decide what to do with it later.

Anna awoke slowly. The roar of the planes intruded gradually into her dream, the sound of death approaching, giving way as she woke to the innocent clink and clatter of the milk float in the street outside. She lay on her back, forcing her eyes to open in the gloom. Dreams. Still such awful dreams. She rubbed her eyes with her fingers, hard, as if she could drive away the images that lay behind them. The bombers droned off into the distance and the milk horse clopped on along the road. She glanced across at the clock. Seven o'clock exactly. She had overslept again.

I'm going to be late, she thought, and heaved herself out of bed in one motion, her usual elegance compromised by her tiredness. Selecting a skirt at random from her wardrobe, she struggled into it, the buttons stretched tight across her expanding stomach, then ran downstairs to the kitchen.

'You're late this morning,' her mother remarked, as her daughter swigged down a cup of cold tea. 'What happened?'

'I forgot to set the alarm.'

'You'll lose your job if you aren't careful. You could end up on the factory floor, welding or packing or something. You wouldn't like that very much.'

'No, I wouldn't.' Anna swallowed the last of her tea, and grimaced. 'I've got to go,' she said.

Mrs Pilgrim watched her daughter leave, heard the front door slam behind her and, now in the full lightness of the morning, she withdrew the envelope from her pocket and looked at it again, tapping it against the fingers of one hand, wondering what she should do with it. She pursed her thin lips in thought, seeing his name printed so neatly on the back. *Woods.*

She was surprised he had written, and was half tempted to open it, to see what he had to say, to know what kind of man he was. But something inside her rebelled even at the thought of it, revolted by the relationship. And anyway, she knew already what kind of man he was. He was a no good Yank airman, all mouth and trousers like the rest of them, flash with his money and his uniform, a man who would run a mile if he knew there was going to be a child. The kind of man who had ruined her own life, the kind of man who would destroy Anna's too, given half a chance.

She fingered the letter distractedly, contemplating its destruction, already decided that it would not reach her daughter. The girl would never know, and once the baby was born and out of the way, it would be a chapter in both their lives they could put behind them and forget.

The gas stove stood right by her, the small flame burning orange and blue beneath the blackened kettle. It would be so easy. She sat for a while on her chair, a shapeless bulk in a dressing gown, hesitating with indecision. Then she turned it over again in her hand. Such neat handwriting, she observed. Small and clear and regular. Like her husband's writing, she thought, on the odd birthday card he had remembered to give her over the years. She couldn't remember a letter from him. Not even when he was away, fighting in France the last time.

For several minutes she vacillated, gathering courage, until finally she stood up and touched the corner of it into the flame. It caught instantly, burning slowly, smouldering black, curling with the heat, the smoke rising pungent into the kitchen. She let it burn, twisting it this way and that, watching the paper blacken and crack and disintegrate into ash. As the flame licked close to her fingers she stepped away from the stove and held it over the sink, until all but one corner was destroyed. Then she dropped it into the water where it hissed and fizzed and disappeared. She turned on the tap to wash away the ash that remained, and sank back into her chair.

Later, the two women talked over dinner, exchanging the gossip of their day in the careful civility that had become their habit.

'How's Morris?'

'He's fine,' Anna replied. 'Working too hard as always. He'll give himself a heart attack if he isn't careful.'

Mrs Pilgrim smiled. 'His father was a hard worker too. Must run in the family.'

'Perhaps.'

'And how are you managing?'

Anna's eyes flicked up, suspicions aroused by the reference to her condition. It was not something that they ever discussed.

'I'm managing quite well, thank you,' she said.

'I'm very glad to hear it.'

There was a silence, and Anna stopped eating, observing her mother, knowing the old woman well enough to suspect that more was coming.

'I've been thinking,' Mrs Pilgrim said after a moment, 'that perhaps you could get the baby adopted.'

Anna laid her knife and fork together on her plate, all appetite gone.

'I beg your pardon?' she whispered.

'I said that I thought a sensible solution to our ... your ... problem, would be to get the baby adopted.'

Anna shook her head. 'No,' she said. 'No.'

'Well, I know that at the moment you think you're doing the right thing, but in the long term adoption really would be the best thing for both of you.'

'Why?'

Mrs Pilgrim sighed, as though having to explain it to an idiot.

'Because you're an unmarried mother,' she said. 'What kind of life do you think you and the child are going to have? There'll always be the stigma and you will always struggle. Life's going to be hard for both of you. And you'll never marry, not with someone else's child in tow. Believe me, I know how hard it is to bring up a child alone.

'I've thought it all out,' she ploughed on, eyes averted now from the disgust on Anna's face. 'We can get Morris to help us. You can go to the country before you get too big. We can tell people you've been transferred. Then you can have the baby there, wherever, and come back without it. No one will be any the wiser.'

Anna stared in disbelief. 'And when did you work all this out?'

'I've been thinking about it for a while,' Mrs Pilgrim lied. 'I mean, it's obvious it's the best thing to do, if you think about it. There's no stigma for anyone, it gives the child the best possible chance in life and it means you've got some kind of future. If you don't, you'll be living off me until I die, and then you'll be at the mercy of the state. And they'll probably take the child away from you anyway. This way, you can find yourself a husband when it's all over and no one will ever know any different.'

'Except Morris.'

'Morris is discreet.'

'No,' Anna said again. 'Absolutely not.' She would never give up her child, Tom's child. Never.

'You aren't thinking clearly.' Mrs Pilgrim was placating, patronising, and Anna flinched with each new sentence her mother uttered. 'I understand that it's difficult,' her mother went on. 'In your condition it can be very hard to see things objectively. I thought that you might be a bit reluctant at first, but if you really care about what's best for the child, and for you, then you've got to admit that this is definitely the best way.' She paused and waited but Anna made no response. She just stared at her mother with silent fury. Mrs Pilgrim waded on. 'Of course, I'm not expecting you to make a decision right away. Obviously you need some time to think about it. But you can't take too long. Your condition's becoming quite obvious to anyone who cares to look and you need to be away before it becomes common knowledge.'

'I don't need time to think about it,' Anna said. 'The answer is no.'

'Like I said, there's no need to be hasty. Take some time to think it over.'

'Mother!' Anna exclaimed. 'You're not listening to me. Listen to me.' When she spoke again, her voice was low and hoarse and shadowed with anger. 'I will not give up my child. I will never give up my child. Do you understand that?'

'We'll see,' her mother answered, tight-lipped, her decision made.

'You can't make me.'

'Just how do you think you're going to manage? There's no knight in shining armour going to come and rescue you, you know. Your American boyfriend is long gone and no one else is going to look at you now. You don't have many options my girl. So you had better think carefully about this.'

'No.'

'A year from now and you'll have forgotten all about it. You're young. You'll get over it. You'll find yourself a new beau, someone nice, and then you'll wonder what you made such a fuss about …'

'Would you have forgotten all about me if you'd had to give me away?' Anna asked then. She touched a hand to her belly, protective, afraid.

'That's different.'

'Is it?'

'Now listen here,' Mrs Pilgrim hissed. 'The only way out of this mess is for you to have the child adopted. I shouldn't have to spend my old age supporting you and your offspring. I've worked hard all my life. I've brought up one child without a father. I'll be damned if I'm going to do it again. I deserve a rest after all these years. Not more stigma and pointing of fingers. God, it was bad enough when your father left. I'm not going through it all again. Not for you. Not for anyone. You'll give the baby up for adoption and that's the end of it.'

Anna lifted trembling fingers to tuck hair off her face behind her ears. She was afraid now, terrified that she could lose her baby, aware that the authorities might take her mother's side, that they might agree the child would be better off in a more stable family, a family with a father. The hospital could easily take the child at birth. It happened. She knew it happened and the fear was real and debilitating. She breathed slowly to calm herself, every nerve in her body twitching, sensitised. Her mother glared, daring her daughter to challenge her, waiting for some response.

Anna stood up slowly, holding the table for support, weak and dizzy. She licked her lips with a tongue that was dry, unsure if she could speak.

'You,' she whispered, 'will never take my child. You'll have to kill me first.' She slid out from her chair and gripped the back of it, leaning heavily.

'Oh, don't be so melodramatic,' her mother sneered. 'If you really cared about the baby's future, you wouldn't think twice.'

'You're hateful,' Anna murmured, eyes clouded with hatred and tears. 'Inhuman.'

'How dare you call me inhuman! After all I've done for you. All I've ever tried to do is the best for you ...'

'You don't care about me. Or my baby,' Anna answered. 'All you care about is you. How hard it will be for you. What people might say about you.'

Her mother folded her arms across her chest, breathing hard. 'You've got no idea,' she snarled. 'I know what it's like to be a mother without a husband. I know what people say. And I protected you from that. You never knew what I went through. I never let you know what it was like. And I'm still trying to protect you.'

'I don't need your protection,' Anna said, finding her strength again, pushing herself up from the chair, standing upright. 'I'm going to my room.'

'That's right. Just walk away. Pretend the problems are just going to solve themselves. This isn't the end of this, you know ...' Her mother's words were muffled as the door swung shut, but Anna could still hear the raised voice as she plodded upstairs to her room. She sat on the bed and hugged her pillow, her cheek against it, anything for comfort.

'I won't let them take you,' she whispered to her child, over and over again. 'I'll never let them take you.'

She slept finally in the early hours of the morning, sinking into the sweetness of forgetting until the dreams came, more dreams of planes and fire, the baby falling with the *American Maiden*, and no power within her to save them.

She took the next day off work, unable to face it, drained. But she got up anyway, let her mother think all was as usual, drinking tea in silence in the kitchen. Then she rang Morris from the telephone box outside the post office.

'I've got to go to the doctor again,' she told him.

'Nothing serious, I hope.'

'No, I don't think so. But it's better to be on the safe side.'

'Absolutely,' he agreed. 'We'll hold the fort until tomorrow then. You'll be in tomorrow?'

'I think so.'

'All right. Until tomorrow. Thanks for ringing,' he said, and she thought she heard a tone of irony.

She arrived at the doctor's with no appointment and told the receptionist she needed to see him urgently.

'I'm sorry but he's fully booked up this morning. I can fit you in tomorrow if you like.' The woman's make up cracked into a smile.

'Isn't there any way you can fit me in?' Anna said. 'I don't mind waiting.'

The receptionist drew breath between her teeth and ran her fingernail over the appointment book. Anna waited with impatience, outwardly self-possessed, inwardly churning.

'Well,' the receptionist said at last. 'I suppose he could see you at half past eleven …'

'That would be fine,' Anna replied. 'I'll come back at eleven-thirty then.'

'And your name?'

'Anna Pilgrim.'

The doctor looked up from his notes as she slid in through the door. It was less than a week since he had seen her last and he was evidently surprised to see her again.

'Good morning, Miss Pilgrim.' His tone was cool but professional. 'What can I do for you today? No problems I hope?'

Anna sat in the chair and stared at him with eyes that were bloodshot and nervous. She had slept little and the thud in her head was almost overwhelming. She could barely speak. The doctor leant back in his chair and observed her, his fingers forming a pyramid in front of his chin, the forefingers tapping against his lips.

'What's wrong?' he asked gently.

'It's n..n..nothing physical,' she stammered out. She took a deep breath and swallowed hard. 'Will you ...' she began tentatively and then stopped, as if she was trying out her voice for the first time, and was surprised by the sound it made. 'Will it be you who delivers my baby?'

The doctor pondered for a moment before he leant forward on his desk, chin supported by his thumbs, fingers still in a pyramid. 'Yes,' he said. 'I think so.'

Anna paused, uncertain how to go on.

'What is it?' he asked, his curiosity aroused.

She took a deep breath, looked down at her hands and said, 'My mother wants me to have the baby adopted. Can she do that? Can they take the child against my will?'

'I see,' he answered slowly, sitting back in his chair again, thoughtful. 'Well, they *can*, if there's good reason to believe the mother is unfit to look after the child. And of course, there are those that believe that, uh, being unmarried automatically renders her unfit.' He paused, allowing her to take in what he was telling her.

'And what do you believe?' she asked him carefully.

The doctor took off his glasses and gently laid them on the desk in front of him. He pushed the heels of his palms against his eyes for long seconds then regarded her thoughtfully, squinting slightly.

'I don't approve of your ... condition,' he said. 'But I'm sure you already know that.' He paused, agonisingly. 'However, I'm of the opinion that a child is better off with his mother wherever possible, whatever her marital status.' He smiled. 'I've got no intention of taking your child away from you.'

Anna felt the tension in her body start to ebb, and she closed her eyes briefly, absorbing his words and the meaning they had for her. They were safe. Their baby was safe. Thank you God, thank you. 'Can I have that in writing?' she asked.

He laughed in surprise. 'My word isn't good enough?'

She shook her head slightly, needing proof, a piece of paper to stop anyone taking her child.

'All right.'

Still smiling at her tenacity, he opened a drawer, lifted out a sheet of letterhead and stared at it as he decided what to write. He replaced the thick glasses on his nose, picked up the fountain pen and began, his left hand pushing the pen awkwardly across the page. Anna tried to follow the scrawl with her eyes, but it was too far away to be easily legible, so she sat back a little in the hard-backed chair and looked down at her hands. The doctor finished with a flourish.

'I think this will do.' He passed her the letter across the desk and she scanned it quickly, checking there was no ambiguity.

'This is fine,' she said, her composure recovered now that the danger had passed. 'Thank you. I'm very grateful. You don't know how relieved I am.'

She folded it and placed it carefully in the envelope he handed her.

'My pleasure.' Dr Weaver smiled and rubbed his hands gently together. 'Well,' he said. 'I suppose while you're here, I may as well have a quick look at you, eh?'

Anna nodded and went behind the screen to undress.

She spent the rest of the day in the library, browsing among the books and newspapers, picking out books that attracted her and flicking through them, losing interest as soon as they were in her hand, too weary to focus. The piece of paper from the doctor sat in her handbag, in the pocket with the photograph of Tom, and she checked it now and then, to make sure it was still there. Its presence comforted her, gave her confidence that she couldn't be forced to give up her baby. She sat for a while, but the temptation to sleep in the peaceful hush was too great, so she got up and went back out into the street to find a tea shop, where she ate toast and honey and drank sweet tea. Finally, in the late afternoon, she wended her way homewards, towards the row that was looming.

It was almost dark when she stopped at the gate, the grey purple clouds low and pregnant with gathering rain. She saw weather differently now, trying to judge if it was good for flying, or bad enough that there would be no raid. The cloud was too heavy tonight, she decided, and thought that men might live who would have died on a sunnier day.

Inside the house she kicked off her shoes with relief, feet aching from walking most of the day, her head beginning to throb again. She walked slowly down the hall towards the kitchen where her mother sat waiting in her chair, large face staring ahead, impassive. Anna stood in the doorway, leaning against the door frame, eyes tired and determined. She observed her mother with detachment, wondering what thoughts lay behind the expressionless face. There was a long silence and an argument broke out between the couple in the house next door, raised voices carrying on the spring breeze.

'I went to the doctor today,' Anna said.

Mrs Pilgrim tensed and blinked slowly, once, lizard-like. She turned her eyes towards her daughter and waited.

'You can't take my baby.'

'I can,' her mother said, 'and it's all but arranged.'

'Dr Weaver is going to deliver my child. And he won't let you take it.'

Mrs Pilgrim lifted her eyebrows in derision. 'You're going to be a long way from Dr Weaver when you give birth,' she stated. 'I've written to my cousin in Plymouth, you know, Catherine, the one that married a navy officer. As soon as she replies, you'll be on your way.'

'Well, you can write again and tell her I'm not coming. I'm not going anywhere. You can't make me go. I'm not a child.' She was calm and confident, no longer afraid.

Mrs Pilgrim sensed the change and hesitated, swallowing, floundering for a way out of this defeat. 'Well,' she said finally, struggling for dignity. She forced the wedding ring she still wore to spin on the pudgy finger, twisting it viciously. 'If that's what you've decided …'

'Yes, it is.'

'Then I suppose it's your decision. As you say, I can't force you.'

'No.'

'But I think you're being very foolish. And I think you'll regret it.'

'It's my decision and I'll live with it.'

'You think you know it all, don't you?' her mother said. 'A week with a man in uniform and you think you've got it made. Well, I'm telling you, this decision is going to ruin your life. You'll be sorry and then you'll wish you'd listened to me.'

'I don't think so.' All emotion had drained from her now. She felt nothing for her mother. Nothing at all.

'Oh, I suppose you think that he's going to come back one day and play the happy father?' Mrs Pilgrim said, and remembered the letter with unease, a sliver of doubt creeping in that perhaps he might come back after all. She went on, regardless. 'I suppose you fondly imagine that one day you'll be a happy family all together. Well, you're living in cloud cuckoo land. It isn't going to happen. If he ever does come back, he's going to take one look at you, and your child, and he's going to run a mile. Probably won't even believe it's his.' She shook her head. 'Well, only time will tell. Only time will tell.'

Anna made no reply. She stared out of the window at the first drops of rain, falling large and singly onto the path with a splattering sound, waiting for the downpour to follow.

# Twelve

The journey to Bordeaux was long and uncomfortable. Twice, officers of the SS entered the compartment and sat across from Tom for a part of the way. Each time, Tom closed his eyes and pretended to sleep, hoping they wouldn't notice the nervousness of his breathing.

There was no patrol on the train. As before, only a ticket collector spoke to him and he passed over his ticket with just a smile in response, but the presence of the SS, and the endless stops and delays made the journey seem interminable. The pretence of sleeping was difficult to maintain.

They arrived finally in the late afternoon, and he stepped down with the others into the anonymity of the crowded platform. The mass jostled forward as one, moving slowly, and he saw with concern the German guard that stood next to the barrier. He flashed eyes at Mike, who had also seen, but there was nothing they could do, and he guessed their best chance was to go through as part of the tide that bore them along. He clutched his ticket, his hand hot with nerves, as first Mike, then Ralph passed through with no problem. They hung round on the far side of the barrier, separate, apparently reading timetables and notices, but constantly scanning the crowd that emerged from the gate.

Tom stepped up to the barrier and gave his ticket to the man. The collector examined it for a moment then looked up and spoke. The words were unfamiliar and the southern French accent rendered them incomprehensible. Tom smiled and nodded, hoping it had been a simple pleasantry, but the man had asked a question and he wanted an answer.

He asked again. This time Tom did not even try to reply, knowing it was over, and he looked the collector directly in the eyes. They were dark and tired and resigned, and for an instant the two men stared at each other with full knowledge of the truth. Then the German guard intervened, his suspicions aroused. He spoke in loud quick French to the collector, and the collector turned away.

'*Votre papiers!*' the guard demanded, and gestured to Tom to move to one side so that the queue could start moving again.

Tom shuffled out of the way, fumbling in his pocket for the papers. He held them out and the German snatched them away. Tom waited, considering his chances of running, wondering if the guard would risk firing at him amongst so many people. But the German's face was hard and unkind, and Tom decided the risk was too great. So he stood and waited, hands dug into his pockets in the resigned and weary way he had observed other Frenchmen endure these checks. Carefully, he avoided looking across to the others, and hoped they'd had the sense to leave already.

The guard looked up from the papers and examined the American's face. '*Je crois que vous n'êtes pas Français,*' he said slowly. I do not think you are French.

Tom said nothing. The man's French was good, and his own small command of the language had already been exposed. There was nothing he could say. He stared back, insolent, and swore inwardly. He could feel the tension in his muscles. The temptation to run was strong and he clenched his fists inside his pockets, restraining the instinct to lash out.

'American, ja?' The German asked. He was smiling, pleased with his find.

'Yes,' Tom replied. 'I'm an American aviator.'

'*Offizier?*'

'First Lieutenant Thomas Blake, United States Army Air Force.'

The German sighed and rubbed his chin between his thumb and fingers. Then he turned and spoke again to the ticket collector. The collector nodded, met Tom's eyes for a moment of apology before the guard took the American's elbow firmly in his hand to guide him out of the station. Instinctively Tom yanked his arm away, recoiling from the German's touch. People in the queue slowed to watch. The guard growled something that Tom did not understand, and reached again to grab the airman's arm. Tom stepped back, out of range, foolish, he knew, but instinctive. He was trembling with adrenalin, sweating, and he saw the German make his decision, saw the change of light in the man's eyes. But the rifle butt was against his temple before he had time to react, a sickening thud that took him out, dropping him to the concrete at the German's feet. He felt a blow to his guts, a boot finding its mark, saw Anna's face behind his eyes, and then no more.

The train clanked erratically across Germany, and through the thick grime on windows that were jammed shut, Tom could just make out a landscape of devastation. Mile after mile of bombed out buildings, broken walls reaching up uselessly from the rubble, towns that were deserted. Montana seemed an impossible place of peace, a different world he must only have imagined, and he could no longer bring to mind his vision of the house he would build for Anna, as though such a future no longer existed. He turned his head away from the glass, depressed by the stupidity of it all, and touched gentle fingers to the swelling above his left eye, trying to gauge again the extent of the damage. It was still throbbing, still tender, and he could not yet see out from under the bruising.

He had been held and questioned by men who spoke little English and who had no skill in interrogation, low-ranking soldiers whose find had made them very pleased with themselves. They roughed him up some more in his cell, taking turns to throw punches, but he told them only his name, rank and number. They soon grew tired of his taciturnity and returned to their card games, leaving him curled on the damp stinking floor to nurse his hatred and his injuries. Slowly, with care, he sat himself up again and watched them through the bars of his cell, aggressive, bored young men arguing amongst themselves over cards, the kind of men who would pick a fight in a bar for the sake of excitement.

Bastards, he thought, as he spewed onto the ground beside him. All of them bastards.

Then, after two days, they had dragged him from his cell, marched him back to the station, and put him on a train.

Now he sat across from a young RAF officer still neat in his uniform. Next to the door of the compartment their guard lounged with his gun slung carelessly across his thighs, feet outstretched. Occasionally he would lift his head and glare at them, a reminder, Tom supposed, that they were his prisoners, before closing his eyes again and slumping back apparently into sleep.

Neither of the prisoners was asleep. They sat in silence on the hard slatted seats, gazing at nothing, eyes downcast, blind. Tom knew only that they were being transferred to a prisoner-of-war camp, and they talked little, preferring the self-sufficiency of solitude. The fetid stink of his own body and the filthy clothes that covered it lingered in the air, like the vagrants who sometimes rode the trains back home, and he closed his eyes to remember better the hot shower at the hotel near the base, climbing between clean white sheets to Anna, the cotton cold against his feet.

There was a sudden shudder and jolt and the train screeched to a stop. The silence was loud after the creaking and clanking.

'What the hell ...?'

Tom peered out of the window through the dirt.

'A station?'

He shook his head and half shrugged. 'We're in the middle of nowhere.'

'Bombers,' the RAF officer said, 'American bombers,' as the approaching drone of their engines filled the small compartment.

The guard leapt to his feet with sudden animation. The compartment door opened and the corridor was full and reverberating with the confusion of panic. He turned back to his prisoners, eyes darting nervously from one to the other, hesitated, then looked up and down the corridor, waiting for an order that didn't come.

'Everyone's getting off,' Tom commented, his face pressed close to the window, watching the passengers stumbling down the embankment, lying flat at the bottom, hands over their heads. The men turned to their guard expectantly as the roar of the engines became deafening.

Fortresses, Tom observed mentally, and in spite of the immediate danger, he drew comfort from their proximity, flying unchallenged so deep into Germany. The guard was still vacillating in the corridor and the prisoners observed him, feigning the apparent detachment of the powerless. Tom's eyes flicked to those of the other flier in tacit question. The Englishman replied with an almost imperceptible nod. They would run if they could, but the moment passed, and there was no chance. The guard moved back inside the compartment and slammed the door, then resumed his accustomed position.

The Englishman slumped into his seat, arms crossed, scowling. 'Marvellous. Bloody marvellous,' he muttered. 'We're going to get killed by the fucking Yanks.' He glanced across at Tom, who smiled, good-naturedly, before returning his gaze to the filthy window. The roar was fading. The bombers had passed over them now and would drop their loads elsewhere. Tom wondered who was dying instead of them and what there was still left to destroy.

They changed trains at Frankfurt, waiting nervously on the platform amongst a crowd of people who jeered and tried to bait them. Tom kept his eyes on the concrete at his feet, and when an elderly man moved too close, his voice raised, almost hysterical in his hostility, the guard stepped forward and blocked him with his gun. The man, thwarted, leant into the obstacle and continued his tirade, waving his fist in frustrated anger at the airmen until the guard shoved him roughly away.

They boarded the next train with relief, and the guard cleared a third-class compartment for them. They slid into their seats under the stares of resentment, and fixed their eyes on the darkening landscape outside.

It was night when the train finally terminated at an unknown station, and as they stepped onto the crowded platform, the air was dank and humid. Groups of people moved aside to let them through, conversations halted abruptly, hostile eyes following them through the throng. Their guard was tense and watchful. A young woman spat at Tom as he passed by her and the spittle just brushed his shoulder. He dropped his eyes, disturbed by the depth of the hatred.

'*Mörder!*' the woman shouted as they walked away. 'Murderer!'

Tom dug his hands deeper in his pockets and turned away, eyes lowered, wondering who it was she had lost, and if it had been a bomb from his own ship that had killed them. As if it mattered, he thought. As if it made a difference whose plane it was. He shook his head and tried not to think about it, to remember that war was fucked up, and that killing people was the only way to win. He was sorry for her loss, sorry the world had come to such violence, but he was harder now and the Germans only had themselves to blame.

They walked on uneasily. The crowd around them was silent now, and their mood dangerous. The guard stayed close and Tom was thankful for his presence. He had no illusions about their fate without him.

Outside the station they moved quickly through the busy streets, slipping on the wet greasy stones, the German gun prodding them forward anxiously across a park towards the tram station on the other side. It seemed they had just missed the tram, and the airmen glanced at each other with eyes that betrayed their tension. Three adolescent boys, Hitler youth, stopped to stare, keeping a wary distance, their fists clenched in impotent anger. A child in dirty clothes, a headscarf tied around her matted hair, ran up to them, brushing against Tom's hand with grimy fingers before darting away into the darkness, laughing with the friends who had set her the dare. More youths joined the group and their hatred was palpable.

Finally, the guard looked up from the timetable and gestured for the men to move on, along a narrow side street that led away from the terminal. The airmen complied, walking quickly between the dark rows of houses, their leather boots loud on the shiny stones.

The youths followed at a distance until the guard tired of them and turned to yell. His voice cut harshly through the quiet of the narrow street, disturbing the night air, and a curtain flicked back in an upstairs window. A woman's face appeared, large eyes staring down into the road, startled by the shouting. Tom looked up, the movement of the curtain catching his attention, and locked eyes with her for an instant before the curtain dropped back into place as she disappeared inside.

The adolescents hesitated, uncertain, still moving forward with faltering steps. The soldier raised his gun in warning. They stopped reluctantly and stood in a disconsolate group, watching the hated airmen disappear into the night.

The camp was a little way outside town and from the top of the lane that approached it the men could see the flashlights that swept the compound in erratic movements, the long fingers of light searching its darkest corners. The high perimeter fence gleamed under the lamps that were hung above it, swinging slightly in the warm summer breeze and Tom felt the cage shrinking in around him. Steel grey roofs glinted as the beams glided over them, and the prisoners were silent as they approached.

Later, in his solitary cell, naked and humiliated by the intimate search, he climbed under the coarse blankets that lay on the lumpy mattress, and tried to sleep. He wanted to shower, to wash the memory of the man's hands from his skin, and he lay wide awake, staring into the blackness, vulnerable and angry.

Just survive, he told himself. Just survive.

A sort of sleep came finally in the early hours of the morning, a light drifting between nightmare versions of waking worlds of planes and bombs and love betrayed, and in the morning he woke up weary when someone opened the blackout shutter on the small barred window high in the wall above the bed. Early summer sun touched the filthy glass, but its light did not filter through into the cell. Tom lay in the gloom, forcing heavy eyes to open before he hauled himself to sit on the edge of the bed. His body was tired, still aching and sore from the beating. Like an old man, he thought, and lifted probing fingers to his eye. It was still swollen and painful, still tender to touch, and he wished he had a mirror to see it, to judge how bad it was.

Looking up at the window, he tried to gauge the time and judge how long he had slept, but the light was too weak to even make a guess. The guards had taken his wristwatch when they took his clothes and he doubted he would see either of them again. The clothes he was glad to be rid of, relieved to be free of the stench, but the watch he regretted, a present for his twenty-first birthday from his parents. Hungry, he wrapped himself in the coarse blanket and sat back on the pillow to wait.

In time the bare light bulb came on, casting a sickly yellow light over the room. Tom looked around him with vague curiosity, but there was nothing to see, nothing but the bed and the slop pail that was next to it. He reached down and shoved the pail under the bed, out of sight, then sat up again.

When the food arrived at last, it was meagre, and he chewed the small hunk of black bread slowly, making each mouthful last, savouring the sour taste against his tongue and forcing down the acorn coffee. It made little difference to the ache in his gut, but it lifted the tiredness for a while.

He thought about Anna, wondering what she would think of him now, half-naked and stinking, his face like a losing boxer's, rage against his captors simmering inside. He was still amazed that someone so beautiful had let him love her, the beauty of her face also in her heart, all he had ever wanted in a woman. Reminding himself again and again that she'd agreed to be his wife, he refused to let the doubts speak up, forcing them below the vivid memory of her love for him. Harry had been right that evening in the restaurant, he thought, he was afraid to trust, and the doubts would not be silenced, coming later, unbidden, finding their way into his thoughts when he was sleeping, mingling with other dreams of falling planes and dead gunners.

The days passed with no interruption but the delivery of food and the slopping out of the pail, and gradually Tom became accustomed to the solitude, the confined limits of his world. Occasionally, the heating was turned up to an almost unbearable level, and then he stretched out on the concrete floor and scraped the sweat from his body with his hand. He lost all track of time, the light switched on and off at random, the blackout shutters closed for days at time. Only the arrival of the food gave him markers to judge that time was passing.

After a few days, or a week or more, he was taken from his cell to an office with a window. He stared out, mesmerised by the colours of the natural world, fragments of blue sky behind myriad layers of grey, greens of trees and grass. A Luftwaffe officer sat behind a desk in the simply furnished room, and observed his prisoner with interest.

'Please, sit down.' The voice could have belonged to a British officer, upper class and fluent.

Tom turned his attention from the outside world and mentally prepared himself, watching his interrogator warily. He felt vulnerable here, wrapped only in a blanket, and the German's steel gaze disturbed him. He sat and waited for the man to speak again.

'Good morning, Lieutenant Blake,' the officer smiled. 'I am sorry you have had to wait so long before we could talk. You must understand that we are very busy with so many airmen being captured, and we can't interview you all as quickly as we'd like. Would you like some coffee?'

Tom said nothing. Name rank number, he repeated mentally. Nothing else. Name rank number.

The German observed him, sizing him up, looking for the weaknesses.

'Please,' he insisted. 'Have some coffee.'

'Okay,' Tom answered. 'I'll have some coffee.' He took the proffered drink and sipped it.

'Excellent blend, don't you think?'

Tom nodded.

'Real coffee is such a rarity in Germany now,' the officer continued. 'We're very lucky to have obtained this. I must admit what we usually get is very bad, very bitter. Still, that is one of the sacrifices we all have to make in this war and it can't be helped. Unfortunately, it's the same for all of us.'

Tom said nothing, remaining wary, resisting the friendliness, aware that to relax was to become vulnerable.

'You are presently being held in the interrogation centre. The main transit camp across the way is much more comfortable than your present condition. There is tea, and food from Red Cross parcels, hot showers, and perhaps,' he smiled, 'even a uniform for you. And of course, the company of your compatriots.' He sat forward slightly, leaning his forearms on the desk in front of him, waiting for some response. The American was silent. 'You can be transferred there at any time, on my orders. It's just next door. Your life would undoubtedly be much nicer if you were to be transferred.'

Tom nodded to show he had understood, and drank more of the coffee.

'But we need to get a few details from you before you can be moved. Just to make sure that you are who you say you are. Formalities only. I'm sure you understand. The bureaucracy of war. There is always so much paperwork to do.'

There was a silence.

'First of all there is the Red Cross form, so that your family can be notified of your whereabouts.'

He pushed a piece of paper across the desk towards Tom, who picked it up and perused it casually before replacing it carefully on the desk. He knew from briefings in England that the form was bogus, and that knowledge gave him courage, a feeling that he was not alone.

'No,' he said.

The German seemed irritated. 'Am I to understand that you don't want your family informed that you are now a prisoner of war? I'm sure they must have been very worried about you.'

'I'm not filling in the form, if that's what you mean,' Tom answered. 'It's bogus.' He drained his coffee and put the cup down on the desk. The German's gaze hardened, and the line of his jaw became tense.

'I see.' He sighed. 'You understand, of course, that you are currently being held by the Luftwaffe?'

'Yes.'

'And that our methods of obtaining information are humane, military man to military man?'

'Yes.'

'You understand also, I assume, that if you do not cooperate with us, then we may be forced to turn you over to another authority, whose methods are somewhat less humane?'

'You mean the Gestapo.' Images of the raid on the Paris café flashed behind his eyes, and snatches of horror stories that other airmen had told at the base. He hoped the man was bluffing.

The officer's eyes narrowed and thin lips twisted into a humourless smile. A cat with a mouse. 'Yes indeed. The Gestapo.' He paused and smiled as though at an intelligent pupil. 'You see, when you were captured, you were wearing civilian clothing. That means you are quite possibly a spy. Without the information you refuse to give, it will be very difficult to verify that you are indeed who you claim to be.'

'I have my dog tags.'

'Yes, but it's very easy to obtain dog tags. There are dead Allied airmen all over France.'

Tom looked away and breathed deeply, calming the anger that threatened to rise. The man was a bastard, he thought, and skilled at his job.

'We need to know details. Your unit number, your squadron and group, your commanding officer, your target the day you were shot down. With this information you can prove who you are without doubt. I have no wish to give you to the Gestapo.'

Tom stared, insolent now, refusing to play the interrogator's game, sick of being afraid. He said nothing, but the hostility in his eyes was eloquent enough.

'And,' the German continued, 'even if you are who you say you are, there is the small question of how you came to be in Bordeaux with false papers. I'm quite sure the Gestapo would be very interested to know who helped you get there.'

There was another silence. They would have to torture him to find that out, he thought. And maybe even then he wouldn't talk. So there was no way in hell just the threat of it was going to break him.

'So you will cooperate?'

'No.'

'You will regret it,' the officer said.

Back in his cell, Tom watched the door clang shut with the same dull fear as before a raid, and hoped again that the man was bluffing.

* * *

The days passed uncounted. He found solace in prayer, remembering words from Sunday school, prayers he thought he had long forgotten, lessons he had paid no mind to in the years that had intervened. He remembered the sunrises above the overcast on early missions, and the sudden understanding of himself that Anna's love had brought him. With her he had become complete, as if he had found the part of him that made him whole, and he spent long hours in their future, building in detail the house he had planned long ago, making changes for Anna, surprising himself with his understanding of what she would like. She had said once she would be happy in a hovel with him, and though he believed her, he wanted only the best for her, the finest home his hands could create.

He was interrogated again, and the hard grey eyes of the German officer regarded the filthy stinking prisoner with ill-disguised distaste. Tom doubted he'd get coffee a second time.

'Good morning Lieutenant Blake,' the officer said. 'Please, sit down.' He pronounced the rank the English way, leftenant, the same as Anna, and Tom smiled, remembering that she had teased him and mimicked his accent. He sat in the chair the German had indicated.

'You smile,' the officer said. 'I think perhaps that your condition is not something to smile about.'

Tom glanced down at his unwashed body then held the German's eyes with his own. He was no longer afraid. The solitude had plumbed deep reserves of strength within him, a readiness for anything, and he held the officer's gaze, challenging the man's authority.

He said, 'You're wasting your time.'

'I believe that's for me to decide.' The German was calm, his voice smooth.

There was a pause and Tom observed his interrogator dispassionately. Pure Aryan. Cropped blond hair turning to grey, chiselled features and ice grey eyes that were capable of cruelty.

The pilot remained wary. The officer resented the scrutiny and stood up to pace the room slowly before he turned and leant against the desk close to where his prisoner sat.

'You know, don't you, that you are the only member of your crew to survive?'

Liar, Tom thought. Harry. Harry made it down too. But the assertion disturbed him and his eyes filled with hatred.

'You think I'm lying.' The officer observed the pilot's reaction with interest. He smiled. 'But I'm not. Your navigator, Lieutenant Woods, was shot trying to escape on the way here. He died very soon after.'

It would be like Harry to make a run for it, Tom thought.

'Perhaps you were friends?'

He's guessing. There's no way he could know that. No way at all. He said nothing.

'Ah, then you were. I'm sorry to have given you bad news.'

There was a silence and Tom stared at the officer with open hatred.

'I will leave you to ponder your options,' the German said, shifting uncomfortably under such hostility, 'and to grieve for your friend.'

Tom stood and followed the guard back out of the office along the dim corridor to his cell. The door slammed shut behind him, reverberating through his nerves, enclosing him in solitude once again. He sat on the edge of the bed, lowered his face into his hands, and wept.

# Thirteen

June arrived in a gust of wind and rain that darkened the sky with looming clouds for days at a time, casting a pall of gloom over a people weary and impatient with the war. Then American troops captured Rome and the weather seemed less important.

'It's official,' Mrs Pilgrim announced two days later, bustling out of the living room where she had been listening to the radio set, as soon as Anna came home from work.

'Yes, I know,' Anna replied, kicking off her shoes and following her mother back down the hall.

'Isn't it good? The invasion has finally started.' Mrs Pilgrim paused at the living room door. 'We've landed in France. At last. It's official. They said so on the news this morning.' The fat face was alive with delight. 'Isn't it wonderful news? We're finally going to give Hitler what for.'

'Yes,' Anna answered. She had been listening to the radio reports at work.

'You don't seem very excited,' Mrs Pilgrim accused.

'I am,' Anna said. 'Of course I am. It's very good news. I'm just tired that's all. And thinking of the awful fighting there must have been.'

'Well, you can't win a war without fighting.'

'I know. But it's still hard for the people involved.' She was thinking of Billy Lawrence. 'Have they mentioned casualties?'

'No. I don't think so,' her mother snorted and turned into the living room. 'I haven't made any dinner,' she called over her shoulder. 'I've been too busy.'

'I'll make it,' Anna offered, slipping gratefully into the quiet of the kitchen, alone with her thoughts.

Suddenly the war seemed close and involving again.

Anna listened avidly to the news every day after that, reading every article in the papers in case there was some clue that would lead her to knowledge of Tom. But there was nothing, and with each day that passed with no word, no contact from him, she began to lose hope that he would return. She prayed each night for him and to him, but it was harder now to talk to him in her head, and his presence was beginning to be more distant and unreal.

A letter arrived from the cousin in Plymouth. Mrs Pilgrim read it silently in the kitchen, tight-lipped, inscrutable. Anna waited for her mother to start, for the argument to begin anew, but the old woman said nothing, folded the letter and put it to one side. Anna watched, made curious by her mother's silence.

'What did she say?'

Mrs Pilgrim looked up in surprise. 'Oh, nothing much,' she faltered. 'It's a hive of activity down there at the moment, of course. Lots of ships and troops coming and going. They've got people billeted with them. Everyone there has. She says it's been very exciting. I should think it was all rather a nuisance myself ...'

'That's all?'

Her mother frowned, as if puzzled that Anna was asking. 'Yes. More or less.'

Adoption was never mentioned again.

At the factory, people had finally begun to notice Anna's swelling stomach, and the girls who had seen her in the tea room that Saturday five months earlier wasted no time in retelling the story. Within a few days it was all round the factory.

'Surprised she didn't get rid of it ...'

'I wouldn't let a Yank touch me ...'

'What's wrong with a British soldier, that's what I'd like to know ...'

'The Americans do look nice in their uniforms though ...'

'And they've got money ...'

'What's she going to do with it ...?'

'And her so prim and proper ...'

'It's always the quiet ones you got to watch ...'

Anna heard the gossip and ignored it. There was nothing that could make her regret that she was pregnant. The little part of Tom she carried inside her made his absence possible to bear, and she didn't care what anyone else thought.

Morris was circumspect. He had begun to view Anna differently since his successful role as mediator, and the cool professional relationship he had always maintained with his secretary had gradually warmed to a more personal interest, an appreciation of her as a human being, as a woman. He became more considerate, careful not to overburden her with work.

'And is everything all right, Anna?' he asked a hundred times a day, provoking sniggers from the other girls. 'I'm not working you too hard?'

Anna shook her head. 'No, Mr Morris. I'm just fine, thank you.'

'Well, let me know if there's anything I can do. Can't have you doing too much in your condition, can we?'

One evening not long after D-Day, when the girls had left for the day, he called her into his office. He seemed nervous and ill at ease, and it occurred to Anna that he might be about to fire her.

'Take a seat, please,' he offered. 'Wouldn't do to keep you standing.'

Anna sat, obedient and too tired to be more than mildly curious.

'Well,' he began, backing towards his desk where he leant nonchalantly, hands clasped lightly in front of his thighs. 'How are things at home now?'

'All right, thank you.'

Morris paused and fiddled with his signet ring. Anna waited

patiently. She had already missed her bus and she had over half an hour to wait till the next one.

'Um,' he started. 'Um ... er ...'

'What is it, Mr Morris?' she said, trying to be helpful.

He looked up sharply, embarrassed, and said slightly too quickly, 'I was wondering if I might pay you and your mother a visit on Sunday. Just for a cup of tea. You know, to see how you're both doing. Pass the time of day.' His lips twitched into a hopeful smile and Anna stared at him in surprise. 'I mean,' he went on, 'I don't want to intrude or anything. If it isn't convenient ... another time would be fine, or not at all if it's too much trouble. I don't want to put you to any trouble ...' He trailed off.

'I'm sure that would be fine, Mr Morris,' Anna answered. She could think of no plausible excuse off the top of her head. 'Of course, I'll have to check with my mother. Can I let you know tomorrow?'

'Yes, of course. Any time. There's no rush. None whatsoever.'

'I'll let you know tomorrow then,' she told him. She wanted to ask why. Why did he want to come? Why would anyone choose to spend time with her and her mother? But she let the question slip unsaid from her lips.

'Well, you'd better be going then, Anna,' Morris said. 'I don't want to keep you.'

Anna rose to her feet, her hand in the small of her back, supporting it, fingers searching fruitlessly to alleviate the point of pain, as they had all day.

'See you tomorrow,' she replied, and walked slowly out past the factory to the bus stop outside.

'Morris would like to visit us on Sunday,' she told her mother over dinner.

'He wants to come here?' Her mother was incredulous. 'Whatever for?'

'For tea. To see how we are.'

Mrs Pilgrim laid her fork down next to the remnants of the pork chop. 'For tea? How very odd.'

Anna shrugged. 'He's lonely, I suppose.'

Her mother frowned.

She tried again. 'Perhaps he feels a bit responsible for us. He did help us out.' She took another mouthful of food, unusually hungry. 'Or perhaps he just wants to renew the ties between the families. We used to be close, didn't we?'

'Yes,' her mother nodded slowly. 'Perhaps that's it. Still, it seems very strange.'

Anna agreed and they continued eating, knives scraping on china the only sound.

'Whatever shall I cook for him?' Mrs Pilgrim said, after a while. 'I mean, we haven't got any food to spare what with rationing, and I don't know what he'll expect. He's probably used to much better than I can prepare.'

'He's coming for tea,' Anna smiled. 'He's not expecting a three-course meal. I'm sure a cup of tea and some sandwiches will be just fine.'

Her mother hesitated. 'Do you think so?'

'Yes. I'm sure. He told me to tell you not to worry and prepare anything special. He's coming for the company, not the food.'

Mrs Pilgrim was still unconvinced.

'Don't worry,' Anna chided. 'Sandwiches will be fine. Really.'

'Well, if you're sure ...'

'Yes. I'm sure.'

The two women finished their meal in silence.

Morris arrived at four o'clock on the dot, smiling broadly on the doorstep, dripping with the thick drizzle that had begun to fall. He stepped into the half-light of the hall and Anna took his raincoat and hung it on the rack.

'Good afternoon,' he said cheerily, scraping the water from his thinning hair. 'Rotten weather for this time of year.'

'It was a big help on D-Day,' Anna reminded him.

'Very true. Very true.'

He followed her along the hall into the living room.

'Please,' she smiled, 'make yourself comfortable. I'll tell Mother that you're here.'

She left him in the overfurnished living room and he wandered round, hands behind his back, peering at the photographs that were hung, apparently haphazardly, on walls darkened with age. No photographs of Mr Pilgrim, he noticed, eyes flicking across the pictures. Not one. But there was one that seemed to be of a young Mrs Pilgrim, smiling and looking attractive on a beach somewhere. He sidled along a step, eyes narrowing in the dim light. A large picture of Anna in a ballet dress moved into view. She must have been fifteen or sixteen when it was taken. She was staring dreamily into the camera, hands resting lightly on the tutu, one foot pointed and resting behind the other. The face hadn't changed, he thought. Still just as pretty. More elegant now, though. Lost that roundness in the cheeks. He stood with his head tilted, admiring, until he heard voices and footsteps in the hall.

He turned as the door swung open and Anna entered, carrying a tea tray.

'I was looking at the photographs,' he smiled, gesturing to the wall. 'This one of you is lovely.'

Anna placed the tea tray down on the sideboard, and glanced in his direction, knowing already which picture he meant. Mrs Pilgrim bustled in and plonked a plate of sandwiches next to the tray.

'I bet she was a lovely dancer, eh, Mrs Pilgrim?' Morris said.

'Yes. She was.'

Anna bit her lip, the anger still rankling.

'You wanted to dance professionally at one time, didn't you?' Morris asked. 'I remember you telling me over the back fence one day.'

'Yes,' she replied. 'It was my dream.'

'You were very good too, as I remember. You won a couple of competitions, didn't you? Destined for great things.' He smiled, innocent and unaware of the sudden tension.

'She was very good,' Mrs Pilgrim conceded. 'But the stage is no life for a girl.'

Morris glanced at Anna and noticed the pretty lips pinched with irritation. He realised he had stumbled on a touchy subject. Mrs Pilgrim went on.

'She went to secretarial school instead, which was far more suitable. A girl needs a trade these days unfortunately. But I'm sure she's got no regrets about it now, have you Anna?'

Anna handed Morris his tea with a small smile of apology. 'Everything happens for a reason, I suppose,' she murmured. Then, following that thought, thinking of Tom, of her baby, she said, 'No. I've got no regrets.'

'There,' Mrs Pilgrim turned to Morris, who sat now on Anna's usual chair by the unlit fire. 'See. A fifteen-year-old has got no idea about the world. Oh, we had our arguments about it. She was very upset at the time. But she was just a child. I told her then that she'd appreciate what I'd done when she was older.' She nodded in Anna's direction, vindicated.

Morris stirred sugar into his tea, embarrassed, wishing he had never mentioned it. Mrs Pilgrim settled herself on the sofa and Anna retreated to the second armchair, rarely used, at a distance from the others.

'So,' Mrs Pilgrim said, in good humour, 'how are things at the factory?'

'Very busy. Very busy. I sure Anna's told you that we've upped production for the third time this year. It's unbelievable the quantities we churn out now.'

'No, she hasn't mentioned it.'

'Of course,' Morris went on, 'it probably won't be for much longer. The way things are going I should think the war could be over in a few more months.'

'Do you think so?' Mrs Pilgrim was eager for his opinion.

'It can't last. Hitler's spread himself too thin. He's fighting on too many fronts. Too many supply lines. He's got the Red Army on the east, the Americans coming through Italy and our boys at him in France. He's overstretched. The Russians seem to have him on the run good and proper.'

'What about the flying bombs?' Mrs Pilgrim asked, as if he were an expert. 'What's going to happen about them? Aren't they awful?'

Morris shook his head. 'Dreadful things. Absolutely dreadful. But we'll knock out their production soon enough. The Americans have got a wonderful air force ...' He stopped, realising what he had said, eyes flicking between the two women. Anna suppressed a smile, and her mother stared, impassive, apparently waiting for him to continue. 'I mean,' he stumbled on, 'I mean, their air force is dedicated to knocking out important installations. They'll do it soon enough ...'

'You're very optimistic,' Mrs Pilgrim said, her buoyant mood somewhat punctured by his tactlessness. She felt less need to humour him now, and he sensed her change of temper.

'Well, it does no good to worry now, does it?' he answered, and Anna realised he had been saying what he thought her mother wanted to hear. 'Anyway,' he said, 'I didn't come here to talk about the war.' He smiled at Anna. 'I wanted to find out how things are with you, Anna.'

'I would have thought you could have asked her that at work, and saved yourself traipsing all the way over here on a Sunday.' Mrs Pilgrim heaved herself to her feet, poured herself another cup of tea from the pot on the sideboard and sat down.

'Would you like more tea, Morris?' Anna asked their guest, embarrassed by her mother's rudeness.

'No, I'm fine thanks. Another sandwich would be nice though.'

Anna rose and fetched the plate for him. He gave her a grateful smile as she sat down again, fingers interlaced across her belly.

'I think,' she said to her mother, 'that Mr Morris prefers not to discuss personal matters at the office. Isn't that right?'

'Yes. Yes, that's right.'

'I see,' Mrs Pilgrim replied. 'In that case, what would you like to know?'

Morris looked down at his sandwich, taken aback by the directness of the question. 'Well, I suppose I just wondered how the pregnancy was coming along ...'

'Fine thank you,' Anna replied. 'Everything seems to be just as it should be.'

'She's twenty weeks now,' her mother told him.

'Almost twenty-five,' Anna corrected.

Her mother frowned slightly and waved a hand as though to stop a fly landing on her. 'And everything's progressing normally.' She leaned forward towards him and lowered her voice. 'Of course, she's over the morning sickness and all that, but she's beginning to get backache now, and feel the weight. She's very tired all the time and I keep telling her she should stop working but she won't hear of it. She's very stubborn.'

Anna yanked savagely at a loose thread on her cardigan.

'Well, she can leave any time she likes. No one expects her to keep working in her condition. We don't want her wearing herself out.'

'I'm fine, thank you,' Anna interrupted. 'Please don't concern yourselves.'

'But I don't know why she won't stop,' her mother said, as if Anna weren't in the same room. 'It's not as though she needs the money. She's got me to support her. I think she's being quite ridiculous. She'll make herself ill, the way she's going.' She paused to glance across at her daughter, then looked again at their guest. 'Perhaps you can talk some sense into her. She certainly won't listen to me.'

'Well, now, it's up to her,' Morris prevaricated. 'If she feels she's coping ...'

'But she isn't coping. You don't see how tired she is when she gets home.'

Morris looked to Anna for help.

'I'm fine,' Anna insisted. 'Really.'

'You see?' Morris said. 'Like I said, it's for her to decide if the job's too much or not.'

'Yes, well, I suppose so,' Mrs Pilgrim mumbled, and the subject was dropped.

The afternoon drifted by. Conversation moved on to less contentious issues and Anna found she was grateful for the third person, relieved not to be the centre of her mother's attention for a time. She half listened to the conversation, half drowsing as they talked about rationing and the black market, fingering the little cross through the soft cotton of her blouse. She wished that she could leave work. Her mother was right. The long days did exhaust her and she worried that it wasn't good for the baby. But she needed to save money for her child while she could. To have some little independence. Twenty-five weeks pregnant. Almost six months since Tom had disappeared. She should have heard by now. She should have heard something. But she wouldn't give up on him. Not yet. Not while there was still a chance. He could be wounded. Or in hiding, travelling a slow and dangerous path home to her. Write to me Tom, she whispered in her head. Write to me soon.

'... isn't it, Anna?' her mother was saying. Anna looked over to Morris who was standing now, ready to leave, and roused herself from her thoughts.

'I'm sorry, what was that?' she asked. 'I was miles away.'

'I said, terrible weather for the time of year we're having.'

'Yes,' Anna agreed, shifting forward to get up. 'Absolutely dreadful.'

'No, please,' Morris said to her. 'Don't get up. I'm sure you need to rest as much as you can.'

'Thank you. If you don't mind ...'

'Of course not. Thanks for a lovely afternoon, ladies. I've thoroughly enjoyed myself. If you wouldn't mind, I'd very much like to do this again one day.'

'If you like,' Mrs Pilgrim said, warmer to him now, flattered by his attention. 'You can just make a time with Anna. We're always at home on a Sunday.'

'Thank you, I shall. I'll see myself out. No need for you to bother yourselves …'

But Anna's mother followed him out anyway, and stood, arms folded, while he shrugged on the still-wet raincoat.

'See you again soon I hope,' he said from the doorway. 'Thank you again.'

'You're very welcome,' Mrs Pilgrim replied and closed the door behind him.

# Fourteen

At the main camp for airmen where Tom was transferred soon after, he was interrogated again, by American officers this time, keen to ensure that he was genuine. 'The Germans plant people sometimes,' he was told. 'So we have to be careful.' He answered their questions, rehashing the details of the last months, showing his scars as evidence, until the officers were convinced of his identity and he was allowed to go.

He wrote to Anna as soon as he could, a letter that was hard to write, struggling to explain to her all that had happened in words that the censors would not deface.

*My darling Anna,*

*At last I can write to you. At last I can tell you that I'm still alive and that I'm safe.*

*There's so much to tell you, so much that I can't put into words in a letter so please forgive me if I'm not making much sense, only I miss you so much, and when all of this is over I never want to go away from you again. I want to be with you always, where I can see your beautiful face, and hold your softness in my arms. Wait for me, please. Knowing that you love me is all that keeps me going, knowing that one day, soon, we'll be together again.*

*I arrived at this prison camp yesterday, and you must be wondering where I've been all this time, what I've been doing. I can't tell you very much, but I was wounded, and people who were good and kind and very brave took care of me until I was well again. Then after I left them to come home to you I was caught and now I'm stuck here and the whole war seems to be between us, though we don't get much news in here. Do the Forts still fly over your house every morning and make the windows shake? Do they make you think of me? It seems such a long long time ago that you told me that, almost the first thing you ever said to me. You were so beautiful that day in the tea room and I remember that I watched you for an hour, hoping all the time you'd been stood up. I don't think I ever told you that. I never believed in love at first sight before, but I do now.*

*Don't fret about me any more. I'm safe now, and we can write to each other, and as soon as I'm free again we'll be married straight away. I love you Anna, write to me soon.*

He sealed it quickly, frustrated by the inadequacy of words to express what he felt. Then he wrote to his family, relieved to contact them at last and put their minds at rest.

When the letters were finished he wandered out into the compound and saw Harry, sunning himself, half-naked on the wooden steps of the next hut, his torso already bronzed with the early summer sun. Tom stared for a moment, speechless and delighted until he found his voice again.

'Harry!'

'Hi Tom,' Harry smiled. Rising slowly to his feet, he stepped down onto the earth and stretched out his arms. 'Welcome.'

The two men embraced, holding each other tightly before they broke away.

'I thought you were dead,' Tom said. 'God, it's good to see you.' He was grinning, overjoyed to see his friend, but behind the smile he could feel tears threatening to come. 'They told me at Dulag Luft you'd been shot trying to escape.'

'You should know me better than that,' Harry laughed.

'Lying bastard,' Tom said, shaking his head, remembering the grief of that night, the desolation of his solitude when he had almost lost all hope.

Harry laid a hand on his shoulder. 'I'm glad to see you too, Tom, though I wish it could've been somewhere nicer ... A few beers, a couple of girls ...'

'... a different country ...'

'Yeah, that would be good too.'

They sat on the steps of Harry's hut and the navigator lit himself a cigarette and drew back hard, lifting his chin to blow the smoke high above them.

'So how the hell are you?' Tom asked.

Harry glanced sideways at his friend before settling his gaze on the pine forests beyond the wire. 'I'm okay, I guess,' he said, but he seemed older, and some of the cockiness of before was gone. There was a narrow scar across his temple that was new, and his nose had been broken. 'You can move into our room if you want. There's a spare bunk at the moment. Be like old times.'

'Without the flying.'

'Yeah, thank God. Without the flying.'

Tom ran his eyes across the high perimeter fence. A guard in a box observed them with detachment, hands folded and resting lightly on the machine gun that was pointed in their direction. The pilot turned his gaze away and looked at his friend. 'What are the chances of getting out of here?'

'Pretty slim. A few get beyond the wire but not many get any further. There was a big break out in March but the Gestapo shot most of them, apparently on Hitler's personal orders. It's been a bit more low-key since then. There's still an escape committee if you're interested, though. It's something to do I guess. Keeps the goons busy.' He nodded up at the sentry. 'Every one of them here is one less fighting at the front.'

Tom nodded, gaze drawn again to the fence and the forest beyond it. He wanted to go, more than anything, he wanted to get out of there and get back to Anna, but he had no wish to get killed trying. 'So what do you do?' he asked Harry. 'How d'you keep that intellect sharp?'

Harry half laughed and dropped his cigarette into the dirt. Both of them watched it fizz and burn slightly before he stamped it out carefully with his boot.

'I read,' he said with a shrug. 'Play chess. Play softball. I've done a bit of forging. It's not a very exciting life. I don't think I'd come here again.'

'How long've you been here?'

The navigator averted his face. 'Since March,' he answered. Then he turned back and smiled, and Tom wondered what he was hiding. 'I wrote to Anna for you,' he said. 'Told her you were okay, and being looked after. I couldn't really say much else.'

'Thanks. I appreciate it.'

'No problem. Let's walk.'

They moved away from the huts and out across the compound to the perimeter circuit. They walked slowly, their feet stirring up the dust. Tom watched it settle on his boots and the cuffs of his trousers, grey and chalky. Through the silence between them he could feel Harry's tension, something hard and unspoken. 'What happened to you?' he asked finally.

'Nothing.'

'Sure.' Tom shrugged it off with a tilt of his head, but he knew his friend was hiding something, and he was hurt by it. He had spent too long alone. They walked on in silence. Once or twice Harry took a deep breath as if he were about to speak, then changed his mind. People passed them, striding quickly for exercise, small clouds of dust puffing up around their feet. They paused to let a group of runners go by and as they moved off again, still sauntering, Harry spoke at last.

'I guess I may as well tell you. I had a little run-in with the Gestapo in Paris.' He glanced sideways at his friend, and touched automatic fingers to his nose and his temple.

Tom grimaced, half closed his eyes with sorrow. It was what every flier dreaded. 'What happened?'

'I stayed in Paris a couple of weeks and managed to fall in love. Can you believe it?' He smiled at the memory.

'Really?' It wasn't like Harry to talk about love.

'Yeah. Really. It's a shock, isn't it? Harry Woods in love. But she was something special. Jesus, what a woman.'

'She got a name?'

'Yvette. She was our courier.' He paused, enjoying the memory until he remembered the story he was supposed to be telling. Then the smile left his face. 'So everything was going fine. I thought this is it, I've found the woman of my dreams. I'm going to take her home to New York after the war and be happy for ever.' He gave Tom a wry smile. 'Then one night the Gestapo turned up at the apartment. We were in bed together, so we couldn't claim she didn't know me.'

'Shit.'

'Yeah. You know, everything you hear about those bastards is true. They took us both to some fucking hell-hole where you can hear them shooting people in the mornings, and you can hear the screams.'

He stopped walking and fumbled in his pocket for his cigarettes, dropping them from the packet into the dust in his haste, hands trembling as he bent to scoop them up. He stood and lit the cigarette, drawing the smoke deep in his lungs, holding it there, calmed by the heat. 'I don't know what to happened her, Tom. They beat the shit out of me, but what the fuck did I know? What could I have told them anyway? I'm just a lousy Yank flier in the wrong place at the wrong time. But Yvette? Christ. What would they have done to her? She's Resistance. She knows names. She knows places.' He closed his eyes as though he could shut out the images of her torture. 'I mean, I could've told them some stuff I guess. I could've told them about you. But I didn't. I didn't say a word. And it wasn't out of bravery, or duty, or any of those things they give you medals for.' He turned to his friend, his eyes clouded with an emotion Tom could not recognise, something deep and disturbing. 'D'you want to know why I didn't say anything?'

'Sure.'

'Hatred. That's all. That's all that kept me going. Pure and simple hatred.' He took another drag on the cigarette, calmer now, and they moved on, continuing their amble, taking their place in the endless trail of men who walked round and round the rim of the compound. 'I couldn't tell you how long I was there. It seemed like eternity but it was probably only a couple of days. I woke up finally in a Luftwaffe hospital being treated by a German doctor who couldn't look me in the face, he was so ashamed of what they'd done to me. I guess I must have looked pretty ugly. I was there for a while and he fixed me up okay, I guess. Physically, anyway. So that's the story.' He turned again to Tom who shook his head, touching the remnants of the wound above his eye and thinking how lucky he had been.

'I don't know what to say.'

'I guess I'll go look for her after it's all over but I think she's probably already dead. In a way I hope she is, because if she's still there ... or in a camp somewhere ...' He trailed off and Tom tried not to think of what she must have gone through. What she might still be going through. His own suffering seemed trivial in comparison, his girl safe in England. Whatever happened in the future, whether or not she waited for him, she would never have to go through that. Anger began its slow burn in his guts, a desire to get back in a plane and take revenge.

'The hatred keeps me going,' Harry said, as though he had read Tom's thoughts. 'And all that guilt I used to feel about the bombs we dropped? Well, I don't have that any more. I want to wipe every fucking German out of existence.'

The ball from a soccer game rolled into their path and Harry booted it back to the man who was chasing it. They stood and watched the game start again before they walked on, moving now towards Harry's barracks, ducking beneath the lines of grey washing that hung between the buildings. Inside it was empty, the men outdoors in the sun. There was a strong smell of crowded imprisonment, fetid and stale, despite the open windows.

'Welcome to my humble home,' Harry said, and he sat at the rough table in the centre of the small room. Four bunks lined the walls, wooden clogs and shoes in neat rows beneath them. Various bits of home-made furniture were dotted about, covered in books and magazines and jars and boxes of numerous items collected and jealously stored. A half-finished chess game sat in the middle of the table, and two jars that had been used as cups, unwashed from breakfast time, stood on either side of the board.

'The bunk above me is empty.' The navigator gestured with his head to the bed nearest the window. 'You can take it.'

The pilot nodded. 'Later.' He stood by the table, looking round, familiarising himself with the crude furniture, the rough surroundings. One of the bunks was immaculate, the blankets folded neatly, books stacked in a tidy pile on the shelf by its head.

'Mack?' Tom asked, recognising the obsessive neatness of their radio operator.

Harry grinned. 'He keeps us all in order.'

'Someone has to.'

'He's going to be real happy to see you.'

Tom picked up a chess piece, a black knight, and examined it. 'Who d'you play with?'

'Mack mostly. Robbie tries but he gives up too quickly. Loses patience. He's good at poker though. We play for cigarettes.'

The pilot replaced the knight and studied the game. Harry observed him, shrewd eyes narrowed, waiting for him to look up. 'You okay?' he asked.

Tom lifted his eyes in surprise. 'Yeah, sure I'm okay,' he answered. 'I was miles away.' He smiled, dragging his consciousness back from the hotel room to the camp, putting Anna away in a corner of his mind to visit later. 'I'll go get my stuff.'

# Fifteen

Anna stood waiting on the path outside the Lawrences' faded yellow door, hot in the bright July sun. She knocked again, hoping that someone was home, but there was no sound from inside and reluctantly she turned away. On an impulse she stopped at the gate and looked back to the house. The door opened just a fraction and Lottie's elfin face, pinched and wet with tears, peered out.

'Oh, Anna, it's you,' Lottie said. She sounded relieved. 'Come in.'

'Are you sure?' Anna asked, retracing her steps up the path.

'Yes. Come in.'

The door closed behind them and Anna stood blinking blindly in the sudden darkness of the hall. Lottie reached for her friend's hand and took it tightly in hers, her face set with determination against the tears. Anna's eyes adjusted gradually to the dimness as Lottie led her silently upstairs.

They sat on the bed in the airless room and though the window stood open, there was no breeze to cool them, just heat and humidity. Lottie sat huddled against the wooden headboard, her arms wrapped around her knees, hugging them tightly to herself, rocking slightly on the soft bed. She kept her face averted from her friend, as though she were ashamed of her tears.

'What's happened?' Anna asked. 'Can you tell me?'

Lottie dragged her knees closer to her body and brushed her cheek against them, wiping her face on her skirt. Anna waited in the tension, needing to know, anxious.

'We had a telegram this morning,' Lottie whispered, her voice barely audible in the silent room. She bit her lip hard and lifted her eyes briefly to her friend.

'Oh God,' Anna said. The same cold dread she had felt that day, waiting alone in the hotel near the airbase, crept over her skin. 'Billy?' she asked, though she already knew.

Lottie jammed her lips tight against the desire to cry and nodded abruptly, once.

Anna hesitated and then, softly, she said, 'Was he killed?'

'Yes.' Her friend wiped her face with a savage hand.

Anna stared down at the counterpane and traced the pattern with her finger. It seemed impossible that Billy could be dead. He was too young. Just a boy. 'Are you sure?' she asked stupidly, still groping to comprehend.

'Yes,' Lottie croaked. Her voice was hoarse with weeping. 'In the Caen area. Somewhere in Normandy.'

Anna closed her eyes, saw the curly-haired boy who had only just enlisted, saw him lying broken on a battlefield somewhere, and wondered if poppies still grew in the fields of France. She wanted to cry out in protest. Tears of rage prickled sharply behind her eyes. She blinked them back and stared at her friend. 'That's all they told you?'

'Yes.'

Anna dropped her eyes again, feeling helpless. Her grief was hot and full of anger, awakening other feelings suppressed for many months. Emotions tumbled over one another in a confusion of loss and sadness and despair and as she looked up at her friend again, it was not only Billy's death that she mourned.

'Anna …' Lottie said, her face crumbling in sorrow. 'My little brother's dead.' She lifted her arms like a child to be hugged, and Anna held her until she pulled away and leant back once more against the headboard. They stared at each other for a moment as Lottie dragged the sodden strands of hair out of her face. There were no words to say. 'I can't even cry any more,' Lottie murmured.

She leaned forward, lifting her fingers to Anna's tears, and wiped them gently away.

'I'm all right,' Anna lied, and they sat together in silent grief. After a while, when the silence became oppressive, she said, 'How are your parents taking it? And Richard?'

'Richard's gone fishing for the day with a friend. He left early. He doesn't even know yet.'

'And your mum?'

Lottie looked down and twisted her wedding ring absently. 'She's devastated. You know how she dotes on him. Doted. She's been sitting in the living room with his picture all day. The one of him in uniform just after he enlisted. Just staring at it. I don't think it's sunk in yet. Dad's been out in the garden all day, digging.' She rolled the back of her head against the wall towards her friend. There was another silence, longer this time. The little face looked older suddenly, the mischievousness beaten out of it, and Anna looked away, depressed. A wood pigeon cooed softly in the heat outside.

'Shall we go downstairs and have some tea?' Lottie suggested finally. 'I haven't had anything all day.'

'Is that all right?' Anna asked. 'I don't want to intrude.'

'I need you,' Lottie replied simply, and got up.

In the living room, Anna settled into the low lumpy sofa, sinking into one of the dips that seemed to make it so comfortable. Mrs Lawrence sat silently at the table, engrossed in Billy's photograph, barely aware of her daughter's friend. Anna waited quietly for Lottie to come back from the kitchen, her eyes held too by the young face that grinned out at her proudly.

'Mum,' Lottie called out. 'Is Dad still in the garden?'

Mrs Lawrence looked up, startled by the interruption of her thoughts. She gazed round the room, confused, her eyes alighting on Anna without recognition before she snapped back into the present. 'Yes,' she replied at last. 'I think so.' She turned again to Anna. 'I'm sorry, my dear. I was quite lost in thought.'

'That's all right. I quite understand. If you'd rather I left ...'

'No, no, not at all. Goodness me, you were like a sister to him. I'm glad you're here. Especially for Lottie. It's hard for her with Evan away so much.' She lifted the photograph into view once more. 'Such a nice picture of him. He looks very handsome, don't you think?' She held the picture at arm's length, admiringly, her head on one side to appreciate it better. 'We were all so proud of him. He looked so grown up in his uniform, I could scarcely believe it was our Billy. Lottie teased him terribly about it, but he took it well.'

'He was used to it,' Anna said.

Mrs Lawrence chuckled. 'They always fought, didn't they? Like cat and dog sometimes. They used to drive me up the wall.'

Anna smiled.

'He was a good boy though,' Billy's mother said. 'Not a mean bone in his body.' The smile froze and Anna saw the tension in her jaw, the effort not to cry.

Lottie slipped out of the back door and Anna followed, unsure if she was wanted, anxious not to intrude. Lottie seemed unaware of her presence and hurried away up the path at the side of the house towards the small vegetable patch that was Mr Lawrence's pride and joy.

He was leaning on his spade, smoking a cigarette, staring far away into space. Anna followed his gaze to the high brick wall that separated the gardens, the overgrown lilac tree that she and Billy and Lottie had climbed as children, Richard too small and left behind, the red-tiled roof that stretched out along the road. The familiar view was comforting.

'Dad,' Lottie said, still standing on the path, not wanting to dirty her shoes in the freshly dug earth. He didn't hear her. 'Dad!' She called louder this time, breaking into his thoughts. He looked around, startled, taking an instant to adjust to the reality around him. Lottie smiled. 'Penny for 'em,' she said, her head on one side like a curious child.

He returned the smile and took one last deep drag on his cigarette before stamping it thoughtfully into the ground. He coughed, picked up the spade and clambered over the rich dark soil to where his daughter stood. 'What's that?'

'What were you thinking about?' she said.

'Oh, you don't really want to know, do you?' he asked, touching her cheek with a muddy hand, playful.

'Yes. I do,' she laughed, wiping the mud away.

He paused, looking down, rubbing the mud off one boot with the other. Then he said, 'I was thinking about the last war.'

He had never talked to her about his war before, although she knew he had spoken of it often to the boys. He stared down at the grass of the path, one hand resting on the spade. 'I was remembering how scared I was, how afraid we all were, and the relief of each night that we'd survived another day. I was just a bit older than your brother then.' He looked up at his daughter and his face was taut with pain. 'I hope he didn't die alone. I hope he had someone he loved with him when he died.' He coughed again and spat into the mud. 'But I suppose we'll never know, eh love.'

Lottie swallowed hard.

'War's a terrible thing, Lottie, a terrible thing. Such a waste.' He shook his head with disgust and threw the spade down hard into the earth so that it stood upright alone in the middle of the fertile earth, like a headstone. Watching from the path by the kitchen wall, Anna shuddered.

'I'm making some tea, Dad,' Lottie said. 'Anna's here.'

Mr Lawrence put his arm around her shoulders and smiled down at her. 'I'd like a cup of tea,' he said. 'Shall we go in?'

Lottie nodded and snuggled into her father, grateful for his protective arm. She would phone Evan soon, working hard in London, and he would come back and hold her how she needed to be held. She smiled up at her father and he squeezed her gently as they walked along the path. They didn't notice Anna ahead of them, slipping silently away into the house.

Anna meandered home from Lottie's the long way, walking slowly in the sultry evening. There was a faint rattle of thunder in the distance, or perhaps an air raid somewhere. Probably thunder. Clouds gathered ominously, heading east, tinged with the green of the approaching storm. A trickle of sweat seeped down her spine, and an old man in a much patched shirt that clung wetly to his back hurried past her, anxious to get home before the storm broke. Anna was indifferent to the coming rain.

It was almost a relief to cry for Billy, she thought. To grieve for his death. To know at least, and be able to mourn. She wondered how long she could bear the not-knowing, how long she could keep hoping for Tom. Be brave, he had told her. Be grateful for the time we have. She could hear his voice in her head and refused to believe he was not going to make it. He will come home, she told herself. He will. He will. We will grow old and wrinkly together. I won't let you die, she whispered. I need you. She touched her hand to her belly and the hard roundness was reassuring. We need you.

She wandered home in the gathering storm.

Anna paused finally at the door of her mother's house, enclosed in the humid dusk. She gripped the little cross tightly and it slipped in the perspiration on her fingers. Her mother came bustling out of the living room as soon as she heard the key in the lock.

'Where've you been?'

'Lottie's,' Anna said. She barely had the energy to talk.

'Until now?' Mrs Pilgrim demanded. 'What on earth were you doing?'

'Just talking.'

'Well, I've already eaten my dinner. Yours was ruined, so I've thrown it out.'

'Have you?' Anna said without interest.

'Yes, I have,' her mother replied. 'So you'll have to make yourself something else.'

'I'm not hungry.'

'You ate at Lottie's did you? I wish you'd tell me if you're going to eat out. We can't afford to waste food like that …'

Anna shook her head. Her mother's persistence was beginning to grate. 'I'm just not hungry.'

'You've got to eat, you know. You're eating for two now. You can't expect to have a healthy baby if you don't eat.'

'I'm all right,' Anna said. 'Please don't fuss.'

'I'm only thinking of what's best for you and the baby …' She turned back towards the living room. 'Come and sit down,' she commanded. 'You can tell me what the Lawrences had to say for themselves.'

Anna sighed and followed her mother into the living room, where she sat in the armchair with her feet curled under her. Behind the curtains the French doors stood open and the heavy fabric lifted and fell gently with the first breath of air all day. The breeze was cool and soothing. Thunder rumbled again, closer this time. Mrs Pilgrim settled herself on the sofa.

'There's a storm coming,' she observed. 'Should clear the air a bit. It's been stifling all afternoon. So, what did Charlotte have to say? Anything interesting?'

Anna hesitated.

'Well?'

'Billy was killed,' she said softly. 'They got the telegram this morning.'

Her mother was silent.

'Somewhere in Normandy.'

There was another silence. Mrs Pilgrim looked down at her hands and forced her wedding ring to turn on her finger.

'You don't even care, do you?' Anna accused, her anger finding a vent at last.

'Of course I care,' her mother shot back. 'It's very sad. Of course it is. But it isn't as though I knew him or anything. Last time I saw him he would have been just a boy.'

'He still is ... was ... just a boy,' Anna murmured. 'He was just nineteen.'

'So many of them are,' Mrs Pilgrim replied, with unexpected softness. 'So many of them are.'

Anna nodded, holding back the tears, and the two women sat in silence once again as the curtains rose and dropped in the growing breeze. When she had control of her voice, Anna uncurled her legs and stood up. She said, 'I think I'm going to go and lie down upstairs.'

'But I've hardly seen you all day.' Mrs Pilgrim was crestfallen.

'I'm very tired,' Anna whispered. 'I'm sorry.'

'Well good night then. I suppose I'll see you in the morning.'

'Yes. Good night, Mother,' Anna replied. Then she went up to her room and cried herself to sleep.

# Sixteen

Anna gave up work late in August when it became too arduous, and she spent the last remaining days of summer warmth wandering amongst the allotments that had been the park of her childhood, or venturing further sometimes to the grounds of the big estate to watch the harvest workers. She spent time too with the Lawrences, afternoons with Lottie's mother, sharing the intimacy of motherhood in a way her own mother could never do. They would talk all afternoon in the cool of the living room, waiting for Lottie to get home from work and join them, to touch the swollen belly and feel the movement inside. She loved these long days, basking in the joy of her pregnancy, and she talked to her friend about Tom, keeping the memory alive, refusing to believe in his death.

'I saw some Yanks today,' Mrs Pilgrim said one evening when she got home, the two of them in the kitchen, getting in each other's way as they worked to make dinner.

Anna stopped chopping the carrot in front of her and forced herself to breathe slowly. 'Did you?' she answered, keeping her voice even with effort.

'Yes. Airmen, they were, packed into a jeep, careering all over the road as though they owned the place. I can't imagine what they were doing round here, except wasting good petrol and making a nuisance of themselves.'

For a heartbeat Anna thought that it might have been Tom, that he might have come looking for her, but even as she thought it she dismissed it as wishful thinking. He knew where she lived. He knew the address. He would have come to the house, and he would have found her.

'All mouth and trousers, those boys,' her mother went on. 'You never see RAF chaps carrying on like that ...'

But Anna wasn't listening. She was thinking of Tom, remembering.

She had asked him once what it was like to fly, and he had told her that she didn't want to know. His reluctance had made her hesitate, not wanting to hurt him, but still she had asked again. She took his hand in hers, entwining their fingers, drawing him to her in the crowded street.

'Yes. Yes, I do want to know,' she had persisted. 'Flying is your world. And if I don't understand, there's so much about you I don't know. I want to know what you do while you're gone. What you go through.'

'I don't want to talk about it,' he told her softly.

'Please Tom. Please.'

He shook his head, biting his lip, silent.

'Please.'

He relented. 'Okay. But only because I love you. Let's go sit somewhere.'

In the tea room she was afraid of what he might be going to say, but the need to know was desperate, and as they sat in silence, waiting for their tea to arrive, she knew his thoughts were elsewhere, searching inside for the right words to tell her. She poured the tea when it came, and he took his cup and blew across the surface. She watched the ripples before he tipped the cup to suck in the scalding liquid.

'I was terrified on my first mission,' he said. 'We all were. Scared shitless and praying like crazy to get home alive. Legs like jelly and brave faces. We didn't know then that everyone feels like that, that you aren't normal if you don't. So we laughed and joked beforehand to hide the fear. Anything to stop ourselves going inwards and remembering our dreams.

'We lost Simpson. He was the ball turret gunner. It's like a little plexiglass dome right on the bottom of the ship. You have to sit all hunched up inside it. I barely knew him. A real quiet kind of guy. I don't know, maybe he was more talkative with his friends, but I can hardly remember two words he ever said to me, except for yes sir. Anyway, he only made the one trip. Fighters came up from underneath us not far off the French coast and somehow he got half his head sliced off. I didn't see him till we got back home and when I did, I puked my guts up.'

Remembering, he felt the sickness in his stomach again, the bitter aftertaste. He had never talked about it to anyone. Even that night, the only time the whole crew ever got drunk together, no one mentioned Simpson's name. But he had thought about him often and seen the severed head in his dreams. He lifted his eyes from the cup he held in both hands to see Anna's reaction. She didn't flinch, nerves steeled against his words, listening and intent. He looked down at the table again, fingers moving rhythmically against the thick porcelain of his cup.

'There's so much I can't tell you. So much I just can't put into words. When I'm with you, flying seems an impossible nightmare.' He stopped, not allowing himself to be angry with her for making him do this, forcing himself to remember that he would have asked her the same if the roles were reversed, that he would have made her tell him everything. But he didn't want to think about it now, didn't want to drag his thoughts away from the pleasure of being with her and dredge up memories that her company allowed him to forget for a while.

She touched his fingers with her hand and his eyes flicked up to her for just a moment.

'It doesn't really get any easier,' he said. 'You're still just as scared each time. More so probably, because you get to realise just how many things can go wrong, how much it's down to luck. But you learn to hide the fear, to push it way down inside you. And it becomes a part of you, like … like …' He searched for words to describe it. '… like an ugly scar, or a heavy weight in your guts. And it's always there, just below the surface. You carry images of falling planes in your mind always.' He paused. 'There are a lot of ways to die in a plane. I've imagined all of them and seen some of them for real. We all have.' The words were coming to him easier now, opening up this one part of himself that he had thought he would never share with anyone. 'They tell us the night before if we're flying. They put our names on a notice-board. No one sleeps too good the night before a raid. In the morning, when you're shaving, you look at yourself real good in the mirror and you think, is this the last time you're going to do this? Is this the last time you're going to see this face? Then you eat some breakfast, and go to the briefing. You see this little piece of red yarn on the map at the front of the hall that shows where you're going that day, and all you can see is how much enemy ter-ritory there is between here and the target.

'Then the colonel tells you the target is Cologne, or worse, Berlin, and you begin to smell the tension in the room. Not one man in there wants to get killed and each of us is thinking, well, hell, maybe I'll go on sick call after the briefing, but no one ever does.'

He paused, took a swig of tea, and avoided her eyes. A waitress walked by and he stopped her to order more tea, a distraction, then looked at Anna, who gave him a small apologetic smile. He half smiled in reply, but it didn't reach his eyes and she looked away. 'Do you want to know any more?' he asked. He was tired of talking.

'You haven't told me about flying. What it's like in the air.'

He smiled at her persistence and shook his head. 'I can't explain it to you, Anna. It's hard work. It's scary. It always seems a hell of a long way home.'

'Thank you,' she had whispered. 'I just needed to know how it feels.'

* * *

With the autumn the days turned cool and clear and as the nights
drew in and grew colder, Anna became impatient for the birth of
her child. She moved heavily now, with discomfort, and the sadness of Tom's absence hurt more than when she had been active.

Her waters broke early in October, and she awoke to the wetness of her thighs in the small hours of the morning. She was
confused for a moment, thinking that perhaps she had wet herself
before she remembered Mrs Lawrence saying, 'You'll think
you've had an accident.' She smiled and wiped the fluid from her
legs in the darkness.

Lying on her side in the quiet, too early yet for the milkman
or the bombers, the beating of her heart was hard and loud within
her stillness. She should get up, she thought, and ask her mother
to call the doctor, but she waited, luxuriating in these final hours
of calm. There was no hurry; there were no contractions yet, and
she switched on the lamp so that she could see the small photograph of Tom by the bed. She must put it back in her bag, she
remembered, away from her mother's prying eyes. He smiled at
her, the shy boyish grin that she'd fallen in love with the first time
she saw it, and she wondered if he would ever see his child. Be
here with me now, my darling, she whispered. Hold my hand
through this. It's easy to be brave when you're with me. She put
the picture away and rolled heavily out of bed.

Later, Mrs Pilgrim scurried along to the post office to ring the
doctor, then she bustled around the house, trotting up and down
the stairs, fussing and anxious. Anna heard her coming and going
and ignored her as best she could. She sat patiently on the bed, or
ambled round her room, waiting for the doctor to come, timing
her contractions, her eyes closed so that Tom seemed closer, and
his presence more real.

By the time the doctor arrived, the contractions were regular
and frequent and intense. He bundled Mrs Pilgrim out of the
room as soon as he got there, irritated by the old woman's inces-

sant chatter, and with no other choice, she retreated. Anna could hear her pacing round the house, muttering to herself. But as the labour progressed she forgot her mother, concentrating her thoughts on the image of Tom she held in her mind so that he seemed to be with her.

The midwife came in the afternoon and the doctor left for a while to attend to other calls. Mrs Pilgrim hurried in as soon as he was gone. She stood over the bed, hands twisting in front of her.

'How are you feeling?' she asked. 'Is everything all right?'

'Yes,' Anna answered from a distance. Her eyes were closed, and her mother's presence unreal.

Mrs Pilgrim stared down at her daughter uselessly. 'Is there anything I can do to help?' she appealed to the nurse who was sitting at the end of the bed, a hand resting on Anna's thigh in reassurance.

'Everything's going very well so far,' the midwife said. 'There's really nothing to worry about.'

'There must be something I can do,' Mrs Pilgrim pleaded. 'There must be something.'

'I'm sorry, there really isn't anything.'

Mrs Pilgrim turned back to her daughter, who lay motionless, glistening with sweat, breathing hard.

'Relax, Anna,' the midwife coaxed, sensing tension. 'Breathe deeply.'

Anna's chest rose and fell rhythmically, her eyes closed in concentration on her image of Tom.

'That's good now. You're doing just fine. You're doing really well.'

'Wouldn't you like me to stay with you, Anna?' Mrs Pilgrim begged. 'Anna?'

Anna ignored her, eyes still shut, deep within herself. Mrs Pilgrim glanced across to the midwife with frustration, but the young nurse was embarrassed and looked away. Then a glint of gold at Anna's neck caught the old woman's attention and she sidled closer to look. The midwife observed her.

'What necklace is that?' Mrs Pilgrim asked. 'I've never seen that before.' She peered at her daughter, squinting to focus better without her glasses. Anna's eyes snapped open as she felt her mother's presence close in.

'Don't touch it,' she breathed, as her mother reached out for the cross. 'Don't you ever touch it.'

A wave of pain engulfed her, but her eyes, wild with fury, never left the old woman. Her mother's hand stopped in mid-air, waiting for the contraction to pass.

'He gave it to you, didn't he?!' she hissed as her daughter sank back on the pillows, exhausted. 'It's from the bastard that did this to you, isn't it?' The hand jerked forward to grab it, to tear it from her daughter's neck, but Anna intercepted the move, her long fingers wrapped around the fleshy wrist, and they hung there for a moment, quivering with the tension of the struggle. The midwife averted her eyes.

'Get out!' Anna whispered. 'Get away from me!'

Then a paroxysm of pain overwhelmed her and she dropped her mother's arm. The midwife stared in disbelief as Mrs Pilgrim backed uncertainly away, eyes dropped to the floor, acutely aware of the nurse's gaze. She stood near the door, enraged and confused, rubbing unconsciously at the smarting wrist before she turned suddenly and left. Anna heard the door slam and opened her eyes. The midwife watched her, concerned.

'Are you all right?' she asked. 'Is everything all right?'

'My mother and I don't always see eye to eye,' Anna answered drily and the nurse smiled.

'Well at least you've still got a sense of humour about it,' she said.

Then another contraction began.

Emma Louise Blake was born late in the evening and Anna cradled her gently, exhausted and radiant. She looked down in awe at the small person she had brought into the world, fingering the tiny red face, familiarising herself with miniature hands that waved uncertainly in the lightness of the air. The midwife sat down on the edge of the bed and the two women exchanged smiles.

'She's a lovely baby,' the midwife said.

'Thank you,' Anna whispered. 'I think so too.'

The midwife laughed and began to pack up her things, preparing to leave. 'Will you be all right now?' she asked. 'Is there anything you'd like before I go?'

'I'll be fine thanks,' Anna murmured, still absorbed in her child.

'I'll tell your mother to come up, shall I?' the midwife asked from the doorway, hesitating.

Anna looked up quickly and shook her head. 'Not yet. Please. Not yet.'

The midwife came back inside the room. 'I'll put her down for you, shall I?' she said, and placed the infant in the old wooden cot next to the bed. Anna watched gratefully, still in awe, waiting while the child fell soundlessly into sleep.

'How about you get some sleep too,' the midwife said, turning to the mother. 'I'll tell your mother not to disturb you for a couple of hours, eh?'

Anna nodded and within seconds of the door closing gently behind the departing nurse, she was asleep.

# Seventeen

As the summer months cooled into autumn there was still no word from Anna. Tom exercised, pushing himself harder than he should on the small rations that they ate each day, but it quieted the nervous energy of his frustration and helped him sleep at night amongst the fleas and lice that were endemic.

'Run, you asshole!'

Tom was lying on his bunk in the afternoon, listening to the sounds of the football game outside, the dull thud of leather being kicked and the shouts of men.

'Over here! Over here! Pass … Pass …'

He lay on his back, head cradled in his hands, picking out voices familiar from the months of proximity, then let the noise drift to the background of his mind. October sun streamed in through the open window, lighting a long rectangle of pale yellow on the bed against the far wall and he watched the dust motes floating in the shaft of light, playing on the air currents in the room. A cheer rose in the compound from half the crowd as somebody scored and Tom turned his head away from the voices, fingering the unopened letter in his hand with frustration. It was not from Anna.

He held an image of her in his mind, her long strong body in his arms, the smooth touch of her skin against his. Almond eyes, lips parted in anticipation, waiting. He breathed deeply, the memory still vivid, still stirring the desire inside him, and he closed his eyes to remember it better.

'Run! Run, goddammit!'

He pushed the shouts of the game out of his consciousness and gave himself up to the memory.

It was still early when they climbed the narrow stairs to the hotel room but the hallway was dark and Tom fumbled with the key for a moment before it slipped into the lock and the door swung open. He went in before her in the darkness, hurrying to light the fire as Anna followed him hesitantly into the dim blue glow, the flames turning orange gradually, shedding their light and heat into the blackness. He drew the curtains against the cold, insulating them from the world outside where a single searchlight probed the sky. They took off their coats, laid them side by side across the chair and stood as before, close to each other in front of the heater, hands outstretched to its warmth.

'It's nicer without the light on, don't you think?' he asked, and she nodded.

'More romantic,' she said. Turning to him in the half-light she smiled, then dropped her eyes once again to the heater.

The room warmed. They no longer reached out to the fire with their hands and Tom turned towards her slowly, but she gazed on into the flames. He watched her, sensed her quick nervous breathing, the anxious restlessness of her eyes that were avoiding him. She was afraid. He knew that she was afraid and he didn't understand then what it was that frightened her so much. They stood close, faces almost touching. 'Look at me, Anna,' he whispered. He wanted to know, wanted to understand.

She turned to him briefly, met his eyes for an instant and looked away. She was shy of him again. He lifted a hand to her face, touched her cheek with his fingers and gently turned her head towards him, her face tilted to meet his. He could feel the warmth of her breath against his skin and the heat rising inside him. Her eyes held his now, afraid and trusting, as though she had given herself up to him, and even as he wanted her he hoped he could honour her trust, hoped he deserved such submission. His fingers brushed the softness of her cheek, his lips close to hers, and in the moment of his hesitation, she turned away, biting her lip. He watched her struggle with her fear and though he knew she would give herself to him in spite of it, its presence saddened him and muted his desire. 'What's wrong?'

She shrugged and shook her head, close to tears, unable to explain. He stood there feeling useless, not knowing what he could do or say to make it better. 'Please don't be afraid,' he whispered. 'I won't hurt you. I would never hurt you.' He would rather die than hurt her.

'I know,' she said with a brave smile. 'I know.'

'Then why?'

She shook her head again.

'We can wait. If you want to wait till we're married, we can wait …' He thought of what she had told him of her mother, wondered if it meant more to her than she thought, but she shook her head.

'No, it isn't that.'

'Then what?' he asked softly, bewildered. 'Anna, I don't understand.'

She turned towards him again so that their faces were close but her gaze was lowered and they did not touch. 'My mother,' she began in a whisper, hard to hear above the fire's hiss. 'My mother told me things …'

'About sex?'

She nodded, lips pressed tightly together with embarrassment. 'Awful things …'

'What things?' He was gentle and touched a hand to her hair, smoothing it away from her forehead.

'Pain,' she whispered, 'and blood and violence.'

He hesitated, uncertain, hating her mother. 'Do you trust me?' he asked at last, though he knew already what her answer would be.

She nodded.

'Are you sure?'

'Yes, I'm sure.'

He smiled, proud and touched by the devotion of her love for him as she lifted her face to his, lips parted, waiting. He swallowed, felt the heat burning inside him as he brushed her mouth with his lips. She shivered, her eyes closed, and he kissed her again, let his lips linger against hers, soft and warm. She stepped closer into him, put her arms around him and drew him nearer to her. She was kissing him now, passionate and full of desire, and he held her tightly with one arm around her, the other cradling her head, caressing her face, then slowly trailing down across her neck and her throat, brushing against her breast. She shuddered.

They broke away from each other, breathing hard with their desire and he searched her face but her eyes were bright with excitement and there was no trace of the fear from before. 'Are you okay?' he asked, and unbuttoned his tunic, tossed it onto the chair behind him with the coats.

She smiled and nodded then they kissed again and he could feel the softness of her breasts against his chest through his shirt as his lips moved down to her neck and she rolled back her head exposing the whiteness of her throat to his kiss. He found her breast again with his hand, his touch firmer now that he knew she wanted him too, caressing her in his palm and she lifted her head to search out his mouth with hers, kissing him hard, surprising him with the intensity of her passion. He slid his hand under her sweater, felt the soft silk of her slip, the rough lace of her brassiere, fingers searching inside for the smoothness of her skin.

And all the time he remembered that he must be gentle, that he must not reawaken her fear. He wanted to slow down, gain control of the desire that raced inside him, lead her gradually towards their lovemaking but it was hard to move back from her embrace and when he did she was watching him, wanting him as he wanted her.

He touched her face and smiled, lifted her sweater over her head, let it drop to the floor beside them as her hands guided him to the buttons of her skirt. Then she was standing before him in the silk slip which clung to the outline of her body as he stepped out of his pants, pulled the shirt and his undershirt over his head. She reached forward, let her fingers touch his shoulders, ran them down across his chest, curled them in the fine hair that led down in a line across his stomach, but her hand stopped at the waist band of his underpants and suddenly she was shy again, but coy this time, not afraid. She smiled at him as he took her face in his hands and kissed her and as she held him against her tightly with her arms he could feel the softness of her belly against his hardness.

He let go of her face, lifted the silk slip, felt the pleasure of her skin against his fingers and she shivered as he freed her breasts from the brassiere and dragged the flimsy slip from her body. His desire was bright and hard now, aroused by her passion, the soft strong body against his, skin on skin, and he knelt, pulled her down with him until they were lying on the faded rug, the heat from the fire burning hot on their skin. 'Are you okay?' he asked again.

Her body was warm and smooth beneath him and she gazed up with eyes that were timid and anxious to please as she asked him what she should do. He told her to lie still and relax so she closed her eyes as his tongue caressed the soft skin of her breast and his hand brushed down across the flatness of her belly, touching her through the cotton of her pants. She shivered with the unfamiliar pleasure as he undressed her completely and slid down her body with his lips and his tongue and his teeth, always watching her, the long strong body in the orange half-light of the fire. Then he lifted himself back over her, kissed lips that were flushed and full with her passion. She gasped with the pain as he entered her but then he was moving inside her and all that she wanted was him deeper and deeper, deeper than their bodies allowed, her hands against his hips pulling him into her and he moved slowly, gentle, careful not to hurt her. The moment lasted forever as she arched her back and he was lost in her, then they lay curled in each other, breathless and exhausted, silent, the only sound the hiss of the fire.

After a while he reached up and pulled the covers from the bed to keep them warm and rolled over and lay on his back, Anna's head against his chest, his fingers stroking her arm. He stared up at the ceiling, barely visible in the glow from the fire.

'What's wrong?' she asked, and Tom realised his thoughts had not been with her and was sorry. He didn't know how long they had been lying there.

'Nothing,' he lied. 'Nothing's wrong.'

She twisted her head awkwardly to look up at him and he smiled at her slightly. 'Tom, please tell me. Something's wrong. I know it is. You're distant. Please tell me.'

He shook his head. 'Nothing's wrong, Anna.'

'Was it something I did?' she persisted. 'Wasn't our love-making good?'

He shifted himself from under her and turned to face her, propping his head on his hand, leaning on one elbow. 'It was nothing you did,' he said, and touched her cheek with his fingers. 'And our lovemaking was ... beautiful.' There was no other word he could think of to describe it, no way to express how she had made him feel. Like he was walking on air, he thought, where nothing could ever hurt him again.

'Then what is it?'

He looked down at the rug between them, traced the pattern of the flowers with his eyes. 'I was thinking about flying,' he told her finally. 'That's all.'

'Can you tell me?'

He smiled at her persistence, but he couldn't tell her, couldn't yet trust her with his fear as she had trusted him with hers. 'I don't want to. I don't want to talk about it.'

'Please tell me. I don't want for there to be any secrets between us. Not any more. We're almost one person now aren't we? We mustn't have secrets from each other.'

He drew in a deep breath, reluctant, not wanting to pollute the magic of their closeness with his nightmares.

'Please?'

'You're very persistent.' He smiled and tapped her on the nose with his finger and she laughed.

'I can be.'

'Okay,' he said. 'I'll tell you, but it's kind of hard to explain ...' He dropped his eyes once again to the rug, reluctant, knowing it was cruel to tell her. But she was waiting, watching him expectantly with those hazel almond eyes, and it was impossible for him to hide it from her. Like she said, no secrets. She touched his lips with her fingers so that he looked up with a half-smile. 'I don't want to die,' he said. 'I don't want to fly any more and risk losing you. I was scared before I had you, but now I have so much more to lose I'm terrified. I don't want to die.' He watched her reaction, saw the tears gather, the line of her jaw harden in the determination not to cry.

'You're not going to die,' she said. 'You can't die. You'll finish your missions and get ground duty and we'll be married and have a family and grow old and wrinkly together. You aren't going to die. You can't.'

'D'you really believe that?' he asked, and thought how his voice sounded too harsh.

She swallowed, blinking back the tears, and he regretted his words immediately, knowing how he had hurt her. He wished he had stayed silent, not told her his thoughts at all.

'I have to believe it,' she said, and her voice was strained. 'I can't let myself believe that you're going to die. I can't.'

'I'm sorry I told you,' he whispered. 'You shouldn't have asked me to tell you.' He touched her face with his fingers, wiping a fallen tear from her cheekbone with his thumb. 'Don't cry, sweetheart. Please don't cry. Be brave for me. We have now. We have this time together now. Let's just be grateful for what we have.'

'You're not going to die,' she insisted.

'I hope you're right,' he replied, then she leant over to kiss him.

'Make love to me,' she had whispered, and they had made love again, desperate, hungry for each other.

When he opened his eyes the light in the hut had changed. The bed opposite was no longer lit, and the sun had left the room. He must have slept. He lifted his hands to his face to rub away the sleep and they brushed against the unopened letter lying forgotten on the bed beside him. He picked it up, surprised by its presence. Distractedly, needing something now to occupy his mind, he coaxed it open with a finger. The writing was defaced, whole lines deleted by the censor's pen, but he read what he could and the news from his parents absorbed him and lifted him from his sadness.

The door to the room creaked open and slammed shut with a bang. He heard the scuff of boots on the floorboards and identified them as Harry's.

'Not watching the game?' Harry asked. He walked across to the open window, leant against the frame looking out on to the yard and lit a cigarette, inhaling the precious smoke deeply. The scar and the leanness suited him, Tom thought, accentuating the high cheekbones and dark features. The pilot sat up and swung his legs over the edge of the bunk to face his friend. 'No,' he replied. 'I didn't feel like it.'

Harry drew back hard on the cigarette and turned slightly towards his friend. 'Yeah, I know. This place gets to you some days.'

Tom nodded, looking down, examining the boots that swung loosely in the air, the letter still in his hand.

'From your folks?'

'Yeah. My little sister's qualified as a nurse. She's on her way to Europe next month.'

'You must be proud of her.'

'She'll make a good nurse. She's got a sweet nature. Takes after Mom.'

There was a pause. The pilot stared down and Harry observed him. Tom sensed the scrutiny, lifted his eyes to Harry then looked away.

'Anna still hasn't written?'

Tom looked up and out of the window, watching the cigarette smoke curl into the afternoon sun. He licked his lips once, considering, then shook his head. 'No,' he said finally, examining his boots. 'She still hasn't written.'

'There's got to be a reason,' Harry said. 'I'm sure of it. I saw you two together and she adored you. You're a lucky man, Tom. She'll be there when you get back, waiting. I'd bet money on it.'

Tom looked down again, gripping the edge of the bed with his hands, knuckles white with the pressure. He raised his head slowly, and the sounds of the game floated in on the silence. He listened to the raised voices for a moment before he spoke. 'Maybe.'

He wanted to believe it. With all his being he wanted to believe it, but she hadn't written yet, and the memory of their last conversation was still clear in his mind. Maybe she had found someone now she didn't have to keep secret, someone her mother would approve of. Maybe she had forgotten all about him. He wished he had Harry's confidence, and wondered why he wouldn't let himself believe in her. He said, 'I hope you're right.'

Harry nodded, then reached in his pocket for another cigarette and counted them carefully, weighing up whether he should save them for later, calculating how long he had to make them last until the next Red Cross parcel. Too long, he decided, and put the packet back in his pocket. Tom watched him, waiting for him to look up again. Then he sprang lightly down from the bunk and stood with his friend at the window, looking out. They could just see the edge of the pitch and the group of men clustered on the sideline. He turned to his friend. 'Come on,' he said. 'Let's go watch the game.'

# Eighteen

Anna waited until the door slammed shut and she heard the hard leather of her mother's shoes tapping briskly down the steps on her way to work. She moved to the window and watched the bulky form hurrying away until it disappeared out of sight. Then she turned to her daughter and smiled. 'You're such a beautiful girl,' she whispered over and over. 'Your Daddy would be so proud of you.'

She lifted Emma from the cot and carried her downstairs in the quiet of the empty house. With her mother gone, the tension of their hostility ebbed a little but she was still uncomfortable in the kitchen where her mother's presence was so strong. She made herself tea and toast hurriedly, taking them back upstairs to eat in the sanctuary of her room.

Mrs Pilgrim had barely spoken to her daughter in the days since Emma's birth, as though her exclusion from Anna's labour had worked irrevocable damage on their relationship, cutting deeper than previous quarrels. Anna devoted all her attention to her child, the only way she had to give her love to Tom, and she guarded Emma with jealousy, reluctant to allow her mother near. Mrs Pilgrim kept a wary sullen distance and the air in the house hung heavy with animosity.

This morning Anna ate quickly, without appetite. When she had finished, she went downstairs and laid Emma in the old pram that she herself had ridden in as a child. She struggled with it on the steps, unused to its unwieldiness, squinting in the brightness of the autumn sun after so long confined to the dim light of the house.

She walked slowly, accustoming herself to the idiosyncrasies of the pram, her attention divided between her sleeping child and the beauty of the cool blue sky. Neighbours smiled at the new-born baby, stopping to talk to the mother in the way that people do and Anna answered shyly, but with pride. No one asked about the father, the war close enough to them all that they were sensitive. She smiled and chatted, enjoying the contact, and wound her way through familiar streets to the vicarage.

At the gate of the large rambling building she paused for a moment, letting her eyes wander over the austere Victorian house half-hidden by ivy and the overgrown garden. Her heartbeat was rapid with nerves as she heaved the pram through the wrought iron gates, strode up the path and pulled the old fashioned doorbell, which rang out inside deep and sombre.

It seemed a long time before the click of footsteps approached the door across the tiles of the hallway inside and she waited, hands tightly gripping the handle of the pram, worn and smooth against her palms. She prayed hurriedly, asking for help until the door opened and the vicar stood there, outlined against the dim hallway, looking flustered. He paused when he saw Anna but he regained his composure almost instantly and lapsed into his easy, comforting manner.

'Anna,' he said, 'please come in.' He sounded pleased to see her although his face had briefly betrayed him.

'The pram?' Anna asked.

'Best leave it here, don't you think? Just bring in the little one.'

Anna followed him into the spacious hall. It was an old house that had once been fine but it had been neglected and had now an air of tired shabbiness. She liked it. It was comfortable and unthreatening.

He showed her into the large room where he met all his parishioners. Bookcases lined the walls and a grand piano stood dustily in the bay window. She sat on the small sofa where she had sat many times before and waited patiently while he made tea for them. She was comfortable in the large room with its worn out carpet and threadbare furnishings and she held Emma close, the baby content and sleepy on her mother's lap.

The vicar returned with a tray of mismatched cups and a chipped teapot. Anna smiled and thanked him as he poured, the teapot dripping into the tray beneath it. Finally, he sat down almost opposite her and regarded her thoughtfully. He took a sip of his tea and said, 'Well, what can I do for you?'

Anna swallowed, still unsure how to phrase the question she had been turning over in her mind since Emma's birth. She could hear her own heartbeat in the quiet room and it was deafening. She hesitated, wet her lips with her tongue. The vicar nodded in encouragement. Finally she blurted, 'Would you be able to chris- ten her?' She stopped, trying to gauge his reaction, but there was no change in his expression and she pressed on, speaking quickly now in her nervousness. 'I realise that she's illegitimate and that it might be difficult for you and if you feel that you can't, well, then I understand. But it would make me ever so happy if you could.' She gave him a small smile.

He said nothing, betraying no feeling, and sipped his tea. Anna waited, the silence heavy, watching him, biting her lip. He finished his tea and placed the cup and saucer back on the table. Then he answered. 'I'd be happy to do it for you.' He smiled. 'I'm not the sort of man who believes our Lord withholds his blessing from little children, whatever the circumstances of their birth.'

'Thank you,' she whispered and took a small mouthful of tea. The hot sweetness moistened the dryness of her mouth. 'Thank you.'

'And what name will it be?'

She took another sip of tea. 'Emma Louise Blake. Blake is her father's name. He's missing in action.'

She lifted her eyes to his and their clarity surprised her.

'I can see no problem with that. No problem at all.'

'Thank you,' Anna said again. 'I'm very grateful.'

The vicar waved his hand. 'Not at all. Not at all.' He stood up and strode across to the piano where his diary lay open. He perused it for a while, pursing his lips, apparently deep in thought. 'I've got time tomorrow at three o'clock,' he offered, 'if that would be convenient for you. I'm sure you'd like it to be as soon as possible.' He looked up. 'I'm assuming that you'd like a quiet service but if you'd like more time to invite people then we can arrange it for another day.'

'Three o'clock tomorrow would be fine,' she replied. 'A quiet service is fine.'

She stood up and Emma yawned, disturbed by the movement, getting hungry. The vicar smiled and touched a gnarled finger to the tiny hand. Small fingers curled in response. In the hall the vicar watched as the mother settled her child into the pram. When she had finished, she turned to him and smiled. 'Thank you.'

He returned the smile and as she was leaving, he said, 'I assume your mother won't be present?'

'No,' she assured him. 'Just a friend, as a godparent.'

'I thought as much,' he murmured, looking down into the pram at the sleeping baby. 'It's a pity.' Then, perhaps deciding that he had been indiscreet, he lifted his eyes to Anna's face and said, 'Of course, I quite understand. In the circumstances it's only to be expected,' and backed into the shadow of the hallway.

'Yes,' Anna answered. Nothing else seemed appropriate.

'Tomorrow then,' the vicar concluded, 'at three o'clock,' and closed the door.

Morris came at his usual time on Sunday and sat in his customary armchair by the unlit fire in silent awe at the new mother and child. Anna knelt by the wicker crib on the floor, smiling and chatting to Emma, who gazed back with intense thoughtful eyes that were already turning to pale brown, the same as Tom's.

Morris stared at her, hands held loosely in his lap, overwhelmed, and Anna played with her child, his presence barely noticed.

Slowly, almost without realising, Morris edged off his chair and knelt in front of it on the rough carpet. Anna caught the movement and looked up with a smile. Encouraged, he shifted forward clumsily on his knees and Emma turned to examine the unfamiliar face, pensive and unsure. Morris smiled, uncomfortable beneath her scrutiny. She looked back at her mother and began to cry.

'She doesn't approve of me,' he said.

Anna laughed and lifted the howling child onto her shoulder, caressing her softly, cooing and shushing until Emma quieted, reassured.

'You're a wonderful mother,' Morris said. 'And she's a lovely baby.'

'Even though she doesn't approve of you?'

'Even though she doesn't approve of me.'

The door swung open and Mrs Pilgrim bustled in with the tea tray, plonking it down on the sideboard. They looked up and Morris scrambled back to his chair, embarrassed to be found on the floor.

'I hope Anna's looking after you,' Mrs Pilgrim said to Morris. 'She's a bit inclined to forget things these days. You'd think no one had ever had a baby before the way she carries on.' She turned to her daughter. 'For goodness' sake, put the child down.'

'Morris frightened her,' Anna said.

Morris looked up sharply from his hands.

'I didn't mean to …' he began, but Anna laughed and he realised she was teasing. He reddened.

'She's making a rod for her own back,' Mrs Pilgrim told him, as though Anna were no longer in the room. 'Spoils her rotten already.'

Anna said nothing and laid the now peaceful Emma back in the crib. Mrs Pilgrim handed Morris his tea and sat down with her own. Anna's she left on the tray.

'So,' Morris said, to break the silence. 'Is there going to be a christening?'

Mrs Pilgrim turned enquiring eyes to her daughter. 'Well?'

Anna hesitated before she looked up from the crib. They were both waiting for her answer, Morris with an expression of curious interest, her mother hostile and impatient. She dropped her gaze back to Emma, and the heat of her nerves spread across her body, prickly and uncomfortable.

'Actually, she's already been christened,' she murmured.

Mrs Pilgrim slammed down her cup and tea splashed onto her lap. She flicked at the wet patch with irritation. 'What do you mean, she's already been christened?' she demanded. 'When did this happen?'

'Friday.'

Her mother was speechless. She looked across to Morris for support but he averted his eyes, staring morosely into his cup. She struggled for words that would not come.

'I didn't think you'd want to come, what with her being illegitimate and everything. I didn't think you'd approve.'

Mrs Pilgrim's lips clamped shut against the torrent of venom that was collecting behind them, and she threw a glance of resentment at Morris, whose presence was all that held the words back. There was a silence. Morris lifted hopeful eyes to Anna but her attention was with the baby. He drank more tea, miserable and desperate, looking from one to the other. When he could bear the silence no longer, he said, 'Emma's a lovely name. Is there any particular reason you chose it? Is she named after anyone?'

Anna nodded slowly and half smiled. He could not have chosen a worse question.

'Well?' Mrs Pilgrim said, turning. 'We're waiting.'

Anna looked up at her mother, at the eyes narrowed deep in the folds of flesh. She felt reckless suddenly, and wanted to laugh.

'She's named,' she said, holding her mother's gaze, insolent, 'after her paternal grandmother. Emma Louise.'

Morris drew back in his chair, his eyes closed. Mrs Pilgrim stared in disbelief.

'How could you? How could you do that to me? After all I've done for you,' she breathed. 'And that woman has done nothing. Nothing. Probably doesn't even know you exist. Did you name her that just to spite me?'

'No,' Anna replied. The recklessness had gone and now she felt nothing, as though she were watching herself from a distance.

'Then why?' her mother said. 'I demand to know why.'

Anna shrugged. 'If you don't understand then I can't explain.'

Mrs Pilgrim opened her mouth to speak. Then she remembered about Morris and sat squirming in silent rage, fighting to control her fury. Emma began to cry, disturbed by the anger, and Anna lifted her once again from the crib, comforting and tender.

'Anna,' Morris murmured. She looked across to him, eyebrows raised in question. 'How about you and I take Emma for a walk? It's such a beautiful day.'

Anna nodded.

They left the old woman sitting rigid on the sofa and ambled behind the pram through the last of the fallen leaves on the broken pavement. They spoke little and Morris turned often to look at Anna's face, hoping for some encouragement to speak. But she gazed ahead, dropping her eyes only to smile at her child, apparently unaware of his presence. He grew nervous and fidgety, awkward in the silence. When they came to a bench that looked out over the allotments, they sat down and watched the gardeners working, digging the heavy soil.

'Your mother seems to be a bit touchy about Emma,' Morris said.

'Yes.'

'Must be hard for you.'

Anna said nothing, rocking the pram gently back and forth on the path, irritated by his manner. She did not want his sympathy.

'So, is she really named after his mother? Or did you just say that to wind your mother up?'

She stopped rocking the pram and turned to face him for the first time. He shrank from the coldness of her stare. 'Emma's named after the mother of the man I love,' she said. 'Does that answer your question?'

'Y ... y ...yes, of course,' he stammered. 'I'm sorry, I didn't mean anything by it ... I just thought that perhaps ...' He trailed off as Anna observed him with interest, waiting for him to explain. He dropped his head under her gaze, like a scolded child. She sighed. 'I'm sorry, Morris,' she said. 'I didn't mean to snap.'

He smiled quickly, grateful. 'That's all right. I understand. You're under a lot of strain.'

Anna nodded and turned back to the pram.

'Rita's coming along very nicely in your place at the office,' Morris told her. 'I think the responsibility has been good for her. She's certainly working much harder now.'

'I'm glad,' Anna replied. 'It must be a relief for you.'

'Yes, it is.'

They spent time chatting about the factory and Anna feigned an interest in a world that had passed out of her life and seemed remote and alien. Gradually they felt the chill of the late afternoon and wended their way back to the house. Morris helped her up the steps with the pram and they paused at the door. 'I won't come in,' he said. 'I think it would be better if I didn't.'

Anna nodded. Morris stood by the pram, close to her, their fingers almost touching on the handle. She stared down at the red brick of the steps and he waited, but she refused to lift her face. 'Goodbye Morris,' she said.

'I'll come over next week, shall I? Same as usual?'

'If you like,' she murmured, and turned away.

He backed down a couple of steps, watching her struggle to manoeuvre the pram through the door, and waited for her to turn to him again and wave goodbye. But once inside she drew the door quickly shut and he left, head hung in disappointment.

Mrs Pilgrim sat opposite the fire in the living room, waiting for her daughter to come down. Her knitting lay untouched on the sofa next to her and she stared down at the ring she was twisting hard round her finger. Lately it had got too small and it dug painfully into the flesh. She wondered why she still bothered to wear it. After all, it was almost twenty years since Jim had gone. Twenty years since she had been married in anything more than name. She'd tried to tell Anna what men were like, warned her time and time again, but she knew as well as any how persuasive a man could be, and how untrue.

More letters had come from Germany, but from a different man, a Lieutenant Blake. She had opened the first to make sure of who he was, and then destroyed them one by one as the others arrived, sure he would soon tire of writing when there was no reply, soon move his affections to easier prey. A man's love didn't last. Not like a woman's. A man only wanted one thing. And airmen were the worst, she'd heard, especially the Yanks. There were tales about them going round that had made her hair stand on end. Well, Anna was out of his clutches now, out of harm's way. She'd get over him in time. She was young and resilient.

And now Morris seemed to be showing an interest, which was surprising. She hadn't thought he had it in him. But he might yet be the saving of them all. A good marriage that would be, if he didn't mind bringing up someone else's baby. He was dependable, Morris, not like most of them. A good boy, still looking after his mother. He'd make a good husband too, if she could persuade Anna to take him, if she could make her see that a good marriage isn't based on love, but on friendship and support.

Absorbed in her thoughts Mrs Pilgrim was unaware that her daughter had entered the room, and she jumped, startled, when she caught Anna's movement from the corner of her eye. 'You frightened me!' she exclaimed, irritated to be taken so unprepared.

'I didn't mean to,' Anna said, curling herself in her chair. Her mother had given up trying to get her to sit properly years ago. 'Emma's asleep.'

'You'll never get her down tonight if you let her sleep now.'

'She'll be all right.'

There was a silence and Mrs Pilgrim's thoughts trailed back to the argument of earlier.

'Morris said he'd come over again next Sunday,' Anna said.

'That'll be nice,' her mother answered, but she was remembering the anger at her exclusion from the christening, digging to resurrect it. 'I'm at a loss to understand you,' she said, after a pause. 'I really am.'

Anna said nothing, regarding her mother with wary eyes, trying to gauge her mood.

'Did you do it deliberately to hurt me?'

'Of course not.'

'Then why?' Mrs Pilgrim turned to her daughter, eyes narrowed in bewilderment. 'Why?'

Anna swallowed, unsure how to explain. Then she said, 'You didn't want me to have Emma. You wanted me to give her away. You said you didn't even want her in the house. Or me. So I didn't think you'd care about her christening. I didn't think you'd be interested.'

'She's my granddaughter, for God's sake! Of course I'm interested.'

'Then I'm sorry,' Anna said, because there was nothing else to say, no other answer to her mother's contrariness.

'Whatever must the vicar have thought?' the old woman went on. 'I suppose the Lawrences were there?'

'Only Lottie.'

Mrs Pilgrim grunted in resentment. Then, 'And she was christened Emma Louise Pilgrim?'

Anna sighed. She could feel the tears rising behind her eyes as the recklessness of earlier melted away, leaving her weary and emotional. She blinked hard, disgusted with herself.

'No.'

Mrs Pilgrim reddened and the fat hands clenched and unclenched with anger, the knuckles alternating between red pudginess and a tense bone white. 'You little bitch! Isn't it bad enough that she's illegitimate, without you trumpeting it loud and clear? What's her father ever going to do for her? Eh? Why should she have his name?'

Anna shook her head, made breathless by her mother's assault.

'What's wrong with the name Pilgrim? Tell me that. Did you give her that bastard's name just to spite me? Just to be nasty? Why?' She sniffed and searched her pockets for a handkerchief. 'Ever since you went off with that man, you've just been horrible to me. Everything I say or do is wrong. And I know you're only here because you've got nowhere else to go. How do you think that makes me feel?' She lifted the handkerchief to her face and dabbed at her tears with surprising daintiness.

Anna hesitated, wondering if the tears were genuine. 'I'm sorry,' she said finally. 'I didn't do it to hurt you. I wanted Emma to have her father's name. He may still come back. She should have his name.'

'And his mother's name as well?'

'I think Emma's a beautiful name.'

'And what's wrong with Margaret?'

'Nothing. I just wanted to call her Emma.'

Her mother wiped at her tears with irritation, annoyed at their presence. 'So,' she said, gaining control of herself once again, settling her emotions back into hard resentment. 'What is Emma's surname then?'

Anna dropped her eyes, reluctant to say, reluctant to give anything of Tom to her mother, holding him inside herself, the thought of him sacred and precious. His name on her mother's lips would be profane. She said nothing.

'Oh for God's sake! You'll have to tell me her name sooner or later. You're being ridiculous.'

'Perhaps.'

Mrs Pilgrim clenched her teeth and the heavy jaw hardened with tension. She glared at her daughter with impotent frustration. 'I'll find out in the end.'

'I know,' Anna murmured, aware she was being unreasonable. 'I know.'

There was a silence and upstairs Emma began to cry.

'Let her cry,' the old woman said, as her daughter rose from the chair. 'You spoil her. She'll be impossible when she's older if you give in to her all the time. She's getting more demanding already.'

'I'm her mother,' Anna answered from the doorway. 'And I'll decide.'

'I'm only trying to help,' her mother began, but Anna had already left.

# Nineteen

Morris arrived at the house at half past three for Sunday tea clutching a ragged bunch of flowers. Anna opened the door to him, and he held them out with an uncertain smile. 'I got these for you,' he said. 'I thought you might like them.'

Anna took the flimsy stalks in her hand. 'Thank you,' she replied. 'They're … lovely.'

She wondered where he had found them now that every garden was used for food, and led him into the living room. 'I'll go and put them in a vase,' she said, and hurried away from him out to the kitchen, aware for the first time of the reason for his visits, her heart dropping and heavy with the realisation. There was a dull insensitive obstinacy about him that she knew from her days at the factory. He would not be easy to put off.

'Flowers?' Her mother was impressed. 'How lovely. How thoughtful of him.'

Anna arranged them without care in a glass vase that had once been her grandmother's. It was too big for so few flowers and she tried without success to get them to remain as a bunch.

'I'll do it,' her mother said.

Anna waited while her mother made the best of it, then she carried them into the living room. Morris smiled up at her as she placed them on the sideboard. She half smiled in return and went across the room to the second armchair where she always sat when Morris was present. Emma lay sleeping in the crib and Anna bent briefly to check her before she sat down. There was a silence, and she wished her mother would hurry with the tea. She could feel the heat of Morris's gaze, and dreaded what he might be going to say.

'Anna,' Morris said at last, with forced cheeriness.

She could hear her mother still clattering in the kitchen. She would be while yet.

'Anna,' he said again.

'Yes?'

'I was wondering,' he began in a voice so low with his nervousness she could barely hear him across the room. 'I was wondering if you might like to go to the pictures with me next week.'

'I'm not sure if I can,' she stalled. 'I mean, it's difficult with Emma, feeding and everything. I'm sure you understand.'

'Your mother will be quite happy to look after her for an evening. She'll be quite safe.'

'Mm,' Anna said, and understood that it had already been arranged. He must have come round on Saturday, when she was with Lottie. It amused her to think of the two of them plotting together, and she suppressed a smile. 'I'm really not sure that I can,' she said.

'Oh come on,' Morris coaxed, warming now, realising it was hard for her to say no. 'A night out will do you the world of good. When was the last time you went to the movies?'

The Americanism sounded unnatural, and she realised how hard he was trying. 'It *was* a long time ago,' she admitted.

'Where's the harm?' he insisted. 'Emma will be fine with your mother. It's only for a couple of hours ...'

'Yes, I suppose so.'

'So, it's settled then? You'll come?'

Anna sighed and could think of no way to refuse politely. 'All right. But only if there's no problem leaving Emma. I won't leave her if she's unwell or fretful or anything.'

'Of course, of course,' he agreed.

Mrs Pilgrim's footsteps approached through the dining room, and Morris stood, hands held loosely behind his back, smiling and nodding to himself. Anna watched him with a growing sense of unease. He waited for Mrs Pilgrim to put down the tea tray and turn to him before he spoke. 'I've got some news for you,' he said, as if he were about to announce an engagement or the birth of a child.

Anna cringed, the implications sinking in with the realisation that her reluctant assent had added timber to his smouldering attachment. She cursed herself for agreeing to go.

'Anna has kindly agreed to go to the pictures with me next week.'

Mrs Pilgrim beamed, showing traces of the woman she had been before life's disappointments had turned her bitter. 'That's lovely. It'll do you the world of good Anna, to get out somewhere different.'

'We're just going to the pictures,' Anna reminded them. 'That's all.'

She thought of Tom, wondering what he would make of it, and saw him laughing at her predicament. The thought calmed her and she smiled, reassured. It would be a perfectly dreadful evening, she was sure, and then Morris would realise he was wasting his time.

The afternoon passed slowly. Mrs Pilgrim and Morris chattered on, Anna's future apparently sealed between them, and her quiet resignation went unnoticed. She observed them with detachment, through a haze, as if they were distant and unconnected with her own life. They were talking about the war, she heard vaguely, about the winding down of the war machine, and she let the words fade into the background of her mind, a low indistinct hum of conversation. She tried to picture Tom again, to see him how he was that first day in the tea room, shy and intense, but it had become harder and harder to call his presence to her side, the connection fading slowly with time. She rubbed at the cross as if it were a magic lamp, but the magic seemed to be losing its power.

Logically, she knew it was unlikely he was still alive. He would have written by now if he were, got a message to her somehow. He had promised that he would. He had promised she would know. But there was still a part of her that refused to give up, a part of her that was still connected, sure of his physical existence somewhere in the world. He could be wounded, still in hiding somewhere, and she knew that until she was told for sure that he was dead, she would keep praying for him, as if her belief in his life could bring him back.

'Morris is leaving.' Mrs Pilgrim's voice sliced through her thoughts, and she looked up, startled, taking a moment to focus, to remember where she was. 'I'll come out,' she smiled, recovering herself, lifting herself elegantly from the chair.

'We have to make arrangements,' Morris reminded her, 'for the pictures.'

'Yes,' Anna remembered, 'the pictures.'

'Shall we have dinner first?' he asked. 'I'll be coming straight from work, so I shan't have eaten anything.'

'If you like.'

'Does Wednesday suit you?'

She nodded.

'How about half past six,' Morris suggested. 'In town.'

'All right. Where?'

'My bus stops outside the Hippodrome. So why don't we meet there?'

'If you like.'

'We'll decide what to see on the night. I'll bring the newspaper.'

'All right.'

'Six-thirty then. On Wednesday.'

'Six-thirty. Wednesday.'

'How nice,' her mother said, as soon as the door had closed. 'Morris is taking you out. Who'd have thought it?'

Anna grimaced and turned back to the living room. She fingered the cross with agitation, irritated with herself and her mother, hating herself for agreeing to go.

'You're a very lucky girl,' Mrs Pilgrim told her. 'There's not many men who'd want anything to do with a woman in your position. And Morris is a good man. He'll treat you well. He's dependable, you know. He'll look after you. He won't go off and leave you stranded. Not like some other men.'

Anna wondered if this was a reference to her own father or to Emma's, but resisted the temptation to ask.

'You've got Emma to think about now,' her mother continued. 'You have to make sacrifices when you have a child.' She paused so that Anna would understand what she meant. 'I know Morris isn't handsome, and it's a shame he's so short, but these things aren't important. You've got a baby to consider and you can't delude yourself into thinking someone else will come along and rescue you. Emma's father has long gone. Either he's dead or he's found some other woman to amuse him. And even if he hasn't yet, he soon will once he knows there's a child. Men like that want their freedom. He won't want to be tied down by the responsibilities of a family. Oh, he might pretend. He might even marry you, take you off to America. But what then? You'll be stuck then, won't you, when he decides he's had enough.'

Anna said nothing, breathing deeply to calm herself, mouth set hard against the rising anger.

'Morris is your only chance, my girl. So don't you mess this up. You won't get another chance if you let him go. That'll be the end of it. You'll struggle for the rest of your life.' She stopped and waited for Anna to reply.

'Yes Mother,' she whispered.

'And don't 'yes mother' me,' Mrs Pilgrim raised her voice. 'I'm telling you this for your own good, you know. You'd have to be a fool to refuse.'

Anna turned and collected the tea cups and took the tray through to the kitchen to wash up.

\* \* \*

Wednesday, and Anna sat on the bus that would take her into town. She touched a gloved hand to the curled hair that had taken her mother hours to set that afternoon, and licked her lips, feeling the unfamiliar texture of the lipstick with her tongue.

'You'll never get a man without a spot of make-up,' Mrs Pilgrim had told her when she protested, and she had relented, remembering how Tom had liked the way she wore no make-up, the way she looked the same in the morning.

She stared out of the window at the dim lights that had replaced the blackout these last few months. It already seemed normal, as if the utter darkness of before were just a dream half-recalled in the waking hours. The bus chugged through the traffic, winding its way along the narrow streets of the old city, stopping and starting, the ancient gearbox grinding until it pulled in across the road from the Hippodrome. She could see him already. He was scanning the crowd for her, brow pinched with anxiety, lips pulled into a thin tense line. Depression crawled over her, and she was tempted to stay on the bus. Get it over with, she told herself. Don't be so weak.

She got to her feet and jumped from the back of the bus just as it began to pull out from the kerb. The conductor shouted something after her but she ignored it and crossed the road, weaving through the bodies towards him, waiting for him to spot her in the crowd. He saw her finally when she was near, and relief passed visibly across his face.

'Anna, my dear,' he greeted her. 'It's lovely to see you.'

She smiled slightly and wondered why he liked her when she was so cold towards him. He offered her his arm, but she declined and they walked slowly towards the restaurant in silence. A group of American air force officers passed them, their voices loud and joking, and she dropped her head in shame. Their accents and their nonchalance touched her sadness and she had to swallow hard against the rising grief. Morris was oblivious and pointed to the various shop windows, drawing her attention to the muted Christmas displays, the first since before the war. He started to talk then, the initial awkwardness broken, chattering on about the factory and the progress of the war. She tried to listen, to concentrate on his words, but they lost themselves in the web of her memory and she had to ask him to repeat himself whenever an answer seemed necessary.

They went to a cheap and busy restaurant where there were no Americans, and Anna was grateful for its anonymity.

'I thought we'd go and see *In the Meantime Darling*,' Morris said. 'It's on at the Odeon.'

'I was hoping we could see *For Whom the Bell Tolls*,' she replied. 'I love Ingrid Bergmann.'

Morris checked through the listings in the paper. 'It doesn't start until quarter to eight. That'll make us a bit late, don't you think?'

Anna lifted her hands slightly from the table in acquiescence. She had no desire to argue over the choice of film.

'*In the Meantime Darling* will be fine.'

The food arrived, placed carelessly before them by a harassed and overworked waitress. Anna ate without interest, silent, letting Morris make the conversation.

'Anna,' he said, between mouthfuls of fish. 'I think it's time we talked about your plans for the future.'

Anna looked up from her meal, resentful of his interference.

'What are you planning to do?' he asked.

'I don't know,' she replied, half-truthfully. 'Until the war is over, I can't really do very much.'

'You can't stay at your mother's for ever. She's an old lady now, and she can't support you indefinitely.'

'I know,' she replied. 'Do you think I like being dependent on my mother?'

'No, no, of course not. I can see that you're a very independent young woman.'

Anna nodded in confirmation.

'But you've got to make plans. You're a mother and you've got Emma's future to consider, not just your own.'

'Morris,' Anna said, irritated by his tone, and the echo of her mother's words. 'I really don't want to discuss this.'

'I'm sure you don't. But there comes a time when the future has to be faced. The reality is that you're an unmarried mother with extremely limited resources. How on earth do you suppose you're going to manage?'

'I'll get a job.'

He shook his head and swallowed hurriedly so he could reply. 'That's just not practical. A child needs its mother at home …'

'She, not it, also needs food in her belly and a roof over her head,' Anna rejoined, hoping her tone might steer him away from the subject.

He looked hurt. 'I'm only trying to help.'

She sighed. 'Morris, please, can we just have a pleasant evening out together? I really don't feel like discussing it.'

He hesitated, wanting to continue taking charge of her future, but mindful that he needed to tread gently. So he said nothing, unsure how to go on in the face of her recalcitrance.

'Please?' she repeated.

'I just thought I might be able to help,' he told her. 'That I might be able to give you some advice.'

'You can't, Morris. I'm sorry.'

'I understand,' he said, but he didn't, and he was hurt by her refusal to confide in him.

In the cinema they took their seats a few rows from the back of the crowded auditorium. Pathé Newsreels showed the Red Army entering cities in Hungary, and the Americans in the Saar in western Germany. Anna scanned the images with a sense of hopelessness, as if she might somehow see Tom amongst the soldiers, find some clue to his whereabouts, and when the dull and sentimental feature began, she withdrew into her sadness, barely aware of the images before her.

Morris too, was only vaguely following the film, turning his head often to admire the woman next to him, absorbed by her beauty, disappointed by her apparent interest in the picture. She felt his gaze even through the wall of her melancholy, and stared resolutely ahead, wishing only for the evening to end. Halfway through, they had to stand to let someone squeeze past, and as they settled themselves again, she felt the pudgy clamminess of his hand brushing against her fingers on the armrest between them. Repulsed by the touch of his flesh against hers, she jerked her hand away and riveted her eyes to the screen for the rest of the film. Morris followed her gaze with sad eyes and folded his hands in neat restraint on his lap. Her diffidence was going to be harder to overcome than he had thought.

As soon as the score rose to its final crescendo, Anna stood up and pushed her way out into the brightness of the foyer, running for the ladies' room. Inside the cubicle she stood with her back to the door, tears of frustration fighting to rise, angry with herself. She could hear other women outside, the patient animated chatter of those who had seen the same film, and reaching deep inside to find some composure, she wiped away the tears and went out to find Morris.

Finally they stood outside the house in Byron Street in the cold. A nascent moon fought bravely to shed her light through the clouds that clung to her, and Anna shivered. A lamp was on in the house, and she could make out the pallor of his face in the half-light.

'Thank you, Morris,' she said.

'It was my pleasure,' he replied. 'We must do it again.'

'Perhaps,' she mumbled and turned away from him to go. Morris caught her arm with his hand to stop her and she swung round in surprise and anger. She paused, waiting for him to say something, but he must have lost his nerve beneath the coldness in her face, because he let her arm drop and said nothing.

'Good night, Morris.'

'Good night, Anna.'

She disappeared into the house and left him standing confused and disappointed on the pavement.

The hall was in semi-darkness, a large irregular arc of light shining against the wall from the lamp on the landing, the shadow of the bannisters huge and misshapen. Her mother was in bed. She shut the door silently, holding down the latch until it clicked into place, hoping that she might not be heard but knowing instinctively that her mother was waiting for her. Like the interrogation after a raid, she thought wryly, and remembered Tom that day after the mission, standing in the lane by the base, his face haggard, intense brown eyes dimmed with sorrow and fatigue.

She leant against the door, kicked off her shoes, letting her head fall back against the glass. Its coldness was soothing and sharp against her hair and for a moment the dreadful evening with Morris was forgotten, eclipsed by the sadness of the memory. She had been so afraid while he was gone, terrified that he would die, and when, finally, she saw him and saw the anguish on his face, she realised that a part of him had, that a part of him died each time he flew.

'Anna?!' Her mother's voice sounded through the fog of her thoughts and she pushed herself away from the door and stepped barefoot, silent, towards the stairs. 'Anna?!'

'I'm coming, Mother,' she replied, and her voice was uneven and weak. The tension of the evening had wearied her more than she'd realised.

'Hurry up,' her mother called, 'and tell me all about it.'

Anna paused at the top of the stairs, wondering what she could say that wouldn't precipitate another row.

'What on earth are you doing?' her mother called again.

'I'm coming,' she repeated. 'I'm coming.'

She dumped her bag and coat outside the bedroom and

pushed open the door. She came into this room rarely, and it had always been a special privilege as a child to sit on the big bed and watch her mother curl her hair or put on her make-up. Sometimes, when her father had still been with them, sleeping late at the weekend, she would creep in and lie next to him on top of the covers until her fidgeting woke him up. Then he would tickle her until she screamed and her mother came running, shouting at them both. She rested lightly on the edge of the bed, half-turned to her mother, who peered over her reading glasses, a library book sitting open on her lap.

'How was Emma?' Anna asked. 'Did she go down all right?'

Her mother waved a hand airily, dismissing the question. 'She was fine. No trouble at all.'

Anna smiled, relieved. Mrs Pilgrim closed her book and laid it on the narrow bedside table. 'Well?' she asked, softer now, more encouraging. 'How did it go?'

Oh God, thought Anna. How can I say this?

Her mother frowned in the pause, sensing her daughter's reluctance. Anna looked away.

'He tried to kiss me,' she said.

'Well, what did you expect?' her mother snorted. 'He bought you dinner, took you to the pictures, didn't he? He's got a right to expect something in return.'

Tom didn't, Anna thought loyally. Tom didn't touch her that whole first night they spent together. He expected nothing.

'I hope you let him,' her mother went on. 'He needs encouragement.'

Anna shook her head slowly. 'I don't like him,' she said softly. 'I don't like him at all.'

'Oh, for God's sake!' Mrs Pilgrim exclaimed in exasperation. 'It isn't important whether you like him or not. He's going to provide for you and your child. He'll be a good husband to you and a father for Emma. Probably a damn sight better father than your airman would have been.' She paused, took off her reading glasses and put them back into their case. 'I know he isn't attractive,' she conceded, 'but that's beside the point. In your situation, you can't afford to be picky.'

Anna was silent. There was nothing she could say.

'You'll have to change your attitude, my girl, or you'll lose him altogether. It won't take much to put him off, you know.'

'I should never have agreed to go tonight,' Anna said. 'Now you both think we're as good as engaged.'

Mrs Pilgrim stiffened. 'I suppose it would've been a different story if he'd been wearing an American uniform.' Her eyes narrowed. 'I'm sure you wouldn't have hesitated to let him kiss you then, would you? You certainly weren't so reluctant with the last one.'

Anna felt the heat spread from her belly, and her face flushed with anger. She stood slowly, containing it, her face averted from the bed.

'And where is he now when you need him, eh?' Her mother was getting into her stride. 'They're all very romantic and charming with their accents and their money, but they've got no sense of decency. He's not here now, when you need him, is he? Left you right up the creek, didn't he, with his offspring in tow.'

Anna was trembling. She lifted her head and her eyes glowed black with hatred in the faint light from the bedside lamp. 'He's missing in action,' she whispered. 'I don't see Morris fighting for his country, risking his life.'

Mrs Pilgrim pushed herself straight in the bed, struggling with the pile of pillows at her back. 'I'll have you know that Morris is doing very important work,' she said. 'His job isn't easy, you know. It takes a lot of skill to run a factory. A lot of dedication. And it's just as important to the war effort ...'

'And a lot safer,' Anna added. 'A lot safer.'

She strode the two paces to the door and heard Emma stirring in the next room, disturbed perhaps by the raised voice. 'Good night,' she said, and slammed the door behind her.

* * *

Morris turned the key quietly in the lock but inside the house was still lit and his mother sat reading at the kitchen table, warmed by the wood-burning stove. He smiled when he saw her, the image of contented domesticity, and pictured Anna there, his loving wife waiting for him, their children asleep in the big bedroom upstairs.

'Hello love.'

Mrs Morris put down her book, slipping the bookmark carefully between the pages. Her hand rested on the dust jacket and between her fingers Morris could read the title.

'More Hardy, eh?' he said, taking his place at the table. 'Too depressing for me.'

'He understands human emotions like no one else before or since,' his mother answered, smiling. 'You should read him. You might learn something.'

Morris laughed. 'I prefer to learn from real experience, thanks all the same.'

'Tea?' Mrs Morris asked, rising. Morris nodded and his mother busied herself with the kettle and the tea pot.

'Did you have a nice evening?' she asked, turning to him for his answer, shrewd eyes looking for the truth.

'Yes, thank you,' Morris replied, with emphasis. 'We had a lovely evening.'

In the silence Mrs Morris observed her son.

'We got along famously,' Morris said, to fill the pause.

'And how is Anna?'

'Quite well. She seems to be taking to motherhood like a duck to water. I've never seen her looking so radiant.' He paused and the fine lines on his forehead drew into a frown. 'But I have to say, I'm a bit worried about her.'

'Oh?'

'Well,' he sighed, 'it's just that …'

'Yes?'

'I asked her about her plans for the future, and to be honest, I don't think she's made any. I really don't. She seems not to have thought about it at all.'

'I'm sure she must have thought about it.'

'Well, she wouldn't discuss it with me. Got quite testy, as a matter of fact. I thought she'd be grateful for a bit of friendly advice, but quite the contrary.'

Mrs Morris sat down and slid a mug of steaming tea across the table to her son. He took it up immediately and sipped it, taking in air with a hiss so that he wouldn't burn his mouth.

'I mean, why wouldn't she at least want to talk about it?'

Mrs Morris sighed. 'Morris,' she said gently, 'think about it.'

He frowned and tightened his lips into a thin line of displeasure. He waited for her to continue.

'You're thick as thieves with her mother,' she went on. 'I'm not surprised she won't confide in you.'

'You mean she doesn't trust me?'

'I'm only guessing, but it seems likely to me, love. I can't imagine she hasn't thought about what she's going to do.'

'But we get on so well.'

'Give her time,' she counselled. 'Don't push her too fast.'

They drank their tea in silence. She's going to break his heart, poor love, she thought. She's going to break his heart.

Anna lay sleepless in the cold night, Emma content and peaceful in the cot by the bed, reassured at last by her mother's presence. The anger had waned now and left in its place a dim sense of despair, the future a dark tunnel with no light at its end.

It was more than ten months since Tom had gone, ten months of waiting, hope fading gradually with his silence. She had heard no more from his parents so she guessed that they too must be waiting for news. She should write to them again, she thought, but she was afraid to tell them about Emma, afraid that they wouldn't believe the child was their son's. They were good people, she knew, and they were the family she wanted more than anything for

Emma, but how could she go there? She had little money; enough perhaps for a passage to America after the war, but she would need more than that. Montana was a long way from New York, and she was scared of getting stranded, alone, with no one to help her. And why should they believe her, that Emma was Tom's baby? That he'd given her the cross was proof of nothing. She shivered and pulled the covers closer round her shoulders, but the coldness went too deep for blankets to warm.

Her mother's spitefulness echoed through her thoughts. She had to leave this house before it poisoned her completely, before it sapped her will to resist it. But how? There was nowhere to go. No housing, no way to work and bring up Emma alone.

Which left Morris. In spite of her coldness, her reluctance to let him come close, she knew that sooner or later he would propose. Thick skinned and arrogant, he knew she had few options. She stared into the gloom, eyes open but blind in the blackness, and thought of reasons to accept him.

He was dependable. He would provide well for her and her child, perhaps rescuing them from a life of poverty and hardship. He seemed genuinely to care for Emma, and to hold no sense of bitterness against her father. He was kind. He would, as her mother had so often pointed out, be a good husband.

But could she bear to be his wife? She shuddered with the memory of the pudgy hand in the cinema, and turned her face to the pillow to avoid even the thought of his lips against hers.

And Tom. What if, somehow, by some freak chance, Tom was still alive?

One day the war would end, and she would know. One day.

She woke in the early hours shaking and in tears, brief images of the nightmare still with her, the story lost to memory. She wiped the wetness from her cheeks with the sheet, the worn cotton soft against her skin, and the images faded thankfully into unconsciousness. Automatically she reached for the little cross and held it briefly to her lips, drawing courage from its sacredness. She could hear her child's breathing, soft and light and regular, and she squinted through eyes still clogged with tears at the luminous figures of her clock. It was only four o'clock, but she knew she wouldn't sleep again that night, the fear of the forgotten nightmare still running in her nerves. She blinked hard, clearing the moisture from her eyes, trying to dislodge the headache that lay behind them. Her vision cleared but the dull pain remained, and she curled up, foetus-like, her face close to the cot so that she was comforted by the untroubled innocence of her baby. Then she fell slowly into fitful dozing that was filled with the daylight images of Morris and her mother, the terror of her nightmares too deep to be touched by the lightness of her sleep.

Mrs Pilgrim struggled to rouse herself in the dark of the early winter morning. Ever since she had found that first letter from the American she had forced herself to rise earlier and earlier with a growing dread that Anna might go down before her and find a pale blue envelope on the mat, though recently there had been none. He must have grown bored finally of waiting for an answer that never came. He probably only wrote anyway to while away his time in prison. She doubted there would be any more now but she still had to check, just in case.

She dragged herself from the warmth of the bed into the icy morning, hurriedly shrugging herself into the old wool dressing gown. Searching for her slippers with calloused feet, she listened for signs of movement in the next room, but the house was still silent. She shuffled out to the bathroom, incapable of quietness, and then down to the kitchen. There was no letter and she was glad.

Lighting the stove for the kettle, she had to fumble with matches that refused to ignite. Finally, the gas lit with a whoosh that took the fine hairs from the backs of her fingers and made her swear. She watched the gas burning and began to puzzle how best to coerce her daughter into marriage with Morris.

Later, Anna came down, pale and quiet, the night's sleepless-ness plain her face, eyes deep and lifeless.

'What's wrong with you?' Mrs Pilgrim asked.

'I didn't sleep well,' Anna answered with effort, too tired even to talk. She made fresh tea for herself and ate toast automatically, without interest.

'Yes, Emma kept me up last night too,' Mrs Pilgrim lied.

Anna apologised out of habit, the lie unnoticed.

'Is Morris coming over this Sunday?' her mother asked.

Anna looked up from her tea with mild surprise. She had not yet thought about Morris this morning and her mother's remark brought him unpleasantly back to mind. 'I don't know,' she replied. 'He didn't say.'

'Didn't you arrange to see each other again?'

Anna shook her head. 'I told you last night. I don't like him.'

'That isn't what I asked,' Mrs Pilgrim told her. 'And anyway, it's not important.'

'It's important to me.'

Her mother ignored her. 'I only ask because I thought we might invite Morris and his mother over for Christmas.'

Anna lowered her cup of tea and stared. 'You hate having people over,' she whispered, shocked. 'Why on earth would you want them to come for Christmas?' Christmas was bad enough with just the two of them. It would be indescribable with the Morrises there as well.

'I thought it would be nice for you and Morris to spend the holiday together, and it would be a good chance for us all to be together, as the family we're going to become.'

Anna lifted her tea to her lips and said nothing, staring dazedly at the cracked tiles on the floor. She shivered, realising that it was cold in the kitchen, and put both her hands to her cup, warming them against the hot porcelain. 'Perhaps I didn't explain properly last night,' she said finally, her gaze still lowered. She couldn't face the determined hostility in her mother's face but she spoke slowly, her voice deliberate and controlled. 'I don't like Morris and I have absolutely no intention of becoming his wife.' Now, in the light of the morning, the idea of marrying Morris became risible, and she wondered how she had even considered it. She thought of Tom, then of Morris, and comparing them, she wanted to laugh.

'Listen here,' her mother ordered. 'I don't care two hoots whether you like Morris or not. You are a mother with a child to look after, and you are going to have to make a sacrifice for her sake. You are going to marry Morris, because he will give Emma the best chance she can expect in life. No one will ever need to know she's illegitimate. If you don't take this chance you won't get another. No other man in his right mind is going to consider taking on a woman in your position.'

'I don't want any other man,' Anna replied. Her breathing was laboured, her anger exhausting.

'You've got no reason to be so proud,' Mrs Pilgrim said, her voice low and dangerous. 'You will marry Morris. Because if you don't, I will no longer support you. If you won't help yourself, you can't expect me to look after you.'

'He hasn't asked me yet,' Anna observed. She watched with sardonic detachment as the colour rose in her mother's face, and saw how the fat cheek quivered as the muscle beneath it twitched with tension. 'He might not ask.'

Mrs Pilgrim began to breathe heavily, the great chest rising and falling, her breath audible in the quiet kitchen.

'Don't you dare,' she hissed. 'Don't you dare jeapordise this. Don't you even think about it.' She glared at her daughter, who dropped her eyes once again to the tiles. 'They will come for Christmas, and you will be gracious and receptive. Do I make myself plain?'

'Yes,' Anna answered. 'Perfectly.'

A cry from upstairs snapped the silence and, placing her cup on the bench, Anna fled to her child.

# Twenty

Anna sat in the dip in the sofa in the Lawrences' sitting room where she spent so much of her time these days, escaping her mother.

'She's so gorgeous,' Lottie cooed, cradling the still tiny child in her arms. 'I'm so jealous. Can I keep her? I'd look after ever so well. Honestly,' She smiled mischievously at Emma, wrinkling her nose at her and the baby smiled with delight. 'You'd like to stay, wouldn't you, Em?' she said. 'You'd like to live with your Auntie Lottie and Uncle Evan, wouldn't you?'

Emma laughed and a little hand waved uncertainly against Lottie's cheek.

'See?' Lottie turned to her friend and grinned. 'She wants to stay.'

Anna laughed and shook her head. 'No, Lottie. She's just being polite.'

Lottie pouted in mock disappointment and let the baby settle onto her lap. 'But I am envious,' she said, serious now. 'Evan and I are still trying, but I'm beginning to think it's never going to happen.'

'It's probably stress,' Anna suggested. 'I'm surprised you even have time to try.'

Lottie laughed. 'We make time. But you're probably right. The pressure's hard on both of us. He's away so much ...' She trailed off, saddened by the thought of his absence.

'He's still in London?' Anna didn't know what Evan did, only that before the war he was an engineer. She guessed he was involved in aircraft design but she had never asked. Secrecy about such things had become second nature.

Lottie nodded and stroked Emma, lulling the child gently into a sleep that she resisted as long as she could.

'You'd be a good mum,' Anna said.

'I know,' Lottie grinned. 'So, what's the news with the Pilgrims?'

Anna shook her head slightly and gazed steadily at the sleeping child.

'That bad?' Lottie raised an eyebrow under her growing mop of curls.

'I'm embarrassed to tell you.'

Lottie looked interested. 'Go on, go on.'

'I went to the pictures with Morris the other night.'

'Whatever possessed you?'

'I don't know,' Anna shrugged. 'I really don't. A moment of weakness, I suppose. And once I'd said yes, I couldn't get out of it. Believe me, I racked my brains to think of a way. I even hoped Emma would be sick, so I wouldn't have to go.'

'How was it?'

'Make a guess.'

'That bad?'

'It was awful,' Anna said. 'He tried to kiss me goodbye.'

'Yuck.'

'And the worst part of it is, he and my mother now seem to think we're as good as engaged. She wants to invite them over for Christmas. Can you imagine?'

'Oh, Anna.'

'She's determined I'm going to marry him. She even threatened to throw me out again if I didn't.'

Lottie drew in air between her teeth and grimaced. 'You've got to get away from her, Anna. That's awful.' Then, 'Why does she like him so much anyway? I thought she hated men.'

'She does. But I don't think Morris counts.'

Lottie laughed. 'What do you mean?'

'He's just Morris, isn't he? He's too dull and unattractive to be any kind of threat; there's nothing sexual about him so he isn't dangerous. I don't even like him, never mind about love him, so she can't be jealous or resentful. And he's not going to whisk me off to America where she can't bully me any more. Whereas Tom, on the other hand … Tom's a Yank, which automatically makes him no good, and he's young and attractive, and I love him.'

There was a pause before Lottie said, 'So what are you going to do? About Morris, I mean.'

'I'm almost tempted to marry him, just to get away from my mother.'

'No!' Lottie ordered, aghast. 'You can't! You're not serious, are you?'

'Not really. But you can understand the temptation, can't you?'

'No. Not at all. He's awful. How can you even think about it?'

Anna smiled.

'Listen,' Lottie adopted a school teacher tone. 'If you marry Morris, you'll have to go to bed with him every night.'

'Lottie, please don't,' Anna begged.

'I haven't finished yet, and you're going to listen.' She wagged a finger at her friend. 'Not only will you have to wake up next to him each morning, but you will have to let him kiss you. And make love to you. You will have to let him touch you the way Tom used to touch you.'

Anna's eyes closed in pain and revulsion.

'Is it working? Are you still tempted?'

'Okay, okay. You win. I won't marry him. Now stop it, please.'

'And if you're still stupid enough to marry him after I've said all that, I'll stand up at the back of the church when they get to the bit about lawful impediments and say something so awful about you that Morris will run screaming from the church.'

Anna laughed and they sat in comfortable silence, watching Lottie's small hand move rhythmically against the baby's back.

'So, what are you going to do?'

'I can't do anything till the war's finished. Perhaps some-where, somehow, Tom's still alive. There's still that possibility. But if he doesn't come back, I'm going to go to America and find his family and just hope they accept us. Tom always spoke with such love about his folks and that's want I for Emma. A loving home.'

'I'd miss you,' Lottie said. 'But I think it's the right decision. And perhaps he will come back. I hope so. I really do.'

Morris came over on Sunday as usual. Emma was restless and unsettled, perhaps sensing her mother's tension. For a while they persisted, Anna comforting the baby in her arms, but gradually Mrs Pilgrim grew irritated, their conversation disturbed by the constant crying, and Anna took the child upstairs gratefully, pre-ferring the cold loneliness of her room to the forced politeness of the company below.

The two women had spoken little since their argument a few days before, and Anna knew she was being punished for her dis-obedience. In the presence of Morris, however, the old woman thawed and chatted pleasantly and Anna hated her. She felt almost sorry for Morris, caught in her mother's trap, but she showed no signs of softness towards him, aware that any kindness on her part would be quickly misinterpreted. So she came in and out of the living room, joining their conversations just briefly, her eyes lowered, avoiding the eye contact that she knew Morris so earnestly sought from her. Then Emma would cry again upstairs, and she would escape with relief.

Insensitive to their visitor's disappointment, Mrs Pilgrim wel-comed the chance to talk to him alone, and to encourage him in his pursuit of her daughter. Morris listened avidly to her advice, trusting her judgment implicitly, never pausing to doubt her.

'How did things go the other night?' she asked him softly, when Anna's footsteps had retreated safely up the stairs. She was anxious for his views, mistrustful of her daughter's account.

'We had a lovely time,' Morris told her. 'Of course she's still a bit reticent, but that's only to be expected. She's a modest girl, and her situation must be causing her some considerable embarrassment.'

'Yes,' Mrs Pilgrim agreed doubtfully. Then, positively, eager to support his opinion, 'Quite so.'

Morris pressed on, oblivious to her doubts. 'We talked a bit about her plans for the future, but she wasn't very forthcoming, so I didn't like to push it. I wanted her to enjoy herself.'

Mrs Pilgrim nodded. 'I quite understand. But she needs to be pushed. I wouldn't waste too much time if I were you.' She was anxious. Another letter had arrived and the constant threat of discovery wore at her nerves.

'I see,' Morris replied. 'Well, obviously you know her best and I appreciate your advice.'

'I'm very happy to help.'

The sound of Anna on the stairs brought the conversation to a finish and when she entered, the uncomfortable silence gave away the fact that they had been discussing her. She walked between them and sat in her chair, embarrassed by the heat of Morris's gaze.

'How is Emma?' he asked, solicitously.

'She seems to be settling now. I'm hoping she'll sleep for a while.'

'That's good. It's such a worry when a little baby's upset and you don't know what's wrong, don't you think?'

Anna nodded, refusing the invitation to converse, waiting for him to turn in frustration to her mother. She felt cruel, and her mother's encouragement of him disgusted her.

'I've asked Morris if he and his mother would like to come over for Christmas dinner,' Mrs Pilgrim told her.

'We'd be delighted,' Morris chipped in. 'Can't wait.'

Anna cringed and averted her face. There was a silence.

'Well, I'd better be off then,' Morris said at last, rising from his chair. 'Let us know what rations you want us to contribute and we can arrange things. You can ring me at the factory if you like. The sooner the better, eh, Anna?'

She looked up briefly and he caught her eyes. She attempted to smile, then looked quickly away. She could feel him watching her, wanting her, and a dull nauseous dread filled her stomach.

'Don't get up,' he insisted. 'You've been up and down all afternoon. Sit down while you can.'

'Thank you,' she replied, her gaze cast downwards, and she noticed the high shiny polish on his shoes. Poor sod, she thought. It's really not his fault.

Christmas Day dawned bitterly cold, the coldest Christmas in fifty years. In spite of the fuel shortages, they had saved some coal so that Christmas Day at least could be warmed by a cheerful fire.

Anna rose late, awakened by the bombers droning overhead, depressed that the raids flew even on this day. Standing at the window, she watched them go until the roar subsided into silence, and wondered how many would return.

She dressed while Emma still slept, peaceful amid the noise of war, then she fed her and gave her the little booties and bonnet she had inexpertly knitted from some wool she'd found in the basket. Emma smiled appreciatively as Anna carried her downstairs to the kitchen, where her mother was drinking her first cup of tea. Mrs Pilgrim scowled as the door swung open, her natural ill-temper at its worst in the mornings.

'Happy Christmas,' Anna said, leaning near the door, Emma slung casually on her shoulder.

Her mother said nothing until she had finished her tea. 'I hope you are going to behave yourself today,' she said at last.

'Of course,' replied Anna, good-naturedly. 'Why wouldn't I?'

She stood up and with the one-handed dexterity that becomes natural to a mother, she poured herself some tea. It was bitter and she grimaced. A tense silence settled and she gave her attention to Emma, who gazed about the kitchen with interest, as if she'd never been there before.

'You know very well what I mean.'

Anna poured the tea down the sink, and put the kettle on for some fresh.

'Don't you?' her mother persisted.

'Have I ever been rude to Morris?' Anna asked.

'It isn't a question of rudeness,' her mother snapped. 'It's a question of doing the right thing.'

Anna took a deep breath and Emma frowned at the sudden tension in her mother's grip. 'Sorry Em,' she whispered and made a conscious effort to relax her hold, stroking the fine hair away from her baby's face. Emma smiled.

'What do you mean?' Anna asked, sucked unwillingly into the argument.

'You know very well what I mean.'

'I'm not sure I do.'

The kettle boiled and Anna filled the pot with difficulty, not bothering to warm it. She carried it over to the bench and put on the tea cosy to let it brew.

'Are you being deliberately obtuse?' Mrs Pilgrim asked.

'I don't think so.'

Her mother sighed.

Anna raised her eyebrows, waiting for an explanation. There was a pause, then finally her mother said, 'I think Morris might be planning to propose to you today.'

Anna's eyes rolled back and the familiar nauseous dread rose up from her gut. 'Oh God, I hope not,' she whispered.

'And if he does, you will accept him,' her mother ordered. 'Is that understood? You will say yes. I've told him that you will say yes.'

Anna was silent, stroking Emma's back to calm herself.

'Well?' Mrs Pilgrim demanded. 'Do I have your word?'

There was a silence.

'Do I have your word?''

Anna nodded, briefly, lips clenched shut, and poured her tea. 'Good,' her mother gloated. 'I'm glad that's understood then.'

They walked silently to church, the big wheels of the pram squeaking in the peculiar tranquillity of Christmas morning, their heels clicking on the frost-strewn pavement. Anna stared down at Emma, her thoughts miles away from her mother and from Morris, and her mother glared stonily ahead, resentful of her daughter's distance.

In church, Anna sang the carols with joy, allowing herself to be swept along on the tide of goodwill until she came to pray for all those who fought, and then the loss of Tom and Billy reawakened her sadness, and she held Emma tightly against her, seeking comfort in her child.

Afterwards, over tea and mince pies in the church hall, the vicar approached them, smiling widely. 'Merry Christmas, my dear,' he beamed. 'How are you?'

'We're very well, thank you, Vicar,' Anna smiled, his cheerfulness impossible to resist. He lifted Emma from Anna's arms and held her with practised hands.

'Such a beautiful baby,' he announced, and Emma grinned with the compliment. 'You must be very proud of her.'

Anna nodded.

'Any word on her father's whereabouts?' he added, kindly, in a lower voice.

'No,' she answered. 'But I haven't given up hope.'

'That's the spirit,' he told her. 'Isn't it, Mrs Pilgrim?'

The old woman turned away, the great jaw set hard in fury. The vicar pulled a face at Anna then smiled sheepishly. 'Must be on my way,' he said. 'I've got a lot of people to wish a merry Christmas to.'

Anna smiled as he placed the child back in her arms and laid a reassuring hand on her shoulder.

'God be with you,' he murmured. 'And your lovely daughter.'

\* \* \*

Anna worked in the kitchen for the rest of the morning, refusing her mother's help, preferring the solitude, grateful for something to do, and Mrs Pilgrim minded Emma in the warmth of the living room. She worked calmly but quickly, preparing as much as she could so that later it would be easier to cook.

The Morrises arrived spot on noon, and Morris showed his mother into the house as though it were his own. Anna ignored the nerves in her stomach and hastened back to the kitchen, where she had already finished as much preparation as she could do. She stood by the oven, warming now in readiness for the chicken, her hands held out for the warmth, screwing up the courage to join their guests in the living room.

'How is dinner going?' Morris hailed her cheerfully when finally she pushed open the door. The room seemed crowded, her mother and Mrs Morris uncomfortably close at either end of the sofa, and Morris ebullient, apparently so close to his goal.

'Fine,' Anna answered. 'I've just put the chicken in now.'

'Fantastic,' Morris gushed, rubbing his hands in anticipation. 'We're looking forward to it. I've told Mum what a wonderful cook you are.'

She sat down, pulling her feet up under her, curling herself into the farthest corner of the chair. She could feel all eyes on her, and dropped her gaze to Emma, who slept soundly amidst the crowd.

'How is she?' Mrs Morris asked Anna, nodding towards the crib. 'She'd be almost three months now, wouldn't she?'

'Nearly eleven weeks,' Anna answered, wondering how much Mrs Morris knew, embarrassed by the whole situation.

'How's she sleeping? Is she going through the night yet?'

'Not yet,' Anna smiled, pleased by her interest. 'She still wakes for one feed. But that's all right. She's no trouble otherwise.'

Mrs Morris bent slightly to see better into the crib. 'She certainly is a bonny baby,' she said. 'Very bonny indeed.'

Mrs Pilgrim coughed, reminding them all of her presence,

and Mrs Morris turned to her, polite and charming. 'It must be lovely to have such a beautiful grandchild. I'm very envious.'

'It is,' Anna's mother assured her. 'Wonderful.'

'And how are you, Margaret? It's been years since we talked. I don't like to think how many years have passed since we moved.'

'Ten,' Morris supplied tactlessly.

'Is it really?' his mother answered, with the natural social grace Mrs Pilgrim had always detested. And then, trying again, 'So, tell me Margaret, how are you keeping these days?'

'Still struggling on,' Mrs Pilgrim replied. 'Still struggling on.'

'Yes, of course. And the war has put a strain on all of us. Still, it seems to be moving to an end at last, slowly but surely.'

'They've laid off all the outworkers now,' Mrs Pilgrim told her. 'They've no need for us any more. So I suppose that's a good sign. Anyway. I'm very grateful not to be working any more. It was too much for a woman of my age. And with a young baby to look after too, I was quite exhausted.'

Mrs Morris smiled in understanding, and Morris tried vainly to catch Anna's eye.

'Excuse me,' Anna said in the silence. 'I've got to see to dinner.'

Morris smiled at her broadly as she brushed past his chair, his fingers wrapped sweatily round the little ring box in his pocket. He wanted to follow her into the kitchen, to be alone with her, but he was afraid of intruding, of interrupting her at work. So he settled instead back into the chair and made small talk with the mothers, catching up on each others' news.

They ate at two o'clock exactly, Anna serving dinner in the cold cheerless room, and the brightly coloured tablecloth that Anna had washed and mended specially served only to emphasise the drabness. Morris carved, jovial and avuncular at the head of the table opposite the woman he wanted for his wife. Emma still slept in her crib in the living room, and Anna listened attentively for the slightest sound. Dinner was a success and the cook accepted the compliments graciously.

'How long is your holiday, Morris?' Mrs Pilgrim asked between mouthfuls.

'Just today and tomorrow. Hitler doesn't stop for Christmas and neither can we.'

Anna remembered the bombers overhead in the morning and was silent.

'The factory's actually open tomorrow,' Morris continued. 'But as manager, I've awarded myself the extra day.'

'Lucky you,' said Mrs Pilgrim, impressed. 'And they'll cope all right without you?'

'I'm sure they will.'

The conversation was fitful. The two older women had exhausted all their small talk and had nothing else to say. Anna ate silently, offering more vegetables and refilling empty glasses.

'Such a lovely hostess,' Morris smiled.

One by one, they finished eating and the silence became uncomfortable. Anna cleared the table, relieved to have something to do in the awkwardness. She slipped back into her seat when the table was clear and Morris coughed quietly.

Oh God, she realised then. He's going to ask me now, here, in front of the mothers. She wanted to get up, run away from the scene, and the familiar sickness crawled up from her gut. She touched fingers to the cross instinctively, asking for help, shrinking into her chair. Please don't, Morris, she whispered mentally. Please don't ask me. Not here. Not in front of them. Please. She gazed at her place mat, externally poised, her natural elegance masking the turmoil beneath.

Morris cleared his throat again and smiled at the two older women. Mrs Pilgrim nodded her encouragement, and Mrs Morris dropped her eyes, unable to watch. He stood up slowly and drew the little box from his pocket. The blue cardboard was smudged and sweaty and he turned it over and over in his fingers with nervousness. 'There's something I'd like to ask you, Anna,' he began.

She closed her eyes.

'Something I've wanted to ask you for quite some time now.'

Heat prickled over her skin and her heartbeat knocked loud and hard in the silent room.

'My dear Anna,' he said.

She kept her eyes lowered, unable to lift them.

'My dear Anna.' He paused again and took a deep breath. 'This is a very special day for all of us here, and I'd like to ask you something that, should you accept, would make me a very happy and very proud man.'

He pushed back his chair and walked round the table to kneel at her feet.

'Anna,' he said, gazing up at her. 'Will you marry me?'

She swallowed hard. An intense embarrassment pulsed through her. Turning her head slowly, she looked down at the small man who knelt at her side, hopefully proffering the ring. She looked into his face and saw the pale skin quivering with tension, the thin lips that were stretched in a small smile of encouragement.

'I'm sorry, Morris,' she whispered. 'I can't marry you.'

The smile froze and the hand was slowly withdrawn.

'I'm sorry.'

'I see,' he managed to mumble, shattered.

She looked away as he stumbled foolishly to his feet and retreated, unsure, to his chair. There was a long silence. Morris sat looking down at the ring, cheeks flushed with humiliation, and Anna slid quietly from the room, hurrying away to her child. She knelt by the crib, trembling, and then she smiled as Emma began to wake, the little face puckering in readiness to cry. She touched her hand to the fine hair and caressed it, smoothing it, watching it bounce back obstinately. Like Tom's, she thought, wayward and rough. She began to croon softly, more to calm herself then soothe the baby.

'*The north wind doth blow and we shall have snow,*'

She paused and Emma smiled.

*'And what will Cock Robin do then, poor thing?*
*He'll sit in a barn and keep himself warm …'*

She stopped, her voice cracking with emotion and Morris finished it for her, surprising her by his presence. She hadn't heard him come in.

*'With his head tucked under his wing.'*

He sang in a low gentle murmur that was pleasing, and she smiled up at him as he knelt a little distance away from her, careful not come too close. Tears glistened in her eyelashes, darkening them, accentuating her ivory pallor.

'I haven't heard that for donkeys' years,' he told her softly. 'Not since infant school.'

'You remember them all when you have a baby. It's strange.' She gazed down at Emma, now fully awake and curious, eyes following her mother's movements.

'Please don't cry,' Morris said. 'I didn't mean to upset you.'

'I know.' She wiped her face gently with the edge of Emma's blanket. 'I think my mother has misled you, Morris. I'm sorry for that.'

He looked down and the ring was still between his fingers. He slipped it back into his pocket and looked up again at her, watching him with kind eyes.

'Why, Anna? Why won't you marry me? I'd be a good husband to you.'

'I know. But I can't. Not while there's still a chance that Tom … Emma's father, might still be alive.'

'His name was Tom, was it?' Morris asked. There was no bitterness in his voice. 'I somehow never thought of him being called Tom. Such an ordinary name.'

'Yes.' She paused, choosing her words carefully, watching her baby. 'You've been very kind. You've helped me and I'm very grateful …'

'… But you've got to wait and see if he comes back.'

She nodded.

'I understand. And if he doesn't come back?'

'I'll go to America. To his family. He said they're good people.'

'I see.' He heaved himself stiffly from his knees.

'I'm sorry, Morris. I really am.'

He looked down at her for a moment. 'I hope he comes back to you, Anna,' he said. 'He's a lucky man.'

'Thank you,' she answered and turned back to Emma. She did not notice him leave.

Out in the cold of the hall he breathed deeply, full of unfamiliar emotion. No sound reached him from the dining room so he guessed the two women were still there, exactly as he left them. He pushed open the door and it caught slightly on the rug that lay behind it, so that it only opened with some difficulty. Both women looked up as he entered and walked slowly round behind his mother's chair to resume his place at the top of the table.

'What did she say?' Mrs Pilgrim asked, and Mrs Morris winced.

'She isn't going to marry me,' Morris replied with dignity.

'She bloody well will.' Mrs Pilgrim began to squeeze out of her place against the wall to go after her daughter.

'For God's sake sit down,' Morris said. 'She doesn't want to marry me and she has her reasons so let's leave it at that, shall we?'

But the old woman was on her feet, adamant that she would not give in.

'Margaret!' The Scottish accent was pronounced and harsh when he raised his voice. 'For God's sake leave the girl alone. Haven't you done enough damage already?'

Mrs Pilgrim hesitated.

'It's over,' he told her. 'Now, sit down.'

The energy seemed to leave her and she sank submissively onto Anna's chair, defeated.

'Are you all right, love?' Mrs Morris laid a hand on her son's arm.

He nodded. 'I understand now. She explained.'

Mrs Morris squeezed his arm and smiled. 'That's good. As long as you're all right.'

'Shall we go, Mum,' he asked, her small boy again. 'Let's go home and enjoy the rest of Christmas on our own, shall we?'

She nodded and they slipped out of the house and into the freezing air that was fresh and welcome in their lungs.

# Twenty-one

A growing sense of restless unease pervaded the prisoner-of-war camp. Uncertainty enveloped the men as the Russians progressed inexorably westwards and the secure boredom gave way to a tense apprehension of the future. Arguments flared, the pressures of their enforced proximity straining under this added burden. The guards sensed it too, waiting nervously for orders to move out, but for different reasons. They wanted to head west to be captured by Americans, afraid of retribution at the hands of the Russians. No one talked any more of escape. No fantastic plans were hatched and plotted in whispers. The Germans still searched the huts, maintaining routine, but the raids were half-hearted, and the prisoners kept watch on their movements with a bored and indolent interest.

The British camp across the wire had a radio, dismantled and hidden in parts each day, reassembled for the BBC news. Signals were sent between the compounds and the prisoners waited for any word of news that might take them home, mentally following the Allied troops across Europe, the names of captured towns located on clandestine maps, their progress marked with pins and talked of endlessly. They followed the Ardennes offensive through the bitter December, outraged by the massacres, and huddled in groups round the poorly fuelled stoves.

No one knew what would happen to them and they tried not to think too hard about it.

\* \* \*

Tom was dreaming, moving restlessly on his bunk in the cold, the silence broken now and then by the snores or groans of the others. He twisted and strained in the nightmare, the bunk shuddering with his movement, waking Harry in the bed beneath.

*The woman whose life is his own glides down the endless aisle of a church he has never seen. Candle-lit, the shadows flicker in the high gothic arches, the cold stone exuding a chill that is unutterable, death-like. The pews are full, but not of people, not people that exist in his waking world, but pale, dark figures, cloaked and mediaeval, an occult ritual that is evil and frightening. The candles shed little light, the flickering shadows eerie and haunting, illuminating only the darkness of this place.*

*He turns back to the bride and the fear knots hard in his stomach, the terror of flying, of dying, lost in the bottomless well of the horror he feels now, watching her move to her end, the sacrificial lamb. And he, entrapped in this limbo, powerless, condemned only to watch. Such a beautiful dress that she wears, the train reaching into infinity, the silken whiteness whispering against the pale ivory of her skin, soft dark ringlets of hair brushing her bare shoulders. He is envious of that hair. His lips ache and burn to be in its place, to caress the elegance of her neck, to kiss the secret nape and sense her shudder with desire. But she is far from him. He is above her and beyond her, no corporeal reality to touch her living flesh. And her glide is inexorable, infinite, onwards and onwards, away from him towards the hands of another.*

*The face of the priest turns toward him. Alone amongst the crowd able to see him, this seeming man of God lifts off his cowl and bares his fangs and laughs, his evil tangible, eating into the strange body, floating, that is Tom. And Anna progresses relentlessly along the infinite aisle to give her soul to the devil.*

He woke in the winter darkness of the early morning hours, and a steady distant rumbling chased away the memory of the nightmare. 'Harry!' Tom whispered into the blackness below him, leaning over the edge of his bunk. 'Harry! Are you awake?'

'I hear them, Tom.'

'How far d'you reckon?'

'Don't know. A hundred miles maybe. Maybe less.'

In the corridor, footsteps tramped past the door on their way to the night latrine. The whole barrack was stirring.

'What's happened?' Mack's voice hissed through the quiet.

'Listen.'

The hut was silent, listening for the thunder far away.

'The Russians?'

'It's not the Americans.'

'What'll happen now, d'you think?'

'The Germans'll probably shoot us all.'

'D'you think so?'

'No. We're worth more alive. Besides, the Allies have too many German prisoners. They'd be afraid of reprisals.'

'Let's hope so.'

'So what will they do?'

'Evacuate us probably.'

'In this weather? Jesus, I hope not.'

They lay in silence and the guns boomed in the far corners of their consciousness, the sound of approaching liberation.

'I'll make a sledge,' Tom said to no one in particular. 'So we can carry more food.'

'Okay.'

'D'you think they'll let us take sledges?'

'Don't see why not.'

'I'll do it after roll call. Any objections if I use the table for it?'

'Go ahead.'

'I'll need some rope to pull it.'

'No problem,' Harry said. 'I'll find some rope from somewhere.'

* * *

'Where's Harry?' Tom asked, back in the hut from the wash-room next morning, fresh from the icy shower, kicking the dirt off his boots against the door frame.

'Cooler. Again,' answered Mack, looking up from his writing, barely visible under the raggedy blankets.

'What happened this time?'

'The *feldwebel* was poking around in here, and Harry, um, how shall I put it, uh, *protested*.'

The pilot laughed.

'You know,' Mack went on, 'for such a smart city lawyer, Harry can be pretty dumb at times.'

'He enjoys it,' Tom said with a shrug. 'He likes winding them up. Gives him something to do.'

'Hmm. I don't think the *feldwebel* is much of a challenge for him though,' Mack observed, then returned to his writing.

'I guess not,' Tom agreed. But he understood the motivation, the hatred that suffused all Harry's dealings with the Germans. He would choose to spend days in the cooler before he would cooperate in even the smallest task, his every action designed to hinder and enrage. Once Tom had asked him about it, and his friend had touched the scar across his temple, and told him that he did it for Yvette. The pilot hadn't asked again, but it saddened him to see his friend so full of hate, the cynicism turning bitter, no longer redeemed by humour and the capacity to love.

Tom draped his towel over the end of the bunk and sat at the makeshift table in the middle of the small room, examining it, working out the best way to construct a sledge. It wouldn't take him long, he decided. Across from him Robbie sat practising card tricks. Of the four men in the room, three were crew of the *American Maiden*, and they shared an easy familiarity born of danger shared, the relief of a mission survived, an acceptance of each other that was rare in the confined quarters of the camp. Robbie was the fourth, and he resented their closeness, saw him-self as excluded and shunned, so he bitched incessantly to whoever would listen and tried to drive wedges between them.

'Isn't it Harry's turn to cook today?' he asked the pilot, throwing down the last of the cards in triumph.

'Yeah.'

'So what are we supposed to do?' he grumbled. 'How come he always gets locked up when it's his turn?'

'It's okay,' Tom said. 'I'll cook.'

'That's not the point,' Robbie argued. 'You shouldn't have to.'

'It doesn't matter, okay? I don't mind.'

Robbie's pettiness infuriated him, and he had to fight to keep his patience. Mack looked up, aware of the change in the pilot's tone.

'But it puts out the whole schedule,' Robbie whined. 'I mean, how long is he going to be in the cooler this time?'

'Two days,' Mack said.

Tom closed his eyes and shook his head. He didn't want to have this argument. He clenched his fists in front of him on the table, holding in the frustration.

'I know you'll cook,' Robbie persisted. 'But it's the principle that matters. What does he think he's trying to prove anyway? That he's too fucking stupid to stay out of the cooler?'

The pilot stood up sharply, his eyes lit with anger, the chair grating on the floorboards as it leapt back from under him.

'Just drop it, would you?'

'All right. All right. There's no need to get so pissed. I was just asking.'

'It makes no fucking difference to you one way or the other, so just leave it alone.'

'Jesus. If I'd known you were going to react so badly, I wouldn't have mentioned it. Talk about touchy. What is it with you guys?'

Tom stood rigid, breathing hard, fists clenched tight at his sides. Mack looked away, grimacing, not wanting to watch. For an instant Tom hesitated. Then, tightening every muscle against the desire to lash out, he strode across the room and slammed out of the door. The flimsy hut vibrated in his wake.

Outside, he paced the circuit next to the wire, the air freezing in his lungs and his still-damp hair, consumed with frustration, wanting to hit out and scream and rant against his captivity, his only outlet to pace around his cage. Like a lion he saw in a zoo once, he remembered, gone loopy with boredom and the desire to be free. He wondered if he would get home to Anna too fucked up for her to love any more anyway, if by then he would have changed beyond her recognition. Then he thought of Harry in the loneliness of the cooler, embittered and full of rage, musing on his hatred.

Other walkers moved out of his way as he strode, his mood recognised and understood. He was unaware of them, absorbed in his own emotion, his helplessness in the face of Anna's silence. Only the thought of her kept him sane, the need to return to her unbroken, but the doubts rose again to the surface of his thoughts, doubts grown strong on unanswered letters. Just trust her, he told himself over and over. Just trust her like she trusted you.

Slowly, gradually, the rage subsided, and his pace dropped to a slow defeated amble until finally he stopped, staring without hope through the wire to the pine forest beyond, an impossible unreachable world.

All day the camp buzzed with rumours and expectation. Sledges were completed and backpacks sewn by attaching braces to kit bags. No one could settle to anything inside the camp any more, all attention fixed on the outside world.

At three o'clock, the German news broadcast announced huge Russian advances towards the camp. Rumours flew that other camps had been evacuated at short notice, and outside, the steady flow of people fleeing westwards had increased to a flood of refugees. Tom stood by the wire and watched them pass, trudging through the biting snow that covered everything, heads bent wearily into the wind, all their belongings in prams or carts or wheelbarrows whose wheels stuck in the snow and made progress slow and arduous. Children cried with the cold, or walked numb and blank-eyed.

How many would make it? Tom wondered. How many would die on the road? He turned away, wearied by so much suffering, and was touched by flashes of the same hatred that filled his friend.

The days passed as the prisoners waited, the Russians drawing nearer, tension mounting. Hockey games were still played and shows went on at the theatre, but there was little interest. All that was in everyone's mind was the uncertainty of the future.

Ten days after they first heard the guns, the Kommandant announced that they would not be moved, and relief and misgiving rippled through the compounds. It seemed impossible that the end could be so easy, that they could just sit and wait for the Russians to come, and be free so soon. In the evening the order was reversed. They would evacuate that night.

'It's finally happening,' someone said.

'Couldn't have chosen a worse time of year.'

'Stop bitching. At least we'll be beyond the wire. I haven't been out in almost two years.'

'What to take? What to leave behind? Decisions, decisions.'

Tom loaded the sledge with food and cigarettes for trading. No one knew how far they would have to go, how long the march might be. He packed as much as he could in the tense hours before they left, and Harry cooked up what was left. At least they would start with full bellies.

In the early hours their compound finally emptied, spilling its occupants into the clarity of the night, the sky velvet black and shot with stars. Tom lifted his eyes to them, and wondered how the same stars could look down on Anna and his family and be indifferent to all of them. He was dwarfed by the thought of it, and the awareness of his own insignificance in the world. As they passed beneath the last of the compound lamps he turned to Harry, trudging silently beside him. Harry sensed the movement and glanced sideways, a flicker of the old smile touching his lips. 'You drive, I'll navigate,' he said.

Tom grinned, encouraged, glad his friend was with him. It was not the end they had hoped for, and he was not alone in his doubts, his sense that it wasn't over yet. Like going into combat again, he thought, the outcome unknown and mostly down to luck.

The column walked in silence, and they took turns to drag the sledge across the filthy slush that now covered the road, the once pristine snow churned by the hundreds of boots that had gone before them. He nestled his face deeper into his scarf against the bitter cold of the night, the scarf his mother had sent in one of the rare parcels that had got through. He could smell her fragrance in the wool, the scent reminiscent of winters back home, chopping wood in the yard while his mother made coffee, glancing through the kitchen window from time to time, her face half-hidden by steam from the pot. The heat of the cup in his hands when he'd finished, sweating beneath his clothes, warm from the exertion.

A crack like a gunshot sounded from the forest to the east and the column froze. Guards trotted away to investigate, nervous, guns unslung and ready. The men waited, adrenalin burning, but there was no one there, and the slow march was resumed. 'Probably a branch under the weight of the snow,' Tom said. Then he dropped his eyes to the road and searched his mind for the memories of before but they had gone and now there was only the awareness of the long march ahead and the cold. A few times he lifted his eyes and glanced round, but he could see little in the darkness, just the silhouettes of the men all around him.

By dawn the whole column had become quiet, the buzz of excitement dying quickly in the harsh environment, all effort turned now to the hard progress westwards. Just the sound of their boots in the snow.

\* \* \*

They trudged until the following night, taking short rests at the roadside, eating hurriedly from their supplies, wanting to move on quickly, the chill too intense to be still for long. With movement at least came some warmth.

They were quartered at last in a brick factory, warm and dry from the furnaces.

'How far d'you think we've come?' Harry lounged against his kit bag on the concrete floor, blowing smoke into the air above them. They had eaten well, and washed, and the rest and warmth had given them some comfort.

'Thirty miles maybe,' Tom guessed. 'Maybe more.' He lay propped on one elbow, relaxing into the warmth, rubbing at the wound in his leg. It was stiff with the unaccustomed exercise and the cold, and he hoped it would hold up.

'It feels like more,' Mack said. 'How much further, d'you reckon?'

'Who knows?'

'Maybe we can stay here. At least it's warm.'

The murmurs of conversation from groups of men scattered wherever there was space died out as sleep came quickly. Tom lay on his back, the concrete hard beneath his shoulder blades, staring into the blackness above him. His last thought before he slept was of Anna, her head against his shoulder, the smell of her hair against his face. He was too tired to dream.

To leave the factory the next morning was hard; to step out again into the bitter winter after the warmth of the furnaces.

Tom lost count of the days. He spoke little to the others, lips too cold and numbed to talk, eyes averted from the snow-covered mounds that littered the sides of the road, clothes or limbs sometimes visible where the wind had blown nature's shroud away. Mostly, he thought of nothing, his mind blank, one foot in front of the other, slipping at times in the snow, the cold relentless against his face, seeping under his clothes. Only at night, in the eerie silence of the crush of bodies packed close under shelter, limbs resting gladly on wood or concrete or straw, did his mind drift unguided to thoughts of Anna. Hazy and unreal to him now, she shimmered prettily in a world that he could barely convince himself still existed, a world of warmth and love and comfort.

The roads were full. Refugees vied for space with the column of prisoners and trucks that were towing other trucks because there was not enough fuel for them all. Each evening brought the fear that there would be no shelter for that night, and each evening Tom waited with the others in some town or village, the dampness of his clothes freezing against his body, while the Germans hunted for somewhere to put them. They were always lucky, and once as they stood waiting, shivering, the village women came out with hot soup for them, offering it round with shy apologetic smiles.

Mornings were the hardest. To haul himself from the forget-fulness of sleep and the half-warmth of close bodies to the bitter drudgery of the march took all his will. He would shake himself awake and force his mind to empty, driven by a vague conviction that each step took him closer to England, closer to Anna.

In time they came, hungry and cold and exhausted, to a railhead to be loaded like cattle into box cars designed for forty men or eight horses. Packed tightly, it was impossible for them all to lie down, so they numbered off and took turns to rest. Blankets were hung as hammocks so that the sickest among them at least could be comfortable. There was no sanitation, no drinking water, no way to prepare food, and the train clanked with maddening slow-ness towards the west, away from the Russians.

In the slow hours Tom stood close to Harry, but they had nothing to say, and anyway no energy to talk. Some of the men played cards, and the mournful sound of a mouth organ being played in a neighbouring car drifted in above the clatter at times, if the wind was right.

The train stopped often, usually for no apparent reason, but now and then the familiar sound of Allied bombers overhead raised a cheer and some smiles, in spite of the danger. The roar of Fortress engines deep in Germany gave Tom hope that soon, soon, it would be over. Soon, he would be with her again, and for a while in their wake he could remember a life other than this journey, and tease his thoughts away from the stench of the train to another time and place.

After two days the train disgorged its load at a semi-derelict station, and he stood unsteadily on the crowded platform, stinking and dishevelled, breathing in fresh air at last, swaying with hunger and fatigue. For a while there was confusion, German soldiers trotting morosely up and down relaying orders and counter-orders. Then the column began to move once again, shambling on to the already overcrowded camp that would be their new home.

Late in April American forces finally set them free.

# Twenty-two

Tom hitched a ride from the base at Little Sutton with a group of young fliers on 72-hour passes, crowded into the back of the truck, laughing and rowdy, their high spirits infectious, soothing his tautened nerves.

He had woken that morning with a dull sense of fear in his gut, and in the interval between sleep and wakefulness he had thought he had a mission to fly, until his eyes opened in the dark and he remembered. But the fear stayed with him, the gnawing sense of dread that ate at his nerves and drained him. He wondered if he would find her today.

The truck bumped and ground through the potholes that led to the city, still unmended after all this time, and Tom stared out at the neat hedgerows that dissected the landscape into tiny squares of meadow, so strange to him when he had first arrived, so small, but now reassuringly familiar, almost home. Even now, this late in the spring, the wind was cold and chill gusts raced across the flatness of the ground. Still weak, he shivered and pulled his jacket tighter around him.

Birwich itself had changed little as the truck followed the familiar road through the stone-built villages, and suburbs still full of rubble from bomb damage years earlier. Some children chased the truck, shouting out for chocolate and gum, but the men had none to give and the children had to be content with American salutes. They saluted back and then ran away giggling, still shy of the airmen, to tell their friends. The group of men laughed with them with childish delight, and Tom watched the small figures receding into the distance as the truck lurched on over the uneven road.

They climbed down near the bus station and the young airmen went off in search of a hotel and some fun. Tom followed them with his eyes until they were out of sight, and envied them their energy and innocence. It seemed another lifetime that he had been like them, a different person then. He turned and went into the depot. The clerk was taciturn and unhelpful when he asked for a bus to Fielding but a middle-aged woman, rotund in her woollens, took pity on him, and told him which bus he should catch.

'Got no manners, some of these boys,' she complained. 'Perhaps if he saw a bit of action himself he'd be a bit more appreciative of what you servicemen go through. My son was in the RAF, killed back in '41, before you lot even joined in ...'

'I'm sorry to hear that.'

'Well, it couldn't be helped I suppose. I've got used to it now, and at least he died a hero. Spitfire pilot he was. We were all ever so proud of him.'

Tom smiled.

'Anyway, you don't want to hear on old woman like me rattling on. So, Fielding was it?' She thought for a moment. 'You can get the number 28 from across the road there, outside, and get off at Fielding post office. Ask the conductor. She'll tell you. And then you can ask your way in the post office, like. Visiting friends, are you?' She peered up at him.

'Yes, ma'am. Visiting friends. Thanks for all your help. I appreciate it.' He smiled at her and touched his cap, touched by her cheerfulness and her help.

'My pleasure, love. Hope you find your way all right.'

'I'm sure I will. Goodbye now.'

''Bye love. Take care.'

The bus ride was short and took him through unfamiliar parts of the town, middle-class suburbs unknown to him, and he realised for the first time that he had scant idea of what kind of family Anna came from, if they were rich or poor, though he knew she had little money of her own. He jumped off at the post office as the lady had told him and went in, weaving his way through the stands of cards and envelopes to the counter, where he waited in line behind a young mother with two wayward boys and a baby on her shoulder. Two old women stopped gossiping when they saw him, and fell silent, examining him over their spectacles. He touched his cap to them but they just stared and he looked away, too preoccupied to care.

'Yes sir,' said the clerk, irritated by his customers' rudeness, and anxious to make up for it. 'What can I do for you?'

'Excuse me.' Tom's voice was low and soft and the clerk had to lean forward over the counter a little to hear him. 'I'm looking for Byron Street. I believe Miss Pilgrim lives there, at number eight.'

The old ladies strained to hear, craning their necks, fascinated, a mystery apparently solved at last.

'Yes, that's right,' the clerk said, and gave him directions.

Tom saluted the old women with exaggerated politeness as he left, but he was unaware of the new hostility in their stares.

The house was close, less than five minutes away, and as he approached his heart thudded loud, the same nerves as before take off, fear in his belly and a bad taste in his mouth. He swallowed against the dryness of his throat. He had imagined this moment so many times. In his dreams, in his waking hours, her image had sustained him, given him hope when the days as a prisoner had stretched out bleak and empty. But now that he was here, close to her after so long, he felt only the fear that her silence had nurtured. He glanced around uneasily. He had forgotten how small everything was in England, and he felt claustrophobic amongst the rows of terraced houses that lined the road, the trees budding and overgrown above his head.

Number eight. He paused on the pavement, casting his eyes

across the shabby exterior, wondering which window was hers, his breathing heavy with nerves. The gate was broken, swinging drunkenly on one hinge. He would fix that, he thought as he stepped through it and up the steps to the door. He was sweating inside his uniform and the breeze failed to cool him as he knocked.

He waited. Please let Anna answer the door, he prayed silently. Please …

There were heavy footsteps inside, footsteps he knew were not hers, and he braced himself as a figure approached, round and distorted through the frosted glass. The door swung open and a stocky woman in late middle age stared at him with suspicion. She wiped her hands on the apron that hung loosely over her shapeless body.

'Yes,' she said peremptorily. 'What do you want?'

Taken aback by her rudeness, he struggled for words. So this was her mother.

'Excuse me ma'am,' he said, looking directly into the hostile eyes. 'I'm sorry to trouble you, but I was looking for Miss Anna Pilgrim.'

He thought he saw the glimmer of a smile playing on the narrow lips. 'Well,' the old woman said, folding her arms across her chest. 'She got married. Almost a year ago.'

The fear in his gut exploded into a billowing wave of pain that rolled through him. He closed his eyes, struggling for control, and said nothing.

'She's a mother now too. Happy as anything.' The woman smiled at him but there was no warmth in her face. 'Can I tell her you called?'

'No. No, thank you,' Tom murmured, backing away in his haste to escape from her, get away from this place. 'I'm sorry to have troubled you. Thank you ma'am.'

'That's quite all right,' the woman replied, and closed the door.

He turned down the last few steps and yanked savagely at the gate. It came away from the wall in his hand and he threw it aside in frustration. On the pavement he hesitated, unsure where he could run to, then he turned away from the shops on the main street and walked quickly, his mind reeling, barely able to think. The pain was blinding, hot gusts welling up from his gut, engulfing him, taking his breath, and he paced fast, the pavement a blur beneath him. It can't be true, he thought. It can't be true. It can't be.

But it was. His worst nightmare his living reality. He wanted to cry out, to beat the ground with his fists, to protest to God, but he kept walking as though the movement could make it untrue and postpone the moment of understanding.

He looked up, suddenly aware that he was no longer enclosed by buildings, and saw a tiny valley of allotments overlooked by houses. Following the path down from the street he found a bench. It must have been a park before the war, he realised, and threw himself down. He wanted to be home, surrounded by lakes and mountains. A tranquillity that caressed his soul, an aloneness that seemed impossible now.

Two dogs chased each other through the growing vegetables, playing, and he remembered the mongrel pup he had left behind in another lifetime, years ago. Tom wondered if she would remember him, or whether she too had found someone else to take care of her.

He leant forward and rested his elbows on his knees, burying his face in his hands, shutting out the world around him. But inside his head was worse, full of images of Anna, full of his pain, so he opened his eyes again and watched the dogs. He sat all afternoon, unable to think or to feel anything but a dull ache that burned inside him and numbed his senses.

Gradually the sun started to drop and the cool of the late afternoon to penetrate, feeling its way inside his clothes. With reluctance he stood up, stretching limbs stiff with cold. Then he climbed the hill to the street and found his way back to the bus stop, walking stiffly, wearily. A woman with a cut glass accent waiting for the bus said, 'They've got no pride these Yanks. You'd never see an RAF man slouch like that.' She stared at him, ice in her eyes, wanting a response, but he turned away, indifferent to the insult. The bus seemed to take a long time to come.

'What happened?' Harry asked back at the base.

Tom sat on the end of the bed, one foot resting on the grey issue blanket. 'She's married,' he murmured. 'With a kid.'

Harry sucked in air between his teeth. 'Shit.' He watched Tom examine his boot, absently rubbing at small imperfections with his thumb. 'Did you speak to her?'

'Her mother.'

'Are you okay?' Harry asked.

Tom rubbed his hands up over his face and through his hair before he looked up and dropped his hands to his thighs. 'Yeah. I'm okay, I guess. Considering I just got my heart ripped out.'

'I know how that feels,' Harry said. Then, 'I'm sorry.'

Tom shrugged. 'It's okay. I'll be okay. I was half expecting it anyway I guess ...'

'Sure.'

There was a pause.

'Hey,' Harry stood up and moved to stand at the foot of Tom's bed. He stood casually, hands in his pockets. 'How about we shoot some pool?'

Tom thought for a moment, staring at his boot, thumb still rubbing away an imaginary stain. He looked up. 'Okay,' he said after a while. 'Why not?'

He stood slowly and the two men walked across to the officers' club, silent.

Anna was in the post office, waiting in the queue to buy stamps for a birthday card for Lottie. The small shop was crowded. Another young mother stood ahead of her and the baby on her shoulder eyed Emma with interest. Emma grinned with delight. The young mother turned to look, saw Anna, smiled briefly and turned away. Anna smiled too, but the young woman didn't notice, her eyes averted from the unmarried woman, friendship between them taboo. Anna's gaze dropped.

The young woman reached the counter and handed the payment book to the clerk. He stamped it and counted out the cash for her. She thanked him and sidled out, anxious not to make eye contact with Anna again. Anna stood back to let her go, looking down to make it easier.

'Morning Miss Pilgrim,' the clerk said, his narrow lined face creasing into a smile. 'How are you this fine morning?'

'I'm very well, thank you Mr Turner,' she replied. 'And how about yourself?'

'Oh busy, as always. And how's the lovely Emma?' He reached across the counter to chuck the baby's cheek. She smiled and wriggled. 'She says she's fine thanks,' Anna said, and they laughed.

'What can I do for you, my dear?' he asked.

'Just a first-class stamp please,' she answered and gave him the money.

'That's all?'

'Yes, thank you.' She picked up the stamp from the counter and dropped it into her purse. 'Thank you.'

'You're welcome,' he replied. 'By the way, did the American airman find his way to you all right yesterday then?'

Anna looked up sharply, and a flush of panic swelled through her. 'I beg your pardon?' she whispered.

'An airman was in here yesterday,' Mr Turner said, 'asking directions to your house. Lieutenant I think he was. Nice fellow he seemed too.'

Anna stared at him, paralysed.

'He'd be the same fellow that sent you the letters from Germany, wouldn't he?'

She nodded, in shock, her mind numb. Mr Turner looked up from his books, struck suddenly that something was wrong. He peered at her over the half-moon glasses. 'Are you all right, Miss Pilgrim? Would you like to sit down?'

'No,' she blurted. 'I mean, yes, I'm all right. Thank you. I'm fine.'

He nodded. 'Well, goodbye then.'

'Goodbye,' she whispered and swept from the shop, face burning, her heart racing. She paused on the step, the fresh air hard against the redness of her cheeks, struggling for breath, and then she ran. The pram forgotten, Emma bouncing in her arms, she ran home, oblivious of the stares of passers-by.

'Mother?!' she shouted from the front door. 'Mother!' She strode through the hall to the kitchen where her mother looked up in alarm.

'What's the matter?' Mrs Pilgrim asked, swallowing hard, wary.

'Tom was here,' Anna hissed. 'What did you tell him?'

Her mother looked down under the rage in her daughter's eyes. 'I don't know what you're talking about,' she said hurriedly, twisting her ring.

'Yes, you do,' Anna said. 'He came here yesterday and asked for me. I know he did. What did you tell him?'

'Nothing,' Mrs Pilgrim spat. 'I told him nothing.'

There was a silence and Emma started to wail. 'Ssshhh,' Anna coaxed, stroking the child's hair, bouncing her gently in her arms. 'Ssshh.' The wails calmed to small whimpers and Anna turned back to her mother. 'I want the letters,' she said.

'What letters?'

'The letters he wrote me from Germany,' Anna answered. 'The letters you kept from me while you tried to marry me off to Morris.' The full depth of her mother's deception was only now sinking in. 'All this time you knew he was alive. All this time you let me suffer. Why? Why did you do it?' Rage turned to bewilderment and tears gathered swiftly behind her eyes, ready to fall.

Mrs Pilgrim stared at the floor, the great jaw clenched in tension, cheeks quivering. 'For your own good,' she snapped finally. 'I did it for your own good.'

'What do you mean?' Anna asked. Her mother's logic was beyond her.

There was a pause before her mother began again. 'He only wanted you for a good time,' she blurted. 'That's all he came back for. D'you really think he'll still be interested once he knows you've got a baby? D'you think he'll still want you stinking of breast milk and nappies? He only wanted you for one thing. That's all they ever want. Then they tire of you and move on to some other fool who's younger and prettier.' She stopped, breathing hard.

And then Anna understood. This had nothing to do with her. Or Tom. It was about her father. Her mother was taking her revenge against the man who had left her all those years ago.

Anna stiffened, feeling her core harden in disgust. 'Give me the letters,' she snarled, her lips barely moving. 'Give me them.'

'I can't,' her mother spat.

'Why not?' Anna was almost beside herself with frustration and rage. She breathed deeply, trying to calm herself.

'I destroyed them,' Mrs Pilgrim told her.

Anna stared in disbelief, then closed her eyes against the tears that started to rise. 'How could you?' she whispered between lips that were trembling. 'How could you?'

'For your own good,' her mother said again. 'To protect you from yourself. My mother should have done the same for me.'

Anna shook her head. This can't be happening, she thought. This just can't be happening. She backed away from her mother, still dazed with the shock, until suddenly she switched into action and fled to her room. There, she dragged the small suitcase from the top of the wardrobe and hurriedly stuffed it full, mostly with things for Emma, but a change of clothes for herself, her post office and ration books, a few toiletries.

'Come on, Emma,' she said when she'd finished, picking her

daughter up. 'We're leaving. We're going to find Daddy.'

Her mother stood on the landing, barring the way to the stairs, arms folded defensively across her chest. 'You're going, are you?'

'Yes,' Anna said. 'And we're never coming back.'

She stepped forward and the old woman hesitated as Anna stared, daring her to stop them. For a moment the two women duelled, but Anna's will had grown strong, and finally her mother stepped back to let her through. Anna squeezed past the old woman's bulk and struggled down the stairs, Emma in one arm, the suitcase banging against her legs. She dropped her key on the table by the door and slammed the door behind her.

She struggled to the bus stop. Emma was heavy in her arm, the small suitcase awkward. She stopped to change hands several times and climbed gratefully onto the bus when it finally arrived. An American airman stood for her and she smiled at him absently, her mind whirring, tumbling with shock and emotion.

Instinct took her towards the base, the only place she knew to start looking and as the bus bore her gradually closer to the depot, the reality of her journey began to penetrate. He's alive, she repeated over and over again in her mind. He's alive and he came for me.

The bus stopped and started, emptied and filled, and a sense of urgency gripped her, a need to hurry, to find him before he left, went elsewhere, shipped back to the States. It was possible too, that he was based somewhere else, that he came to Birwich solely for her, that she had missed him. She tried to calm herself, to quell her impatience with each load of passengers that climbed so slowly aboard. Emma whimpered and wriggled, unused to her mother's anxiety until the airman winked at her and pulled faces.

'A beautiful baby, ma'am,' he observed.

'Her dad's American,' Anna told him. 'An airman.'

'Well that explains it,' the American laughed, and she smiled, the contact reassuring, her tension easing.

She changed buses at the bus station, standing on the concrete amid the commotion and noise, the revving of engines and the shouts of drivers echoing round under the high steel roof. There was nowhere to sit, and Emma was weighty in her arms. She watched the clock ticking round, each minute a lifetime until the bus pulled in at last and then chugged out again on its way to Little Sutton.

There were few passengers and she made herself comfortable, calming herself gradually, less anxious now that she was actually on her way to the base. Emma slept on her mother's lap, made drowsy by the rocking motion of the bus. Anna patted her, but her mind was turning on the knowledge that he had written to her. When did he write first? she wondered. How many letters had there been?

All this time he had been waiting for her replies. All this time waiting, wondering, as she had done. She wanted to vomit, the sickness of regret physical and real. He must have worried and thought the worst, as she had. She screwed up her face in pain and sorrow. She should have known. She should have realised. She cursed herself for not thinking to ask in the post office months ago. But how could she have known? How could have known her mother would be so cruel? So twisted? She turned her eyes to the window, staring out, blinded by emotion, and wiped her face with a handkerchief, blinking her eyes back into focus so that she could watch the town become suburbs dwindling into countryside, the landscape familiar and ancient, soothing.

It was just after noon when she stepped down off the bus, taking her suitcase from the conductor who helped her, kindly. The bus pulled away with a grinding of gears and she watched its hulk retreat into the distance, turning left at the end of the village to resume its tortuous trip back to the city. She gazed round at the old stone buildings, unchanged in centuries, felt the clean air cool and fresh in her lungs. A group of fliers walked by, awakening memories of a more innocent time. The sorrow left. Now

there was only the desire to find him, the excitement of anticipation, the dread that he might have gone already, the joy of
knowing he was alive. She stepped into the hotel, asked them to
look after her suitcase, then hurried through the village on her
way to the base.

The lane was longer than she remembered, stretching out
ahead of her between the green and budding hedges. A robin sat
on a gate and watched her, twittering, the redness of his breast the
only colour against the drabness of the fields. She walked on, her
arms aching with the weight of the baby, striding quickly, anxious,
still filled with a sense of urgency. A B17 flew low overhead on its
way back to the airfield and she followed it with her eyes, never
breaking step, cradling Emma's head protectively against the roar.

Near the base she slowed, nervous now, afraid that he may not
be here, and she approached the gate cautiously, timid under the
watchful eyes of the young serviceman on guard.

'Yes ma'am? Can I help you?' he called out, encouraging her
closer.

She nodded and stepped closer. 'Yes. Thank you.'

'What can I do?'

She hesitated, licking her bottom lip in a moment of uncertainty before she spoke. 'I'm looking for someone who used to be
stationed here.' She smiled slightly, apologising with her eyes for
bothering him. 'His name is Tom Blake. Lieutenant Thomas
Blake. He was a pilot.' She examined his face to see if the name
meant anything to him and he smiled.

'You've come to the right place,' he told her. 'He's been back
just a couple of days. A whole group of them released a week or
so back. I'll phone through to the office for you.'

He retreated into the little sentry box and picked up the
phone. She could hear him talking but the words were lost in the
breeze before they reached her. She waited restlessly, Emma no
longer heavy, the knowledge of his proximity almost too much to
bear. She wanted to run past the guard, to run through the camp

and shout his name till he came to her. Standing here, helpless, she was excited and impatient, the guard's phone call too long.

'Sir?' The small voice was lost in the hubbub of the officers' mess. 'Sir?' The young man stood behind the lieutenant awkwardly, wondering how to catch his attention.

'Tom,' Harry said. The messenger smiled with gratitude. 'Behind you.' He motioned with his head and Tom turned slowly, without interest. The young man reddened under the officer's idle scrutiny.

'What is it?' Tom asked.

'Excuse me, sir,' the messenger said. 'There's a lady at the gate who is asking to see you.'

Tom's countenance changed perceptibly; lines of pain etched swiftly into his indifference, and the set of his jaw hardened as he fought to control his emotions. The young man waited for the lieutenant to respond, made uneasy by the pause. The silence lasted for almost a minute until finally Tom said, 'Tell her I don't want to see her.' He turned away from the messenger, facing Harry once more, his gaze lowered to the half-empty plate in front of him. His breathing was hard and laboured and he was trembling.

'Yes sir.' The young man saluted, confused, and left.

Harry leant forward on his forearms, pulling his chair in close to the table. His face was close to Tom's. 'Tom,' he said.

The pilot didn't reply.

'Tom,' he said again, more urgently this time.

Tom looked up but he didn't meet his friend's eyes.

'You've got to talk to her, Tom.'

Tom shook his head. 'I can't,' he whispered. 'She's somebody else's now. I don't want to see her.'

Harry reached over and gripped the pilot's arm, squeezing hard. 'This is your last chance,' he told him. 'Give her a chance. She must want to see you or she wouldn't be here.'

Tom dropped his gaze. He knew Harry was right, knew he

should hear what she had to say, but he couldn't face her knowing he could never have her again.

'She's come for you,' Harry pleaded. 'You have to go see her. You'll always regret it if you don't.'

Tom swallowed, hesitating, his mind still full of the images of his dreams. The navigator's grip tightened on his arm.

'She's alive, Tom,' he whispered. 'And she's here. I'd give anything for this chance with Yvette. Now go, before it's too late.'

'Okay.' The pilot nodded once, persuaded, and looked up, holding the eyes of his friend. They were dark and still touched with the memory of things unsaid. 'I'll talk to her. But only to keep you happy.'

Harry's mouth widened into a wry smile. 'Good. Now go.'

Tom took a deep breath, stood up and followed the messenger out of the hall as the narrow back hurried between the Nissen huts on the way to the gate. He watched him step off the path into the mud for a group of officers, saw him salute and continue. He kept his distance, approaching warily, her presence disturbing, stirring up the pain. He could see her now, the woman at the gate holding a baby. Someone else's baby. His guts twisted.

He drew closer and saw her step forward, eager to meet the messenger. There was a pause as they talked then she staggered and the young man had to support her with his arm. She was bent almost double for a moment, almost dropped her child before she recovered, pulled herself upright, backed hurriedly away from the messenger.

Tom was near now, near enough to see her face, to see the pain and the incomprehension, the battle to hold back tears. She turned away, walked on unsteady legs from the messenger who watched her go, and then she was gone, out of sight behind the hedge.

He moved to the gate and stood next to the messenger. They watched her together for a moment, in silence, then Tom was running after her on the road. He caught up with her quickly. 'Anna!' he called, breathless from the exertion, still weak. 'Anna!'

She turned, startled by his sudden presence at her shoulder. 'Anna,' he said again, devastated by her tears.

She moved back from him, confused and hurt, eyes evading his. He reached out a hand, resting his fingertips on her shoulder, and she stiffened under his touch. She looked up at him briefly, eyes full of mistrust. 'Why?' she whispered. 'Why did you send us away?'

Tom ran his eyes over her face. His whole body rebelled against the knowledge that she was no longer his to hold, and his fingers lifted trembling from her shoulder to her face, touching the wetness of her tears. 'You're not mine to love any more,' he said simply, and his hand dropped to his side, the contact with her skin too painful.

'I don't understand,' she said, regarding him warily.

Tom hesitated, finding the words difficult to form, wondering why she needed it explained. 'You're married. You have a child.'

She stared, looked away, eyes searching the road for an explanation, and then back to his face. She shook her head. 'I'm not married.'

'But your mother ... she told me ...'

'I'm not married.' Her voice was choked with emotion, the desperate need to make him understand. 'I waited for you. All this time I waited.'

'My letters?'

'I never got them. My mother destroyed them. The man in the post office told me you'd come, told me you'd written. I didn't know until today. I didn't even know if you were alive.' She watched him, her eyes hopeful behind the tears, and he looked away, wanting to believe but afraid.

There was a silence. Then Emma squirmed and twisted in her mother's arms, wanting to see, to touch the man behind her. She reached out with a small fist, brushing the rough cheek with her hand, laughing at the unfamiliar sensation. Instinctively, Tom smiled. 'She's mine?' he asked.

Anna lifted her gaze to his, met the eyes that searched her face for answers. She nodded. 'Emma Louise.'

Relief rushed through him in a torrent, knocking him back, taking his breath away. He smiled and lifted his fingers once more to her face, shivering with the touch of her skin. She moved her head against his hand, like a cat. Emma squirmed, wanting attention, and he turned to her, lifted her from her mother to hold her in hands that seemed huge against the tiny body.

'Hi, Emma Lou,' he whispered. 'How're you doing?'

Emma grinned and he held her high against his shoulder. Then he bent to Anna to kiss her, briefly, lips touching for only a moment.

They walked on in silence, too much to say to be spoken, so they talked with the closeness of their bodies, his arm around her shoulder, protective, hers around his narrowed waist, Emma sleeping content on her father's shoulder, secure in the strong arm that held her. The lane was silent save for the tread of their shoes on the rough surface of the road and the occasional raucous cry of a crow flying low over the fields, out of sight behind the hedgerows. Nothing seemed to move in the stillness of the afternoon. Glistening puddles lined their path, pools of rainwater that reflected the sun and the ponderous clouds, so that it seemed to Anna that they were walking in the sky.

# Acknowledgements

I am indebted to many authors and books about the Second World War, but especially to the following: Philip Kaplan and Jack Currie, *Round the Clock: The Experience of the Allied Bomber Crews Who Flew by Day and Night from England in the Second World War*; Angus Calder, *The People's War: Britain 1939–45*; Arthur A. Durand, *Stalag Luft III: The Secret Story*; John Hackett, *I Was A Stranger*; Martin Gilbert, *The Second World War: A Complete History*.

I am also grateful to Jane Campbell, Jo Riccioni and Shannon Powell for their invaluable feedback, and most of all to my husband Steve for his unfailing belief and support.